Son of Paul

Son of Paul

John Moehl

RESOURCE *Publications* · Eugene, Oregon

SON OF PAUL

Resource Publications
An Imprint of Wipf and Stock Publishers
199 W. 8th Ave., Suite 3
Eugene, OR 97401

www.wipfandstock.com

PAPERBACK ISBN: 978-1-7252-5891-4
HARDCOVER ISBN: 978-1-7252-5892-1
EBOOK ISBN: 978-1-7252-5893-8

AUGUST 2, 2021

This is done in honor of, and in partnership with Elisabeth. Throughout my life, she has cast a long and loving shadow, offering wise counsel and a calming hand. I would also like to dedicate this to my uncle and aunt who both recently left this temporal world we shared for more than two-thirds of a century, but not without first baptizing me a writer. I do write. I hope one day to live up to my uncle and aunt's expectations and become a writer.

Proverbs 22:6

Start children off on the way
they should go, and even when
they are old they will not turn from it

Contents

Note to the reader

THIS IS A STORY with several themes. Among these, it is a story of international intrigue and criminality. This is also a story that is intertwined with some characters and entities found in *Closer to God*, *The Agate Hunter*, and *Waiting—almost there*.

This tale starts with a Biblical quotation. Interwoven throughout the story, you will find more verses from the Bible. These passages all share the same reference, the New International Version of the Bible (https://www.thenivbible.com) as transcribed through Bible Study Tools (https://www.biblestudytools.com/niv/) employed by the author.

Author's Note

WHEN I WAS A kid, my mother used to make Spanish rice. There was nothing Spanish about it. She took whatever she found in the fridge, added a bit of aging rice, mixed it all up, and threw it in the oven. I liked it.

Perhaps Mother's Spanish rice imprinted on my brain or my digestive system or both. Years later, as a Peace Corps volunteer, in a small restaurant in my town, I used to always order *un peu de tout* (a little bit of everything)—in many ways, not dissimilar from my childhood Spanish rice.

A friendly critic told me my tales were really only travelogues—suggesting, or at least implying, perhaps my niche in life was with the tourist industry. Maybe.

I do see life as a voyage. I am sure many of us do. However, less abstractly, my hope in spinning my tales is that I am able to concoct a tasty serving of *un peu de tout*—describing places that may be new to some, depicting emotions and concerns that could be common to many, and adding a sprinkling of history to try and provide context.

As a disclaimer, I am unaware of any existing or past companies or entities named Equatorial Management or Delpro. Any connection to any functioning or former firms, businesses, or groups is purely coincidental—all actions and events attributed to Equatorial Management and Delpro, or any other enterprise or organization in the following story are completely fictitious. Equally, all actions or events attributed to any public or private agencies, individuals, or groups come solely from the imagination and are not based on any facts. While these characters and actions may occur at real places—past and present—these are in no way intended to recount true happenings at these spots. The story is completely a work of fiction, as are the characters. The acts of these characters as told in the following story are also completely fictitious, both in terms of time and place. Hopefully the human emotions are not.

The Herder

The wind ripples across the savannah,
the heads of the grasses balancing in precise rhythm.

Over the hill, a herder appears, chaperoning a small group
    of long-horned zebu;
the cattle guide him.

The band moves slowly through the tall grasses, surefooted and alert,
the herder softly humming, shaded by the brim of his straw hat.

The cows swat persistent flies with their tails, their herdsman ignoring
    the nuisances.
The flies assail the secret place of the boy—hidden in the nearby gulch.

The boy watches the beasts sweep the drying stocks that bend
    under their hooves,
envisioning an invading army of fierce Fulbe warriors—
    he the last salvation.

The zebu vanish, the wind quiets to a whisper, the boy has won;
he has saved all from the horrors of the would-be conquerors.

Leaving the gulch, the boy marvels at his imagination.
He wonders when he might grow up—unsure he wants to.

Prologue

HE WAS BORN IN the District Hospital in Bole, Northern Region of Ghana. His mother wanted to name him Peter in honor of the Apostle Simon Peter. His father worried about the impact of any of Simon Peter's denials of Christ that could have filtered through the centuries to taint his son.

His mother may have won, but his father held tightly to his hopes that his son would follow more closely in the footsteps of the Apostle Paul than those of Simon Peter. This was not because his father also had an apostolic name—he was Paul, named after the great man others called Saul of Tarsus by his parents who had been missionaries. Paul the father in no way compared himself to Paul the Saint. He considered himself to be far too flawed to be his son's model—but should Peter closely follow Saint Paul's teachings, he knew his son would be in good shape.

After all, albeit Saint Peter was viewed by many as the prolocutor— almost the chief— for all the Apostles (a good thing, Paul the father thought), it was Saint Paul who was the Herald of Christ. It was Paul who had traveled far and wide in His name as decreed in Acts. It was down Saint Paul's path they all tread.

Thus, a young Peter, son of Paul, ran barefoot over the savannah of Ghana while his parents, Baptist missionaries like his grandparents, tried to make inroads in a population where Christianity was a close second to Islam, but where Protestantism was a tiny minority. As he ran, Peter had no idea if he followed in the footsteps of Saint Paul or of Sumaila Ndewura Jakpa, the founder of the Kingdom of Gonja in the White Volta Valley that surrounded Bole.

CHAPTER ONE

Homecoming

Wondering how deep the roots have grown

AKWAABA.

These good wishes, painted as a multi-colored mural on the terminal wall, welcomed Peter as he deplaned at Kotoka International Airport after his flight from London via Nairobi. He quickly maneuvered through immigration (being a Ghanaian resident) and customs before emerging in the entry hall one floor below. The hall was overflowing with meeters and greeters—some legit, others more nefarious, ready to prey on the unsuspecting first-time visitor.

Among the elaborate placards for big-name hotels and the smaller signs of drivers awaiting the arrival of someone from their organizations, there was a slight gray-haired couple with big smiles on their faces—Mom and Dad.

It was like fighting your way out of Wembley Stadium, but after an amazingly strong (for two old folks) embrace, the trio struggled through the swarming crowd, making their way to the dusty Pajero in a back corner of the large airport parking lot.

As usual, his father drove and his mother insisted he take the other front seat. She leaned over his shoulder from the back bench to look at her son—her child who, as a boy, had (none too happily, she remembered with a bit of a smile) left home for his studies abroad. She eyed the young man now seated before her as they drove northeast, out of Accra, to Kpando, on the shores of Lake Volta, where the couple had their current mission.

A dozen years ago, Lynn and Paul Volman, American Baptist missionaries originally from Gravois Mills, Missouri, had moved from Bole to Kpando—their new post almost 200 miles to the southeast, as the crow flies, from their initial congregation—twice that distance by road.

The shortest route home from the airport was via Akosombo—site of the dam that, in 1965, created Lake Volta. As Peter had arrived in the late morning, they decided to immediately enter into the fray of mid-day traffic—the "go slow" as city dwellers called it—and then stop for lunch once they had left the metropolis behind. Just south of Akosombo a number of resorts dotted the Volta River, downstream from the dam, offering good spots for a relaxed and tasty meal.

The immediate in-the-car conversation spiraled around, carefully avoiding key subjects, keeping to the mundane: the trip, the food on the plane, the weather in UK. Early afternoon, they arrived at River Shores, where they could sit on the bank of the surging water, almost feeling its pulse as they rested on the riverside. They ordered chicken and chips—Lynn and Paul having Fanta, to their surprise, Peter ordering a Star beer.

The exchanges around the small riverfront table were still garden-variety welcome-home chitchat, interwoven with flashbacks to earlier days in the Gold Coast. They reminisced of difficult days in Bole. They thought back to the challenges of the hot and dusty dry seasons when they frequently went without water for days—their kerosene fridge often not able to keep up with the excruciating heat.

They talked fondly of Peter's little sister Lydia who had been christened in honor of Saint Lydia of Thyatira. Native of the region of Greece, Saint Lydia was the cloth merchant met by Saint Paul during his travels, also known as the "Woman of Purple" and widely considered as the first European Christian convert. They recalled how their Lydia too had had a connection to the color purple—wearing until it was literally in tatters her favorite purple T-shirt with the name of the Ghanaian national football team, the Black Stars, stenciled on the front.

They laughed at how people sometimes mixed up the names of Lynn and Lydia—confusing mother and daughter (some of their flock in Kpando stumbling over the alliteration of Lynn and Lydia, having difficulties pronouncing the "L").

Lydia, like Peter, had attended mission primary school (starting in Bole but finishing in Kpando) and then gone to secondary boarding school overseas—this paid for by the Church Missionary Society as part of the family's benefits' package. Lydia had chosen to go to America while her big brother had decided to pursue his schooling in England. She had even managed to reconnect with the extended family in Missouri. Four years Peter's junior, she was just beginning her university studies—having a tough time gaining traction as someone who was not the most studious nor farsighted. The less controlled environment of college, compared to the conservative religious high school she had attended, only increased her struggle to do well both in her studies and her newly adopted home.

They wished Lydia could have shared this moment with them.

Eating the appetizing food as the river silently slid by, the conversation continued to skirt any topics of significance, moving to a briefing for their son of the most relevant events in the country that had been an anchor of stability in West Africa over recent years. When Peter ordered a second beer, Paul caught Lynn's eye, but neither said anything.

Soon, they were back on the road, crossing the river a little way upstream, at the Adomi Bridge. They continued along the eastern lakeshore for another sixty miles to Kpando—a town of nearly thirty thousand. At their current post, Paul proudly announced, the religious map was nearly the opposite of Bole. Muslims were less than one in fifteen. Christians were a big majority. Nonetheless, Catholics and Pentecostals shared almost a third, each, of the pious, while Protestants were nearly one-quarter of the churchgoers. Baptists competed with Anglicans, Lutherans, and a few other faiths that seemed to come and go through the years.

The road was in relatively good shape, and as they sailed along, Paul moved into center stage, opening an oration (of which Peter had heard many earlier iterations) on education—highlighting that one-in-seven Kpando residents never sets foot in school—let alone reaches seventh grade. Although the Baptists did not have their own school, they actively promoted all levels of education—focusing chiefly on primary school where Paul was (again) proud to report that nearly half of enrolled children, and (with emphasis) more girls than boys, now finished primary school. Yet, this achievement notwithstanding, attendance in secondary schools was appallingly low—less than one in one hundred. And, critically, this was the case in spite of the fact that Kpando had, in addition to primary schools, a public high school and another public technical institute—these accompanied by the Bishop Herman College for boys and the Evangelical Presbyterian Junior High School. People just weren't pursing their studies! Paul figured this was because, in some ways, things were too good. For those who wanted to work, most found jobs, women as well as men—albeit the majority of these duties were in the informal sector. Half the town's families—Paul reminded his passengers—farmed and raised animals. In addition to traditional row crops and animal husbandry, Peter's father recalled (as Peter already knew so well) that people practiced a number of specialized activities including raising a variety of unconventional birds (beyond the ever-present chickens, there were doves, ducks, Guinea fowl, ostriches, and turkeys), propagating grass-cutter (a large indigenous rodent), silkworms, bees, snails, and even fish. Then, for the fish, there was, of course, a lot of employment in the very large artisanal fishery on the lake. There was just a lot to do and the huge market of metropolitan Accra to suck up all the produce.

This was not, Paul stressed (for the umpteenth time, Peter thought), to say people were well-off—they weren't. Probably, they were better off than their former devotees in Bole, but most were far from prosperous. The Church, their church, tried to help. It tried to build the moral and spiritual strength to move ahead—to do better each day. They—Lynn and Paul—only hoped they were, with God's blessings, having some positive impact.

As if planned by a celestial being (just maybe, *The* Celestial Being), they reached the city limits of Kpando just as Paul's sermon reached its end. They drove by the two banks, the central market, and the post office—turning left, toward the lake, they passed the Catholic and Evangelical Presbyterian churches, and rode another half-mile to a small and tidy compound on the right. Continuing through a low cement-block wall with an (always) open iron gate, they passed in front of a small church with a short steeple adorned by a hand-carved teak cross. The cross had been a gift to Peter's father upon his arrival, bestowed to him by the Paramount Chief of the Akpini (one of three traditional chiefdoms among which the municipality was divided, the others being the Gbefi and the Sovie). This was not to say the chief was one of Paul's parishioners—he wasn't. He was, however, someone who welcomed all with good intentions to his community—a position not always held in some locales.

Behind the church, in the shade of avocado and mango trees, there was a modest but comfortable three-bedroom bungalow—the rectory—that had been Lynn and Paul's home for more than a decade. And, behind the bungalow was a very small two-room abode that was called by most "the quarters"—the lodging for household staff. Bankole, known in the household as Kole, and Yewande, called Wanda, had been with the Volmans since Bole. The Nigerian couple, Christians, had fled religious fighting in Jos—finding themselves adrift in Ghana, Lynn and Paul offered a roof and a degree of steadiness in exchange for house and garden upkeep.

As the Pajero came to a stop in front of the house, Kole and Wanda seemed to materialize from nowhere to give Peter a big hug and a modicum of kind words. Then they vanished as mysteriously as they had come, feeling the family should not be bothered during this important homecoming.

The travelers got Peter's luggage out of the back of the car and headed into the house along the frangipanis-lined pathway that led to the front door. Immediately, Peter noticed several window-mounted air conditioners sticking out of the facade like warts. He was happy that his parents would be able to live more conformably in the hot and humid surroundings after years of trying to make do with fans and gallons of iced tea, but the machines seemed somehow incongruous with the more spartan lifestyle he knew his parents wished to portray.

Once inside, Peter was installed in one of the two extra bedrooms—the one that Lynn still called "the kids' room." The family then gathered in the dining room where, after prayers, they shared a very light meal before Peter went to bed.

Unlike in more northern latitudes, sunrise was a constant in the tropics—a little past six o'clock every morning, throughout the year. Just before sunrise, every morning, just as much a constant as the sunrise, Paul went to his church to pray.

The main doors, embellished with small replicas of the cross on the steeple, faced the parking area just inside the compound's wall. However, the building, of cement block with a corrugated metal roof, was L-shaped. Entering the vestibule, a worshiper would turn right into the nave—the altar at the East end of the structure.

In Paul's mind, this was a stately edifice compared to the much more unassuming thatched-roof chapel they had had in Bole. Yet, even in the humble setting of the North, Paul had appealed to the Missionary Society to invest in a simple stained-glass window to adorn the altar—insisting they needed something to make their place of worship special, given the far more elaborate structures receiving the votary of other churches and other religions. Now in Kpando, in a more affluent and—according to

Paul—sophisticated social setting, he had managed to persuade the society to move things up a notch—procuring a large, variegated window with an image of Christ at its center.

When Paul knelt at the altar for his morning prayers, the rising sun shone brilliantly through the stained-glass, Paul imagined it burning an image of Christ on his forehead.

Every morning Paul prayed for the uninitiated—the ignorant and the negligent who had not found Christ's ways. He prayed all would find God—many of these, too, finding their way to his congregation. He prayed for peace in, seemingly, as always, times of trouble. He prayed for his family. Today, he added a particular prayer for Peter and his homecoming. Then, as every day, he asked God to bless his work and, when it was fulfilled to His satisfaction, to welcome him in his own homecoming into the Kingdom of Heaven.

Today, memorable for the fact it was the first time in a long time his son had slept under his roof, Paul thought back over nearly three score of years that encapsulated his life. How bizarre—how wonderful—how blessed—that a kid, born in Central America, with roots in a Midwest hamlet, would find himself in West Africa. How blessed that he found himself where he could spread God's Word to try to bring salvation to those who so, so badly needed to find it. How even more blessed that this same person should be where he was with his childhood sweetheart—the love (after God) of his life. To say Gravois Mills—what he saw as home—was a small community was to greatly exaggerate—it was tiny. This made it all the more exceptional—all the more Divine—that he had met his soulmate among those few families who had clumped together in the silty clay soils of the Ozarks, fifty miles southwest of the great Missouri River, to make the village—a village much smaller than Kpando—even smaller than Bole.

Paul's parents had been Baptist missionaries in Costa Rica. Paul was the fourth of four children, his parents in their late forties when he was born. As with his own children, Paul's parents had sent him "out" for his high school studies—getting him back to Missouri where he could speak English and learn how to become a real American. However, unlike today, the added expense of a boarding school was not covered by the society.

Paul's father, Mark, had grown up in El Dorado Springs. His mother, April, was from Myrtle, in Oregon County, right on the Arkansas border. They had met at a Greyhound bus station. After a short courtship, they had married, and Mark had been ordained in the denomination of a parish in Springfield through the American Baptist Conclave—the same pathway followed by his son.

Unfortunately, the Springfield congregation assumed no direct responsibilities for the education of their missionaries' children. Mark and April had farmed out their first three boys across the state to various extended family members. When Paul's turn came, he ended up being sent to live with his mother's sister, his Aunt Rose, who worked at the post office in Gravois Mills.

Lynn's father, a third-generation Gravois Mills' native, ran a bar near the boat launch—the community located at the north end of the serpentine Lake Ozark. The two children, youngsters really, had met as freshmen in high school. There was an immediate spark. She was wearing his letterman's jacket (Paul had been quite an athlete) by her junior year, and the two married two years after high school graduation (in the interim, doing odd jobs around town).

His life was blessed. Not only had he found his bride on the shores of Lake Ozark, but the two had wed in the Baptist Church where they had found their God who would guide their lives. This was no easy feat in a borough heavily dominated by Methodists (including Lynn's parents). Yet, through His Mysteries, they had been shown that the true way was through baptismal with the Baptists, and this decision required them to regularly travel eight miles south to the Baptist Church on Highway Five, where their nuptials were performed.

After the wedding, they relocated to Springfield to follow in Mark's footsteps—to become ordained missionaries (actually, Paul being ordained, and Lynn blessed as his spouse). They had then spent six months getting to know their Springfield brothers and sisters in God before traveling to Ghana to open a mission in Bole.

It had all been too wondrous to believe—yet, it had all been truly by the grace of God. Paul took a deep breath, nearly tipping forward into the altar, feeling the Holy Spirit fill the very marrow of his bones as he thanked God for his blessings, hoping he could be God's instrument to bless the lives of others.

Paul's knees hurt and he felt light-headed when he stood up to go back to the house for breakfast with Lynn, and today, joyously, with Peter too.

When Paul came into the kitchen, Lynn already had made coffee and was heating a baguette they had purchased in Accra to serve with scrambled eggs—the scrambling to be done when their fatigued offspring would wake to enjoy his first day home.

In the quiet of the morning, over cups of hot coffee, Paul carried Lynn back into his reflections of their life together and the good fortune they had shared through God's grace. They comfortably chatted about Gravois Mills, that funny little church on Route Five, the bats that flew at night about Bole, and the ballooning price of petrol in Kpando. Their conversation made great arcs through their merged lives. Yet, as in the drive up from Accra, they seemed to avoid the burning subject of the day: what was Peter going to do?

Lynn let her mind follow the nostalgia of her husband.

"Dear, remember that day we first arrived? That was the old airport—what a mess! I perspired a bucket and was sure we'd never get out of that place—and all those unsmiling black faces that seemed to want to bore into our very souls—what a beginning to this now wonderful tale."

"Ya know, honey." Paul seamlessly picked up the conversation. "I never thought we'd make it—but we did."

"We sure did! People cried when we left Bole. Here you are now, respected by one and all—God has held His hand out to His son Paul, and you have shone like a sun. I am so proud of you! You have done so much to help these poor people—these ignorant folks who are so much in need of your guidance and wisdom. You work so hard. I hope they realize how lucky they are to have had God send you here."

"Shhhh," Paul cautioned, "you know, all I am able to do, all I am able to accomplish is only possible with God's help. We are but tools of His word."

"Of course, dear, we are God's servants." Lynn built, as frequently, on Paul's base, "But it's also a question of genes—good genes. You followed your father. You were born in a mission. It's in your blood."

There it was. It was out in the open. No more dancing about—the covers had been pulled back.

"I did," Paul said, fully opening the topic, "what I thought was best. That's what we all have to do—isn't it? Maybe it's genes—I don't know. But I am so thankful for the road we have taken—we, you and me—we, the family."

"Yes." That was all Lynn felt necessary to add.

"Yet, honey," Paul continued, "we are all products of God—He alone knows what's best for us—how best to use us. And, we must have faith in Him that He will guide each and every one of us in His way."

"And?" Lynn remained monosyllabic.

"And." Paul swallowed, going full throttle ahead, uncertain where this was going, "we don't know what God has in store for our beloved Peter. We have no idea if he will maintain the family tradition. I have prayed to God he does. But it's his decision—his and God's."

"Can't we push, help, or do something?" Peter's mother worried.

"Not now. He's not ready," his father concluded.

"Maybe. But at his age." Lynn's uneasiness persisted, "When we were his age, you and I, thanks to your steady hand on our future, had already chosen our pathway—we had already become responsible adults. Why, in spite of my uncertainties, bolstered by your keen vision, we were married and serving as God's messengers in Bole. He's a man."

"Dear, put it in God's hands."

"OK."

"You sure?"

"No, but I'll try."

"OK, pray—it helps."

"I'll try."

"Fine. Now how about topping-off my coffee?"

"Ahem . . .."

Lynn and Paul looked around to find a tousled Peter standing behind them—unsure of how long he had been there—what he had overheard?

"Coffee dear?"

"Thanks Mom."

"Want to go to the church with me to pray son—it's a beautiful day."

"Maybe later, Dad."

Lynn scrambled the eggs, Paul and Peter sipped coffee; the kitchen was quiet enough to hear the doves cooing in the avocado tree outside the backdoor.

CHAPTER TWO

Lost in Thought

Choices—real and imagined

PETER HAD OVERHEARD MUCH of his parent's conversation. He was not surprised. This only added to the burden that weighed on his shoulders. He felt he had slipped into the river and was now uncontrollably being carried by the current. He had done his studies, obtained his degree in business (not theology as his parents had hoped), and he was now expected to do something. What?

For him, it was not the same. It was not easy. His classmates went home after graduation, to a quaint English village or town, most likely, where they had been born and where their family had roots. They might strike out on their own. But they might go into the family business. Or, they might even start a new business in a community where they were known as an established member in good standing.

This didn't apply.

His family tradition was being a missionary—being a missionary in a foreign land. Yes, he had been born in Ghana. Indeed, he could probably become a full-fledged Ghanaian citizen and live the rest of his life in a country that he found nice enough—not a bad choice for a future. But he was not culturally nor by birth-right a Ghanaian. He was an American (by nationality). He was almost a Brit—having spent most of his adolescence and early adulthood in the UK. He wasn't sure what he was.

His parents wanted him to be a rerun: return to Springfield, be ordained, and then go somewhere—preferably as a married person and probably (highly likely) not back to Ghana.

He wasn't ready.

He had, he thought, nothing against his father's vocation and his mother's passion. He had no inherent antagonism toward missionaries nor to the possibility of even someday becoming one himself. Yet, he felt no attraction either.

There was religious fervor in his parents—adoration and devotion.

He felt none of this. He was OK, he guessed, with God. He imagined there probably was, maybe should be a God. He knew many people believed with their very essence there was a God. There must be, he supposed, a God.

He didn't know.

This was not something about which he thought a great deal. While his personal religious convictions were in flux, his desire to immediately become a proselytizer of his father's god was almost nil.

He was too young.

There was too much to do.

There were too many choices.

It was unfair to assume, to presume—to pressure— someone to follow one direction as if predestined when there were so many options.

He needed time to think.

Peter didn't tell his parents anything about his concerns. Over breakfast, and afterward, he simply underscored he was tired after a long journey and fatigued by his recent end-of-year exams and graduation. He wanted to rest some. He wanted to relax. He wanted to, at least for a short bit, be like a carefree tourist and visit some places around the country where he had been born, but from where he had been absent for so long.

He started by just wandering around town, seeing the sights.

He was a white man—but he wasn't a real stranger because all knew he was "Mister Paul's son."

He could communicate in a few basic greetings in Ewe (the most prominent local language) and was able to migrate through most situations with ease.

He went to the market. He chatted with people in bars—getting a beer (or two) for himself since his teetotaling father and mother would not allow such a drink in their house.

He walked over to the lake. He watched the fishermen, following them to the landing where they beached their canoes and bartered with powerful ladies, market queens—buy'em-sell'em's—for their catches of tilapia and catfish. Some of the fish would remain to garnish the tables of Kpando, but most, he knew, would head to the capital—many ending up in *maquis*—small bar-restaurants that served grilled fish with *attiéké* (a cassava dish) or fried plantains.

For long, there had been stories about how the fishers used children they purchased from other families as their helpers—slaves. There were similar stories about local traditional healers, reportedly demanding a family to pay with one child, a soon-to-be slave, for treatment. There were lots of stories. Peter listened to them all but took few seriously. He was basically apolitical. He was, in fact, pretty agnostic about everything. He had enough to worry about just to figure out what he was doing—what he was going to do.

He wandered about. He thought. One day he spied a handbill glued to a telephone pole: UNDP Interns. It announced the United Nations Development Program—UNDP—had a short-term project to introduce people to (big) international administrations. In effect, they were looking for cheap labor (not all that different from the fishermen or the healers, Peter mused) to sort and file a backlog of documentation. They had cloaked the tedious tasks in a covering as an internship. They would pay little, provide no benefits, but they would have some training and seminars to justify this philosophical approach.

Peter was not really interested in diving into heaps of humdrum UN papers. But he knew Accra pretty well. It was a multi-million-inhabitant highly-decentralized megalopolis, composed of many nearly self-contained neighborhoods—Labone, Cantonments, Nima, Kaneshe, Asylum Down, and on, and on. UNDP was located between Labone and Osu, near Oxford Street where there were more European-style stores. It was also adjacent to Osu Castle—built by the Norwegians and the Danes in the 1660s and the seat of colonial and post-colonial governments—and Independence Square; not that far from the massive Makola Market. In short, it was as close to the city center as one could probably get.

Going to the capital, under any pretext, seemed a good option at the moment.

Predictably, Peter's parents were (mildly put) unsupportive. Nevertheless, he was an adult, and they could do little other than advise and then stand on the sidelines and either cheer or complain. If he were selected as an intern (and why would they ever select a missionary's son?), his stipend would pay for his expenses, so Paul could not even threaten to hold back needed funds.

Peter was determined.

Although he had just returned, he needed to get away from his parents for a while. This was, he assured himself, no indication of any dampening of his love for them—he just needed some space.

He applied to UNDP. He was accepted (to everyone's surprise—even his own). Within a month, he'd packed his suitcase, taken a taxi to the city, and found a small—very small and very expensive—studio apartment in North Ridge, walking distance to UNDP and just below the ceiling of the organization-set limits for reimbursable rent. Within two weeks, he felt he was up to his neck in unfathomable paperwork and wondering if this had been such a good idea.

However, once accustomed to the job, he found the internship itself to be very underwhelming. It was monotony personified. After the initial wave of pending documents had been handled, the day-to-day tasks were menial. There was little direct supervision. In the morning, there was a heap of papers for the interns to sort, collate, categorize, and file. When the pile was gone, if there were no seminars or other training activities, the crew was apparently free to do whatever—including leaving until the next day.

The team of interns consisted of five—the other four a little younger than Peter. The quartet, three girls and one boy, was comprised of current university students—two from University of Legon, one from the University of Cape Coast, and another from University of Kumasi. They were all studying political science or a related field—thinking the time spent at UNDP would not only contribute to their studies but give them a leg up in finding a high-paying job in an international organization after graduation. More interesting to Peter than their academics or their career hopes was the observation that all four had links (not direct, but extended family, in-laws, or just good friends) with employees in UN agencies who had helped them get the six-month assignments—the intern's ration far more than students could get elsewhere for a temporary job.

Indeed, when Peter weighed the activities against the intern's stipend, he felt he was paid pretty well. But he was clueless as to why he had been selected. He knew no one in the UN. He didn't think his parents did either. He seemed a strange choice for many reasons. Then, one day, it became clear. Their supervisor, Mr. Agbogahe, made a highly unusual appearance near the end of one day's paper sorting.

"Hey Petey," Mr. Agbogahe spouted before leaving (Peter hated being called 'Petey'), "you going back home for a visit while you're here in the big city?"

"Don't know," Peter replied.

"Well, if you do, you need to say, 'thanks' to Chief Nana (the Chief of the Akpini), he reached out to us when he heard you had applied. His recommendation got you here."

All explained. The chief had helped with more than the steeple. Peter would need to acknowledge this, especially since Mr. Agbogahe had now opened the door. For the immediate, he assured his supervisor he would thank the chief and, with due deference, bid his benefactor all the best. Conspicuously, it was all about contacts.

Away from the boredom of agency archives, Peter had a lot of free time and was unsure how best to use it. Some feminine companionship, particularly now when he was outside his parents' shadow, would be welcome. He had had a number of liaisons while studying in the UK—going back to his time as an innocent secondary student and becoming more frequent and intense as he moved through university. Some had been heartfelt, others almost lascivious—none had lasted.

It wasn't that his partners had not been intelligent and affectionate—many had. It was not that they had not enjoyed each other's company—both in and out of bed. They had. It was not that they had reached a natural endpoint. Several, if not most, could have gone on longer. It was, he guessed, that as the fervor calmed, as the new became ordinary, he thought it was time to move on. He had no idea to where.

Hence, for whatever reason, he was now a concupiscent young man with no ties. A young man, he reminded himself, who sought no ties—at least not now.

There were many options.

Nonetheless, he felt the trio of attractive, even attentive, girls with whom he now worked was off-limits. He was, in principle, opposed to mixing work and play. Given the political contacts of his coworkers, any physical interlude with his female colleagues seemed all the more ill-advised.

As in any city (or town or village, for that matter), there were (what were locally called) free women—not truly free in a financial sense, but free of commitments and worrisome tomorrows. While, just as with his views of missionaries (he noted, to his own surprise), he had nothing against the vocation of what some called sex workers—having availed himself of their services occasionally at times gone by—this was not what he was looking for today. Having concluded this, he realized he was not sure what he was indeed seeking.

After an initial period when he visited many of the local haunts— bars, nightclubs, dancehalls, and the like—he decided he favored a more low-key social environment. He settled on Labadi Beach.

This public beach nestled between two five-star, beach-front, full-service tourist hotels, was frequented by many—a true cross section of the city's varied residents. Some came to swim (although the waters were a bit iffy given the megalopolis' effluents), some came to tan, but most came to enjoy the ambiance, the sea breeze, and the never-ending dramas provided by the beachgoers.

In addition to the omnipresent boy-girl theater, there were roaming vendors selling everything from clothes to art objects, there were acrobats or gymnasts hoping for a tip, there were restaurateurs (the local equivalent of fast food) along with barmen and barwomen. And everything was *bon marché*—bargain-basement pricing to attract clients from all segments of the citizenry.

Peter would find a rickety table halfway down the beach and install himself with sunglasses and a good book. He'd sip frosty beers, munch on brochettes (aka shish kebabs), bouncing his eyes back and forth from his book and the never-ending theatrics that surrounded him.

One Sunday afternoon, when he had already invested several hours in his new advocation, the caretaker even placing a parasol over his seat to prevent him from turning lobster-red, a girl—a young lady—more correctly, ran into the corner of his table, a bulldog-type canine, from who knew where, at her heels—agitation on both the lady's and the dog's faces.

A long-time member of the brotherhood of dog lovers (many people locally extremely afraid of any hound or mutt—perhaps due to a preponderance of rabies), Peter managed to shoo the offending mongrel away, offering, with great gallantry, a seat to the now-hyperventilating woman.

She gratefully slid into the plastic chair across from Peter, thanking him profusely in melodic English that was distinctly non-Ghanaian. She introduced herself as Ruby and, with little prodding, announced she was a Liberian refugee. She added, spontaneously, she was originally from Sanniquellie, the capital of Nimba Country—the area where the civil war started in 1989. Her parents were initially from Guinea—leaving due to political and economic instability. Her father had been a schoolteacher, and she had hoped to follow the trail he had blazed. Sadly, Ruby's father had been killed early on in the war, and her mother and two siblings fled to Ghana where she had been for far too long—wanting desperately to go home.

Peter was taken aback by this autobiographical outpouring. It seemed unnecessary—almost incongruous given the general seashore joviality. But, when he took a gulp of his beer to cover up his ogling of the lady who now shared his table, he saw, bedecked in a colorful bikini, a most shapely and athletic female for whom one should make allowances—even if she did seem to gush her story totally unexpectedly.

In one quick soliloquy, Peter said his family lived up on the lake (avoiding any reference to missionaries) and he was here for a while on a training program. He asked if she would like beer.

She would.

It was done.

They had several beers, several brochettes with piping-hot chips, and then left to Peter's studio, hand-in-hand.

It was not a one-night stand—albeit there was no planning to the contrary. It simply turned out that Ruby and Peter got along—they got along well.

They returned often to the beach. They also went to the movies. They even went to the theater and a concert.

Ruby would always return home to her mother—never spending the night, although sometimes only getting into her own bed just shortly before her family, early risers, got up to meet the new day.

Their relationship was pragmatic, if, at times, wanton. They realized all too well—perhaps truly too well—they would ultimately each go their own way—Ruby hopefully returning to Liberia and Peter following his guardian angels.

All too soon, what had been foreshadowed happened: the internship was over. Peter briefly considered staying in Accra with Ruby, but, with no income, he could not support himself, let alone his significant other (as he had begun to think of this charming person who, over the past weeks, had nearly become his double).

After a last night of poignant loving, Ruby helped Peter fold the clothes for his suitcase and then accompanied him to get a *Tro-Tro* (kind of hybrid bus-taxi) back to the shores of Lake Volta.

Paul and Lynn were delighted to see their son back in the nest—but unsure of the context, and loath to ask. They did all they could to deal with it casually, as though he had just returned from an overnight fishing trip.

Peter was, he hoped, polite to his parents—rerunning his practice of walking about town—at times, deep in thought, at times enjoying a clandestine beer (or two). On regular intervals, Lynn or Paul would ask if he needed anything, if they could help with anything. Peter deflected politely, getting back to his roaming—what his father saw as moping.

After a fortnight, he felt the pressure was unbearable. Under the pretext of needing to get back to UNDP to settle final accounts, he headed back to the city. Ruby, surprised and elated, eagerly accompanied him to a small hotel in Tesano, a neighborhood far enough from the urban center to be relatively affordable.

For four days, the couple only left the room for light evening meals at a nearby *maquis*.

This may have relieved the pressure, but it in no way resolved the situation. Peter was now even more befuddled than when he had returned from the UK. Not only did he have to plan his whole life, but he had to decide if this plan had a permanent place for Ruby. The questions were staggering.

Again, there was a heartbreaking goodbye and a forlorn return to Kpando. There was more strolling, more head-scratching, more beer drinking—but not more answers.

Again, this time after a month, there was a reprise of the need to go back into the city—for a second time the excuse being delays in the final UNDP paperwork and payments. However, this time, when Peter showed up unannounced at the tiny home Ruby's mother had rented, the rooms were empty. No one was there.

Peter inquired of neighbors, several from Liberia. There seemed consensus that Ruby's family had gone back home, having received some sort of message from a family member who was apparently well-placed in the government in Monrovia. Something had changed. They were gone.

Peter was devastated.

Back in Kpando, he returned to what had become his routine: wandering.

His parents were concerned.

They were seated around the kitchen table—a fresh pot of coffee and a plate of just-out-of-the-oven Grandma April's oatmeal cookies adorning the space. This was the normal format for a serious family powwow—the last one having been when Peter stupefied his parents by declaring (demanding, more like it) he'd go to school in the UK and not go back to Missouri. He'd felt it was too good a chance to miss to see another part of the world, they'd seen it as too good a chance to miss to get to know one's homeland and extended family. There had been no compromise. Obviously, in the end he had not gone back to his perceived roots.

Now, with stern faces, they were seated again for a tête-à-tête, this time convened by Paul, the worried father—supported, as always, by Lynn, the worried mother—to, in their words, "Try to help."

"Son." Paul started in that soft voice he used to build up to his sermon.

Peter, attempting to maintain his composure, struggled in his chair—he hated being addressed as Son. He knew who his parents were.

"Son," Paul repeated, apparently not getting the reaction he had wished for from the first intonation, "we know how difficult growing up can be."

Peter wriggled uncomfortably (indiscernibly, he hoped)—this was potentially going to be a tough round.

Still getting no response from his son, Paul continued as though he had not missed a beat, "Growing up isn't easy—we all need God's help. Your mother and I were oh so lucky—we met early, saw our future together clearly, and were quickly able to get to the work God had set before us. Everyone is not so lucky. We know this . . ."

"Oh honey," Lynn interjected, "we really do know how hard it can be for some."

"Son." This now seemed to be Paul's anchor. "None of us can go it alone. We need God's help. Grandfather Mark and Grandmother April did so much to help us find our way—it seems they were able to do what your mother and I cannot do. But everyone needs guidance. Deciding on one's life is a big, big task—too big for you alone—even too big for the three of us. We all need God's assistance."

Another wiggle, but no other reflex from the object of the discussion.

"Son," Paul said, yet again, "you've laid a strong foundation. You did well in school. You've a good education—far better than your mother's or mine. Of course, we'd like to see you follow God's ways. We'd like to see you keep up the family tradition and be His shepherd to support those so, so in need. But only you and He can chart that course—your mother and I are here, and always will be, to give you a helping hand. To give you, if you want, advice. To give you encouragement. And, even though perhaps less welcome, to point out errors, few though they certainly will be, if we think it is absolutely necessary. Nevertheless, at the end of the day, it's up to you. It's your life. It'll be your decision. You need to pull yourself up by your bootstraps and get on with it. Son, it's time."

Peter exhaled, he trusted surreptitiously. This should be the end, he thought, for this congregation of one. His father had wound it all up, hit his high point, and hopefully he'd now reached the closing remark.

"Peter," Mother joined in as a postscript, "we pray for you, honey, many times a day. Put your faith in God and He will show you the way."

Peter felt he needed to say at least a few words. "Thanks, Mom, Dad, I know you're worried—I know you're praying. I also know it'll all be fine. I just need some time, that's all."

"It's in God's hands," his parents said in unison.

Peter picked up his coffee; *thus endth the lesson*, he thought.

Peter was fretting. He was sitting under a Denya tree at lakeside, watching a solitary fisher in his dugout check his nets—feeling as isolated as the fisherman—equally adrift—but he himself, unlike the fisherman, felt he was in unknown waters. His thoughts flew across the lake, and he did not hear the light steps that approached.

"Any luck?" asked a deep baritone voice.

Startled back to the here-and-now, Peter looked around to see Kole slipping to the ground to sit next to him.

"It looks like you're a fisher of men today, and I was wondering if you're getting any bites."

Then only a small, "uh-huh," from Peter.

"Ya know," Kole continued, unimpeded, "lotsa folks would love to be sit'n where you are."

"Uh-huh."

"You bet. Why, not to talk about being a fisher of men, there's white guys like you who come up from the city to go fishing in this ol' lake—lotsa 'um. Ever think about fishing for our lake's delicacies? Highly thought of pastime. Highly appreciated sport. Might even settle the nerves."

"Not much of a fisherman, of any sort," Peter finally glumly replied.

"Don' know. Really a highly regarded activity—both in that Bible of your father's and around here. Maybe you ought'a try it?"

"Not my thing."

"Don' know—fish'n 's pretty grand for lots folks. But, like we say back home, '*Nearly no dey kill bird*,' either you've got it, or you don't—guess you don't."

"Yep."

"OK. Then how about a little gossip about this ol' village to lighten your load?"

"Uh-huh."

Thereupon, the circuitous chat began—starting with the weather and the level of water in the lake, slowly moving toward the target, Peter's fretfulness.

Peter, finally with a grin and a mild guffaw, assured Kole his mind was in a passive and pleasant place—happy to be back among his family, underscoring he felt Kole and Wanda to be very important parts of this family—recalling how, years ago when they had first met, he used to chant incessantly to this ballast of the household, "Kole in Bole, Kole in Bole, Kole in Bole . . ."

Undeterred by his erstwhile charge's assurances, Kole pursued the target. "Peter, ya know what we say back home? We say, '*Becos Lizard day nod im head no mean say evritin day okay*.' You de hear? Just because ya nod your head and smile, it doesn't mean that everything is fine."

"Honest, Kole, it is."

"My young friend, don't try and kid me—I've known ya far too long."

"Me?"

"You," Kole emphasized, with a big smile.

"So?"

"So," Kole jumped in immediately, "ya need to clear your head. In Jos, sometimes we'd give our kids a big dose of *pepe*—they'd sneeze, and everything'd clear up. Ya need to sneeze."

"But Kole, I eat plenty *pepe*—I love hot peppers—and I don't sneeze."

"No," Kole persisted, "but ya still need to clear your head—get grounded—get your balance. We say, '*laif de lek basko, fo get balans yu get fo di waka.'* To keep your balance, young man, ya have to keep movin'. Na so?"

"OK, where's my *basko*—my bicycle?"

"For me, and ya know, this is just from me for you, I think ya *need* go waka. Ya need to stretch your legs—get away, really away, for a while. Not as a student when you're tied to ya books, but as a young man—get a job, see something new, see someone new, decide where ya want to be. But that's just me."

"OK."

"This isn't easy, Peter," Kole continued, "ya may not have known, but I was an instructor at Hillcrest School in Jos—one of the top schools, not only in Nigeria, in the whole of Africa. Can you imagine? Can you really imagine? Look at me—today I'm a houseboy *cum* gardener. Look at me. Imagine the shift. One day in a respected position in a highly respected school. Another day, wash'n floors and trim'n bushes. Now—get me right. I'm in no way ashamed or even unhappy wash'n floors and trim'n brushes. I'm with the woman I love. I'm in a peaceful place with nice people. Many, many people have it much, much worse. I know why I'm here— how I got here. I'm fine with it all. I don't bring it up as complaining, but to shine a light on how dramatically the lives of all of us can change—go in directions we never fathomed were possible.

"When I was your age, finished with my own school'n and start'n off in a prestigious position, I'd never have believed it if you'd have told me one day I'd be takin' the clothes of other people (he thought, but did not specify, 'white people') off the clothesline, clothes of others that my wife had washed, so that I could help her with the iron'n. We're unable to appreciate nor understand the twists that await us in our lives."

"Father says we're in God's hands and He guides us according to His plan."

"I'd not dare contradict your father. I, too, am a Christian. Yet, I don't exactly share your father's convictions that God is always guiding us. If this were truly the case, we'd all be where He plans, doing what He requires. I'm not sure this is the way things are. I think each and every one of us has to take responsibility for his own course in life. Maybe God helps out—maybe he doesn't—I don't know. But, for me, it's up to each of us—we can't just sit back and wait for God to do it or we'll be waiting forever."

"I agree," Peter finally replied after a long pensive pause, "my parents seem to have a direct line to God—I have never been so connected. It seems I should be. At times, I feel I should be ashamed I am not. But I am not. I do not receive Divine messages—I do not hear God's Word."

"My friend, count me among your numbers. I've no Divine connection. I feel I have to steer my own canoe, or it will simply sink in the waves of a messed-up world. This, I know, is a bit dramatic—nearly humorous. Still, when we look out over the lake, think of each of us as fishers in our own canoe. I have to guide mine and go where I can catch enough to sustain me—you have to do the same."

"I'm OK with that—it's just that I haven't a clue which way to turn. When I look out to that guy in the canoe, I see myself treading-water over in the middle of the lake, not even able to make it to the canoe—let alone to dry land. I feel I'm sinking."

"There you are. You want me to think you are fine, but in truth you're sinking."

"Hmmmmm."

"Yes. You need a life vest."

"Fine. Throw it to me."

"Alright. Why don't you think about a trek over to Nigeria? It'll be different. You'll see a lot—good and bad."

"OK."

"OK. Let me talk to Wanda, and we'll have some ideas for you to throw at your parents."

A few days later, Peter was leaving for his now habitual promenade when he crossed paths with his father—Paul on the way to the church.

"I've got to start my work on next Sunday's sermon, Son," Paul, with somewhat forced gaiety, proclaimed, "you've done a lot of desk work recently with all your studies and such, but writing a good homily is still a real struggle for me—so how about coming with me to the sanctuary and we can ask for God's guidance—for both of us?"

"Thanks, Dad." Peter stumbled over his words, not wanting to offend his father and not wanting, even more, to go to church. "Maybe we can do it another time? I've gotta run."

"Sure, son," Paul responded in a rather glum voice, realizing that the church held no magnetism for his beloved offspring, "you go ahead with your plans and possibly we can have a visit with God tomorrow—I think it would help."

"Fine, Dad, see ya soon."

Unlike most days, when Peter's roamings were practically completely random, today he, in fact, did have a plan—a rendezvous. He and Kole
were going to meet at a small cabaret—locally called a spot—for a beer
and a follow-up to their lakeshore discussions.

As arranged, Peter found Kole seated at a rather ramshackle table in
the rather ramshackle drinkery, a cold beer already in front of him. Ordering two more brews, Peter sat down, carefully testing the shaky chair
before applying all his weight.

"*Ben-ben rod ova long,* my friend, *ma kombe.*" Kole smiled. "We're
all traveling along a twisting road, my friend."

"Well." Peter frowned dramatically. "I'm personally getting dizzy
from all the curves."

"Can I help?"

Only a hum from Peter.

"Wanda and I had a good conversation about you, my friend—our
friend. We agree, as you and I chatted earlier, it's hard to get the full picture from a seat in Kpando. Maybe ya do need to go elsewhere to be able
to look through another window."

"Hmmm."

"For this, in our corner of the world on the shores of the lake, Lagos
is about as far away from Kpando as one can easily get. Wanda's uncle,
Silas Otuaro, has been a doctor in Lagos for years and years. If ya think it
would interest you, Wanda can reach out to him to see if he'd be OK with
a visit by a young man (he didn't say, but it was understood, young 'white
man') named Peter."

"Sure."

"Peter, I want to be clear. This *waka,* this West African safari is
simply a possibility—a choice—an option. Of course, we're suggesting
Nigeria and we're Nigerians. I suppose, if I'm honest, this is a little bit of
home-country nostalgia. I suppose, if I'm still honest, it is also a bit of
Nigerian swagger—wherever we end up, we always manage to maintain
the idea that we're special—you'll remember I told you at one time Benin
City had a signboard at the entry to town proclaiming, 'Welcome to the
Birthplace of African Civilization.' I guess it's natural that we'd like you to
visit our homeland.

"But this is truly not about our roots—it's about yours. We know all
too well how hard it can be to find one's way—and how shocking it can
be to have this way totally turned upside-down by forces beyond your

control. We know how we all have to expect the unexpected. And, very importantly, we know you and we know your family. We would never want to do anything, suggest anything that'd make problems for ya, or that would upset your parents.

"Wanda and I are Christians. My real professional life was teaching at a Christian school. We admire—I guess, we love—your parents. We know they're devout and committed to giving their lives to Christ. We respect this. If, right now, ya wanted to do the same, this would be a good choice and an honorable choice. We're not trying to push ya in any direction—simply trying to let ya possibly see another twisted pathway that ultimately may well lead ya back to the same destination. Or, it might take ya to somewhere ya never thought you'd go."

The long speech had made Kole's mouth dry and he took a big swig of beer, eying Peter over the rim of his glass.

Peter hadn't committed to Kole's suggestion, his possibility, then and there.

They'd finished their beers, had one more for the road, then each had gone his own way—Peter drifting back in the direction of the lake.

As Peter floated through the now overly-familiar sites of Kpando, as he saw the same houses, the same dusty roads, the same busy market and unbusy banks, the same kids going back and forth to the same schools, he knew he was overflowing with sameness. If Nigeria was different, and, if even half the stories were true, then he should choose this option—he should visit Uncle Silas in Lagos.

Feeling it best to keep things as simple as possible, he did not mention his discussion with Kole to his parents. He knew from the onset this would not be something his parents would support—he was unsure if it was even something they would accept. Nevertheless, he was an adult, and it was not something they could refuse.

He chose a quiet morning moment when his father returned from his prayers to inform his parents he had been invited by a friend from school in the UK to come for a visit to Nigeria. He didn't provide much detail, and his parents, instantly disturbed by the subject of the discussion, did not even ask about how such an invitation had even reached their son in Kpando. Their concern was Nigeria. Nigeria! Why on earth would their son want to go to this place? This place known for all manner of ills from terrible diseases to drugs and even murder. Nigeria!

"Peter, honey," Lynn almost implored, knowing she could not stop her child, and that the more she resisted, the more he could become headstrong, "maybe Nigeria isn't the best place to visit."

"Son," his father picked up the baton without a slip, "your mother's right—Nigeria isn't a good place right now—lots of problems. I'm sure, if you're looking to travel a bit—become a tourist like you've said—we can think of somewhere else and then somehow find the money to get you there."

"I know you're only thinking of me," Peter said, trying to start off with a conciliatory tone, "but this is really not a big deal. First off, remember how you always told me how people in Missouri think of Africa—in their minds, we must be having lions and elephants running through our yard in Kpando—these chased by natives in ostrich-plumed headdresses, decorated egg-shaped shields, and long, long spears!"

His parents could only nod.

"So," Peter continued, while Paul marveled at what a good preacher he would make, "these stories about Nigeria are simply not all true—or at the very least, totally overblown. And there, I will be among friends—I will be far from any lion's den."

Paul and Lynn sipped their coffee.

"I met many Nigerians through my studies in the UK—they're great folks. Silas (Peter thought it best to try and at least keep the names straight as he spun a tale) was a close classmate and, as they say here, he's only a stone's throw away. Now, before I settle down (he knew these words were reactants for his parents), I have a chance to visit Silas and see some new sites—a short outing next door—nothing to be concerned about. I'll be back before you know it—you'll never even have time to miss me—I promise"

"But Son . . .."

"Oh," Peter interrupted, "one more thing, I don't expect you guys to pay for my jaunt—you've done too much as it is (he added for good measure). I managed to save some money from my internship. It's not a lot, but it'll just manage to get me through my quick run over to our big brother Nigeria."

Adding Nigeria at the end made his mother visibly shudder. His father was still admiring his son's oratory skills—a little unpolished but effective.

Paul and Lynn could have dug deeper for other excuses for their son, their dear Peter, to NOT go to Nigeria, but it seemed pointless. He was decided. In spite of that feeling in the pit of their stomachs that this was an ill-fated voyage, there was little his parents could do to dissuade him, and nothing they could do to actually block his scheme.

Peter made his plans to visit Nigeria—*Naija* as some of his Nigerian schoolmates used to call it.

CHAPTER THREE

Tasting the Waters of Naija

Experiencing unaccustomed ways

WHILE MANY FELT NIGERIA was right next door to Ghana—both key parts of British West Africa until not all that long ago—in fact, the principal coastal road joining the two states passed through Togo and Benin—two small francophone countries sandwiched between the two much larger anglophone nations.

Geography, therefore, required Peter to not only get a visa for Nigeria, but to also obtain transit visas for the two maritime French-speaking countries. As a Ghanaian resident, in theory, he could get the necessary documents at the border. However, this inevitably required *dashes* (cash gifts to expedite processes—bribes in most unvarnished conversations) at each crossing—negotiations for these sums leading to slow and unpredictable results. The best thing, if one had the choice, was to get the visas in advance at the embassies in Accra.

Peter decided he needed to make another trek to the capital. After getting all his visas, he would swing by home to reassure his folks, letting them know all was in order, and then take the back road down to the Togolese border where he could get public transport all the way to Lagos.

It would be too much to say everything in Accra went splendidly. Nonetheless, after more than a few delays, seemingly endless forms and questions, and no small amount of fees that made it seem as though he had paid his share of *dashes*, he had all the travel documents he needed and headed back home, crossing the Adomi Bridge and moving north to the lakeshore.

He had no rigid schedule and ended up spending two nights with his parents to try to better dampen their fears about his solo travels in, as they saw it, the dangerous monster—Nigeria.

Ultimately, sensing, in spite of his best efforts, all his parent's trepidations were still firmly in place, it was time to go. He gave his folks a warm hug in the predawn coolness, preempting his father's prayers, and headed off on his journey—at the gate, embracing Kole and Wanda who had come to wish him *good waka*. His small duffel bag in hand, he quickly passed through the town's byways he knew so well to the taxi park where he got a *Tro-Tro* to Ho, the regional capital. There he changed into another equally uncomfortable and cramped contrivance for the ride, following the Togolese border, down to Aflao—the Ghanaian border town that was really a suburb of the Togolese capital Lomé. Moving through immigration and customs formalities with minimal difficulties, he joined another vehicle—this time a bus—to Contonu, the capital of Benin.

The road skirted the seaboard, adorned with pristine sandy beaches and pulsing palm trees of almost postcard splendor. At Aneho, he crossed over into Benin, into that little shard of Benin that sits below the body of Togo like a sliver under a fingernail. Here, the crossing mirrored that of Aflao. He then continued eastward, crossing the Mono River into the body of Benin, ending up in the main taxi park of Contonu.

At that point, he entered a much larger, nearly plush, bus for the last leg to Lagos. The final border crossing at Akraké was more tedious given the large volume of people and vehicles of all sorts. Twelve hours and 260 miles after leaving Kpando, he entered the outskirts of Lagos.

It was like starting at the headwaters of a major river—following the surge downstream. As Peter moved forward, at first slowly, then quickly, the flow increased. The road was awash with traffic. It became engorged. Then, it came to a standstill—there was simply too much to funnel through—he had reached the infamous go-slow of Lagos.

The flow seemed to have a yellow tint—nearly a sunflower yellow, if one could imagine the color beneath the layers of grime that bedecked most of the vehicles. This was the amber of the Lagos city taxis—taxi taken in the largest possible context. There were all variety of passenger cars from broken-down Fiats to nearly new Mazdas, there were old Blue Bird school buses from the states, there were Toyota and Nissan minivans, there were even Tuk-Tuk's (auto rickshaws)—it was a phantasmagoria of conveyances.

The bus ride finally ended in the taxi park in the Orile Iganmu neighborhood of the massive megalopolitan concourse that was Lagos. There was no other way to describe it: it was huge!

There was movement everywhere.

There was noise everywhere.

There were people scurrying everywhere.

There was a vitality there verged on utter chaos.

It was almost inexplicable. One must, Peter felt, really see it to believe it.

His instructions from Kole were to take a taxi to Silas's clinic in the neighborhood of Idi-Araba—near the teaching hospital. The clinic was manned twenty-four seven and, since no one knew exactly when Peter would get to the city, once he got to the clinic, someone would call Silas who would come to pick him up.

It was well after sunset when Peter got into a taxi for the clinic. But, from all indications, everything was still in overdrive. People, cars, motorcycles, pushcarts, even goats—everywhere there was something doing something. In spite of the driver's assurances that traffic was light and they'd get there in no time, from Peter's seat (torn black vinyl in the back of a dilapidated canary-yellow Corolla that shook as it slowly crept down the road) it seemed as though the whole world was on the move.

A tremendous amount of honking of horns, yelling of drivers, and near misses with other cars and pedestrians notwithstanding, they did, after what seemed like a very, very long time, ultimately reach the clinic. As promised, there were staff on duty and, to Peter's surprise, they even knew he was coming.

He was offered a plastic chair in a corner of a waiting room and then someone brought him a warm Coke and some semi-sweet crackers—confirming Silas would be there soon.

Peter was struck by the concept of soon. Nonetheless, Silas did come, a big smile on his face and an outreached hand, just before midnight.

Wanda's Uncle Silas was almost the exact opposite of her husband Kole. Kole was a hefty guy—broad-shouldered, with considerable girth, and an ebony complexion. Silas was wiry and slight, a large polished bald head siting on a sinewy toffee-colored frame.

Following an impressive hug and perfunctory greetings to his staff, Silas shepherded Peter outside into an aging lime-green Mercedes. Without even a wince, Silas, with a blast of his horn, entered into the river of humanity that was still flowing in front of the clinic.

Once he had asked Peter the standard questions about the trip and the family, including Kole and Wanda, of course, he informed his guest that for more than three decades he had lived in Akoka, a neighborhood to the east, on Lagos Lagoon. His wife had passed a few years ago, their three children were in the UK and the US, but he still stayed in the old home even though it was now far too big for his needs and the neighborhood far different from when they had moved in all those years ago.

He anticipated Peter's possible questions, continuing that the neighborhood today was probably no worse off than many around the city—times were stressful for most and the local government had a hard time addressing everyone's needs.

These were strange days, he concluded. It was nearly, he added, as though everything and everyone had been poured into a giant blender—a sticky human paste the result. All was mixed together now. Former residential areas were filled with businesses—even industry. Bars, dancehalls, and even cemeteries seemed to pop up everywhere. It was all now just an anthropological ooze that, like a lava flow, continuously leaked into the lagoon.

Peter practically cringed at the image. Yet, as he peered out through the smudged Mercedes' windows, it seemed somehow apropos.

Peter must have dozed off, for, as he felt the car slow nearly to a stop, he looked out the window to see a church's steeple—thinking he was back in Kpando.

Silas, noting his passenger's consternation, explained, "That's the Gospel Church of Ilajai Road—my across-the-street neighbor—we're home."

Peter peered more deeply into the darkness only minimally alleviated by the dim ivory-tinged illumination from the time-worn streetlight. Silas was inching into a litter-infested parking space on a street already replete with all variety of vehicles—some apparently functioning, others obviously having been immobile for years. Immediately next to their car, a single incandescent lightbulb barely lit a signboard proclaiming, "Odukoya Electric: the place for all your electrical needs." The establishment itself was a low structure of cement block and corrugated roofing sheets with a heavy welded set of iron "burglar bars" protecting the store's entry while, Peter thought, someone with a hefty machete or a chisel and hammer could just cut a hole in the wall or the roof to carry away all that was of value in the blink of an eye.

Silas fixed a long bar to the car's steering wheel, locking it, Peter hoped, with a prayer as it didn't seem a suitable deterrent to anyone who really wanted to steal the car—admittedly any thief having many better options than a too-old-to-be-good Mercedes. Peter and Silas then exited the car, Silas making a great show of locking the doors, and Peter, duffle bag in hand, followed his host into complete darkness—a small alleyway to the right of the electrical supply store.

Peter could see tiny flickers of light reflecting off Silas's polished dome as he blindly followed his host down the claustrophobic and malodorous corridor until he literally walked into his sponsor who had stopped and was, obviously through long experience, unlocking a door in total darkness.

A push of a heavy door and the flip of a switch and Peter, blinking to adjust to the new brightness, found himself in the entryway of an old and stylish home.

Silas turned with a wink and a smile, "Welcome—welcome to my humble home."

Peter retuned the smile as best he could and mumbled a gracious, he hoped, thank-you.

Further on, they entered into a clean parlor with a well-used set of leather-covered armchairs and sofas. One wall was occupied by book-shelves, the tomes interspersed with wooden and bronze sculptures. Other parts of the room were decorated with a wide variety of photographs, most black and white, of people Peter assumed to be Silas's family.

Silas motioned to Peter to take a seat, disappeared for a moment, returning with two bottles of beer. After passing a sweating bottle to his guest, Silas said, "It's really late." He took big gulp of the golden liquid.

Peter noticed on the wall clock it was three in the morning but said nothing—not wanting in any way to make it appear he was uncomfortable with the hour or the surroundings.

"Let me quickly tell you something about here." Silas returned to his conversation as if a time-honored dialogue. "As much in the city, it takes some getting used to."

"Sure," Peter uttered automatically.

"First, don't be mistaken. We don't have NEPA (the electric utility that was more off than on). The light is thanks to an automatic genera-tor—everybody's got them—we haven't had reliable public utilities—elec-tricity or water—for years."

"Gosh," Peter said—another automatic response.

"You won't really have to do anything special—I just wanted to let you know. We have big water tanks in the back to capture what is rarely released by the water works—we even add to this water from the rain gutters—and the generator is a pretty good system that only occasionally lets us down. With luck, you'll never notice anything wrong."

"Fine." Sleep now pulled heavily on Peter's marrow.

"You'll have my son's old room upstairs—so, make yourself at home—you're certainly most welcome and it will be good to have someone else in this big place."

"Thank you." Peter hoped the words actually came out of his mouth, he knew he had thought them, but couldn't be sure he'd actually said them—as he was really slipping into the abyss of fatigue.

"Your beer's tipping there, Son." Silas tried to pick up the pace. "Take a big swallow—it'll help. I've got just a few more little things, then we'll both head to bed—stay with me."

"OK," Peter managed to say, as beer dribbled off his chin.

"This place is now surrounded by all manner of things—nothing to be worried about—but things to get to know slowly. I suggest you stay inside through the day—sleep as much as you like—there's plenty of food and beer in the fridge and, as you see, lots of books to read—there's also a TV in the study down the hall. So, make yourself at home, but rest inside and I will come home early to further introduce you to where you are. For now, lets' get to bed."

He was being crushed by a spinning mass of cotton—a white whirling daemon swooping down upon him from above. But his body was too heavy to flee—his throat too tight to scream. His eyes opened in panic. He sat up.

He found himself in a bed with a simple wooded headboard, sunlight streaming in through less-than-sparkling-clean windows. Was he in a hospital? Had he had an accident?

Hearing a whirring noise, he looked up to see a fan slowly spinning in the middle of a snowy-white, if a bit smudged, ceiling—the daemon explained. But where was he?

The mist continued to clear. He realized that this foreign place was Silas's—Silas's son's room—he was in Lagos!

The early morning discourse with his host dripped back into his memory—food in the fridge, books on the shelf, TV in the study, stay inside . . .

He looked at his watch on the bedside table—it was one in the afternoon—he'd had a long and much-needed sleep.

Having gained his bearings, he sat motionless in bed, listening. If he did this at he's parent's home (he was still unsure if he wanted to designate the home in Kpando as his home), aside from the desultory rooster crowing or neighbor's child crying, there was silence. Here there was a din—a commotion that seemed to vibrate through the walls in spite of the house's obvious solid construction and its off-the-road location. His ears could hear no distinguishable elements—only an ebb and flow of the clamor of a continual hubbub.

It was time to join the fray.

He found a clean bath towel on a hook behind the door. Down the hall was an ample bathroom with a big shower that, as Peter sampled its performance, had good pressure, was nice and hot (almost too hot), but whose water had rather a straw color that Peter hoped came from rust in the pipes rather than other possible more organic origins.

Putting this thought aside, he concentrated on the hot water undoing the knots that had developed in his back as he had traveled across four countries yesterday. Then, feeling more presentable, albeit still in his travel cloths (only two and a half changes available in his duffel bag), he decided to explore the kitchen. He was hungry and ready for a beer.

As promised, although Peter had forgotten, Silas appeared on the scene around teatime—bearing a bag of takeaway in case his visitor was not able to find his fill in the fridge.

Peter and Silas sat around the kitchen table, not having tea and crumpets, not having a hamburger and fries, but enthusiastically gobbling up the jollof rice and fried chicken Silas had brought—this, of course, accompanied by cold beer.

After politely asking about how his guest had spent the night, Silas got into the mechanics of Peter's presence. "I'm glad you're getting your feet under you—you were knackered this morning."

"Sure was," Peter offered through a mouthful of rice.

"Well, as I started to say earlier, this is, as you have now seen, an old house. Years ago, it was somewhat set apart from the neighborhood—sitting back off the road on an oversized lot going back to the preferential zoning of the colonial time. But things change. It's impossible to hold onto big chunks of land in this city unless you're truly wealthy and powerful. Little by little, for various reasons, our plot shrunk like a waning hibiscus—soon we had withered to a space just slightly larger than the house itself—all the surrounding areas jam-packed as though it were a vacuum being filled. At first there were some small houses, then there were small business, then there were sheds and lean-to's. We were left, like a conspicuous wart on the nose, a large venerable home surrounded by the outgrowths of humankind—an island—a monument of times gone by. We were only connected to the outside by the tunnel-like alley that not only leads to our front door but is also the main outlet for several of the smaller homes and business that have sprouted-up. Each time I come and go, I imagine I am a monk secretly leaving the abbey through a covert burrow used to flee the coming hordes. However, don't be concerned. There is no real problem or danger—just a lot more noise and clutter. I'll give you a key and you can come and go as you wish.

"Wanda didn't tell me exactly what your plans are—but I believe this is your first time to our city. So, I have taken the liberty to arrange a guide for you—I hope this is OK? Tomorrow, if you come by the clinic, I'll introduce you to your could-be chaperone and we can make some clearer plans."

"Sounds, great—I really don't know how to thank you."

"Not to worry—my pleasure. It's been a long time since I've had something special to do."

"I don't know what I'd have done if you weren't here."

"I am happy to have you—happy to help."

The next day, before noon, Peter surfaced from Silas's, feeling a bit like he was a rabbit emerging from his warren. While the ambient noise inside Silas's was far above that of Kpando, when he exited the tunnel, his ears were instantly assaulted by a piercing cacophony and his eyes assaulted by brilliant light.

Adjusting to this new atmosphere, his gaze immediately fell on the church steeple across the street—his mind flashing back again to his family—he somehow saw himself, as his father undoubtedly wished to see him, as Father Peter, entering the church on Ilajai Road. He had to physically shake off the image, forcing himself to concentrate on finding a taxi to take him to the clinic.

When he entered through the double doors of the health center, the polite lady decked in white at the front desk promptly directed him to Silas's office. After a knock and a rapid "come in," Peter found his host seated behind a stout metal desk piled high with papers, across from him an attractive young woman, also dressed in white.

As Peter approached, both Silas and his guest stood. Silas made the presentations, "Peter, this is Daberechi—kind of a mouthful, meaning one who is dependent on God—you can call her Dabi like we all do."

Peter shook hands with the grinning woman of about his age, immediately appreciating her raven skin and her statuesque form accentuated by her nurse's uniform.

Before he could say anything, Silas continued, "She's volunteered to usher you about and I've agreed to give her a leave of absence to do just that if you'd be OK with it?"

Peter was.

Peter realized he was definitely OK with spending time with a comely young lady, who, he was finding out, had a winning personality and was very sharp indeed. But, and Peter felt like he was inventing puzzles for himself, this was, certainly through Silas's eyes, a means to an end. What end? What end would be achieved by an extended guided tour of Lagos? Enjoyable though it may be on multiple levels, what would it bring that Peter was seeking?

Was this a pre-scripted play with Peter as the principal actor? Had Wanda, Silas, or whomever tried to craft events to help Peter? Was he (possibly once again) getting ready to live out others' solutions to his problems?

He honestly didn't know.

But that was no reason not to go ahead—and he did.

Lagos definitely does not have all the attractions of London—museums, art galleries, historical building and monuments—they're there, but of different scope and in more limited supply. More than drinking in the past as can be done in London, in Lagos it was, for Peter, more a question of sipping the culture of now—getting a taste, little by little, to understand what was beneath the apparent chaos that was so overbearing.

In some ways, to Peter the unceasing throb of this city was almost like living inside a drum—being inside the boba drum of an Ewe group of Gahu musicians—the beat of this master drummer not random nor rambling, the drum navigating for the group—setting the pace for life.

Peter mentioned this to Dabi one afternoon when they were, after a long and hot walk through one of the never-ending commercial centers, enjoying beers at a small off license.

"This city pulses at its own rhythm, a hectic rhythm," Peter observed, "it reminds me of the Gahu drummers in Ghana—a thumping that enters your bones."

"You know," Dabi replied, "we Lagosians seem to have almost developed calluses to the, what others see as bedlam all around us. I can assure you that for everything that seems totally out of control to you as an outsider, there is a logic and a structure—people here have learned how to adapt and adopt—becoming very effective at moving through and across the tides of the city."

"It is amazing," Peter acknowledged—being truly taken aback by his surroundings.

"And, Peter, my friend," Dabi continued, "you might not know this, but the Gahu style actually originated here from the Yoruba People and their Kokosawa music."

Peter was impressed, yet said nothing, only taking a big swig of beer.

From music to a fondness for beer and spicy food, Dabi and Peter quickly realized they had a lot in common. While the sightseeing was short-lived, their relationship was not. They started with a few dinners together that soon led to Peter spending the night at Dabi's—both agreeing it would be unseemly at the very least for their romantic dalliance to take place under the roof of Dabi's boss and Peter's host.

This was not the fiery lust he had experienced with Ruby where, nearly like soldiers at the front, they realized from the onset their connection was destined to be ephemeral, trying to engulf each day together in unprecedented passion. This was tender. His intimate relationship with Dabi was almost calming, as though, in the isolation of their bedroom, they sought the opposite of the clamor that enveloped their outside world.

Indoors or outdoors, they were grateful to Silas for serving, as it turned out, as a matchmaker. Yet, their feelings notwithstanding, they appreciated all too well their bond was fragile—probably transient as Peter was, it seemed, just as likely to float away as he had floated in.

"You know," Peter started, as they were enjoying a beer in their favorite haunt of the moment.

"About us?" Dabi swiftly picked up.

"Uh-huh," Peter continued around a big swallow of beer, "about us—and, about life."

"So."

"Well, first, I think we have to tell Silas. There's no reason he'd be anything but happy . . ."

"OK. He's my boss, ya know. So, if he's not so happy, I'm the one in his sights. But I agree, let's go ahead."

"Fine. Good. Then, it's clear to me, and I imagine to you, that I'm not here to see the sights."

"And?"

"And, I don't know. I really don't know why I'm here. I needed to get away. I needed to think. I needed to do something. Wanda said, 'Go to Lagos', and I came to Lagos. I still don't know what I'm looking for."

"Yeah." She smiled, "that was clear from the first day."

"Ya know, Wanda could probably have said, 'Go to the moon,' and I'd have tried to find a way. I really needed to get away from Kpando. Away from my folks. Away from that church. Just away."

"And, now you're here."

"This all doesn't mean I won't go, don't want to go back. God! I just don't know."

"Well, you know Silas is very clever. There's lots of girls at the clinic who'd love to go out and about with a young American—'cus that's what you are. But he chose me—I don't think it was by chance. I bet he figured I could help—don't know how or why— but he doesn't do things willy-nilly—that's your word—you Americans—not good Nigerian Pidgin."

They both laughed and drew deeply on their beer bottles.

They decided, after they'd told Silas, Dabi would go back to work—there was no reason she should forego pay just to sit and drink with a lost soul. They could still see each other every day after she got off work—maybe even at Silas's, depending on his reaction to their liaison.

It was a plan—short-term—very short-term—but a plan, nonetheless. They ordered two more beers and began discussing where to have dinner.

There was a new rhythm for Peter. He still felt the echoes of the boba, but it now shared the stage with a multitude of sounds that began to resonate less as caterwauling, more and more as distinct and not unpleasant reverberations.

He would rise at his leisure, feeling nearly the grand gentleman in the manor-like home of Silas. He would eat a bit, read a bit, and tipple— sometimes a bit more than a bit. Slowly, still like a rabbit making his first sortie of the spring, he would wander about Akoka; he was never totally sure he knew where he was, but sure he was somehow always close to a city taxi that could take him to the clinic and his afternoon rendezvous with Dabi.

Silas had greeted Peter's "friendship" (as he, Peter, described it) with Dabi with aplomb—in no way surprising Dabi, but in some ways startling Peter who remained unclear as to what Wanda had told Silas and whether or not Silas had, in his own mind, some sort of master plan for the young American seeking to find himself.

Despite Silas's nonchalance, Peter remained mildly uncomfortable being under his roof while engaged in amorous pursuits with Dabi. Thus, they continued to retire several times a week to her apartment in the Mushin neighborhood of the city—an area even more embedded in the urban madcap mayhem of the municipality than the (historically) more sedate lagoon-side borough where Silas lived.

As Peter would sit in Silas's parlor, preparing to meet Dabi, listening to Silas's stereo, reading Silas's books, savoring Silas's beer after eating Silas's food, the impermanence of his situation definitely did not escape him. He had traveled hard to exchange his parent's nest for Silas's. He had traded one bubble for another.

Was this progress?

He didn't know.

The knotty question was: what did progress look like?

He didn't know.

Was this all about predestination?

Maybe.

From his earliest memories in Bole, it seemed as though everyone, not just his parents, everyone, looked at him as a missionary in waiting.

His father often observed, as a second-generation evangelist, "It's in the blood."

Was it in his blood?

Was he, childlike, circling around the inevitable?

Were, as had flashed through his mind when he saw the church on Ilajai Road, his church and his congregation waiting?

Was he deluding himself? Was he forestalling the ordained by going on a wild goose chase? Should he not succumb and don the robes awaiting him?

At what cost?

He convinced himself and others that he admired missionaries. Did he?

He thought not.

This was a terribly thorny question.

He assumed he loved his parents—he was their child. Children loved their parents.

His parents had not abused him. To the contrary, they had tried to do their best for him.

Still—did he want to walk in their shoes?

Honestly—no.

In truth, he didn't really admire missionaries. He felt they lived in an artificial world they created for themselves where they justified their narrow view by the imagined fact that they were leading the disheveled, unknowledgeable, and uncultured masses to God—delivering them, the masses, to their salvation. The "they," not just his parents, they, the larger group of proselytizers, lived in just as much of a bubble as that from which he now was trying to break free.

Their paternalistic views were so condescending to people who lived complex and sophisticated lives—lives completely unknown or overlooked by those who considered themselves as God's messengers.

Peter never told his parents he had African girlfriends—not even close African classmates for that matter. In the UK, at least half of his relationships had been with Africans—a group with whom he felt he shared a kindred spirit—but about whom he had never told, would never tell his folks.

He knew full well his parents would swear they were not—could never be—racist. He knew full well his parents honestly believed all were God's children. Yet, through their patronizing behavior and deep-seated beliefs, if someone were able to extract the very essence at the core of their beings, he, sadly, knew his parents would profoundly believe that white, Anglo-Saxon, protestants were quite simply better—it was God's way.

This was too harsh.

It seemed too cutting—too grim.

Possibly, too honest.

Maybe.

He didn't know.

He was, after all, in his own bubble.

Was this a bubble of his own making? His parents'? Others'?

Where was the exit?

Where was inner peace?

Wasn't, in his father's words, God the pathway to inner peace?

Shouldn't he be following God's pathway?

Weren't his parents (and grandparents) correct? He had a birthright—he had an inheritance—he had a tradition to follow—he had God's ways to follow.

Wasn't he truly called to do God's work?

Didn't the impoverished and the impecunious reach out to him, as they did to his parents, to enlighten them with God's words and God's ways?

Wasn't it destiny?

Wasn't it God's will?

This was all too, too much!

He needed to spend less time cloistered in Silas's comfortable home drinking beer and embroiled in his own mental gymnastics. He needed to get out.

He needed to focus on the newness.

So much was so different.

He was in the heart of Naija.

Sitting with Dabi in a small chophouse eating a steaming plate of pounded yam and vegetables, washed down with large volumes of icy beer seemed to be the elixir to clear the spinning ruminations from his head. Dabi recounted several strange tales from the day's ministrations at the clinic. Peter listened with one ear while the other filtered the racket emanating from the other patrons, intermingled with the clang of pots and the hollers of cooks from an outbuilding that served as the kitchen.

He decided to try and compete with the commotion. "Dabi," he started, "I think I need to be doing something. You know this. I know this. We've talked about this. It's always been a question of what."

A refocus of her eyes indicated she had changed gears, now far from the clinic and trying to see from Peter's perspective. She took a big swallow of beer, hoping it would help, but said nothing.

"I still have no idea. So, I've decided, let's look in the papers—look in the want ads or anywhere where any jobs might be posted—let's just roll the dice."

"So?"

"So what?"

"So, eat your yams."

He did, enjoying the smooth, almost sweet taste of the tubers, accentuated by the bitter and fibrous vegetables—all emboldened by the pungent flavor of good palm oil.

After a dessert of fresh mangos, they walked about, buying some newspapers at street-side kiosks, before retiring to a nearby bar to review their harvest. As they enjoyed their after-dinner beers, they pursued the three Nigerian papers and the *International Herald Tribune*—both uncertain why this latter had ended up in their search for a job.

Before pouring over the local press, they were attracted to a back-page story in the *Tribune* that detailed the alleged machinations of one Sir Horace Barthley—these coming home to Nigeria.

Sir Horace, pictured, who knew where, in dress reminiscent of a Gaucho, was reported to be an errant philanthropist with loose linkages to some of England's best families, but also connections to several less sterling groups—some suspected of a wide variety of international acts of corruption. The specific saga featured by the *Tribune* involved accusations that Sir Horace, through a Chinese intermediary, had been surreptitiously purchasing large tracts of land in Nigeria, claiming to be operating on behalf of the government, preparing to build a new federal highway, whereas the ill-gained lands would be peddled at exorbitant prices and under questionable titles to companies seeking sites to build new oil and gas pipelines.

"See," Dabi huffed, exasperated, "it's not like we don't have enough crooks here at home, we even import fake nobility to further torture our citizens!"

Peter slid a copy of the *Daily Post* under Dabi's nose, deflecting, "Let's leave Sir Horace to his shenanigans and look for something for poor ol' Peter."

They dug as deeply as they could through the local papers, deeming Peter unsuited to the nursing, teaching, lorry driving, welding, heavy-equipment-operator, and pipe-fitting jobs that appeared to abound. They then ordered a couple of beer chasers, deciding there was always another day.

After a week of "other days," they were no closer to their objective. Then Dabi had a breakthrough.

Over after-clinic beers, she announced, "A long-lost cousin came by work today. He lives in Port Harcourt. He works for Shell. We had a cup of coffee—I hadn't seen him for fifteen years."

"That's nice."

"Yes, it is," she almost boasted, "but you don't know why."

"OK."

"Guess."

"Hmmm."

"Guess!"

"Humm—he's going to give you a hundred million Naira and we can go off and live on the beach with no worries."

"Not quite, but close." She frowned, not appreciating Peter's frivolousness. "He's pretty high up in Shell. He can get you a job."

"Wow!"

"Yes, Mister triviality. Yes, I've got a lead for you. What do you have for me?"

"Huh?"

"This is Nigeria. There's no free lunch. I help you, you help me."

"Hmmm. Fine. I'll help you. Tonight, when we get to your place. Just wait and see. I'll really help you. Then you'll be so, so happy you helped me. In fact, you'll owe me tomorrow for all the good times you'll have tonight. OK?"

"A little too narcissistic for me—but, OK."

"Oh, aren't we the one with the grandiloquent vocabulary—not even Pidgin (finally, he rejoiced, a chance to use that word that had come up on his A-levels so long ago)! What you may see as pompous today, maybe pompous like good ol' Sir Horace, you'll see as honesty tomorrow—you'll be so grateful to have seen the honesty, the wonder, for yourself."

"I think you've had enough beer."

Dabi's cousin, Kelechi (Dabi said the name meant "Glorify God"—Peter felt God was following him and called the cousin "Kele"), was a godsend if not God's Glory. The three met at the Federal Palace Hotel on Victoria Island where Kele was attending a seminar on security organized by the Nigerian National Petroleum Corporation.

Kele, a rather plump and smiley person, was a pivotal part (his words) of Shell's PR team in Port Harcourt, a major petroleum city nearly 350 miles to the southeast of Lagos on the margins of the Niger Delta. After the general pleasantries, Kele explained that Port Harcourt had been a principal refining center going back to the 60's. Pipelines, like a spider's web with a hub in the Delta, carried petroleum products across the country. Many of these pipelines were on the surface and pipeline vandalism, called "bunkering," was a big concern. Large volumes of refined products were stolen at a huge cost, not only to the companies but also the communities. People hacking into the pipes created spills that frequently resulted in long-term environmental troubles—some so severe entire villages had to relocate. Furthermore, the thievery often ended in fire and death. Hundreds of pipelines were vandalized each year, and over the years, thousands of people had lost their lives. In short, Kele concluded with an accentuated theatrical frown, bunkering was bad—bad, bad, bad.

Shell and the Petroleum Corporation were trying to do all they could to minimize bunkering—both by increasing security and by trying to educate communities as to the risk while also trying to provide some incentives to residents to be more supportive of the big petrol businesses.

One pipeline that was especially problematic was the 2E that ran almost due north from Port Harcourt, 140 miles to Enugu—paralleling the Niger River on its eastern shore. Shell and the Petroleum Corporation, in collaboration with community organizers and leaders, were in the process of putting together a team to monitor the 2E—to try and reduce the damages while fostering goodwill among people sharing their space with the pipeline. The good news was that there was an opening on this team if Peter was looking for a job.

Before Peter could react, Kele added the post-script: this was real general stuff, as he explained it. There were no real requirements other than being willing to bounce up and down the pipeline and talk to people.

Peter took the job. Kele had been right, and with his recommendation, it was really just a matter of course for Peter to fill-out a contract for short-term services and get his ID as a paid member of the very large Shell workforce.

The compensation, while barebones, was enough for Peter to pay his bills while he sampled a new part of the human banquet. The downside was that he had to leave Lagos and Dabi—Silas, too. Nonetheless, as is often the case it appeared with oil company work, it was flexible. Peter would spend ten days with the team going up and down the pipeline, visiting villages and villagers, inspecting and photographing infrastructure. He would then be able to get on a Shell flight from Port Harcourt to Lagos and have one week there, before flying back to the Delta and the pipeline.

Once again, the rhythm of Peter's life changed. And, for the first time in some time, he seemed to feel this was a change for the better. This was certainly not a career path. It was also not a get-rich-quick stunt. But it was something that occupied his mind and body. There was a lot of exercise walking around villages, over fields, and along streams. There were always challenges—at times big ones—raised by local communities. He and all the team members had to be able to think on their feet. It was not just reciting some platitudes from Mother Shell, Inc.—these people had real worries and they wanted real answers. They deserved (in Peter's view) real answers.

While he hoped he was contributing, he was learning. He learned about local life and politics. He learned about corporate scheming and (often) greed. He learned about the engineering demands of building and maintaining pipelines. He learned about why people hack pipelines. He learned new ways to think and communicate.

Interspersed between his open-air classroom sessions were intra-mural sessions of concupiscence with Dabi during his regular returns to Lagos. As a now duly employed staffer of Shell, he was able to bring a few carefully selected gifts to his paramour as well as make arrears by contributing to Silas's larder.

After one nearly exhausting session in Dabi's apartment, the two were savoring refreshing beers at a local off license, when Peter began sharing details of a recent rather unusual encounter along the pipeline.

"We were just coming into a village near Ozalla, just south of Enugu," Peter described, "when we found the road blocked by scores of villagers, most with large sticks which they swung threateningly at our minivan—seemingly ignoring the big letters 'SHELL NIGERIA' painted in bright red and yellow on the side."

"Not a good sign," Dabi inserted, downplaying the drama Peter felt.

"Not at all," he continued, "a few even took swipes at the front of the van. They were chanting, 'Oyebo, Oyebo, Oyebo.'"

"I'm guessing that was not in your honor, albeit you're certainly an Oyebo—a white man."

"Not at all a welcome—not even a little bit," Peter resumed, "I was really quite uncomfortable. I was the only Oyebo in the van."

"As usual."

"Fortunately, our driver was from Enugu and he knew the local dialect as well as some of the people in the village. He, and I must say, not without a good case of the jitters, was able to get out of the vehicle and talk with some of the leaders."

"And?"

"And, you probably know of this already, the villagers were all riled up and seeking vengeance because another vehicle—a big black Mercedes, evidently, with an Oyebo in the back seat—had hit a kid who was running across the road. Luckily, the child was not too badly hurt, but the community still wanted retribution. If they couldn't catch the offending car, they'd settle for any replacement—including a Shell Nigeria van. They really wanted to beat our vehicle and its Oyebo passenger to a pulp to pay for the crime of hit-and-run—even though it was committed by another. An eye for an eye—any eye apparently."

"Yep."

"You'd think that'd be quite enough for a noteworthy yarn."

"It wasn't?"

"No. And this bit is very weird—not that beating an innocent stand-in to a pulp isn't weird to some people."

"You among them . . ."

"Yes—definitely yes—but moving on. When everyone cooled down and we were back on-the-job with one of the engineers going over a pipeline map with the village leaders to flag any worries, I opened my haversack to get my pad to take a few notes. I had forgotten I had put that old *Herald Tribune* in my bag in case I needed, but could not find, a toilet roll."

"And?" Dabi pushed.

"And, it fell out, open to the picture of Sir Horace. Now here's the really unbelievable part: the village leaders saw the picture and said that was a picture of the *Oyebo* sitting in the back of the black Mercedes."

"Agreed. That's almost unbelievable."

"So strange."

"And?"

"No real and. There were heated comments after seeing the picture—comments I could not follow and could only evaluate as being seething. But palm wine appeared, and tempers seemed to relax. Just another day on the pipeline, I guess."

The work had no real endpoint. If there was the pipeline and as long as people lived along its path, there would be issues. Sometimes big, sometimes almost negligible—but there were always questions. A number, possibly even the majority of these concerns could not be answered by Peter's team of lower-tier on-the-ground grunts. But they were conscientious. All matters were duly noted, copies of the report given to the elders, and the originals pushed up the twisted chain of Shell administration.

Peter got to know the 2E intimately, almost like getting to know the intricacies of a new lover—but the 2E was no lover. In his mind it was the opposite. He saw the serpentine metal tubes as anathema to society and nature—to God (or the gods, he wasn't sure). So much toxicity flowing so strongly over such long distances was a sure recipe for problems—big problems. Management blamed the villagers and truly they were the instigators of many mishaps—some catastrophic. Nonetheless, human error and mechanical failure were unavoidable. There was always an accident waiting to happen.

Still-and-all, being there, trying to help—it seemed a good thing to do. He wondered if his parents would call it "God's work."

The days melded into weeks and the weeks into months. Days in the hot sun and the drenching rain following the intervolved conduit that carried the economic lifeblood of the country—the quintessence of the state for which men schemed and plotted to see who would get the bigger slice of the national cake. This was now the soul of the realm—replacing traditional crops like rubber, palm oil, groundnuts, and cassava that had previously driven the fiscal motors of the Federal Republic since independence.

Peter would try to flee the politics of petroleum when he flew back to Dabi and a Lagos he was, to his great surprise, actually getting to know and even slightly understand. They would have an enjoyable respite that was always too short—all too soon be was back in bed with the 2E.

In spite of his often-lumbering thoughts, Peter did not *not* enjoy his work. He was outside—each day with new people, new places, and new predicaments. Questions of right and wrong, of God and country, aside, he felt free. He agonized much less about tomorrow and lived much more in today.

He would write his parents before each break in Lagos, giving the letter to Silas to put in the clinic's mail. Paul and Lynn would follow the same channel and there was always a letter waiting from him at Estate Silas.

He and his folks engaged in written chit-chat; the weather, the cost of food, the craziness all around the world. There were no references to Peter's future, to his current activities or relationships, to his religious bearings, or to his pious plans. It was a sort of reliable system for them to exchange the core message: "I'm OK, you're OK, we're carrying-on".

Then, Peter's contract needed renewing and was renewed. He understood he wasn't going to be following the 2E for the rest of his life, but for the moment it seemed like not such a bad place to be.

CHAPTER FOUR

Other New Lands

A parable comes true

PETER WAS FASTIDIOUSLY PUNCTUAL. He attributed this to his Germanic roots. He recalled his father proudly proclaiming the family heralded from Bavaria where Volman meant "man of the people"—surely a sign that being a shepherd of God was foreseen in the family genealogy (Peter had tried to look more deeply into the pedigree when at school and discovered that the old Volmans, or Vollmans, were, according to some reports, a vicious warrior clan with shifting allegiances—not quite the same image as his father's).

Peter was never really sure how his parents jumped freely from Bavaria to their emphasis on Anglo-Saxon mores as the foundation for God's ways. He guessed that, as he had learned in his lessons in the UK, this was because his folks also knew the Anglo-Saxons had evolved from Germanic invaders, possibly around the fifth century. Did this mean Bavaria was included? He didn't know. He really didn't care that much.

His solution, when finding convoluted histories or uncertain syntax, had generally been to not look too closely (don't pull at scabs, his mother had always said). Perhaps curiously selecting the same antidote his parents often used when encountering difficult knots to untangle—not wanting to turn over too many stones muddled in mire—opting for the least-said-best-done tactic. He remembered his father's readings from Saint Luke at Christmas, "*But Mary treasured up all these things and pondered them in her heart.*" He too stuffed things in his heart (or wherever) to ponder later—always feeling he had more than enough to occupy the present.

Today none of that mattered.

Peter had been called into the office in Port Harcourt—no reason given.

He knocked on his supervisor's door at precisely ten o'clock.

"Peter," Abeo, the rather rotund junior pipeline supervisor for the northern river eastern-shore zone, said with no sign of cordiality, "right on time as always. Haven't you heard of African Time? Time is flexible—soft and pliable like fresh latex from a rubber tree. It shouldn't be molded and hardened. Take time, boy."

Peter had only met Abeo three times before. Dabi had told him the name meant "bringer of happiness"—he had never seen any happiness brought forth from Mr. Abeo's perpetually scowling face. His only inference for the summons could be that somehow he was in trouble. He smiled humbly, remained standing, and simply said, "Good morning Mr. Abeo."

With the mien of an endlessly disconsolate spurned tortoise, Abeo continued without looking Peter in the eye (an ill omen from Peter's position), "You know, these pipelines are a problem. Everyone's trying to steal our products. We can't win."

By this time, Peter certainly understood that petroleum exploitation and human society were yin and yang. Petroleum was an extractive mess for the communities concerned. Petroleum was big bucks for those on the top.

This was not, however, a discussion to have with Mr. Abeo. Peter blandly added, "Indeed, Sir, it's difficult."

"Well, we're not alone. Everybody who's trying to help the world out of its energy crisis is having problems—especially here in Africa."

"Of course," Peter said, noncommittally.

"So, the African Petroleum Association, founded here in Nigeria, is holding a seminar on community relations in Luanda, Angola. You know, Angola is also a big producer with lots of American dollars streaming into the country in spite of the civil war."

"That's good."

"It is. And you're going to represent our zone."

"Excuse me?"

"No excuses necessary. We've decided you'd be the best guy to go to Luanda for the seminar."

"But . . ."

"Now no reason to worry. Whatever you've heard—the war isn't in Luanda. The capital is perfectly safe—why, as safe as Lagos I'm told."

"But . . ."

"No need to thank me. We'll take care of all the arrangements and we know you'll do fine by us there. We hope there'll be interpreters. You know Angola is Portuguese-speaking."

"But . . ."

"No. Not to worry. We'll do the needful and let you know once all is ready."

"But . . ."

"Happy to help. See you next time."

It was done.

Peter told his team he would be going to Angola (they already knew), informed Silas of the same, and whispered it into Dabi's ear while scribbling the news on a letter to Kpando.

Peter reached Luanda via Johannesburg—all told, two days of travel required.

The arrivals area was a madhouse. His plane, a TAAG (*Linhas Aereas de Angola*) 747 had been full to cracking—if it wasn't petroleum, he had no idea why so many people were coming to the city. Nonetheless, the reality was that the immigration, customs, and baggage facilities were stretched over their limits to handle the 400-plus passengers flooding into the terminal building.

Language and just available space complications led to long delays. It was well after sunset when he finally got to the venue for the seminar, the *Hotel Presidente*, a four-star hostelry on Luanda Bay, just four miles west of the refinery.

It was Tuesday night. He had the next day to rest and then the two-day seminar started on Thursday with his flight out early Sunday morning. If all went well, he would be back in Lagos before sunrise the next Monday—he was already ready to get back.

First impressions were, as all knew, crucial. Peter's first impressions were not very glowing.

Admittedly, anywhere suffering the effects of war is at a disadvantage, but Luanda was far from an appealing site. Police and military were everywhere—undoubtedly with good reason. There were also everyday people everywhere—not like Lagos, though, where people scurried about intent on the actions of the moment. These were people who seemed to be in fear of now and unsure of their future. They were furtive. They were disheveled. They seemed completely ungrounded when compared to their counterpart Lagosians.

Peter's taxi driver from the airport added some of the backstory. He turned out to be Mozambican—a refugee of the war there—coming to the sister Lusophone country where petroleum raised hopes even if politics did not. He was originally from Chimoio, not far from the Zimbabwean border and managed quite well in English. He was clearly in Luanda for economic and not patriotic reasons, underscoring to Peter that, aside from their colonial and linguistic histories, Mozambique and Angola had little in common. Here, when there was a strong wind of independence blowing, the Portuguese left the lands they had occupied since 1484—literally fleeing overnight—leaving many businesses and services without staff or leadership. They left many buildings empty and construction sites unfinished—structures that have remained uncompleted to this very day—these skeletons now housing thousands of refugee squatters—many dying from disease, attacks by bandits, or simply toppling off the multistory structures in the dark of night or in the vapors of the local moonshine that was all such impoverished individuals could afford. The driver finished by literally warning Peter to watch where he stepped—the war-related influx of the misplaced, the displaced, and the unwashed was uncatered-for. There were no specific public or other services. There were even no toilets or other hygiene facilities. Hence, the streets were strewn with all sorts of offal and flotsam—quite a bit of a very disgusting nature.

It was a tantalizing picture.

Peter felt in fairness he needed to see more for himself. He needed to get a taste of the city.

But he first needed to deal with the seminar.

After a good rest on Wednesday, he managed to suffer through two days of meandering, often meaningless, discussion about people and oil—this supported by mediocre interpretation at best. It was evident, like his own presence, most of those seated around the hotel's conference tables were there because they were told to be there. There was little spontaneity. There was little thinking outside the box. There was more excitement about lunch than the subject at hand.

By the end of the second afternoon, it was obvious to all that the African Petroleum Association wanted to try and show it cared as much about people as money. This theatrical event was their trivial and superficial effort at making convincing arguments that they were socially responsible.

Well, thought Peter, it was what it was.

On Saturday, after a lay-in and a big English breakfast, he decided to walk around the lagoon and out the thin knife-like peninsula that separated the bay from the Atlantic. This seemed to be the major tourist center with places named Miami, Coconut, and Del Mar—a worthy destination for his last few hours in the Angolan capital.

He followed the main road out the peninsula—Avenue Murtala Mohammed, named after the Nigerian military leader who was assassinated in 1976—thinking how ironic that he was here from Nigeria and would hike down a major thoroughfare named after a Nigerian commanding officer during the Biafran Civil War and past head of state. The road followed the crest of the narrow finger, with sandy beaches and shoreside bars on the left where the waves of the Atlantic slowly rolled in, in some places meeting the polluted effluents from the city and the lagoon.

He had just passed the Hotel Panorama when he saw a sign for Restaurant Monteiro ahead. He thought this would be a good place to get out of the sun and have a cold beer. Concentrating on his pending refreshment, enjoying the fresh onshore sea breeze, a most welcome change from the stifling ripe drafts that wafted from the city, he was startled when he felt a tap on his shoulder. Stopping and turning, he saw a grinning young man in shorts and a T-shirt—the youth asking him in halting English if he had the time. He was in the process of looking at his wrist when he felt more than saw shadows at his back as two pairs of hands grabbed him with tremendous strength, forcefully dragging him, despite his fighting and screaming, into a small alley off the main road.

Then there were only swirling silhouettes and excruciating pain. Later, he had no idea how much later, he regained his senses, managing to crawl to the shoulder of Avenue Murtala Mohammed where he again collapsed.

It was now early evening and, in spite of the dusk light reflecting off calm seas, he was clearly visible at the edge of the road—a bruised and bleeding mass of flesh huddled in fetal position. Beachgoers, couples heading to the nearby night clubs, hotel residents, shopkeepers, and the numerous denizens of the waterfront were all out and about—some even side-stepping his form so as not to trip over his recumbent and motionless frame—no one stopping to help. He was just more refuse on the streets of Luanda.

Peter awoke, not knowing where or when.

He looked about. White bare walls, blinking and clicking machines, the smell of disinfectant—he was in a hospital. He looked about again.

Sitting in a metal straight-back chair near the foot of the bed was a tawny-skinned man in his late thirties or early forties. He was reading a magazine, unaware Peter was awake.

Peter struggled unsuccessfully to sit up, the rustling of the sheets calling his movements to the attention of his unknown roommate.

The swarthy man stood up. He was wearing shorts and a T-shirt. He came to Peter's side and in a soft, gentle voice introduced himself in accented but comfortable English, "I'm Raul. I found you on the side of the road. You were in bad shape."

"Thank you—thank you so very much. I am so grateful—but where am I?"

"You're in Clinic Sagrada Esperanças, at the end of Avenue Murtala Mohammed, the road where I found you."

"Oh. Thank you!"

"You've been sleeping for over twelve hours—they gave you something when we came in—something strong before they dressed your wounds."

"I am so grateful—"

He was interrupted as a white-clad nurse entered the room and exchanged a few words with Raul. Raul then turned back to Peter. "They are glad you are awake. This is a small clinic. They are not able to do all that is needed. They are not able to make sure there's not something seriously wrong inside. They've stopped the bleeding, sewn the gashes, and applied medication to the wounds and abrasions. But they can do little else."

"What do they suggest?"

Raul again deliberated with the sister and then liaised with Peter. "They think you should be somewhere else where they can make sure everything is fine. They think you need to be under observation for at least seventy-two hours. They suggest you transfer to the Luanda Medical Center—a really good place the sister says. It's in the Cidade Alta part of town, on the bluff, on Rua Amilcar Cabral. But they have to have your permission to make any such arrangements."

"I am so sorry to inconvenience you further," Peter replied, "but please tell the good sister I'll do whatever is recommended."

Raul had another tête-à-tête with the nurse and then resumed with Peter. "They have, of course, some forms to be filled. They need more information. They need to know who you are—we found no ID, so you are listed as an unknown white man. They need to know where you stay. They also need to know who will pay. It's, as always, very complicated."

By this point, Peter's head was as clear as could be expected. It was truly complicated. He gave Raul his room number at the *Hotel Presidente*. He had fortunately left his passport in his room when he had gone out on Saturday. He confirmed to Raul what they already suspected; he was an American. He gave his full name and date of birth.

The sister promptly contacted the hotel and was able to confirm the general details of Peter's identify—at least enough for them to move forward. If they had to complete all the formalities now-now, Peter would not get to the medical center for another two days and they wanted him checked out where there were more tools and more staff. The formalities would have to wait.

In about an hour Raul told Peter an ambulance was on its way to transfer him to the larger facility. Peter was in the process of thanking his savior when Raul said he could not in good conscious leave Peter now. Clearly Peter was still suffering from his attack and, equally important, he did not have the language skills to tell the attending medical staff what they needed to know—he would go with Peter to the center.

When the ambulance driver would not allow Raul to travel with Peter, he hailed a cab and followed the white van with the flashing red lights. He was at Peter's side as he was wheeled through the emergency entrance and, after far too many delays, wheeled into a room on the fourth floor. By this time, Peter's injuries were throbbing and aching painfully. The center's staff gave their new patient a strong sedative before beginning a battery of tests to complement those already done by the clinic.

In nearly a rerun, when Peter finally returned from the drug-induced never-never land, he again found Raul seated at the foot of the bed. This time, however, Peter knew where he was and who his visitor was. Moreover, Raul was able to update Peter; the most pressing tests had been done and they needed now to wait for the results. Raul then called the nurse who made sure all was in order for the patient—both medically and administratively.

Raul translated the sister's report. Through the hotel the hospital had been able to get in touch with Shell by fax. Shell had assumed full responsibility for Peter's medical and related expenses. So far, all was fine.

After the nurse left, Raul offered, "You may have noticed, my Portuguese isn't great."

"Couldn't prove it by me," Peter said.

"I'm Cuban," Raul continued, "as you know, Spanish is my native tongue. We can communicate pretty well with our Portuguese brothers and sisters, but there are some gaps. I think I've given you the true story—but some of the details may change due to this language thing."

"It doesn't matter. I couldn't have done anything without you."

"Oh, it's fine."

"No, without you I might be dead."

"Oh, I'm sure if it wasn't me it'd be someone else."

"Not at all—not at all!"

"Well, let's just be happy things appear to be OK now and I'm glad I could help."

"You've done so much . . ."

"I'll stick around a while if you don't mind."

"But you've got to have other things to do . . ."

"No, it's fine."

"We'll, I'm so grateful."

Peter's words fell away as he drifted off.

He came back, unsure of how long he had been dozing, to find Raul reading a Bible—a Bible in English.

Again, Raul heard Peter move and looked up, holding the black book, "The sister gave me a magazine at the clinic but here they gave me a Bible . . .don't know . . . .. maybe they think I need redemption."

Peter held out his hand for the book and, taking it in shaking fingers, thumbed through the pages. This was the core of his father's faith—the core of his grandfather's faith. He had been raised with The Book. He knew all too well how to navigate its chapters.

Now, strangely, he knew exactly where he was going. He turned to Gospel of Luke and read aloud to Raul:

Luke 10:25-37 The Parable of the Good Samaritan

*"On one occasion an expert in the law stood up to test Jesus.
'Teacher,' he asked, 'what must I do to inherit eternal life?'
What is written in the Law? he replied. 'How do you read it?'
He answered, 'Love the Lord your God with all your heart and
with all your soul and with all your strength and with all your
mind'; and, 'Love your neighbor as yourself.'*

*'You have answered correctly,' Jesus replied. 'Do this and you
will live.'*

*But he wanted to justify himself, so he asked Jesus, 'And who
is my neighbor?'*

*In reply Jesus said: 'A man was going down from Jerusalem to
Jericho, when he was attacked by robbers. They stripped him of his
clothes, beat him and went away, leaving him half dead. A priest
happened to be going down the same road, and when he saw the
man, he passed by on the other side. So too, a Levite, when he
came to the place and saw him, passed by on the other side. But
a Samaritan, as he traveled, came where the man was; and when
he saw him, he took pity on him. He went to him and bandaged
his wounds, pouring on oil and wine. Then he put the man on his
own donkey, brought him to an inn and took care of him. The next
day he took out two denarii and gave them to the innkeeper. 'Look
after him,' he said, 'and when I return, I will reimburse you for any
extra expense you may have.'*

*Which of these three do you think was a neighbor to the man
who fell into the hands of robbers?*

*The expert in the law replied, 'The one who had mercy on
him.'*

Jesus told him, "Go and do likewise."'

"You are my Samaritan," Peter emphasized as he completed the
reading.

"Not at all," Raul countered, "the Good Samaritan was good not
only because he helped someone in need, but because the someone was
somehow a foe—helping your needy adversary is indeed special—helping someone like yourself should be just routine."

"What?" Peter asked.

"Pass me the book," Raul followed-up—quickly perusing the pages
as someone familiar with the text.

"Here it is." Raul pointed at a page, "John 4:9—'*The Samaritan
woman said to him, 'You are a Jew and I am a Samaritan woman. How
can you ask me for a drink?' (For Jews do not associate with Samaritans.)*

"And here too, Luke 9:51-53, '*Samaritans did not welcome Jesus when he was on his way to Jerusalem*'"

"So?"

"So—so, Jesus was a Jew. The Samaritans and the Jews didn't like each other all that much. To put it in terms closer to home, it's like the MPLA and UNITA fighting here—they don't much like each other. By the way, I should know, I'm, though I've never told you, a military advisor to the very same MPLA.

"So, if you were from UNITA and I helped you—now that would be special.

"If you're just someone with whom I share the road and I find you fallen on that road, it's not special, it's to be expected that I help you up."

"OK," Peter offered, "let me come back to special later, but I've a question for you. I've heard the parable of the Good Samaritan all my life. How do you know the injured man was a Jew—it doesn't say?"

"It was Jesus—he was a Jew."

"How do you know? Jesus tells the tale, but he never says he was the traveler."

"True. But if the victim of the attack wasn't Jesus, how would he know all the details?"

"He was Jesus . . ."

"He was the traveler."

"You are, regardless of what you say, special—many, many thanks."

With that, the introspection into the Samaritan's good deeds in Angola ended. The nurse came, giving Peter an injection for the pain and he was gone to the world.

Peter awoke in his hospital room at a random moment when his meds wore off. Raul was gone. There was a short note scribbled on a scrap of paper left on the chair he had recently so assiduously occupied: "Gone back to MPLA."

Peter spent another three days in the hospital. The pain from his bruises and gouges slowly diminished—needing less and less drugging to make the hours tolerable. As the results from all his tests were collated, the doctors found no urgent concerns. Just as on the outside, inside there were considerable contusions and signs of abnormal stress. Of special note was the spleen, which was bruised. However, the doctors felt the present condition did not warrant transfusions nor surgery—much to Peter's relief (his alarm not just about the quality of the care given the wartime surroundings, but also the risks of contracting AIDS).

After the additional three days of bed rest, while he was not ready to run any races, he felt he was able to get back on a plane and return to Lagos.

As on the inward journey, he transited through Johannesburg. He again traveled on a TAAG 747—the wide-body parking over a mile from the O. R. Tambo International Airport terminal. Buses dropped off the 400+ passengers at the building for arrivals. Once up in the departure area for the two-hour wait for the flight northward to Lagos, Peter wandered down the long and crowded corridors housing an assortment of shops that greedily grasped voyagers' last few coins—selling everything from wine to perfume, biltong (jerky) to *objet d'art*, safari clothing to diamond jewelry. At the end of the tightly stretched shopping area, there were enterprises taking care of passengers' other urgent needs including bars and cafés.

Peter sat on a barstool, drinking a series of *Castle* drafts, watching the multitude of motley gypsies ripple up and down the *couloir* as planes landed and departed. This was a global polestar for air travel, linking Africa with all four corners of the world—nonstop flights to Asia, North and South America, Europe, and the Middle East. The multiplicity of clothing and languages reflected the diversity of destinations. It was kaleidoscopic.

As he swung around on his stool for another vantage point for the endless human theater passing in front of his eyes, he watched droopy café patrons chat over mouthfuls of sandwiches and salad. Standing out, at a small table in a far corner, two men were having a much more animated discussion. He watched as arms flailed and faces contorted with grimaces.

Then his own face slightly contorted. He recognized one of those in what could have been an almost-polite altercation. It was Sir Horace—he was nearly certain. Different attire and demeanor from the *Tribune* snapshot—but Peter was practically sure it was he.

For a moment, Peter had the flirtatious intention of getting up and asking the peppy gentleman if he were indeed the reportedly at times scandalous nobleman. However, prudence overcame impetuousness. Peter simply ordered another beer and wondered what potentially villainous, if one believed the worst of the paper's now dated portrayal, actions had brought Sir Horace south.

Peter thought back to the gentleman's rumored land dealings, the ignoble events in the village near Ozalla, and to all the behind-the-scenes high jinx that were rampant in places like Nigeria and Angola—Ghana, too, for that matter. If Sir Horace's business was funny business, he had more than ample opportunity to plot and deceive.

It appeared the apparent fallible nobleman might well have the ingenuity and cleverness to make things happen—even if these were illegal, immoral, or both. This led to far more thinking than the weary traveler that Peter was could muster, so he had another beer.

By the time Peter's flight was called he was eternally grateful that airplanes had toilets because he had a lot of beer to filter out.

Peter had called Silas from O. R. Tambo so, after a good nap on the flight north, and an uneventful arrival and taxi ride, when the old beat-up, yellow Toyota (underscoring, Peter thought, as if necessary, the contrasts between Johannesburg and Lagos) dropped him across from the Church of Ilajai Road (the steeple staring sternly down at him as if to reprimand him for his absence), Silas was ready for his unpredictable visitor. The two shared ample portions of good whiskey while Peter provided his host with the short version of his time in Angola. Then, on unsteady feet, Peter shuffled off to bed in what was becoming his room.

The next several months assumed once again the comfortable pre-Luanda cadence. Peter was back following the 2E and spending his free time with Dabi. It felt as it should, except for one little thing. Peter didn't have his accustomed stamina. After a day tracking the pipeline or a night pursing more pleasurable tasks with Dabi, he was tired—really tired.

He didn't mention this to Dabi, but did talk with Silas—after all, he was a doctor.

Silas, who Peter now considered more of a godfather than an innkeeper or protector, did have the young man come into the clinic where he gave him a quick going-over—the remnants of Peter's beating still clearly visible. Doctor Silas also critically noted all the meds Peter had had thrown into his veins in Luanda. Overall, his conclusion was that things had been very serious, but his charge was healing. Nonetheless, it would take time—quite some time. And there were still no guarantees that some more far-reaching issues could not appear as his body continued mending.

It was not the nothing-to-worry-about resumé Peter had hoped for, but it was not all that dire. More on-the-job convalescence and, Peter imagined, all should be fine.

Then there was another thing—this one not so little. Dabi was, as she proudly repeated often to Peter, a Lagosian—her parents were Yoruba from the city—her father starting off years ago as a young solicitor in private practice.

Her father had been very good at his job. He had been named to a rather minor post on the bench of the local judicature in Ogun State—serving in Sagamu, only thirty miles from Lagos. As his jurisprudence skills increased, he attained higher and higher posts, further and further away from Lagos. At the climax of his professional trajectory, he was Chief Judge in Ogoja, at the extreme north of Cross River State, four hundred miles and two days east of Lagos—only sixty miles from the Cameroonian border.

When Dabi's father had died—six years earlier—her mother had decided to stay in Ogoja where she now had her home and her friends. Of late, however, her mother's health was failing, and the family wanted the matriarch to return to Lagos where they could look after her and where she could get the best medical care.

But she was having none of it. She rejected all pleas to relocate—underscoring that her unmarried daughter was a nurse so if the family really cared for her wellbeing, they could look after her in Ogoja.

As Dabi told him the story, Peter realized he really had known very little of the personal life of this woman in whose embrace he had spent so many joyous hours. He was only belatedly learning that she was her parent's youngest child—the "follow-back" as she told Peter. She had two older brothers and an older sister—all having worked at various occupations in Lagos and, the youngest of the trio more than twelve years Dabi's senior. With the age difference, all her siblings were presently much less active in their advancing years. Clearly, if someone had to go to take care of their mother, it was Dabi.

This was not her choice.

The situation was delicate and complicated.

Finally, and reluctantly, the four children agreed to at least temporarily accept their mother's demands. They felt if Dabi could be with her for some time, she could really convince their mother that her health required better care—better care only offered in Lagos. Then, just possibly, they could persuade her to come home. She was, by all accounts, a very strong-headed woman and the outcome was far from certain. Nevertheless, there seemed to be few options so Dabi had to leave for Ogoja, in the lowland rainforest, on the margins of the Cross River National Park—Dabi was leaving for the bush.

Separation was not unknown to Peter. This particular parting was all the more accepted because their union had always been engulfed by the unexpected. While they had not had a live-for-the-moment, evanescent relationship—their bonds slowly but steadily pushing their way through mostly untilled soil—they had always known that they did not know their future—it was a known unknown. They would poke at it. They would try to rely on it. But they each understood they could realistically make few honest plans for what lay over the next hill.

Now, after a painful and physical final night together, Dabi was off to the forest.

Peter went back to the 2E feeling even more lead-footed than usual these days—and these days were pretty laborious.

One evening, after a particularly heated discussion with village leaders near Awgu, the team was spending the night in the Ckisem Hostel near the junction of the Old Port Harcourt-Aba Road and the Port Harcourt-Enugu Expressway. This establishment was typical of the many shoddy inns where they spent their work nights—a rambunctious generator for electricity, big poly tanks for discolored water that sometimes made it to the shower in the room (if the room was lucky enough to have a shower), starched sheets on a mattress with its own ecosystem, and a TV that didn't work (and hadn't in recent history). But there was always a Bible stuck away somewhere in the room.

After a barely edible plate of rice and sauce—washed down with several bottles of beer (the brew's label proudly exclaiming it would "Make you feel good!")—Peter returned to his room not feeling all that good.

It had been a long day. He was tired.

As needed sleep evaded him, he nosed around the room until he found the omnipresent Bible—knowing, in all probability, the Good Book would, as usual, have somniferous effects. Unlike his parents, he was not a doyen of The Word. He had, he supposed obviously, been in close proximity to the Bible throughout his years at home. His father would read what he felt were relevant passages to the family when he felt (rather regularly) there were relevant events that justified an additional dose of God's guidance. His father would also sometimes test his Sunday sermons on the family—going into excruciating details as to the Biblical references. His mother, on the other hand, would read the Good Book every morning when she got up and every evening before going to bed— never hesitating to share the best parts with her children. In short, this text was no stranger to Peter, albeit not a frequent companion nor his top choice of reading material.

As he opened to a random passage, he thought back to the Good Samaritan—he had truly found his, but he still wondered if the Biblical counterpart to his own guardian angel, or so he seemed, had actually ministered to Jesus. How much credence could one give to passages, some more than two thousand years old, most originally spoken and noted in other languages? The writings of yesteryear sermonized today were certainly not literal. Did they even reflect real events? Had there been an original Good Samaritan or was this quite simply an endorsement of man's better instincts—which most hid most scrupulously? How could so many follow passages in a book upon which they themselves did not agree?

Was it only an agreement in principle?

His thoughts were interrupted as, almost dozing, the book fell open on his knees—open to Acts 15-18. This was strange. He read the pages that were now visible. Paul, addressing the apostles and Christian elders in Jerusalem, was questioning whether or not Gentile believers needed to be circumcised—the accepted practice that, following Moses' position, males should be circumcised—a position strongly adhered-to by the Jewish community. Peter the Apostle reportedly previously made a statement that, since God was all about choice, circumcision should not be a requirement. Rather, he suggested, the people should be encouraged to refrain from immoral sex acts, from eating the meat of "strangled" animals, and from food stained by idolatry. This message was then carried forth; among the messengers, Paul and Silas—Paul and Silas later continuing their journey through Syria and Cilicia (located in present-day Turkey).

Strange. Apparently by happenstance, it was all there—sex and sectarianism, right and wrong.

Stranger still, the actors were there: Paul, Peter, and Silas.

Peter imagined his father would say that, just like the helping hand offered by Raul, this was a sign—God was showing his child the road to salvation—the way to Grace.

Peter knew his mother would say, "Listen to your father, Son."

Not too far off this mark, Dabi would likely say, "It's a warning—a directive from the ancestors—take time!"

However, Peter the son did not think of a chance act, like what page appeared when a book fell open, in any of these terms. He remembered another thing his mother often said, "Honey, never forget, Catholics prefer Paul, Protestants prefer Peter."

He had no idea to what his mother was referring. It was of no real importance to him who among the apostles was the preferred messenger of God. He was not about superimposing the ancient past on today. He was about seeing how today could lead to a better tomorrow.

In some infusion of all these thoughts seeping through his tired brain, he concluded that, in the present, Peter, like Paul, should be a voyager—not carrying the words of Jesus, but carrying energetic curiosity (although he had to admit the energy was a few notches below normal levels of late). As he fell into welcome sleep, he dreamed of running across the savannahs of Bole.

CHAPTER FIVE

In the Name of the Father

Divine Providence—will the anchor hold?

BOLE WAS ON LYNN's mind too.

Bole and Peter—her dear, now vagabond son.

Lynn would lie in bed, listening to the grumble of the old window air conditioner and the competing mumbling of her sound-asleep beloved husband. She would think of the stream of days, of years, that had brought her to the here-and-now. She would think of the pile of letters in her dresser drawer, carefully folded and tied with a ribbon (like missives from a secret lover, she imagined), received from Nigeria from Peter—carefully crafted, saying nothing, leaving so much unanswered. She remembered Peter the boy, running unfettered across the hills of Bole. She shuddered at views of her boy in the vulgar and fetid (as she fancied them) byways of Nigeria—the land of fiends and terrible dangers.

Her boy.

And, of course, her girl.

Lydia, while not, Lynn hoped, facing the imminent dangers of Peter, was in a strange new world—an unwelcome permutation of the reality that had been so comfortable to them all.

It was hard to face what so many called modernity.

She hoped God could help.

Lynn had always tried to be the obedient (to God and Paul—in that order) spouse her husband wanted and needed. This was a work in progress.

But, with even more gumption (using her dad's word), she had tried to sculpt herself into the good and caring mother who could truly help mold her children's lives. Much like her husband, she tried so hard to build her children's inner and outer strengths—in her case, not with spiritual and religious passion, but with maternal devotion to help her kids grow up and find true happiness (a gift she herself was unsure if she had found).

Lynn had been no great student. She was certainly not academic in her outlook on life. Still, she had a deep appreciation of the need for a good and well-rounded education. So, every day, when her son and daughter finished their classes at the mission schools (the Baptists didn't have their own schools, in Bole the children had gone to a Catholic school and in Kpando to the Presbyterians), she had a homemade blackboard she'd push into the garden and the children would review their lessons with their mother.

During these sessions, Lynn would try and talk about the US—the people, the places, the politics. She wanted her children to always know—to never forget—they were Americans.

Lynn would also try and dig up parts of her own studies to share with her kids. There was not a whole lot to work with and much had faded with age. If anything at all, she fancied herself a student of the classics to which she had had, perhaps surprisingly, a fleeting exposure in high school—but with which she had formed a lasting affection (academic or otherwise). She would randomly mix odd quotes and passages from the ancient Greek writings with the ever-present preachings from the Bible (Paul's shadow far-reaching) to try to, in her own way, broaden her children's horizons.

She so wanted her children to have choices.

She so wanted her children to be able to meld seamlessly into a complex and frustrating world.

She so wanted her children to become happy and healthy adults.

She so wanted her children to find real peace.

And now, as she thought of her dear Peter and Lydia, she was filled with trepidation. She was afraid.

Sometimes, to try and get grounded, Lynn would furtively (and she herself did not understand why she felt a need for stealth) remove from her closet (behind her two extra pairs of practical pumps—was this a hiding place?) the small polished wooden chest from her great-great-grand-mother. Opening the well-worn latch, she would wistfully stare into the box, her sole heirloom, her only thread to her forebearers, looking at the bits of jewelry and souvenirs from a woman she had never known.

Lynn's family was not one to talk much about ancestry. There were few choice fruits hanging from their family tree. The exception was Annabelle: her father's great-grandmother.

In the 1820s, as the Erie Canal was nearing completion and John Quincy Adams was president, Annabelle moved from the banks of the Rhine River in Alsace to the embankments of the James River in Virginia as a mail-order bride. While few details had filtered through the years, and these most likely tainted with some romance and color over time, by any account, Annabelle was the master of her own destiny. She was a brave and determined young woman who had lived to old age to see the outcomes of her self-assurance.

She had fled a scurrilous and enfeebled old man who had literally purchased her as his child bride. She had fled with jewelry and coins the old man had tried to use to buy her affection. She had fled west and, as a single woman, homesteaded and then had a daughter with an adventur-ous young man who had professed a desire to put down roots but who had later been unable to overcome his wanderlust.

Nonetheless, through it all, Annabelle had remained resolute and steadfast. She had always known that she could rely on herself.

Gazing into the polished chest, Lynn knew she could not do the same.

Lynn, sadly, knew she had to accept that she was tied to Kpando and the man she loved.

For her, this mission was as much a stockade as a pathway to God's Grace.

She knew this was why her son had fled.

She knew her son was lost.

Was she, too, lost?

Would she finally wipe away from the family's genealogy any trace of the brave Annabella?

~

Unlike her husband (but possibly like her son), Lynn had not clearly known, foreseen her destiny. After all, she was not the child of missionaries—missionaries who intuitively and unequivocally considered following and leading in God's ways as their path to God and His Divine Providence. Missionaries whose complete fealty to their God was their anchor—their lifeline to weather the storms of everyday human suffering.

No, Lynn had not been born with her life's path plainly laid-out before her by God's Grace. As her father before her, Lynn had been born in Gravois Mills. Her father, Ben, had been born to a single mother—scandalous in those days. Ben's mother, Irene, lived with her father—the owner of one of the village's most popular taverns. Irene's mother had died of tuberculosis when Irene was six.

It wasn't for nothing that Ben's granddad, Howard (everyone called him Howie), was a barman—he was his own best customer—generally ten sheets to the wind before noon. It was up to Irene to manhandle her groggy parent to their upstairs apartment and then take over the bar—putting-up with the clients groping her thighs and breasts while her young son washed glasses, swept the floor, and swabbed out the muck of the local boozers—of whom there was no shortage.

No one was surprised when young Ben, just a teenager, fled home, fled the bar, fled Missouri, and ultimately ended up in the army. He saw action in the European Theater and with VE-Day, returned to the Ozarks with a new New Jersey wife, Denise, ready to make a new start in an old place.

This meant tackling the family bar. During Ben's absence, Howie had died and Irene, after too much work and maltreatment, had become a frail old woman. Ben and Denise (she used to like to say she was "Denise from Depford") had the best intentions. They worked hard to renovate the old alehouse. Denise, an above average cook, modernized the kitchen and offered a new menu to accompany the spirits. Slowly, their efforts seemed to pay off and the rough grog house was transformed into an upscale pub that attracted families in addition to the community's hard drinkers.

When they had finished, they had built a respected establishment, and, in so doing, had also established respected positions for themselves in the community—the army guy and his Jersey gal.

As stability entered their lives, they decided to start a family. Lynn was born just a few months after Grandmother Irene died—the grandmother's sickroom turned into a nursery.

Life became routine. Lynn started school. Denise started to talk about making a baby brother for their now big girl. But no little brother came. Quite to the contrary, one day Lynn came home after a typical day in the fifth grade and her mom was gone. Lynn never knew what had happened, it just did. Her mother was gone.

Her father tried to act as though nothing had happened. He tried to carry on as he always had. Still, he couldn't. It was too much. He was devastated. He was broken. He was changed. Soon he was drinking more than Howie ever had. But the similarities stopped there. As opposed to having his child take over the bar's management, he nearly sequestered his girl—only allowing her to go to school (as was the law) and then detaining her in the upstairs apartment while he tried to wash away his anguish downstairs with cheap sour-mash.

Then Lynn entered seventh grade and puberty at the same time. Her father changed again—again for the worse. In addition to being her overseer and jailor, he began to be her abuser. While he never actually violated her, he would come upstairs, barely able to stand, and caress her hair, her face, her budding breasts—saying how she felt just like her mother—Oh how he missed her mother!

So, as she shifted to high school, as she met Paul, and as she wore his letterman's jacket, it was, she knew, just as much to get away from home as it was to enjoy the company of this exotic young man recently arrived from Latin America.

Lynn knew Paul's aunt. Everyone knew Rose at the post office. She was friendly. She was kind. And she made sure you got your mail.

Before she had met Paul, Lynn had never been to Rose's home. But Rose and her husband, Herbert, an aging couple with grown children, were well-thought-of by all in Gravois Mills.

When Lynn had known Paul well enough to be invited over to his (adopted) home, Rose and Herbert seemed to live up to all expectations—affable and generous. As she got to know them all better, the only observation she had, based on her impressions of Paul's faith, were that Rose and Herbert were not at all as God Fearing as Paul (and probably his parents).

And, as the Lynn of Kpando thought back to the Lynn of Gravois Mills, she realized what a clear reflection of his parents Paul must have been. Although a high school athlete, and an average student with an average (she guessed) social life, there had always been something abstemious about the young newcomer from south of the border.

While Paul did not go about the school yard reciting the Bible, he seemed to have a bottomless quantity of Biblical references when he did comment on something—anything, from the weather to the over-salted casserole in the cafeteria. He was always able, and ready to juxtapose nearly everything anyone did to some sort of devotional rendering.

Most of the kids either ignored these comments completely or gawked at their agent with such bewilderedness that it was unquestionable that the boy from Costa Rica would be seen by many as some sort of alien abnormality who would never really fit in.

Now, looking back over the years, Lynn guessed this had been true: Paul had truly never fit in. Thus, while she was scurrying from a family run amok, he was running from a community within which he himself felt he did not fit.

At first, Lynn was simply amused by Paul's, as she saw it, "religious bend." This was a complete contrast to the environment in which she had been raised. She viewed it definitely more out of curiosity than passion.

Her family, probably for generations she thought, had never been churchgoers. They, her family, had not been bad people. They had not been unholy. Not going to church had never been a conscious decision. It had been a subject that never came up.

Her forebears were not even agnostic. They had never given religion enough thought to be agnostic (let alone know the word, she guessed). They had been simple folks just trying to stay afloat—fighting in close quarters each day, with no time to think of the higher order of things—to think of Divine Providence.

Most of her family had, one way or another, lost this fight. She knew, having Paul as her anchor, had allowed her to survive—even if not to excel.

She must say, she mused, that she had not hooked-onto Paul as a drowning person puts a life-lock on flotsam. It had indeed started as curiosity. Religion, God, and all (what her father would have called) the falderal were just as alien to her as Paul the émigré seemed to be to many of his classmates. It was, she imagined (as a Midwest girl who had never seen the ocean), like someone sticking their finger into a sea anemone to see what happens. She reached out to Paul to see what happens—not to immediately seek shelter or solace.

From Paul's perspective, she supposed, she was initially not a girl, certainly not a potential girlfriend, she was simply someone who smiled and had the patience to listen to his ecclesiastical epilogues.

She was never able to counter his pontificating with religious points of order or even with complementary biblical citations. But she (having been around a bar far too much) did know how to engage people in banal conversation. She would ask him how this or that compared to his child-hood growing up in Costa Rica. She would ask about the weather, the food, or any of an assortment of everyday things in that country that was anything but everyday to her.

At first, he was very guarded, speaking little of his family or his birthplace. But, as others looked on him askance, he, perhaps ironically, began to see Lynn as his anchor. He began, drop by drop, to tell her of the wonderful (as he saw them) times he had had growing up in the Garden of Eden with parents who were, by the grace of God, clairvoyant and virtuous. Soon he spoke zealously of how his father and mother had been blessed by God and had, in turn, ensured their children were so blessed. His life had been surely foretold by the pious acts of his parents. He was not only one of God's flock, he was compelled to be a shepherd of this flock.

Lynn was impressed. It was not the zeal of her new friend that im-pressed her—albeit this was impressive. It was the certainty with which he viewed the future. The conviction with which he viewed his coming years. This was all totally antithetical to the insight (Lynn even doubted there had been any real insight) of her family—a family that lived hour-to-hour and never looked further ahead than the next weekend crowd at the bar.

There had been, of course (she hoped), in addition to the initial inquisitiveness, a genuine physical attraction—Paul and Lynn seemed to just get along. While each was running from and to something, they were also eager to connect with someone. They wanted to share and be shared. Before they knew it, Lynn was wearing his red and white letter-man's jacket and they were acknowledged by all as a (strange) couple.

Following a driven and undoubting partner had never been easy for Lynn. After years of trying, she had had to accept that she did not have the infallible fortitude to assuredly move on day by day, never questioning the road ahead. She was never sure. She continuously felt calamity would strike—if not today, tomorrow.

Nevertheless, her husband's unwavering certitude allowed her to push her misgivings to the background—into the shadows of her mind. She allowed the slipstream of his energetic gush forward to pull her along—not resisting, and often not totally understanding.

In point of fact, she felt as though she were more times than not being sucked into a vortex. When she shared these feelings with her husband, he assured her this was the power of God moving within her. She quietly hoped it was not really the equivalent of being sucked down the drain.

These misgivings notwithstanding, Lynn gave it her all. She immersed herself, or at least tried as best she could, in her husband's dogma. She set private milestones for herself, reading the Bible (every day, morning and night) to be able to contribute in a seemingly complementary fashion to Paul's continued ecclesiastical epilogues. She began openly praying several times a day—more to demonstrate to herself than her husband her growing (even if still nascent) faithfulness in His Word.

She tried to show, not as an affectation but as real dedication, a new and hopefully resolute religionism—as much for her own self-confidence as her husband's. She tried hard to believe. She thought she did believe.

When Paul and Lynn moved to Ghana, the transition, at least in the eyes of others, was complete and indisputable. Lynn was not only the devoted wife; she was also the supportive and demure wife who staunchly back-stopped her husband's assertiveness and fervor. She was the smiling and plain spouse of the brave man who had crossed the ocean to bring the needy the word of God.

Lynn completely transformed into the role of Pastor Paul's adoring wife.

She was the sounding board for the sermons. She was the companion faithfully at his side at the doorway for the greetings at the end of the service. She was the welcomer for evening Bible study and the consoler for the bereaved. She was the mission hostess and the church cleaner. She was whatever she needed to be—whatever her husband wanted her to be.

As reward, God blessed her with two wonderful children and a stable life where she was able to get up every day and know it would be much like the day before—calm and dependable, even if hot and muggy. There was food on the table. There was a sense of community. There was a safe harbor.

Yet, as Lynn had known throughout her life, change was inevitable. As much as she tried to cling to the peaceful days when her young children were by her side as they proudly looked up at Paul at the pulpit delivering a stirring sermon, she knew nothing was forever.

Her children, unavoidably, drifted away. She told herself this was temporary. But she knew this was not so. Her dear daughter would likely never again cross the seas to these shores. And now her cherished Peter was in the grips of terrors she could only imagine.

To add to her agony, Paul, too, had changed his routine and was no longer the omnipresent bulwark to allay her uneasiness. When they had first arrived, Paul had always worked at the kitchen table—almost every morning spending several hours honing his next sermon—bouncing ideas off Lynn as she made a fresh pot of coffee or prepared the evening meal.

Then things changed.

Paul began leaving home midmorning, only coming back for lunch. Sometimes he even missed lunch. When Lynn asked if everything was alright, Paul would only reply that he needed to walk about to get his thoughts for his sermon straight—to get his bearings. He wanted to better feel his congregation—to walk their paths—to be fully able to craft His words for his wards.

Lynn knew they were all changing—Paul affirming this was all part of God's Plan.

As always, Lynn could only acquiesce.

Contrary to all appearances, she felt powerless.

Lynn had no real friends. Kole and Wanda were there, yes. She honestly liked them—maybe she loved them. But, at the end of the day, she was the "*patronne*." She had to maintain her distance. She had to maintain her standing. This was not a friendship.

There were many others in the community—people of all positions and standing. There were inevitably those who could be her friend. Maybe or maybe not?

She and Paul were the only permanent resident foreigners—"Europeans" as they were sometimes called, although certainly not from Europe, they were white. At times there were various white volunteers in the community from the US, Europe, or elsewhere. But these were folks who came and went. These were not full-time residents of Kpando. Paul and Lynn were, unlike others, now permanent citizens (trustfully, in good standing) of Kpando.

Lynn had, in many ways, moved (or tried to move) from viewing life as us-and-them to being one of them. Though white, though an American, she formally resided in Africa—in Kpando. She was now from here and not there.

Even so, after what seemed a lifetime in this land, she remained unsure of her footing. She remained unsure of her status. She remained unsure of what was correct and what was incorrect. What would God want her to do?

She tried so hard to follow God's ways. She tried so hard to follow Paul's example. She tried so hard to be good person.

Still, she was filled with doubt.

She knew all were God's children. She knew that skin color, that ethnicity meant nothing—all were of the family of God.

But somehow, she couldn't really embrace her neighbor as she knew God wanted her to do. She could not in all truthfulness join hands with those with whom she shared the walkways of the village and say, "We are all one."

In spite of all, she still felt they were in fact different. She was different. White people and black people were different. Africans and Americans were different.

Different was not necessarily bad, but she could not shake the idea—preconceived though it may have been—that somehow, she was from a higher plain. She was not necessarily better; she was just somehow above. She could not avoid the reality that she considered most of those with whom she shared her space as children, not in age but in knowledge. These were the needy, the uneducated, the weak. She was not part of them, but she was with them. They were her children, not like Peter and Lydia, but they were the frail and childlike—the unanointed. Through the power of God, the Father, through the shepherding of her husband, they too were her children.

She was their guardian, but not one of them.

But now, today in Kpando, as lunch got cold while she waited for her husband to return (from where?), as she painfully envisioned her son in the grips of unknown dangers, while her daughter was challenged with new cultures and new thoughts, Lynn was unsure if she had been able to follow the teachings of God the Father.

Had her anchor slipped?

Surely, if she had been able to loyally adhere to His way, if she were a good and true Christian, a real believer, she wouldn't be questioning—she wouldn't be doubting. It was she, the skeptic, who was becoming the infidel. It was she who was undermining the good work of her husband, the shepherd Paul—Paul, the herdsman of his community. It was she who was casting dispersions on the lives of her true children. It was she who was, as was apparently hereditary in her family, bringing chaos into the calm.

She would pick up her Bible and look for the right passages, the right words to strengthen her resolution, to confirm her faith, to atone for her sins. She could find none.

Lynn was flooded simultaneously by regret and misgivings. Above it all, she was overcome by a feeling of fear; a very focused feeling, not for herself but for her treasured (for he was her treasure) son, Peter. She felt more than knew her child was teetering on the edge of perdition because she knew her son was in Nigeria.

She was very afraid.

CHAPTER SIX

Walk-About

In the footsteps of Paul

PETER WAS INDEED IN Nigeria.

He spent another eight months in Naija, chasing the 2E and her dramas.

But this was a different Peter. The book of Dabi had seemingly closed. This was now a young man determined to chart his path himself. This was someone who had taken the first steps and successfully entered into the pandemonium of Lagos and who was now looking for the next step. This was someone with renewed focus.

His downtime (most referred to this period as the leisure time spent not working, Peter thought of it as time when he felt even more dejected than when he was following the arteries of Nigerian petrol) was now mostly spent at a Shell guesthouse in Port Harcourt where the maintenance costs were minimal—rarely going to Lagos to see Silas. He saved his money. He argued with himself. He looked at possibilities. He made plans. Piece by piece, he began to put together a jigsaw of his fate. He still wrote his weekly missives to his parents—these now most often a mishmash of hokum—platitudes telling them what they wanted to hear (no mention of a renewed focus).

Then it was time to change—time to act. After he gave the mighty Shell Ltd. notice, he made one more trip on the petroleum giant's shuttle to Lagos to say goodbye to Silas.

Back in Port Harcourt, unemployed, with no small level of uneasiness, he put his plan into action.

He took a boat upriver to Lokoja, at the confluence of the Niger and Bénué rivers. Finding a cheap room at the Adankoko Seminary (two blocks from the river and a block from a pizza palace), he spent a few nights in the capital of Kogi State. He walked around, visiting such unusual places as the European Cemetery and the World War I Cenotaph. The early British explorers noted they had founded this city in 1857—with their chronic myopia, ignoring centuries when the peoples of the Owono, Nupe, Hausa, and other groups had inhabited this area.

Part of his stay was a result of delays in finding a boat up the Bénué to Makurdi. This was the first of a series of hopscotch moves following the Bénué—to Ibi, through the Kambari Game Reserve, onward to Imburu, to Hamdalla on the Cameroonian border, and then to Garoua.

This was all seemingly slapdash, but there was a design that had its origins in plans made months earlier in Port Harcourt. Garoua was an important, but seasonal port. Once the rains had drained from the surrounding Sahel, the river was virtually dry. Peter's travels had to follow the rains. He arrived in the capital of the Northern Region of Cameroon in late June as the waters were still rising, absorbing the daily deluges that fed the thirsty grasses of the encircling savanna.

Garoua was, however, a benchmark and not a destination. Over the next several weeks he migrated in a generally southeastern direction, intentionally or not, moving though the slot between Bouba Ndjinda and Bénoué Game Parks (not visiting either), traveling by public transport (Peugeot 504 taxi or Saviem minibuses, also called "mammy wagons")—basically drifting, following whatever energies that seemed to prevail on his sense of place.

In more of an after-the-fact view than preplanned charting, he seemed to meander down the N13 Highway until he reached the trigonal borders of Cameroon, Chad, and Central African Republic—the latter frequently referred to simply as CAR. Having no visas for either new country, he made appeals at both border posts, deciding to move ahead where he got his first authorization—employing skills learned well in Nigeria to try and expedite the processes.

CAR won and he was soon meandering down that country's RR4 roadway (not really meriting the title highway), ultimately ending when this track met the more robust NR3—the major axis joining the CAR capital of Bangui with Cameroon through the principal passage of Garoua-Mboulai.

Traveling down the RR4 was a learning experience—possibly just the type for which Peter was looking. The 125-mile trip reportedly could be accomplished in three or four hours—the operative word being could. It was rainy season. Moving south from Ngaoundel to Bocaranga and Bouala before reaching Bouar at the NR3 junction required three days— three days encrusted with and slipping through mud of a quantity and quality he had no idea even existed.

The entire event took place in a battered Peugeot 505 with seven other passengers, a driver, and a heaped roof rack including a basket of chickens. More times than not, or so it seemed, the passengers were actually outside pushing the vehicle through waves of mud—once through a small river. The last day on the road was the worst—a voyage through muck and mire. At night the crew slept in what was termed an "auberge." This was a cluster of small, thatched sleeping huts with straw mats and a kerosene lamp. A larger, centrally located hut was the equivalent of the bar-restaurant. Inside, the space was occupied by low stools around empty beer crates that served as tables where the patrons could eat boiled cassava, washed down with horrifically fiery moonshine. Food and accommodation for a night was less than one US dollar—so at least the price was right.

When the taxi finally limped into Bouar, Peter was exhausted. At the taxi park, he was directed to *Chez Robbe* as the best place for a *blanc* to get board and room. He got in a Citroën 2CV *"Deux Chevaux"* town taxi that somehow managed to move down the street on wobbly wheels, with smoking exhaust, cracked windows, and broken seats—assured by the driver in equally broken English that everyone knew Robbe.

The decrepit car screeched and slid to a stop in front of an establishment that looked like it would be more fitting in an East African game reserve. With a high-pitched roof and surrounding wide and shady veranda, the facade of the building itself was split bamboo. The bamboo motif continued inside where there was a long and polished mahogany bar surrounded by a covey of tables and chairs—apparently now a lull in what would seem to normally be a busy place. The single occupant, a large, bulky white man was standing alone at the bar drinking from a cola bottle.

"Excuse me." Peter approached and said, "I'm looking for a room and a shower."

The hefty man finished a swallow of cola and replied while licking his lips, "Well, young man (this in nearly unaccented English) you've
come to the right place. I'm Robbe. You're welcome."

"Thanks . . ."

"You're welcome," Robbe continued, "but you really, really need to
clean up. You look like shit."

"There's a lot of mud on the road and . . ."

"No explanation necessary," Robbe went on, almost ignoring his
soon-to-be lodger, "if you saw the crap that comes through here, you'd
think you were just another typical grunt looking for a beer."

"Well . . ."

"Of course," Robbe moved behind the bar with unexpected agility,
"you need a kickstarter." With a smile and a bow, the proprietor of *Chez
Robbe* offered the newcomer a sweating beer that Peter sucked down in
nearly one motion.

This was the first time in a long time that Peter had felt some aura
of real hospitality—real welcome. In fact, it had not been since his arrival
at Silas's most accommodating residence that he had really felt at home.

Peter quickly adapted to Robbe's ambience. During slow periods in
the dining and drinking that generally occupied the premises, the two
would sit in the cool(ish) shade of the veranda, Peter happily drinking
beer while his host sipped cola. As a level of comfort developed between
the two, Robbe began to tell his story to his young guest—evidently happy
to share his past with an honest broker.

He was Belgian. Actually, as he emphasized strongly, he was Flemish—not the same. He had been born in the small town of Nazareth—ten
miles southwest of Ghent—obviously a very Catholic community. His
father, a common laborer, sadly, had been a collaborator with the Nazis
during the occupation. This had led, perhaps logically, to stressful relationships with the residents of Nazareth, even after the death of his father
so detested for his traitorous acts.

Robbe had always been one of those very clever and dexterous
people who could fix anything—it just seemed to come naturally. With
only a primary education, he was able to start a very successful electronic
repair shop—successful in the sense that the town folk all came when
they needed help, not that he was successfully integrated into the local
society.

It was not easy. Robbe had to go to Ypres, near the French border,
to find a wife—local girls literally shunning him as the son of a filthy

collaborateur. But, in spite of all, he was able to start a family and had a business to support this family.

Then, one Christmas, he had put a Santa Claus—a Saint Nicholas—in the shop window. A sister, coming in to get one of the convent's irons repaired, commented that this was not the true spirit of the season. Robbe ignored her—he didn't go to church. The next day, the local priest came by and, with much less compassion than his female cohort, informed Robbe he MUST remove the profanities he had used to garnish his shop. He MUST!

Robbe did not follow the priest's dictates—he was not one prone to caving-in in the face of what he felt to be false powers. As a result, the shop was black-balled—no more clients, no more business.

Robbe, still a young man, had joined the Office of Development Cooperation to go to the Congo as sort of a jack-of-all-trades—a "*bricoleur,*" a handyman, to help the variety of projects supported by Belgium in the country. This was a difficult assignment in that he often had to travel to remote parts of the vast country. The Cooperation, as it was called by all, did not pay for dependents to come out and share the struggles of such strenuous assignments. His wife had to stay in Belgium—in Flanders.

As the years passed, he enjoyed less and less his annual vacations at home. He was one of those for whom, as someone once said, "Africa was like malaria or shisto, it got into your blood."

At first, as he rationalized, simply to cool his ardor, he began a sexual relationship with the young girl who served as his cook and housekeeper. What started as only transactional became deeply emotional—he fell in love for the first time in his life, he supposed. Alphonsine—he generally called her "Al"—became the most important thing in his life.

They passed a contented decade. They had a daughter. Al became the head of the household and a mother—both to her delight. Robbe, rather than going home on vacation, managed to get the money into his wife's bank account. She was satisfied. They had an arrangement.

Al was originally from Bukavu, on the shores of Lake Kivu. In 1967 she had taken their daughter home to spend some time with her family. Whether through the wrath of the gods or just stupid bad luck, Robbe's family was in Bukavu when the city was taken over by Jean Schramme and a group of Belgian and Katangese mercenaries who were fighting the president, Mobutu Sese Seko Kuku Ngbendu Wa Za Banga. The mercenaries held the city for weeks before Mobutu's forces attacked; the white mercenaries fleeing to Rwanda, leaving many dead in their wake.

As always, the casualties included more innocent civilians than fighters from either side—Al and her daughter terribly among the departed.

Robbe had been devastated. He had tried to burn the pain from his brain—drunk for weeks, for months, he couldn't remember (he no longer drank). Finally, numb but somehow functional, he had simply left Congo—going north—never formally resigning nor attending to any exit formalities. He crossed the Ubangi River, kept going north on the NR3 until he ended up in Bouar. Again, whether through an act of the gods or just luck, totally by accident he found an old auberge for sale. This led to the birth of *Chez Robbe* and his now long-time residence in, what some called, "the heart of darkness."

In concluding his tale, Robbe added the footnote that his life seemed somehow entwined with the netherworld of the warrior. He had lost his family to professional combatants. Now, as Peter had undoubtedly noted, his major customers were soldiers—some from the CAR, but most from the locally-based French Foreign Legion—hardened troops of operation BOUAR Africa (*Éléments français d'assistance opérationnelle* (EFAO))—their emblem the Cape Buffalo, also called the "Black Death."

Peter let out a sigh before finishing his bottle of now lukewarm beer. He felt, at least more than some, he understood the annals of Robbe. While very different in many ways, they shared a certain gnawing—an incessant voice deep in their souls always asking "why?"

The next day, as Peter was going down the steps from *Chez Robbe's* veranda, he collapsed—crumbling to the ground, unable to get up due to the excruciating pain.

It was like a repeat of Luanda. Again, Peter awoke not knowing where he was—his surroundings resoundingly hospital-like. The odor of antiseptic. The hum of machines and soft voices. The clean white walls and shiny waxed floor.

Any questions he had, did not take long to be answered.

A few minutes after he regained consciousness, he found the faces of Robbe and another white gentleman—clean-shaven, crewcut, bulb-nosed—peering intensely at him. Robbe smiled and presented Dr. Jacobs.

The healer, not mimicking Robbe's smile, and with a flat but stern voice, provided all the needful through Peter's aimless sedative-reinforced thoughts, "Son (there it was anew, 'son'), you probably will never know how lucky you are (of course not). Clearly (to whom), you were injured sometime back. Now (you mean now-now?), when there is a lot of tissue damage (you're damn right there was a lot of damage), some things can cover up other things. Today (what day is it?), there are only faint marks of those external wounds, but inside things heal much more slowly (naturally, they're inside). You had what we call a traumatic abdominal wall hernia (of course you would call it that). This can be very serious and is very painful (holy shit, yes!). Fortunately, we were able to put everything back in good shape (damn straight) and you should be fine after some good rest and a solid antibiotic treatment (bully!)."

Jacobs had been right; Peter had been lucky. As one would hope, as their business depended upon the human condition, the Buffalos had the best possible medical care. The camp's small hospital was surely better equipped than anything in Bangui, and probably anything across the border in Cameroon.

This fact notwithstanding, under any conditions, Peter's condition was serious. He ended up spending three weeks in the hospital bed as fears of post-operative infection grew. When he finally did leave, he was weak and emaciated. Once more his guardian angels (or fairies or whatever) had shown-up, however, and Robbe continued to demonstrate that he was really a good guy.

Peter was still a paying lodger *Chez Robbe*. At the same time, he was about as close to family as someone could be. On the business side, his host only charged him a token fee for his long-term accommodation while he recovered—his meals at no charge. The pub's staff took care of him—took care of him as though he were nobility.

When he first returned from the hospital, Robbe's "people" (as he called them, somewhat overly paternalistically) helped Peter in and out of bed—to and from the bathroom. They fluffed his pillows. They changed his sheets. They brought him his meals on a shining bronze tray. They, once the go-ahead was given by the doctor, brought him far too many icy beers. They told him tales to pass the time—tales of the last night's carousing by the legionnaires or tales of misadventures of townsfolk—tales of wives cheating on their husbands and leopards stealing goats.

Once he had regained much of his strength, he was able to take his meals in the restaurant or on the veranda. He was even invited to Robbe's private quarters in the back corner of the compound—a place off-limits to nearly all. Robbe had a neat and well-appointed apartment that was a surprising contrast to the earthy and sportsman-like atmosphere of the bar-restaurant and guest rooms. Here, if you didn't know better, you'd have thought you were in Belgium—Flanders, as Robbe would quickly correct you if you got the locale wrong.

The living room fanned out from a small, rarely used fireplace, comfortable chenille armchairs and a settee situated close to *barbinga* (locally, as he learned from his benefactor, called rosewood) end and coffee tables, with a good-sized matching dining table in a bay-window nook. The walls were kind of a cream color and the drapes a deep wine tone. In the corner there was a Victrola. It was very homey. The mantle and the end tables were blanketed with photographs, most back-and-white, some sepia, in a variety of frames ranging from sterling to mahogany—most of an ebony-complected young woman and a *café-au-lait* girl, some of an older, stouter white woman, and only a few with Robbe himself.

On those special occasions when Robbe invited Peter into his personal space—his refuge—there were treats with all the fixings. Most of the time it was to sample an exclusive Flemish dish like *carbonade* or *chicons au gratin*, accompanied by fresh bread and good wine. Once Robbe served Flemish pancakes (a mix between a French crêpe and an American pancake) with fresh mangos and an amazing sherry. Robbe knew good things.

As Peter began to heal, he began to ponder where he should go. As always, Bouar was not a destination, just an extended wayside rest stop. During busy periods, Peter and Robbe would sit at the table in back of the bar where the boss could survey the goings-on—breaking up, for example, a group of seriously drunk legionnaires who were trying to see who could take the bigger bite out of his beer glass.

During less hectic moments, Peter and Robbe would sit on the veranda, watch Bouar flow about them, while Robbe recounted tales and technologies.

Peter's host was truly a marvel at understanding how things worked—he knew how just about anything functioned. One day, as a case in point, while Peter nursed three beers, Robbe explained in excruciating detail how a Xerox machine worked. Alas, when Peter stood up shakily, he understood no more about the innards of a copier than when he had sat down.

Peter felt he was staying long enough in Bouar to apply for residency. In fact, he was there long enough to establish a contact point for his mail. He wrote the same banal letters to his parents—imagining that from the Bouar post office to Kpando would take months. He also contacted Silas and was surprised when his Nigerian liaison sent him a big manila envelope with the mail that he had been holding from Ghana and elsewhere.

Peter did not want to delve into family matters (who else would write?) nor to be weighed down by his parents' romantic religious notions that he was on his youthful rite-of-passage that would ultimately lead him to head his own congregation. Accordingly, he put the khaki envelope, missives unread, on the bottom of his duffle bag under his spare pair of jeans.

On a sultry afternoon, as the duo sat on the veranda—Peter thirstily downing beers while Robbe sipped cola—the hotelier in the depths of a monologue about the latest shortwave radio technologies when Peter unceremoniously, some would say rudely, interrupted.

"Whadaya think?" Peter almost mumbled as he stared into an empty amber bottle, "Where should I go?"

As he regained his strength, Peter felt he should also regain his odyssey. Looking back over his experiences on the Bénoué and the RR4, Peter was undecided if the next leg of his journey should be by water or land. Neither would be easy. Both would be illuminating. He needed an inspiration to plot his course.

"Well, kid." Robbe smoothly changed gears, moving from shortwave operator to trip advisor, "I guess that question itself means you're feeling well enough to get back to following your stars?"

"Guess so."

"You're young." Robbe smiled, "tough and energetic. I say, 'have at it!'. Much sooner than you'd wish, you'll feel yourself slowing down and hating it. It's your time."

"Sure. But what should I do, flip a coin?"

"You lament about your overly-devout parents. You now know, of course, that I too have been affected by, I would say, been the 'victim of' religious folk. I am certainly no acolyte of the church. I still remember how the old priest, who ultimately was responsible for shutting-down my business, always quoted scripture before he destroyed something—God's Word covering the acts of a zealot—not unusual, unfortunately."

"Yep."

"Well, this ol' guy was ranting about me doing God's Will—or, rather NOT doing God's Will."

"Uh-huh."

"He kept quoting Proverbs 16:9—'*The heart of man plans his way, but the Lord establishes his steps.*'"

"I seem to recall dad chanting this?"

"Yeah. I guess folks use it a lot to say, 'plan how you wish, but in the end, follow God's ways.'"

"I planned, but I didn't plan to be here!"

"Well, like I say, 'It's your time.' And I interpret that stuff from Proverbs as saying, 'Make your plans and plan well—but you never know tomorrow.' I read somewhere that they figure Saint Paul traveled over 10,000 miles years and years ago. Today, as the son of Paul, the road is yours."

That night, Peter asked Robbe if he had a Bible. To no one's surprise, among his considerable collection of printed material, stuck in an alcove of his suite, he had several versions of the Good Book. Almost furtively, Peter borrowed a tome and returned to his room to unaccustomedly peruse the book that was the bedrock of his parents' lives and that he had found so obnoxious during his youth.

Peter was unsure why he even thought of the Bible. Was it because of Robbe's references to the priest and the scriptures? It was strange. He sought guidance and, while his parents were absolutely sure the Bible, as the Word of God, guided their lives, he put about as much credence in the book as he did in the prophecies of the soothsayer in Bouar market (who would foretell one's future for the price of a beer).

He sought common-sense advice, not thousand-year-old hocus-pocus—as he saw much of what was touted as divine enlightenment. He knew all too well that the scriptures were no crystal ball. If they had been, his father would have vaulted to much higher heights. And, he thought sadly, his mother would have found the serenity she so wanted.

He might accept that, if you scraped off all the hyperbole, ritual, and supplication, the Bible might simply be a collection of short stories— maybe like those of Kipling. These stripped-down stories possibly did, like the shared wisdom of the village elders, provide some lessons learnt and even perspective on human behavior (if, like Peter, you presupposed that humans, *Homo sapiens*, were pretty much the same—both through space and time).

Nonetheless, he largely felt of the Testaments as an uncomfortable tie to his past and not an insight into his future.

Then why had he asked for the book?

It was not the welcoming of an old friend. Still, Peter had had (mandatorily) more than a passing acquaintance with the Word of God. Lying in bed, he thumbed through the pages, more asking himself why he bothered than actually looking at the words printed there-in. The text's soporific effects began to overcome Peter's hesitations. Before falling into a deep sleep, he managed to flag a passage.

The next morning (following his mother's routine, he wistfully reminded himself), he picked up the book (good or otherwise, he wasn't sure) and read the selection he had pinpointed the night before:

> Ezekiel 47:9—"*Swarms of living creatures will live wherever the river flows. There will be large numbers of fish, because this water flows there and makes the salt water fresh; so where the river flows everything will live.*"

It was the river. As his parents had taught him, as the American poet, Henry W. Longfellow had written about Paul Revere's Ride, "One, if by land, and two, if by sea". It was two—just not by sea but by water—the river.

Rethinking his thoughts, Peter told himself it was insanity to rely in any way on some words—random passages at best—from a source which he held in such low esteem. He remembered when, as a child, his parents would try to direct him in applying the scriptures, while he did his best to do the exact opposite. Now was he endorsing The Word?

He took words attributed to some old fart who lived over two thousand years ago and used these as the beacon for his next step—the determinant for what to do now. It was crazy.

Yeah. It probably was, he speculated. But it was no worse than throwing a coin in the air and then taking action based on which side of the piece landed face-up.

Maybe, he concluded, the Bible was just his divining rod. It was, after all, familiar, even if uncomfortable. So, in the absence of other consultation, he might as well consider it as the secular opinions of the ancestors.

Thinking back to Robbe's comments, Peter resumed his 10,000-mile journey.

With great gratitude, and a bit of sweet sorrow, Peter bid goodbye to Bouar and *Chez Robbe*. He traveled by taxi to Bangui where he waited to get visas for the two Congos. He then booked passage on a boat down the Ubangi River.

He soon had game reserves and luxuriant forests of the two Congos occupying both banks of the river. It was awe-inspiring—it truly seemed that "swarms of living creatures" had homes on the river's shore.

He continued downstream to the Ubangi's confluence with the massive Congo River. He then changed course and went up-river, stopping briefly at Kisangani before continuing upstream to the main artery of the Congo, the Lualaba River, onward to Kindu. This city had been a major trading center at least since the nineteenth century when Arabs moved gold, ivory, and slaves from here to Zanzibar.

At this juncture, Peter left the waters to return to the land. He took a taxi reminiscent of the vehicle that had carried him to Bouar, this time going to Kasango—150 miles from Kindu—a distance that required two days to cover. Stanley had reportedly visited this town in the late 1800s, but Peter was in no way following Stanley's footsteps, even if he were spiritually following Saint Paul's.

Peter then continued another 300 miles and four days to Bukavu, skirting the *Réserve Nationale d'Itombwe* and arriving on the shores of Lake Kivu, vividly recalling Robbe's tale of his wife and daughter's savage deaths in this very city.

With the scent of old battles in his mind (and the holes from motor shells still visible in the walls of Bukavu's buildings), Peter followed Schramme and the other Belgian mercenaries who, not all that long ago, had abandoned their Katangese counterparts and fled across the border into Rwanda. He managed to get a transit visa at the border and rather quickly—considering the speed of travel inside Congo—crossed from Cyangugu to Bweyeye where he entered Burundi—traveling down the highlands to Bujumbura on the beaches of Lake Tanganyika.

Peter was weary—really weary.

He had lost most of the prescribed post-operative fattening undertaken by Robbe. Traveling could be hard work.

Here, on the lakeshore, he was, by air, two-thousand-miles away from that other very different lakeside where his parents awaited his genesis. This southern lake, shared by four countries was old, clear, and deep—very deep—four-times larger and nearly the antithesis of the relatively new, shallow, and sometimes murky waters engulfed by Ghana.

If he were a rich Shell executive with a corporate jet, it would take him five to six hours to fly from Accra to Bujumbura—four times that long by commercial carrier. If he had been able to drive the 3,000-plus miles in a good Land Rover, it could have taken, non-stop, ten days to two weeks. By his chosen means of conveyance, it had taken months—at times, moving seemingly aimlessly.

River travel had been new to him and he had experienced all variety of riverine vessel from small "freighters" (really nothing more than slightly enlarged fishing boats with outboard motors) to large passenger scows. None of these were luxurious cruise ships. None even had any relationship with the word "comfort." Some had excrement-encrusted heads and lice-laden bunks—serving beer and bananas. Others had no facilities (those needing a toilet were handed a bucket). These were quite simply pragmatic means of transport—be the cargo produce or people— to service the throngs moving up- and downstream.

The harsh and often cramped conditions were, however, overshadowed by the magic of moving through the Continent's major water arteries. It was an ever-changing cinematic wonder. There were the to-be-expected hippos and crocodiles among the river birds—swimming and wading. There were the songs—human and not—coming from the surrounding forest. There were antelope coming for water. There were the scents. There were the colors. There were hard-packed paths where villagers came to beaches used by their ancestors to wash clothes, cassava, and themselves—children splashing happily as their families went about their chores, not thinking of water-borne diseases such as bilharzia, river blindness, and, of course, malaria.

Any time Peter peered over the gunwales of his current courier, he would see something different, something to appreciate, something to study.

Still, it had been a long slog. He was weary.

Although his reserves were running very thin (his cash-at-hand as stressed as his energy levels), he decided he needed to take a short break—after all, what was the hurry? Was he rushing to or from anything? He honestly wasn't totally sure—but he thought not. He needed to, as Dabi used to say so often, "Take time."

Bujumbura had been a relatively cosmopolitan lakeshore center of trade for a very long time. At least as early as the seventeenth century, Arab slavers from the Zanzibar Sultanate penetrated into the interior from East African beachheads. By the mid-1800s, Europeans, led by missionaries (the White Fathers or *Pères Blancs,* at the forefront), had established their own presence in the lake basin. The presence of outside forces was formalized at the end of that century when Burundi became part of the German East Africa colony.

One of the stalwarts going back through recent history was the Burundi Palace Hotel—once the paramount residence for visitors—this preeminence now replaced by the modern glass and plastic chain hotels that occupied the centerpiece for tourists.

The Palace currently catered for more long-term lodgers. There was an active black-market trade in a variety of articles in high demand—many of these originating in Congo and then transiting through Bujumbura en route to European vendors. A large number of the local intermediaries apparently resided at The Palace, doing business on its ever-active veranda.

Cheap rooms and a lively terrace—what more could one want?

Peter took a room for a week.

Peter did a lot of nothing for the next seven days. He would get up late in the morning and, after a surprisingly hot and invigorating shower, walk to the Greek bakery for a fresh croissant and coffee. A noticeable Greek community had been established in Burundi after the Greek Civil War—there was even a Greek fishing fleet on the Lake using the same gear and methods their forefathers used in the Mediterranean. He would then stroll about town, ending up in the late afternoon at the *Cercle Nautique* where he could sit at a table right on the water's edge, drink cold beer, munch fresh sardines from the lake, and top it all off with a plate of *brochette-frites.* As he started on his after-dinner-beer, the sun was setting, the fishers were lighting their lamps for the evening's fishing, and, snorting and farting, the hippos came into action, getting ready for the nighttime forage along the banks. As the sun set over the mountains of Congo, he would meander back, ending up on the terrace of The Palace for a beer and a "movie."

It was not a real cinema movie—it was just another night on the terrace. But it was compelling drama. The black-market movers and shakers came out of their rooms or moved from shadowy corner tables into the lights of the veranda. The girls—spectacularly appareled—arrived and, with great deference, examined who among the patrons would want or need some female companionship. The hucksters would then come selling all manner of handicrafts, knickknacks, or treasures from carved statues to "guaranteed Congo diamonds." There was never a dull moment.

Peter would welcome others to his table, curious as to the denizens of the evening promenade. He readily offered a seat to any of the girls, but (possibly for health considerations, possibly for other reasons) made it clear upfront that he was glad to buy his companion a beer and chat, but he had no intentions of having things go any further. Some left immediately. Others drank a welcome free beer and then absconded. Yet, a few stayed for more than one drink and told fascinating tales of village life and the tribulations of being a "free woman" (as they often referred to their profession).

One evening there seemed to be a penury of ladies—*papillons de nuit* as some called them—and Peter was surprised when a middle-aged-plus gentleman in conservative dress asked if he could sit down.

Peter was pleased to have someone with whom to talk and immediately offered the newcomer a beer.

"Your offer is most respectfully accepted," said the man in slightly accented English, "I am Brother Mike from the Brothers of Piety. Our monastery is in the south of Rwanda."

"Ahhh—what do I call you, 'Father'?"

"No. No. No. I'm not a priest. I'm Mike, Michael, brother, or whatever—but not father."

"OK, Brother Mike," Peter replied, a bit too cheekily, "I'm guessing you're not here for the chippies. But who knows? There's some truly memorable beauty on display, even though the *papillons* seem to have delayed their major coming-forth tonight."

"Oh, my young and new-found friend," Brother Mike quickly rejoined, his tone a bit guttural, falling back to the resonance of his Flemish mother-tongue, "you have no idea as to the souls sought by a monk. But, no, I am not seeking female camaraderie—else I wouldn't be here chatting with you."

"OK."

"I am," Brother Mike continued, feeling he was now committed to telling some sort of story as to his being on the terrace, "here before you to savor the excellent *steak au poivre* from The Palace's able kitchen while in town to buy fish for my community—on behalf of my brothers, I come to Bujumbura two or three times a year to purchase a good supply of the delicacies offered by the lake."

"At least now, then, not a fisher of men?"

"Ahh. Well, from my experience, I have no need of casting nets to catch any of my fellow travelers on this Earth—each and every one of us creates enough traps for ourselves as we move along life's path—I need not complicate matters."

"So, you don't convince people to come to your God?"

"I try to do good—to help."

"Sure."

"If I succeed—and it seems I do not do so as often as I would wish— I might hope that my example will show others that there are options— there are choices."

"So?"

"There are many alternatives, of course, for us all. Choosing is not easy for anyone. The choices abound—good and bad. The perils ever-present. We all stumble. We often fall. We are all too frequently unsure— doubting. This is the human condition, I fear."

"OK. Then . . ."

"I do not mean to, do not want to preach. You are young—you have your life in front of you. I do not. But we share the same realities—the same weaknesses and strengths.

"I have chosen my path, yet I still have doubts. I then doubt my doubts. I then question my doubts and my decisions. I then wonder. I am getting old. If I could do it all over, would I do the same? Was I right? Was I wrong?

"You see, the terrace is not just for enjoying beer, good *frites,* and the glory of women—it can also be a place of deep introspection.

"So, there you have it, young man, far more than you thought you would probably get from a stodgy old brother from Rwanda."

Peter took a big gulp of beer. He examined his new drinking partner—the older man evidently now staring into a world of his own making, thinking of his own words; at that moment, in a different place and time. Peter exhaled and decided.

"Brother Mike," he started slowly, "I had thought we'd talk about the rains or last season's harvest—even the way forward for the Church in the green hills of Africa. To my surprise, I guess to my satisfaction, you have taken a different path.

"I am the son of missionaries—from the other side of the river, but still rooted in the Christian God—my mother used to say you people prefer Paul, while Protestants prefer Peter. Anyway, Peter or Paul, as you say, it's all about choices. Damn! It's all about choices."

"For us all."

"Sure—for us all. But a million others carrying stones from the same quarry does not take the weight off my shoulders."

"No but asking for help might."

"Help? No one else can carry my load."

"No, they can't, but they can try to help you make your own load lighter."

"I doubt it—like you, I'm a doubter."

"Maybe I should have said questioner and not doubter. It is good—it is even better—to question. But it is also necessary to find answers—even if these are incomplete—even if these are somehow in error."

"Where are the answers?"

"Maybe on the terrace?"

"Sure!"

"The world is full of surprises. I'm quite certain you've already discovered that."

"My people don't like surprises—they like constancy and continuity—they admire unquestioning devotion—they require their own expectations be met, regardless the cost—regardless the circumstances. They know they know, and they want you to accept that they know—no wavering allowed.

"My people—my parents and grandparents—expect—no, they quietly demand allegiance. There is no room—no space for anything but complete devotion.

"But devotion to what? Devotion to their personal beliefs—to their personal prejudices and preconceptions.

"They portray themselves as humble servants. However, all too often, it seems they are just the opposite—they, consciously or not, see themselves as the masters—the masters of truth—the masters of salvation—the masters of others.

"They unequivocally insist all are God's children—all equal in the eyes of God. They almost vehemently assert all life is precious—all are cherished parts of God's creation. Yet, they see all outside their personal realm—what they absolutely perceive as God's kingdom—as being ignorant, weak, and inept.

"They steadfastly swear—and believe—they are helping others—saving others. Yet, they know nothing at all of those they profess they are rescuing.

"They live in their own world. They are adamant their world is 'The World'—the only way forward—not just for them—for everyone."

That was a lot. Peter had just, as though exhaling from deep in his lungs, voiced things he rarely even dared to think. He ordered more beers, draining his glass in a matter of seconds. He had totally uncharacteristically and candidly admitted thoughts, conclusions, and emotions of which he seldom, if ever, spoke—confessed to ruminations he had had on the lakeside or footpaths of Kpando. These most private and personal contemplations were not things to divulge on a terrace populated by hookers, black-marketeers, hawkers, and chiselers. And, he had done so to a complete stranger. He should be feeling uncomfortable, he was sure. Yet, he was not sure if he was feeling as he should—he almost felt better.

Brother Mike shattered Peter's reverie, "My young companion whose name I don't even know, no one ever said it would be easy."

"I'm Peter, sorry," he said, changing channels in his mind, "I should have introduced myself. I know it's not supposed to be easy, but I never knew it would be so frustrating.

"This space we share—this life we each experience—we each sample—it's truly mixed-up—so often baffling.

"I grow up. Everyone's fine. They say, 'He's a good bloke' or 'There's a guy whose gonna go far'. Go where? I have no idea I only know I need to find my way."

"Sadly," Brother Mike opined, "few of us have any success at reading our own tarot cards. Be assured that I, many years your senior, still have misgivings—still spend hours contemplating decisions made and possibilities not explored—wines untasted, mountains and valleys unseen.

"Rare is the person who wakes up one day and says, 'I'm an adult now' and just goes forward with the first choice that pops up—never looking back—never questioning.

"We all seek that what we can accept as the truth. We all enquire about the 'why's' in our lives. Why me? Why now?

"As any of us, you can move ahead on faith. You can move ahead on self-confidence. You can move ahead like you're walking on thin ice. But you, and all of us, we are all destined to move ahead—even when we don't want to or when we don't know where we're going.

"As a religious man, I suspect I should be going from day to day on faith. I should be calm and satisfied I am being guided by the God I serve. Perhaps, I should be more like 'your people'? Perhaps, I should be more adamant? Perhaps, I should be more sure? Yet, truth be known, every day I am concerned and confused. And I don't think this will ever change. The more we see, the more we do, the more we question—and the more we may realize the answers are not quick in coming. It's life."

A waiter, a black bowtie a little askew above a less-than-spotless white shirt, came and slightly bowed to the good brother—the two seemingly having more than a casual relationship.

"Ahh," Brother Mike nearly crooned, "my steak is ready. This fine gentleman so elegantly appareled, is Fostan—I'm sure he can help you if you need anything. He and I, through my years coming to the Lake, have become good friends. He makes sure my steak is the choicest and my pepper sauce the sweetest.

"Fostan, my new young terrace-mate here, Peter, is one of your guests. I'm sure he'll see you if he has any needs.

"Peter, sport, I will take my savory meal inside in the dining room where I can do it justice. It has been a pleasure chatting with you. Good luck and God's speed on your journey—I hope you find what you're looking for. I will think of you in my prayers"

With that, Brother Mike followed Fostan inside.

Peter ordered another beer.

He thought of Brother Mike's commentary.

It seemed queasiness with regard to one's place in the universe was, in the Brother's view, a typical mystification—almost an integral part of the human species.

Peter wondered.

Before going to bed, Peter thought more of the evening's discussion—still amazed at his own candor—his venting. Life could infuriate, inflame, and incense (beer, of course, helped loosen the tongue, he had to admit).

He thought of his parents. He thought of his parents' life.

He thought of faith. He questioned his own convictions.

He thought of Jesus' brothers Peter and Paul.

He recalled his father recounting in minute detail Paul's third voyage—travels to Galatia, Phrygia, Ephesus, Tyre—places that were just names, Peter having no idea where they had been nor who had lived there. He saw Paul afloat in a largely unknown world, much as he himself.

When during this voyage, Saint Paul encountered the Christians of Corinth, whom he saw as uncertain and questioning their fealty, he extolled them, as Peter's father had told it, referring to Corinthians 16:13—"*Be watchful, stand firm in the faith, act like men, be strong.*"

Paul the father had frequently referred to this passage when trying to encourage his son to seek the right path in life—tacitly, that being the path his father had chosen for him—the path, of course, that God had chosen for him. Paul, the father, had further referred to Paul the Saint as the seasoned voyager—a sojourner, who like Peter his son, always and steadfastly followed God's ways and who, hopefully also as Peter the son, was forever mindful of God's Words.

Saint Paul had shown a light on the way forward—at least according to Paul the father. That holy light persisted as a beacon for Peter the son.

Moreover, and most importantly, Paul the father had sermonized, in spite of all odds, Saint Paul persevered. He had been perpetually faithful to his God. In what was seen as his fourth voyage, he had had to overcome horrific obstacles—obstacles Paul the father ensured his son that had strengthened the man's, the Saint's, perseverance.

But perseverance cannot overcome all obstacles, be they ever so unjust. Saint Paul had been imprisoned in Palestine by King Herod Agrippa. Wrongfully, as Paul the father had highlighted. Paul the Saint lamented in Acts 26:31—"*After they left the room, they began saying to one another, 'This man is not doing anything that deserves death or imprisonment.'*"

Of course, there were reprehensible and unfair people everywhere, at every time.

However, ignoble and dishonest actions can be corrected (with God's help, according to Paul the father).

Saint Paul, as Peter's father had retold the tale, was indeed released in Palestine, only to be later imprisoned in Rome. He went before Nero and again, in Paul the father's view, due to Divine Intervention, was released—Paul the Saint referring to this in 2 Timothy 4:16—"*At my first defense, no one came to my support, but everyone deserted me. May it not be held against them.*"

Peter's father frequently accentuated the point, the exhortation of God the Father as lived by Saint Paul, that it was up to them, their family, to take the high ground. It was up to them to be loving, even in the face of hate. They were, after all, among God's chosen few. They were the bringers of God's Words—the heralds of salvation (all a bit much, Peter thought).

Paul the father had so often told his child, the son he saw as his scion, "If there is one thing I can advise, it is this: follow in the steps of Paul—not Paul your Father, but Paul your Saint."

Two days later, as the sun rose above the Serengeti over 400 miles to the east, and the pied crows cawed in the acacia trees along the lakeshore, uncertain if he were in fact following Paul's footsteps, Peter boarded a ferry to go Mpulungu, in Zambia, traversing the lake's 350-mile north-south axis (the distance by road, 520 miles). The vessel lazily sauntered down the lake over a period of three days. Ten days later, after passing through Chirundu and Beitbridge and points in-between, Peter arrived in Johannesburg—over 4,000 miles from the shores of Lake Volta—over 4,000 miles from Paul the father.

CHAPTER SEVEN

The Letter

Still entangled in the net

JOHANNESBURG. THE HEART OF so much history, so much politics, so much wealth. A place so different from the rest of the Continent—the great landmass of Africa hanging above South Africa like a giant hot air balloon looming over a tiny basket below—a basket filled with a weird assortment of individuals—individuals who were seen as both a threat and a friend.

Once again, although more of a stopover than a destination, Peter looked for a way to establish a temporary base.

His resources were exhausted—his savings from the good folks at Shell now effectively gone.

He needed to find something to do—something to do to make money.

And, he was, of course, among flocks of people gushing into South Africa, trying to get their small piece of the high-energy economy—seen as an opportunity of a lifetime with the new leadership now in place. Malawians, Zambians, Zimbabweans, Mozambicans, and Angolans abounded. Many said there were more men from Lesotho and Swaziland working in South Africa's mines than there were men still residing in their home countries.

However, rather chagrined by the realization, Peter recognized that he was not competing in the same job market as the majority of the other émigrés. While apartheid as an official policy and lifestyle had recently formally come to an end, apartheid—racial inequities—was still very much a part of day-to-day life in many circumstances. Old habits die hard. Things adjust slowly. The distribution of wealth—big money—was still largely unaffected by the winds of social and economic change that were fiercely blowing across parts of the country.

In this setting, many white entrepreneurs and managers wanted white mid-level staff—there was a market for college-educated white males. Peter just needed to find it.

Here, there was no Silas to guide him nor Dabi to help him. He had to ferret out the answers himself.

Peter had taken a comfortable bus from Beitbridge, south, down the N-1 right into Johannesburg. His first night, he splurged, nearly emptying his pockets for a room in the four-star Mapungubwe Hotel, not far from the city center.

The next day he set about seriously looking for more affordable, longer-term accommodation. He knew no one and he knew there were areas of Johannesburg best left unvisited. He could only ask about and hope (he forwent prayer, knowing this would have been his mother's choice).

Ask about he did: at his hotel, at a nearby by bar, at the restaurant where he had his breakfast, even at the cobbler's where he went to get his shoes repaired. The consensus uniformly seemed to be to look for a guesthouse in the Yoeville-Bellevue East area, slightly north of the town center.

After extended traipsing around the target neighborhoods, Peter settled on the Mountain View Guesthouse—although, there was no mountain in view. It was across the street from the Gbezua Butchery and the Africa Kitchen, in between the Church of Jesus and the Sthole Truck Stop—four blocks from the Yoeville Police Station. But it was not the location nor the neighbors that made the decision for Peter. It was cheap. Furthermore, while cheap, it was relatively clean. The clincher was that the manager, a genial Indian gentleman, agreed to let Peter have a room for a month just on his signature—no deposit. Most unusual and most welcome to someone who was truly out-of-pocket.

Next, it was a job.

His starting point was Mister Khan, his new innkeeper. Mister Khan seemed to know something about everything. His best tip was that his wife's cousin's daughter's husband was an architect. His firm had been busy planning new industrial buildings not far from the airport—in Bredell, near the intersection of the major highways R-21 and R-23.

According to Mister Khan, the recognized end to apartheid (real or imagined) had led to the opening of major intra-African markets to South African entrepreneurs—many of these new ventures were close by in the southern African region while a growing number were all across the Continent as South African began to stretch her legs and invest throughout the territory. South Africa was, after all, the African—or at the very least, the Sub-Saharan African—industrial leader, offering (or destined to offer) South African goods and services from the Cape to Cairo.

Mister Khan, knowledgeable as always about the subject, had to underscore that South Africa's perceived supremacy—economic and not racial, he added with a twinkle in his eyes—was now being challenged on left and on the right by China.

The Chinese could offer any product made in South Africa at a fifth of the price—the fact that it lasted a tenth of the time was not a general consideration, as Mister Khan had keenly observed.

So, as Mister Khan had analyzed the situation, South Africa had to look for her comparative advantage. There was, of course, mining. South Africans were investing, and sometimes operating, mines in Ghana, Sierra Leone, Liberia, Mali, and elsewhere. But there was also agriculture.

The Chinese reportedly, according to Mister Khan's information, had a tough time feeding their mammoth population. Thus, for the moment, it seemed China would not be exporting too much food to Africa—but no one was sure for how long?

This opened a window to South Africa, as it had been explained to Mister Khan, to send temperate-climate crops—apples on the top of the list—and related foodstuffs around the Continent. South African exporters were sure they could compete with the old colonial powers of France and England who had been the provisioners of these foods heretofore seen as luxury products only for the upper classes.

This brought Mister Khan full circle, back to Bredell. This area had been chosen for the processing and packaging of foods for export—less than ten miles from the airport, for products going by airfreight, and close to major roads for other items traveling by surface.

Mister Khan was sure the time was right for Peter to get involved.

Mister Khan was able to get some names for Peter from his wife's cousin's daughter's husband—contacts that Peter followed-up promptly. And, whether through insight or just the luck of the draw, Mister Khan's prediction proved to be true. It was apparently a good time as Peter got a job as timekeeper on the construction site for one of the buildings designed by Mister Khan's distant relative.

The site was big—from Peter's seat, it was really big—but he had little to use for comparison. Much of the work involved manual labor and the overseers used two fifty-man teams a day.

The pay was far from great and the bosses were not all that particular about who the workers were as long as they were there working. To this end, they had established a rather flexible system to try and keep the workforce at full capacity. They had fifty-four-inch brass circles, each stamped with a number from one to fifty. For each day in the time book, there were two columns with fifty rows.

At the start of work, a worker passed through the main entrance and showed his disk to a guard seated at the front gate. The guard wrote down the disk's number in his notebook. Much of the work was "task work," the laborer leaving once the assigned task was completed. Thus, when someone exited the main gate, the guard *cum* record-keeper would circle the number when the worker showed his disk—a circled number representing a completed day's work. Sometime later, frequently not very long after the first man had left, someone else would show the guard the same disk and the process would be repeated for shift two.

The first thing each morning, Peter would be given the pages from the guards' notebooks that represented the previous day's work. He would then transpose these into the official time book. Not too difficult.

No one knew, in fact, most doubted, that it was only one person per number per shift per pay period. Indeed, the bosses felt this was a plus. If someone could not come to work due to illness, family problems, or because they just wanted to get drunk, they could give their disk to someone, anyone who would do the work for that day. The company, in truth, hired numbers and not people.

Every two weeks, Peter would calculate one hundred totals—the numbers of hours spent on the two shifts over the half-month. Different jobs—different numbers—had different daily rates. For each number on each shift there was an official contact name. Each fortnight this person had to present himself (for better or worse, all the workers were men) with ID to receive the pay—how these monies were later distributed among various individuals who had been involved in the exercise was of no interest to the company.

The system appeared to work, and the construction progressed ahead of schedule.

After eight months as a Mountain View lodger, the factory-warehouse for food exports near the intersection of highways R-21 and R-23, dubbed Orange River Foods, was more than half completed. The overseers began thinking about operations as much as construction. They needed to line-up the required staff so as to be able to start processing food as soon as the building was certified as completed and operational.

While Peter's assignment during the construction phase had been rote and mundane, he had kept at it and kept at it with good spirits and a positive air. This impressed the overseers—particularly the new Orange River Foods' General Manager, Mr. de Woordvoerder. He offered Peter a job as a supervisor once the building was finished. Peter accepted.

Peter had managed to save a bit while staying at the Mountain View, but not really enough for him to be able to travel very far if and when he decided to leave. He needed to find alternative lodging.

While the building was going up and Peter was making plans, farmers and others in food-related fields were making contact with the new company to try and negotiate good prices for their products. These would-be partners often came around the job site to get a feel (as they said) of what things would look like.

One day a Mr. Wewege stuck his head into Peter's mini office to ask some questions about the timeline for the completion of construction. After the work questions were asked and answered, for reasons he himself little understood, Peter decided to enquire of Mr. Wewege if he happened to know of any accommodation for a newcomer in need of a roof over his head.

Again, whether the luck of the draw or the gods smiling, Mr. Wewege explained to Peter that his major activity was the nursery business—he only tangentially engaged in actions that might relate to food export. Business was good and he had recently purchased a neighbor's nursery. The new acquisition was easily merged into his operations, but the extra nursery came with a small house, a cottage really, that was now vacant. Unused things deteriorate quickly. Mr. Wewege would be happy for someone, a reputable someone he inserted (the racial inuendo just barely perceptible by a half-smile as he eyed Peter), to live in the dwelling as long as he kept it in good shape and paid all the utilities.

Effectively rent-free lodging—Peter could not ask for more.

Peter paid his bill with Mister Khan, thanking him profusely for all his kindnesses. He used his savings to buy a used Kawasaki 650 and then moved into the little house at the nursery in Slaterville—only six miles from his job site.

He had a new base.

Peter wrote to Silas, giving him his new address and just the slimmest of details as to how he got to where he was. He thought about writing his parents but decided now was not the time—he wasn't sure why this was so, but he was quite sure this was the case.

He then adopted his new routine. Up early, light breakfast, refreshing ride to Bredell, work (generally monotonous, verging on stale), then a few after-work-beers at any of a number of pubs before retiring home to another light meal before bed. His main focus was to save enough to be able to do what he wanted to do—he figured this was probably the aim of most people walking the Earth.

To this end, he kept his social life to a minimum—only evening beers, rarely going to restaurants or other evening attractions and, avoiding establishing any close relationships—be they male or female. In many ways, he was still testing the terrain.

The new food complex was completed and inaugurated. The company changed modes and Peter was now supervising a component of the multi-compartmented firm that packaged fresh fruit for airfreight to supermarkets around the Continent that were part of a large and expanding South African grocery chain. The work was only slightly less plodding than his timekeeping. He had seen his old job as a game of Bingo—one-hundred squares to cover each day, and that was about it. Now he oversaw a team of eleven people—eleven fruity people (he thought with a smirk, unsure if the pun was even applicable—probably not). They would bring in pallets of produce from the unloading docks; sort, wash, box, wrap, palletize, send to the loading dock. Every day was a mirror image of its predecessor.

Then the tedium was somehow dislodged.

Peter received a big envelope with Silas's return address. Inside, there was a concise note from his old counselor, stating how happy he was to hear from his young wayfaring friend, how far this friend had traveled, how he hoped his friend was in good form, how they all, including Dabi, were fine, and how he was happy to now be able to forward the mail he had been collecting.

There were then a dozen smaller envelopes with Ghanaian postage and one with US stamps. Peter did not feel ready to meet the challenge of reading his parents' mail, but he was intrigued by the envelope from the States. Opening it, he found a letter from his sister, Lydia:

> My dear brother,
>
> I feel we are almost strangers. This is such a shame, but I guess it is the world into which we were born. As I write, I am unsure how to "speak" to you. I am unsure of what you look like, what you like, what you dislike, what you're doing, where you're going?
>
> I write to Mom and Dad every week, and they are pretty good at keeping the conversation going. So, I know you have left Ghana to go to Nigeria to see new sites and maybe experience new things. Our folks think you've probably left Nigeria now, for points unknown, so I am even more unsure if this will ever reach you wherever you are?
>
> You have always followed a different road than I. When Dad said you should go to Missouri to continue your schooling, you said you'd go to the UK—I said I'd go to Missouri. When Mom and Dad tried to get you to build bridges to our family here in the States, you blazed trails over new horizons—I kept to the known and comfortable, readily embracing all those in this state who have known two generations of our family. We have simply been so different.
>
> This difference, as I am sure you know, is visible at all levels—even the smallest. While we each spent our childhood in Ghana, your anchor was Bole while I was much more a part of Kpando—I still love the scent of the lake, the musty aroma of the soil, and the waifs of fish frying in palm oil laden with chilies.
>
> This brings me closer to the main reason I am writing. I guess I just need someone special with whom to talk—no one here could really listen the way I need to be listened-to—I don't know if you can? But you're about all I've got left. This is a very difficult topic to discuss—letter to write. I don't know what to do. I'm crying and need help—I need my big brother.

Let me try and fill in a few of the blanks—quickly so you don't, as I know you want to, put the letter down because you think it's just more bla-bla-bla.

As you know, I'm now in college. It's OK and I'm doing fine. Still, I miss home. For me, I guess like you, home is always Ghana. I think of myself as an American, but I think of home as Ghana. I am always a stranger here—even if an American. I so miss the sights and sounds—the people—of where I grew up—of where my family lives.

To try and have a little taste of home, I'm a member of an international students group here on campus. We meet once a month, have food from somewhere special, and then talk about life in these United States. It helps.

Last week we had our regular meeting. There was a new girl from Ghana, and low-and-behold, she was from Kpando—imagine that! What are the chances?

While she didn't know me—or you, for that matter—she knew Mom and Dad's church and knew them by sight. Although she'd never met them, she had an aunt who was part of Dad's congregation.

My new friend's name is Ama. I was so happy to find someone with whom I could talk about home that I immediately invited her to go out for drinks and we were together last night—this the reason I'm writing today.

You may not know it—probably don't—but unlike you, I'm not a big drinker. I like a beer, but two will do me just fine—even the tasteless watered-down local beers. Ama, however, seems to follow closer to your tastes—she did some damage last night. I wouldn't say she drank so much as to be sloppy drunk—although she probably could have if I'd kept filling her glass—but she was more than a little tipsy.

We were talking about Kpando—going over the town as though we there walking the roads and paths. We were looking across the lake, talking about the market—almost going from stall to stall. Then she said, did you know that 'spot'—that bar—behind the market—the place run by Chantal? Then she said, "Oops"

I immediately asked what she means by, "Oops?" Then, the conversation, greased by the beer, took a nosedive. Without boring you with all the specifics Ama provided, details that I myself didn't need to hear, the just of the issue is that, according to Ama—and, unfortunately, I do believe her—Dad has been having an affair with Chantal for years. In fact, apparently Chantal and her family and friends consider her as being Dad's second wife.

This is terrible!

I don't know what to do.
I feel so ashamed. I feel so embarrassed. I feel so dirty.
I feel so, so sorry for Mom.
I feel so helpless.
I can't tell Mom. I can't accuse Dad. I can't do anything. I'm in college in Missouri.
I'm leaning on you from far, far away. I know you, too, probably can't do anything. But I needed to try to talk to someone—and I knew not who else.
Peter, what can we do?

Peter re-read the letter three times. He was flabbergasted. He was not flabbergasted about a man cheating on his wife, nor a white man cheating on his white wife with an African—not even by a religious person cheating in defiance of the Ten Commandants. He was flabbergasted by the fact that these things were being done by HIS father.

Under any other circumstances, he would have said this was pure rubbish—totally and completely impossible. Not HIS father! HIS father could never, never do these things—things that, after all, weren't, in Peter's view, in the bigger picture, all that catastrophic—but things that could never be done by HIS father. Never! Yet, as he put the letter down, he knew it was true.

What was it that people in Nigeria said all the time, "Never say never?"

Chantal was his father's lover—in reality, in the situation his father himself had created, she was truly his second wife. Chantal, second wife of an American missionary—an American pastor! Chantal, Pastor Paul's *co-épouse.*

As Lydia had said, there was little he—little they—could do. Uncovering the years of deceit and deception would only wound the innocent. This could destroy their mother and wasn't even honestly fair for Chantal, as no one had forced his father to jump into her bed.

If Peter had been there, face-to-face with his father, undoubtedly, he would not be able to control himself and he would pull his father into a quiet corner of the church, his father's church, and accuse him righteously and mercilessly. He would demand his father stop all his duplicitous and sacrilegious (in the eyes of a pastor and the eyes of his God) activities immediately. He would demand contrition and repentance forthwith. And, he would demand his father never, never speak of this to his mother. Peter would bring his father to task.

But Peter was not there. There was no bringing to task. There was no blaming—no uncovering the truth. There was no disgrace or humiliation. There was nothing to do to a cheating father 4,000 miles away.

All Peter could do was to write to his sister. And even then, what could he say?

There was so much to say, but so little that could be said. Lydia knew. She asked, "What can we do?" The answer effectively was: *nothing.*

When Peter had drafted his reply to his sister—drafted and redrafted—re-touched and re-done, he added a postscript:

> *PS: Lydia, my dear sister, as you have so eloquently indicated, your roots are in Kpando—on the lake's shore. This, and our father's hypocrisy and dishonesty, made me recall one of those verses he chanted to us so often. I have had to borrow a Bible to get it right—not being much of a Bible-beater myself, as you know full-well—but you will certainly remember better than I one of his favorites: Matthew 4:19—"'Come, follow me,' Jesus said, 'and I will send you out to fish for people.'"*
>
> *Our father was certainly a fisher of men—and he caught many. Yes, he was a disingenuous fisher. Nonetheless, a fisher who knew so well how to set his nets to fool others—us included.*
>
> *But, of course you will recall, the Bible also warned in Isaiah 19:8—"The fishermen will groan and lament, all who cast hooks into the Nile; those who throw nets on the water will pine away."*
>
> *Even I, who do not share your deep beliefs, have to believe that ultimately our father will reap what he has sown—he will pine away.*

Peter knew his missive was woefully incomplete, but there were few choices (in spite of, Peter bemused, Brother Mike's statements about all the choices we all have). Neither child could undo what had been done—what was (probably) being done. Neither child could fix the problem. The best they could do was probably do nothing. They could only hope their mother never found out and that these acts, what had become part of their father's hidden life, remained hidden. There was little else to do.

Peter felt his letter was completely inadequate. Still, it was all he could do—all anyone could do. Things were as they were. If Lydia was so inclined, she could pray—other than that, there wasn't much else.

After Peter had posted his letter, he thought about his sister. She was so right, they were strangers—or nearly so. She was only four years his "follow-back" (as Dabi had referred to herself—thoughts of this special Nigerian, Lagosian, lady still painful). This wasn't really that big a differ- ence to account for their near estrangement—many children are sepa- rated from their siblings by more than a decade (this, Peter thought, far too big a gap—nearly generational).

No, he and Lydia were separated more by space than time. They had always occupied different spheres. It was more than the contrasts of Bole and Kpando—although that could be part of the distinction.

They had looked through different prisms.

Peter had always been agnostic—incredulous of all the religious incantations that he felt were elixirs to cover the eyes of the embittered. In spite of how much he might try to think to the contrary, he saw his parents as salesmen trying to sell miracles to people who often really needed the basics for survival. He couldn't shake the conviction, as he had surprisingly uttered out loud to Brother Mike, that his parents' work was solely self-serving.

But it was not so with his sister. He could still see her sitting stoically in the back of the church as the nave filled with melodious cries, "Yah- weh, Yahweh, Yahweh! All praise, all glory, and all blessing to Yahweh! Yahweh, Yahweh, Yahweh!".

To her credit, Peter felt Lydia was not a cultist. Not a deaf, dumb, and blind believer, regardless the realities. Not an ardent fanatic like some (he wondered, if like his parents?). So many zealots, his folks undoubtedly among them, seemed to toe-the-line under any and all circumstances. This did not apply to his sister.

Lydia, at least the little girl he remembered, seemed to honestly believe in the need to be a good person—feeling the church, if adding no other value, helped people be good. He had always thought this idea naive, but he respected her aspirations.

He really knew so little about her—little about the young girl in Kpando and even less about the coed in Missouri.

The main memory in his mind was of Lydia with Kofi—the loving mongrel pup someone had given their father. Lydia and Kofi seemed so alike—so full of life. They wanted to play, they wanted to be with people, they wanted to do good. And, they were both highly sensitive. On the outside seeming to be the rambunctious youngsters—inside highly

responsive to the slightest criticism or grumble. An insensitive gruff retort could easily send either of them into timidity.

Today, Peter imagined Lydia had lost much of her timidity. Had she
also lost her faith—her faith in doing good? He wondered.

As Peter thought of his sister and brooded over his father and his father's
selfish acts, he was unexpectedly contacted by a Mr. Koopman.

Mr. Koopman was an acquaintance, if more of competitor than a
friend to Mr. de Woordvoerder. However dicey their relationship, the two
entrepreneurs managed to have a drink together from time to time to talk
about their common interest in growing the country's food exports. After
maybe just one beer too many, Mr. de Woordvoerder was bragging about
Orange River Foods' new plant and the company's top-notch staff, including, by name, Peter (apparently noteworthy as an American import).

Mr. Kooppman wanted to meet Peter.

Mr. Koopman was starting a small agricultural export business.
Unlike Peter's current employer with grand global visions, Mr. Koopman was targeting what he saw as growing, but more limited markets
in neighboring countries. He had perhaps a less grandiose view of the
opportunities for moving into other parts of this vast Continent.

While more modest in his expectations, Mr. Koopman was very aggressive in his product—he wanted to sell only the very best. He wanted
to market top quality for top prices—be this considered as feeding luxury
clients—so be it.

Mr. Koopman felt that the best products come with contented
employees. He was, therefore, convinced he needed to pay significantly
higher wages to attract the best people—he wanted to hire Peter.

Peter was well aware he and all his colleagues at Orange River Foods
were unquestionably underpaid. From the onset, the company had had a
bulldozer approach—push everything out of the way. If someone didn't
like it, they were more than free to leave.

Peter figured this was an opportunity and a good time to leave.

After giving notice, he joined Mr. Koopman without even a contract.

His mind was still embroiled in the chicanery and perfidiousness of
Kpando as he started a new job in Vlakfontein—only two miles from his
old employer.

Another page was turned.

Work at Koopman Farms, as it turned out his new employer was so-
named, was indeed more rewarding than at its predecessor—both financially and professionally. Here it wasn't a repetitious, nearly robotic,
production line. Here it was all about quality and not quantity. Specific,
and relatively small, orders were filled—generally with a mixture of
hand-selected fruits or vegetables. It was almost as though each product
was an individualized fruit basket attentively assembled. There were no
compartments nor components. There was only a relatively small team
of roughly a score of workers just as attentively assembled as the fruit
baskets. Numbers would fluctuate with the seasons, but Peter found he
was part of a smaller nucleus that monitored the entire workspace and
the overall operation from in-coming to out-going. Throughout the day,
throughout the plant, Peter and his co-supervisors ensured all was as it
should be.

A new routine was established—not very different from the previous pattern. Peter was still focusing on building his bank account—se-
verely depleted (again) with the purchase of his Kawasaki.

Still and all, things were good.

Mr. Koopman was an innovative man. While he fully accepted that he
needed to pay a good wage for good work, he was definitely not averse
to lowering his overall costs. One of his rather ingenious tactics was to
court volunteers.

While not an overly religious man (as far as Peter could discern—
and Peter felt he had a good eye for such things), like many Afrikaners,
Mr. Koopman acknowledged his historical Calvinist origins and was, at
least in name, a member in good standing the Reform Church (*Gere-
formeerde Kerke in Suid-Afrika*). Mr. Koopman understood, moreover,
that (as Peter was so painfully aware) religions had hooks. Afrikaner
Calvinism shared basic principles with a number of US congregations:
the Reformed Baptists, the Presbyterians, the United Church of Christ,
and others. Accordingly, Mr. Koopman sent regular notices to "sister"
churches, highlighting the importance of farming in Africa, and welcoming any volunteers who would like to come and make a difference (Mr.
Koopman offering nothing more tangible than a hearty embrace upon
arrival).

As Peter entered his fourth month at Koopman Farms, the first volunteer arrived: Katherine from Iowa—she asked to be called "Katy." To Peter's amazement, when Katy was introduced to the group, it was explained she had a master's degree in agricultural marketing from Iowa State University.

Peter could not imagine why she had decided to come here—but here she was.

It was perhaps natural that two Americans would gravitate to each other. Katy was overwhelmed by being in Africa, by being so far from home, and by being side-by-side with someone like Peter who had done and seen so much—done and seen things she could not even imagine.

For Peter, it was unclear why he had opened the door—wanting female companionship—wanting to hear about his homeland (or one of his homelands)—or plain curiosity why someone with her qualifications would choose to do what she was doing. Yet, for whatever reason or reasons, open the door he did—figuratively and pragmatically.

Since Mr. Koopman provided no support for volunteers beyond a big smile, Katy was pretty much on her own in terms of how she lived in South Africa—where she stayed, how she ate, how she did laundry, how she saw, if need-be, a doctor—how she survived. Thus, after a few nights in a modest guesthouse, Katy came to Peter, asking about cheap accommodation—a subject, she assumed correctly, about which Peter had first-hand information.

Katy was worried—her church had almost no budget for supporting volunteers. Her family had tried to kitty-up to fill the void, but there was very little with which to work. She had a round-trip ticket and a few traveler's checks, but that was about it.

Peter wanted to help. He wasn't sure of his motives, but he wanted to do something.

The house Mr. Wewege had so generously put at his disposal had two tiny bedrooms—one vacant. It didn't make any sense at all to have someone in need like Katy and to have an unused bed that could be slept upon at no charge. He offered her a position as roommate.

Within three weeks, the position had changed, and they had become something more than friends. It didn't take too long before there was a vacant bed once again in Mr. Wewege's cottage.

Much as Katy proved herself to be a reserved lover, the path to Peter's bed had not been direct nor immediate. She had come to Africa with a mission if not as a missionary. She had not come to get laid nor to be a tourist—points she spelled-out clearly for Peter when accepting his kind offer of lodging.

Over the first few days—both at work and home—Peter was able to piece together much of Katy's story. Her parents, devote Baptists, were third generation farmers in northeast Iowa—growing corn and soy. She was the youngest of six children—her oldest brother fifteen years her senior. She was the first in her family to go to college—her five siblings engaged in farming in Chickasaw County in one way or another. For her family, Chicago was a far-off place—no one even thought of Africa.

But Katy was going to be different. She was not revolting. She loved her family and greatly respected their lifestyle and priorities. She simply felt she was different and should do different things. She suspected that she would ultimately find herself back in Iowa, back in a farming community—probably back in Chickasaw County. Yet, at this point in her life, she knew she needed to do more—to experience more.

Her studies had been bifurcated—marketing and human nutrition. She was, in fact, according to her interpretation, here because, in their initial exchanges, Mr. Koopman had indicated he was interested in starting a new series of products highlighting, in addition to their quality, also their important health benefits. He wanted to mount an "eat this, it's good for you" campaign with Katy's help.

Katy saw this as an ideal opportunity to put her studies to work and to, at the same time, realize her hopes of experiencing more—seeing new and diverse things. She was excited. However, she was also extremely serious and principled. The jury seemed out as to whether or not, overlying all this, she was also very religious. Much like Lydia, she appeared to be pragmatic while determined to do the right thing—God's role in this process still pending (as seen from Peter's vantage point).

As Peter was putting together the Katy jigsaw puzzle, he provided a barebones recital of his own life—son of missionaries, educated in the UK, now traveling about to see what the world had to offer. He took extra care not to embellish nor to add too many distractions—what he saw as boring technicalities.

Peter, as he rehashed events, had not immediately seen Katy as a lover nor even a convenient solution to an overly long period of celibacy. He had seen her as someone who needed a place to sleep—full stop.

However, beneath her somewhat austere exterior, Katy was, as Peter was learning, a frank and funny person with great warmth and keen senses of humility and tenderness. While her get-the-job-done facade was, in truth, a real reflection of her dedication and capabilities, she had a real need for guileless human connections. Quite simply, she honestly liked people.

And as she welcomely settled into the Slaterville cottage's life and lifestyle, the passing weeks witnessed her liking of Peter the friend transformed into something deeper and more emotional—Peter the admirer (and the admired). When this conversion was complete, even if it did seem to be preordained, she was happy to climb into his bed.

Katy was a gentle partner—quite a contrast to Ruby or Dabi. Thinking back to secondary school physics, Peter (a little ashamed of himself for doing so) thought she was more like potential energy, while the others were kinetic energy. Continuing the analogy, to himself he added, this potential could very rapidly be energized.

Katy and Peter were attentive to one another. In the embraces of pleasure, they often seemed to float away to their own placid place—far from everything—engulfed in oneness. Their relationship, however, was considerably more than one of seeking solely sexual gratification. They were like a single bipolar being, each portion relying on the other, but with its own discrete essence.

Peter badly wanted to suck Katy's cultural marrow from her—finding the core of what it was really like to be an American.

Katy, similarity, wanted to absorb from Peter the knowledge, the cognition of her surroundings. She felt so foreign—so out-of-sync with her new environment. Through osmosis, she wanted to understand—to be a part.

It was a binary but mutually symbiotic alliance—synergies arising from their dualism.

At work, they rarely saw each other—even taking measures to not be seen together, to not be known as a couple. Peter was, after all, a supervisor—moving about the facility, checking on everything—alert, always the sharp observer (the traits Mr. Koopman had admired before hiring the young man). Katy, for her part, delving into nutritional health, was most frequently either in the small cubbyhole Mr. Koopman had given her as an office or moving about the metro area in a company car, checking on products and markets.

Nonetheless, once the bell sounded and the crew left Koopman Farms, Katy unabashedly got on the back of Peter's Kawasaki, and the two would go for a pint at one of the several pubs they frequented (Peter's after-work-beer habit hard to break).

Then, once they were seated at a table in the bistro, they would dive into lively and often thought-provoking discussions about Missouri and Nigeria, about churches and mosques, about rivers and lakes, about corn and maize, about hot dogs and *beignets*, about shish kebabs and *brochettes*, about men and women. Each had a thirst. Each was like a parasite on the other's nature—trying to absorb the soul of another culture.

It was hard to gauge any real impact one had on the other's character—the other's essentiality. Each learned from the other. Through knowledge, there was, as hoped, growing understanding. And, through these processes, there was a growing bond between the two young adults.

Peter took some sort of curious comfort in hearing Katy describe how challenging it was for her to grow up in a family of all older people—all very conservative, conventionalist older people—people to whom the land and the farm were everything—the only thing. Peter understood all too poignantly the struggle in grappling with the need to do things that were completely antithetical to your parents' expectations—Katy's family fully believing she would, as she should, marry and become a good farmer's wife. Her parents knew their little girl would stay in the tightly knit community in Chickasaw County, adding a fifth generation to the family homestead. They were stunned when this very same little girl proved to be, in their view, strong headed—obstinately insisting on continuing her studies and traveling abroad (Katy underscoring the fact that she had, to try and lessen her parents' resistance, followed agriculturally-related curricula—but this made no impact on her folks).

Katy shared with Peter the near misery she endured knowing she was moving ahead, unsure of where—but without her parents' blessing—without her parents' backing. Peter empathized with her (thinking, but not saying, "At least, your father was not a lecherous old man").

Peter, indeed, did not reveal this family's—his father's—shame. However, he did share how he, too, was upset with his relationship with his parents. How they, too, wanted him to follow in their footsteps. How their lives, too, were tied in a net of strict conservatism and traditionalist theology—a net they so hoped to be able to throw over their son.

Peter, possibly in an effort to lighten a weighty topic, even referred to the passage in Matthew that he had referenced in his writing to Lydia.

He, Peter, was unsure if, through the church, his father had become a fisher of men—he suspected he had, as his church was full most Sundays. But unquestionably, his father wanted to be a fisher of one man—his son.

Nevertheless, during a quiet moment, after returning to the cottage, Peter assured Katy, as much as they would like to do as their parents wanted, they must lead their own lives. Today, these lives had led them to this bed in Slaterville. Saying so, he grabbed her around the waist—pulling her to him.

Some days later, pleasantly installed at a pub for an after-work brew, Katy opened the door with no preamble, "Is it working?"

"Is what working?" Peter replied incredulous.

"Your pilgrimage."

"Pilgrimage?"

"Of course." She smiled, "you're a pilgrim. You're a wanderer looking for a sacred place—not a sacred place to find your God—a place to find yourself."

"Hmmm."

"Am I wrong?"

"I guess not."

"So."

"So?"

"So, as you've told me ever-so-many times, you're now 4,000 miles from home. Is this far enough? Have you traveled enough? Do you now know yourself? Have you reached your destination?"

"No," Peter said, almost agonized, "I don't think so. I sure don't feel I'm at my destination. I really, honestly, don't feel much different than when I started. I have the same uncertainties. I have the same questions. I continue to wonder."

"And."

"And?"

"And", she continued, looking nearly annoyed, "what does this mean? What does this tell you?"

"I don't know."

"Well, guess. You know I, too, am nearly in your shoes. Go on, guess."

"I guess," he went on, practically painfully, "it means it's hard to find yourself by walking away. I have found many things. I have seen many things. I have understood many things better. But I am still what I am. I am still conflicted. I am still seeking, yet still unclear for what I am really seeking. Is that an answer?"

"Sort of. At a minimum, it is a warning to me. Vigilance may not be the answer—albeit I'm always keeping my eyes open. Changing the scene many not be the solution—albeit I'm anxious to see as many scenes as possible. So, I go on—undecided."

"We go on."

"OK, we go on—at least for now. Still, as you know better than I, our merged paths could just as easily separate as not."

"It's all about today."

They ordered more beer.

While neither Katy nor Peter could find the keys to the riddles that plagued their futures, they were far more successful at finding the insights they each hoped to assimilate from the other to enlighten the present.

Peter slowly but surely began telling Katy the details of his travels—the places and people, the sites, the sounds, the smells, the good, the bad. For himself, this was cathartic—helping him order and fix in his mind where he had truly been and what he had really seen. He hoped for Katy this was informative—improving and expanding her understanding of very complex landscapes and social tapestries.

For her part, Katy, greatly appreciative of Peter's perceptions into a geography that had heretofore only been something seen in *National Geographic*, helped Peter see more clearly the America she knew. She was able to contrast American and South African matters, ultimately bringing them both to the conclusion that people were pretty much people and things weren't all that different.

As usual, always wanting to dig a little deeper, over beers, Peter asked his roommate, "So we feel things are pretty much the same everywhere, yet all we hear on this side of the Atlantic is about America as 'the land of opportunity'—'American exceptionalism.' If there's a commonness, how are these extraordinary statements possible?"

After some thought, Katy replied, "Now that I've seen the little I've seen here, I can't be sure. If you'd asked me back home in Iowa, it'd have been simple, I'd have said, 'We're just the best.' Now I don't know. America may have the biggest of some things—many things. But who cares about the biggest hamburger or the biggest airplane? America is, however, a really big country. This means there are lots of everything. Still, when I hear you talk of Africa—Africa, too, is a really big place. Today, since you asked me, I'd have to say that people are exceptional and that America, like many other places, offers a lot of opportunity. Not definitive—but maybe good enough for today."

"Maybe?"

"Well, if you really want more," she interceded, "I will speak more expansively as a young college-educated woman of liberal persuasion—not the mouthpiece for the country where I was born and the country where you feel you still have your cultural roots. So, I may be, as all too often, a spectator in my own world. Thus, may I pass on to you the words of the, some feel, great President Reagan, who had long been a much more highly placed spokesperson than I.

"As I learned in high school, and wrote down in my notebook to memorize, Mr. Reagan, as far back as the 50s, had said, '*I, in my own mind, have always thought of America as a place in the divine scheme of things that was set aside as a promised land.*'

"Later, just before being elected, the Reagan President-to-be, as I recall from Civics' notes, was reported to have said (once more, from memory), '*I have quoted John Winthrop's words more than once on the campaign trail this year—for I believe that Americans in 1980 are every bit as committed to that vision of a shining "city on a hill" as were those long-ago settlers . . . .These visitors to that city on the Potomac do not come as white or black, red or yellow; they are not Jews or Christians; conservatives or liberals; or Democrats or Republicans. They are Americans awed by what has gone before, proud of what for them is still . . . a shining city on a hill.*'

"This is possibly a pertinent concept here in South Africa?"

"I guess, to go full-out, if there is, in principle, a special part of the American story, it is this declaration of the additive advantage of having a melting pot. As you have explained to me, across Africa, in many cases, tribal and ethnic bonds are much deeper than national ties. As you have described, in your home, Ghana, the Ashante, the Ewe, the Fante, and the Ga all have their own space—their own niche. They may think of themselves as, for example, Ashante first and Ghanaian second. In America we are supposed to think of ourselves as Americans first.

"As you've told me, your ancestors came from Bavaria—mine came from Sweden. We are, nonetheless, expected to say we are Americans—not Germano-Americans nor Scandinavian Americans—simply Americans.

"Now, especially today, and looking at our surroundings, this is probably more theory than fact. As America becomes more and more a cosmopolitan melting pot—not just melting a variety of European Christians together, but a whole montage of the globe's peoples—it is harder and harder for there to be universal acceptance—general assimilation—seamless incorporation.

"Some, today, would say we are no longer even trying.

"I don't know. But I do imagine that at some point I will go back, and I will try to try myself."

Peter was once again impressed by Katy's perspective and commitment. He wondered if his own spirit was even half as tenacious as hers.

CHAPTER EIGHT

Shadows on the Wall

Getting too close for comfort

ALTHOUGH KATY AND PETER took some pains, chiefly at work, to not be seen as, not to act as a couple; they were a couple. For the first time in both their lives they entered into a formal, if unofficial, spousal arrangement. They shared their lives.

Moving slowly, trepidatious at first, their two self-reliant and self-confidant individual lives began to become an interconnected twosome. They shared a home (a cottage really). They shared a space. They shared a life.

As always, there was a learning curve—a comfort curve. It wasn't just sharing a bed, it was sharing the bathroom (and all the pleasant and not-so-pleasant activities undertaken there-in), sharing chores, sharing dreams.

There were good days and bad days. There were happy and sad days. But, inevitably, most days the "I" had changed to "we"—the "my" to "our."

They were a team.

And they both enjoyed it.

The unspoken figment that floated above them was the question of now versus tomorrow: how long could this last? How long should this last? Katy was a volunteer—a non-paid person working under a hazy, open-ended agreement with a company that assured her official status in a country where she was an outsider. Peter, whose immigration standing was arranged by the same company, was also an outsider coming from a completely different direction. If they left, they would follow divergent points of the compass.

Was it all an illusion?

Each hoped not, though they seldom even opened the door on the subject.

While their relationship grew to new (they hoped) heights, their work felt like it was growing in the other direction. As all too frequently, the polish was now tarnished—the jobs were monotonous—more so for Peter than Katy.

Katy still had new ideas to explore in terms of establishing a "body-building and healthy" regional food market. She was putting together model menus, contacting retail outlets like the big supermarket chain, *Shoprite*. She was exploring options for school lunch programs as well as charity programs for the vulnerable. She was busy.

Peter was still as scrupulous as always—but the newness was gone. It had become drudgery—recent challenges became chores.

They discussed and decided the best short-term remedy was a vacation. After all, they were due some personal time. They approached Mr. Koopman with the proposal that they take ten days off—to try and push the decision in their direction, they agreed for this to be ten days without pay. With a minimum of decorum, Mr. Koopman agreed.

As it turned out, they first needed two months to make all the arrangements. After looking over the options, they concluded the best thing was for them to fly to Malawi and spend their down time doing what tourists do. They booked a week at the Monkey Bay Beach Resort on the shores of Lake Malawi (also called, they learned, Lake Nyasa or Lake Niassa, depending upon from which shore you viewed the lake).

Katy and Peter took it as a good sign that they had to wait two months to get the delightful (as advertised) beach-side bungalow of their dreams (as advertised). This meant (they hoped) the resort was a popular attraction worthy of their visit—worthy of the wait.

Nevertheless, this also meant they had to find some rather exceptional ways to keep themselves occupied to fill in the gap—over and beyond the job and ardent amorous activities that were now (sadly) at times all too familiar.

The wanted to go to Cape Town or Windhoek, but these weekend destinations would require airfare that would cut into their skimpy vacation budget, as this was play with no pay. They decided, accordingly, the next best choice to add something new was to see if they could visit the capitals of comparatively nearby countries. Mbabane (Swaziland), Gaborone (Botswana), and Maseru (Lesotho) were all a little over 200 miles away—easily within the range of the Kawasaki. As it was summer, the longer days would allow them to reach these centers in a little over four hours—less if they pushed it at the risk of meeting an unfriendly SAP officer. This also meant taking un-scenic toll roads and driving after dark. Still, in spite of the possible downsides, it was a way to see heretofore unseen sites and, most importantly, allow Katy to see some of the African world outside South Africa.

They were excited. They even added Maputo (Mozambique) to the list, although this city was over 300 miles away—really taxing their ability to enjoy it on a weekend. This gave them four destinations. If they were on the road every other weekend, they would be quite busy until they left for Malawi.

Things went pretty much as planned. The major thoroughfares connecting the capitals were fast-moving and, even when going to Maputo, they were able to keep their night driving to a minimum—this critical since the roads were shared with all variety of contraption, these materializing out of nothingness in the dark nights. They were also able to avoid any of SAPs finest, although Peter always exceeded the posted speeds and was fretful that a traffic cop would pull him over at any moment.

Gaborone, Mbabane, and Maseru were rather sleepy cities after the never-ending rush of Jo'burg (not to be confused with the tumult of Lagos, Peter reminded himself). While many would consider these capitals as "more African," the South African influence was obvious. Commercial and industrial sectors were highly dominated by their muscular big brother, RSA (South Africa referred to as Mzantsi in Zulu and Xhosa languages—a local slogan «*Mzansi fo sho!*"—South Africa for sure)— citizens of nearby countries like Botswana, Swaziland, and Lesotho often (maybe too often) relied heavily on their weighty neighbor's goods and services (as Messrs Koopman and de Woordvoerder, along with many of South Africa's finest businessmen, hoped).

The economic circumstances apart, there were marked differences. Peter explained to Katy that he saw it as an ink blotter. South Africa was a big, thick blob of ink that had been blotted. The ink had slowly diffused from this epicenter—the closer to the blob the thicker the blotch (possibly the stain, Peter added). For emphasis, he inserted that his folk's home in Kpando was so far from the blob's core that there was only the faintest tint of ink reaching the shores of Lake Volta—but a tinge, nonetheless.

The countries they were visiting—the capitals more correctly—were very, very close to the blob—they were darkly colored by the ink.

When they were enjoying a beer at the bar at Masa Square in downtown (such as it was) Gaborone (their second weekender after Mbabane), Katy observed, "There seem to be a lot of women here, and by the look of it, not your everyday hookers?"

"Well," Peter chimed-in (somewhat amazed Katy would put things in terms of "everyday hookers," but saying nothing this regard), "according to Philip at the farm, who's originally from here, financially the Batswana—the people here—are comparatively pretty well off. Most have some disposable income—even at the lower end of the scale. One, possibly unanticipated, effect of more money is more heavy drinking. Apparently, lots of guys drink a lot. Then, if they're knackered, their wives get together and go out on the town. So, if Philip's telling is spot-on, lots of these women are just out for a good time while their husbands sober up (or not). It remains to be seen if they're looking for some masculine companionship for this good time—but Philip didn't go there."

"Well, good for the girls," Katy concluded.

"Yep. And good on Botswana for being able to care better for her people, even if there is abuse—there's always abuse."

"But, you know, Peter, when we've gone out on your bike back in South Africa, like when we went west to Lichtenburg or East to Carolina, things outside the city looked very much like things here. I really couldn't tell the difference."

"Well, Botswana has big ticket industries like diamonds and beef. These attract South African interests. For all intents and purposes, you are probably right, here isn't too different from rural South Africa right next door. But what would you expect?

"Remember two weeks ago in Mbabane, not too different there either. Swaziland, though a kingdom with a very prominent and deep-rooted African culture, has always been surrounded on three sides by South Africa. Another story is that reportedly, when during apartheid, miscegenation was seriously enforced, white South African men (Peter imagined it was only men) used to frequent bordellos set up in Swaziland for their solace.

"Yet, whether in the hills of the Swazi governed by King Mswati III or on the boarders of the Kalahari overseen by the Kgosi, the chief of the Tswana, regardless of the growing footprints of what we might see as 'modernization,' or, perhaps better described as South Africa's finger-prints, many of the people still live much as they have for generations—experiencing (whether by choice or not, Peter thought, as he recalled his time spent with people living along the 2E pipeline) modest incremental changes through time—changes some claim as 'development', others call-ing 'disruption.'"

"Back home," Katy lamented, "most folks think it's all about lions and elephants. They fully expect me to see Tarzan. Or, for the old folks, they may think I'll actually run across Tracy and Hepburn—still alive in the Dark Continent, albeit dead and buried in the US—and the *African Queen*."

"Tales."

"Indeed. Tales. Be on the lookout for *Cheeta* the Chimp."

"So." Peter inhaled, knowing he was getting up on his soap box and probably taking the conversation into a trench where Katy would not typically go, "tales abound. I've mentioned Silas. He was a real thinker—he had a wonderful collection of books. Silas was most satisfied to turn my own thoughts away from Africa and back to my professed homeland of America—your native land—our native land, I guess.

"Silas took almost wry pleasure in highlighting to me, knowing I had never really lived in the US, the actions white men had taken against Native Americans. He marveled, however, that some observers, centuries earlier, had had a deeper understanding—standing out from the crowd. He loved to read the quote from Benjamin Franklin's *Remarks concerning the Savages of North America*, where he wrote, '*Savages we call them, because their Manners differ from ours, which we think the Perfection of Civility. They think the same of theirs.*' Yet, to most of the invading Euro-peans, indigenous peoples were quite simply sub-human savages.

"Silas would then jump across the ocean to talk about white men on this side of the Atlantic. He noted about the same time Franklin had writ-ten his words, reportedly in France there were a number of Europeans, now called philosophers, who were writing about 'savages.' This topic was frequently referred to as 'the noble savage' or, for the French, *'le bon sauvage.'* These so-called 'thinkers,' as Silas told it, included, among others, Jean Jacques Rousseau who wrote *Discourse on the Origins of Inequality Among Men.* To these self-professed intellectuals, native peoples—savages—were often categorized as kind beings in tune with nature—simple folk. Indeed, it was this simplicity that outside aggressive intruders saw as a passivity and gentle ignorance that allowed these foreigners to colonize and extort those they considered as 'noble savages.'

"Ironically, Silas, referring again to Franklin's writing, was surprised that an old white colonialist in the Americas would pen, *'Perhaps if we could examine the manners of different Nations with Impartiality, we should find no People so rude as to be without Rules of Politeness; nor any so polite as not to have some remains of Rudeness.'*

"Silas was very certain that what Europeans saw as passivity among the 'noble savages' was an inherent politeness to strangers. And, equally, what was seen as the seed of independence was the 'rudeness' to which Franklin referred. Silas liked to say, 'abuse politeness at your own risk.'

"All this, I suppose, is a very long-winded way to say we need to be careful how we interpret what we see. We are visitors. We are, in some ways, interlopers. These are complex times, complex places, and complex people.

"I do not pretend to understand well. If my travels since leaving my family have shown anything, it is to show how little I really know."

"A lot there," Katy smiled, "a lot more than finding *Cheeta.*"

Peter chuckled, amazed at how clearly, and how much of Silas's allocutions he was able to remember (he felt a physical twinge as he thought of his host from Naija, wondering if he should have stayed, thinking of Dabi), "As my ol' prof used to say, 'Life ain't easy.'"

They ordered more South African beer in Botswana.

Their tour of close-by seats-of-government wrapped-up in Maputo. Here the contrasts with the South African colossus were more stark. While there was a growing influence and presence of the "big boy of the South," Mozambique was unquestionably what Peter saw as, with a dose of vexation at himself for his over-generalization (a trait he truly detested—having seen it expressed far too often in his parents' views), "more African."

Like her Atlantic Coast lusophone sister (Peter not necessarily cherishing happy thoughts about the older sibling, Angola), Mozambique had had the great misfortune of having to endure a horrible civil war. This had led to so much death and destruction. Now, however, the capital and the country were being rebuilt (South Africa, of course, a major player).

Saturday afternoon, as they took a taxi to a well-reputed Portuguese restaurant, having left the bike at the guest house where they were staying, the driver surprised Katy and Peter by speaking good English.

"Still a pretty city, isn't it?"

"You speak English?", Katy and Peter said almost in unison.

"Of course." The driver smiled, "I'm from next door in Swaziland. Most of my brothers went to work in the South African mines. I'd rather make some money sitting on my butt in a cab than scurrying about holes in the ground."

"Makes sense."

"I came here during the war," the chatty chauffeur continued, "terrible time. Look there. See those birds in that tree? During the war, no birds. People ate them all. But they've come back. We all hope this is a good sign."

Katy and Peter were touched.

They found the capital to be vibrant (Peter, again making comparisons, finding it diametrically opposed to Luanda, as he described in great detail to Katy). It was the largest of their recent landing-places—immersed in a very different history.

They discovered quite a distinctive city from their earlier destinations, enjoying the people and the still remaining totems of the Portuguese period very much—just as much as they enjoyed the spicy food like Peri Peri Grilled Chicken and the Portuguese baked goods—especially sweat pastries such as *Travesseiro de Sintra* and *Pastel de Belèm*.

They also enjoyed the history, which was still visible via *Fortaleza de Maputo*, the red stone eighteenth century fortress near the waterfront of Delagoa Bay, at the estuary of the Great Usutu River. This fort, cannon included, was indicative of the seesaw of Africa's relationships with Europeans. Early in the eighteenth century, the first structure at this site was a rather primitive enclosure built by two boatloads of Dutch expeditionists from Cape Town. These folks were then displaced and replaced by several boatloads of British pirates who were in turn replaced by Austrians before the Portuguese took control toward the end of the century.

It had been an admirable destination (and excellent diversion from the growing sameness of Jo'burg) well worth the long ride. For Peter and Katy, and hopefully for the Mozambicans they had encountered, it had been a good time.

Back in their Slaterville cottage, it was now time to pack a bigger bag and get on the flight to Blantyre for the little over two-hour trip from Jo'burg's O. R. Tambo Airport. They had, at a painful additional cost, arranged their itinerary to start in Blantyre, the commercial capital of Malawi, and leave from Lilongwe, the political capital, so as to be able to see as much of the country as possible—covering the distance between the two capitals in a rented car already reserved at Chileka International Airport in the country's business hub.

The nearly four-hour drive from Blantyre to Monkey Bay was generally uneventful, but memorable from the point of view of the number of people they encountered using all means of transport. Sheer numbers were impressive—the Southern Region of Malawi having nearly four-and-a-half times the population density of South Africa. There were a lot of folks ogling Katy and Peter who, in turn, ogled them back. There seemed to be little farms and little houses everywhere. Peter, as he told Katy, thought it resembled looking down at all the olives on a fully loaded pizza from *Trabella Pizzeria Illovo*—one of their favorite haunts about a half-an-hour from O.R. Tambo.

Once installed in their lakeshore bungalow, all their expectations were met. They had an unhampered view across the great lake—the fourth largest freshwater lake in the world. They would watch the wind whip waves—in moments the lake's surface changing from sublimely smooth to challengingly chaotic.

Lake Malawi, in addition to being impressive simply as a big, deep lake, was all the more impressive when one looked below the surface—choppy or calm—to the water's fishes. In terms of diversity, some compared the lake's aquatic environment with the terrestrial environment of the Amazon rainforest. There were more than seven hundred fish species—many unique (most textbook examples of evolutionary radiation, as Peter was to learn). The distinctiveness of the lake's piscine residents made spying on them—skin- or scuba diving—a popular pastime for tourists. However, the presence of bilharzia in the lake made the waters' margins risky—underwater explorers needing to boat out some distance from shore before entering the tepid waters to avoid the slow-swimming parasites that occupied the littoral zones and were responsible for the disease.

Bilharzia or no bilharzia, Peter was enthralled by the colorful fishes. Katy, not much of an underwater person (she said it was too much corn in her blood that made her bob up), accompanied him in the resort's skiff. For hours they would float offshore, —Katy mesmerized by the animated lakeside as the boat seemed to pulse with the lake's own energy while Peter snorkeled, marveling at the fantastic array of creatures with which they shared the waters.

On the third day, Katy almost pouted that Peter spent more time in the lake than he did in their bed. Upon hearing this, he immediately picked her up and carried her into the bungalow's comfortable bedroom—the two surfacing the next morning.

Their evenings were spent in the complex's main pavilion, starting in the dining room where they had quite good meals, often including the lake's prime relish, *chambo*, following the plates of these delicate fish with an aperitif on the veranda, overlooking the sleeping basin.

Over their evening drinks, they would discuss the country. Peter gave Katy a thumbnail sketch of the post-Independence Anglophilic "Life President" Banda and the almost puritanical standards he embraced, including blackballing such popular things as miniskirts on women and long hair on men. Nevertheless, through apartheid, Malawi had been one of the few African countries to keep its strong ties to South Africa—benefiting, in return, from considerable South African assistance, including the designing of their capital city, Lilongwe.

Peter off-handedly pretended his wealth of local lore was purely an innate gift—a special nearly osmotic clairvoyance. He hoped Katy fully appreciated his unique abilities.

Grievously for Peter, Katy knew all too well the truth. For the two months of their prep time, Peter had been pumping every Malawian he encountered in Jo'burg for details of their country and customs. She finally had to openly reveal him as a charlatan—yet, a charlatan of whom she was very fond.

They both enjoyed the easy banter. Still and all, in the back of Peter's mind, when he heard "charlatan," he could not help but think of his father.

Rather tardily each morning, Katy and Peter would trek back to the pavilion for breakfast—a full English breakfast. Over the eggs, sausages, kippers, fried tomatoes, kidneys, and other tasty parts of the impressive breakfast buffet, Katy took a great fondness to the coffee mugs—each embellished with an image of one of the lake's many prismatic fishes.

As they were preparing to leave, to climb to the plateau about 1,800 feet above the lakeshore where the political capital was to be found, Katy asked at the reception if she could buy a pair of the wonderful coffee mugs. With thespian regrets, the receptionist unhappily informed her departing guest that they did not sell their tableware. However, the mugs were made by potters in Dedza—certainly the couple could pass there and buy mugs to their hearts' content.

To accommodate Katy's search for wonderful coffee mugs, they had to change their anticipated route. Initially they were going to follow the M5 along the lake to Salima before climbing the plateau to Lilongwe. Now they would have to take the M10 to join the principal thoroughfare, the M1, to find Dedza snuggled-up very close to the Mozambican border. But no effort should be considered too much if the end result was to have Lake-Malawi-fish-adorned coffee mugs in their cottage in Slaterville.

It took them about two hours to reach Dedza, the town of 15,000 people sitting at over 5,000 feet in elevation and just on the shoulder of the M1 Highway—spitting distance from the Mozambican frontier. The pottery shop itself was about two miles out of town, on the secondary road called the T372—to Katy and Peter, more of a trail than a road.

As they pulled up to the potter's, they were surprised to be greeted by a white man—an American. It turned out Robert, as he introduced himself, originally from Duluth, had been a Peace Corps Volunteer, met and married Olivia, a daughter of Dedza—the two following their dream and setting up a combination potter's shed and tea house.

Happy to have some country folk on the premises, after introducing the visitors to Olivia, the four sat on the pleasant patio enjoying cups of local Chombe tea served in pots, saucers, and cups from the pottery. While they sipped and chatted, Olivia had her staff wrap a pair of carefully-selected, fish-bedecked mugs—a gift to what they all hoped would be new friendships.

After several cups accompanied by savory scones, Katy reminded the group that she and Peter had to get back on the road if they were going to make it to their hotel in Lilongwe.

Robert, acknowledging it was probably time, recalled to his visitors that Malawi was a small country. If they went back to the M1, they would probably be at their destination sooner than they thought. Thus, he proposed they continue on the T372 which would finally rejoin the M1 but allow them to see much more of the hinterland.

This seemed like a good option. After goodbye embraces, Katy and Peter got back in their rental Mazda sedan—Peter silently hoping the car was up to the road ahead, if the small sample of the T372 they had already experienced was any reflection, the road ahead would be anything but quick.

Peter had no idea of how prophetic his thoughts were.

Only ten minutes after leaving the pottery, they had a flat tire.

This was promptly changed, and they carried on—a little more slowly, now with no spare.

Then, only a few miles down the road, Peter had to pull off beyond the shoulder to let some cows pass. As he moved back onto the lane, the car thumped and swayed as it went—not a good sign.

Upon quick evaluation, it appeared that, by misfortune, there had been some broken beer bottles off the road where they pulled onto the shoulder—these puncturing the two left side tires.

They were sunk.

Katy just kept saying, "Bad luck, bad luck, bad luck . . ."

Peter was trying to decide if it was the fault of old, worn tires or jagged beer bottle parts. Between analyses, he could only think, "Oh shit!"

After their reactions stabilized, they realized that they had to do something and that that something involved seeking someone to help.

There were several homes on nearby hills, so they selected one and, grabbing their small catch-all before locking the car, headed off, crossing the fields in the direction of the house—whose house, they had not a clue.

It wasn't, in retrospect, perhaps all bad luck.

Their target house was indeed occupied (many in rural areas weren't at midday since families were working their farms) and the owner opened the door at their knocking (many wouldn't).

They pointed to their car on the other side of the fields, indicating they had had a breakdown, asking if he could help. Almost as an afterthought (Peter thinking of his conversation with Brother Mike), they introduced themselves and baptized themselves as visitors.

The homeowner, a white-haired man of indeterminate but advanced age, presented himself as Chimango (Peter unsure if this was a surname or a given name), politely asked them to come in, showing them to well-used foam-cushioned chairs around a small coffee table. He then disappeared momentarily, returning with glasses of fresh water—feeling they, or their nerves, must be thirsty.

After they were seated and had sipped their water, forcing themselves not to think of its origins, hoping it was as safe as it looked, Katy picked up the conversation, "We thank you very much for your hospitality and kindness. It is wonderful that we've found you and fantastic that you speak English."

"My pleasure." Chimango smiled. "As to your first point, we are simple farmers—politeness is in our nature (Peter thinking back to Franklin's words). As to your second point, while a farmer at heart, I am a retired schoolteacher—I used to teach at Saint Bernadette's in Chipasi—only about a mile from here. By the way, this place is called Chentcherere. It's an area of honest maize farmers—a backwater for both the government and visitors like yourselves—so, you're most welcome."

"As Katy said, we're so thankful," Peter inserted, not wanting to be rude through silence, "we're really quite unsure what to do?"

"My suggestion," Chimango smiled even more broadly, "is to relax."

"Relax?", his visitors responded as one.

"Of course. You really can't do anything now-now. Therefore, you might as well relax. My home is your home. Here in these hills, we know all too well that the unexpected is a frequent caller—we're never really prepared—we truly need to count on our neighbors and our family. As strangers, it is correct—it is customary—that I, as the person you have sought-out, take the place of friends and family who are not here to help you when the unexpected has called."

"We are ever so grateful." Peter felt the ball had somehow been passed to him, "but we're at a loss."

"Of course," Chimango continued, almost as if Peter had said nothing, "just relax. I imagine you were trying to get to Lilongwe today?"

His guests nodded.

"Well," their host went on, with less of a smile, "I don't think you'll make it there today. But not to worry. I've lived here for forty-five years; my wife and two children are buried nearby. My other two children have left this backcountry for the cities—one in Mzuzu and the other in Blantyre. You see, I've plenty of room. The Good Lord has guided you to a good spot. You can relax and we'll see about your problem."

"We really need to be in Lilongwe tonight." Peter hurriedly almost gasped.

"I am sure you do." Chimango smiled again, "but I doubt you will."

"We've bookings . . ." Katy added for emphasis.

"Undoubtedly. But they'll understand. Things happen."

"I doubt it—we've a deposit and all," Katy continued.

"Certainly. But now you're here."

"OK." Katy seemed to gradually accept the inevitability that had been clear to Chimango from the onset. "What's next?"

"I have a nephew on the next farm." Chimango nearly beamed. "You'll have to wait a few minutes while I go over to get him. He's a strong and clever lad. Also, he's got a bicycle. And he even speaks a little English. The nearest phone is in Chimpando, not too far, about six or seven miles away. My nephew, his name's Blessings—so we know we can't go wrong with him (Chimango chuckled)—will ride over to the Chimpando and call your hotel. Hopefully they'll then be able to send out someone to help. Or maybe someone will come by who can carry you to the city. But we don't get much traffic here."

"Splendid," Peter intoned, hopefully with sincerity, "we've a plan."

"We do indeed," Chimango acknowledged as he headed to the door, "make yourselves comfortable—I'll be right back."

Katy and Peter were truly surprised how quickly Chimango was back, refilling their water glasses—telling them that good custom was to never let a visitor's cup run dry. His guests had no idea how far he had traveled to get to Blessings' house, but they'd seen the lay of the land, and it wasn't right next door. They looked at each other with admiration, each thinking, "This old guy's got it together."

Hardly had their glasses been filled to the brim when there was a knock at the door and a young boy of about fifteen or sixteen came in. Chimango introduced him as Blessings. Their keeper's nephew was as polite as his uncle as well as being reserved and respectful around elders and strangers as befitted his position in the grander scheme of things. He had a lithe body covered solely by a soiled pair of shorts and an equally dun-colored T-shirt whose original hue was indiscernible. He wore no hat, and his feet were barely covered by a pair of refurbished flip-flops.

After the formalities, Blessings and his uncle spoke seriously for a few minutes, Chimango excusing the fact they were speaking Chi Chewa, the most prominent local vernacular, as he wanted to make sure they understood each other perfectly and his nephew's Chi Chewa was understandably better than his English. Then uncle and nephew joined Katy and Peter sitting around the coffee table.

Chimango asked Katy to give his nephew all the details; name and phone number of the hotel, name and date for the bookings, as well as the particulars about the car if it were a rental (Peter was again impressed, Chimango was on top of it). The uncle then confirmed from the nephew in Chi Chewa that all was well understood. He then shooed him away to rush to a phone in Chimpando.

After Blessings' departure, Peter asked if they shouldn't have given the boy some money to help if he needed anything. Chimango only replied, "All is fine. You're our visitors."

Once more Katy and Peter were surprised. In less than two hours Blessings was back. During that time, Katy had chatted with their guardian about his family, about teaching, and about the maize harvest. Peter watched the road—sure that a car headed for Lilongwe would come along in the next three minutes. No car came.

To assure optimum communication, Blessings briefed his uncle in Chi Chewa and Chimango then informed Katy and Peter: Blessings had been able to talk to the receptionist at the hotel where they had made their bookings, they understood the circumstances and would hold the room for forty-eight hours assuming the problems would be resolved by then. By good luck, moreover, the office for the car rental agency they had used was located on the hotel's premises. The receptionist had been able to transfer the call to these people and they had told Blessings that if renters had problems they would come to their aid. Blessings had given them clear directions and they said they would have someone there before noon tomorrow.

It was done.

There was nothing more to do than hope—to have faith that things would work out as Blessings had indicated.

Peter moved to give Blessings a gratuity—a small stipend, but Chimango stopped him mid-stride, repeating that it was customary to help strangers in need—that was that.

Blessings went home.

Chimango informed Katy and Peter that he would prepare a bed in the room that used to be for his eldest son—immediately assuming the two shared at least a bed if not a name. He added that once the sleeping arrangements were completed, he would get an evening meal together—finishing with, "I hope you're hungry."

Katy and Peter wondered what dinner at Chimango's would be like.

If Katy and Peter had lived in Malawi, they would have known the answer to their question: *nsima*. *Nsima*, a stiff corn porridge, or its local variant, was the staple food of much of Southern and Eastern Africa. *Nsima* was served as a firm, almost doughy, ball with sauces, called relishes, on the side—the maize and its accompaniments eaten together like mashed potatoes and gravy.

Once this realization hit Peter, he recognized that this type of meal was very common indeed. There were many variations on a starchy ball and a sauce. There was *fufu* in Nigeria made with cassava. There were *banku* and *kenkey* in Ghana made with fermented corn. There was *foutou* in CAR made from pounded plantains. Other groups used pounded yams, some even targeting mashed kidney beans. This was the Malawian version of a very prevalent plate.

As the sun set, Katy, Peter, and Chimango sat around a modest dining table, kitty-corner from the coffee table, the dining table's center occupied by three enamelware bowls—a matching enamelware plate in front of each of them. The largest bowl contained balls of *nsima*. The other two, as Chimango explained, were the relishes—one beans and cabbage and the other prepared with dried Lake Malawi sardines called *usipa*. The fourth seat at the table was occupied by a flat wick kerosine, Chimango called it "paraffin," lamp that almost provided enough light for them to see what they were eating.

After blessing their repast, Chimango served his guests a ball of *nsima* and the prerequisite two relishes, noting there was a fourth ball remaining that was for the ancestors but that could, he thought according to custom, be for visitors if they were still hungry. As the lamp fluttered, projecting dancing shadows on the mud block walls, the old teacher addressed his visitors, "I am most happy to have you at my table."

Licking fingers laden with relish, Katy and Peter could only grunt their gratitude.

"I am sorry you have had misfortune," the pedagogue continued, "but it has been a long time since I have had newcomers under my roof, and I am most indebted to you for accepting my humble hospitality."

This was met by more gratified grunts.

"This afternoon, while Blessings was away, I had a lovely chat with the endearing Miss Katy. This brought back memories of my time as an educator. My grandmother, who lived to be over one hundred, always said, 'A day you don't learn something is a wasted day.'"

More gleeful grunts.

"Thinking back over my enjoyable chat with Miss Katy, I realize, or I hope I realize, that she, probably you both, are interested in learning—understanding."

Still more grunts as the *nsima* balls vanished from Katy and Peter's plates.

"With your kind permission, with your kind tolerance of an old man, I would like to tell you a sort of story—would that be alright?"

Nods accompanied the grunts.

Chimango settled back in his chair, his own food nearly untouched, leaned on his elbows, and once again felt like a teacher at the head of the classroom. He told a serpentine and multiform narrative:

> *My new friends, I hope I can call you my friends, as this is how I see you. I hope you are enjoying my unpretentious meal—this is how we eat. Amazingly, maize is the core of our diet. Yet, maize is not an African crop. Three or four hundred years ago maize came here from South America—it's imported. The plates and bowls, the lamp, even the big spoon for serving—these all come from China. Imports. The cooking oil for the relish came from gallon containers given by your country to the Mozambican refugees just across the border—it's written in big letters "Not for Resale"—but of course, some of the refugees sell their ration and buy beer or cigarettes.*
>
> *We are a small country. We are proud. But we are so dependent on the outside—an outside we often pretend does not exist.*
>
> *Here we are the Chewa People. Our ancestors came from far away, from the Congo. We share this land with the Ngoni, people who came from the South—from the Zulu.*
>
> *We follow the "bele lineage"—we are matrilinear. Women are, in many ways, our elite. Our social system is based on our mothers. Inheritance follows the woman's line—although the beneficiary is typically a man. It's confusing, I know. But, for example, I am able to live here and hold on to my farm even though a widower—although the lands belonged to my wife. In some villages, I would have been driven out when my wife died, but here, I can stay. Yet, when I die, it is not my son who will inherit—it is my wife's nephew—yes, it is Blessings.*
>
> *This is one of the reasons my boy is in Blantyre and not here. Why work so hard for dry and infertile fields when they will ultimately go to someone else? Better to work at a petrol station. It's complicated.*
>
> *And it is not only our ancient customs with which we have to deal. There are new and horrible things. High on the list is*

HIV-AIDS. Look around. What do you see? You see lots and lots of young kids—really young kids. Lots of AIDS orphans. We are approaching one million affected people—this in a country of about ten million. We're losing roughly twenty-five thousand people a year. As the older ones die due to lasciviousness, the fields go untilled. But people still die—the malnourished more quickly. Yet, like my long-time, now dead neighbor used to say, if you'll excuse my lewdness, "What can you do in these hills at night except screw?"

People die. The population becomes younger and younger while our schools become poorer and poorer. Who wants to be a teacher today? No one.

It is, with this background, that I sit in front of you. You, visitors, are trying to understand a new place—a new attraction—before you go home. I, an old man, am trying to understand a new place—but this place is the place I call home.

We consider ourselves as lucky that we have not suffered the civil war that has pushed our brothers and sisters from Mozambique right up to our door. And we are lucky.

After thirty years on seat—nearly on a throne—our Life President has departed the presidency. We have managed to change leaders without tearing ourselves apart. This is good.

But we have so many problems—problems that seem to never end. Too little land. Sometimes too little water. Too little food. Too much disease. Sometimes too much water.

No money. All too often, no hope.

It isn't easy.

When I was a boy, if someone in the hills had a bicycle and a transistor radio, they were rich. We had a hoe and a panga—a machete for you outsiders. That was about it. We had one good set of clothes for church—if fortunate, we had one pair of shoes. We had so little. Still, we had so much. We had enough to eat. We had good harvests that filled our granaries. We had each other. We were happy.

Today no one is happy. Someone who has a bicycle wants a motorcycle. When they get the motorcycle, they want a car. They want a television. They want jeans and sneakers like people wear in your part of the world. And, mostly, they want money.

Money! And, do you know, back in the 60s one of our Malawi Kwacha was worth more than one US dollar! Today it takes nearly sixteen Kwacha to reach a dollar. Imagine. And look at what we import. How do we pay for all these foreign goods? With dollars!

It's a mess.

True, we've become independent from our overseas masters. But what independence? We are certainly not self-sufficient. We rely on many. And many abuse this reliance. It's a mess.

If you were my students, back in the day, I'd tell you, "Study hard, because there's tough times coming."

This is probably not the story you came to find on your touristic interlude from South Africa. This is not all roses and accolades—yes, we do have roses here in Malawi, thanks to our colonial history. This is not the story most tell most white people as they saunter across our African lands. But this is the story an old teacher feels needs telling.

And it is not a story of black and white. Of course, we've been abused by the yoke of colonialism—but no more than by the yoke of economic dependency. We still have powerful outsiders abusing our people—just look at the labor conditions on many of the tea estates in the South. But we also have powerful insiders who are taking advantage—abusing just as much from their own nationalistic seats.

No, it's not about skin color. There are all types with different insides and outsides. Just look at Asia's grab on what little we have.

I tell this not with anger nor with melancholy. It is what it is. Like I've said, "The unexpected is a frequent caller." All of us living on the land know that we cannot count on tomorrow. In fact, we can barely count on today.

We have faith. We pray to the Good Lord. We ask Him to look over us—we believe—we hope he does. We offer our prayers. We ask for help. Some ask for even more. We have faith. We pray. We wait.

But as we in these hills wait, the world moves oh so quickly about us. It changes. It changes our lives. It changes the way our children think. It changes the way our leaders lead. It changes everything. And we are still in the hills. We still have faith.

Therefore, when you go home, remember the people in the hills of Malawi who are here with faith—for better or worse.

Katy and Peter were entranced—their state as much affected by the ambiance as their host's words. The room was now awash with the scent of kerosene—this bathing the shadows that flickered across the earthen wall and the sounds that reflected off the corrugated metal roof as the countryside fell asleep—today much as every day, yet different from any other day. Peter thought of the noble savage. Life is never simple.

Carrying a smaller kerosene lantern which he left with them, Chimango accompanied Katy and Peter to their bedroom. Removing only their shoes and jeans, the two jumped into a bed they found both clean and comfortable. As soon as her head hit the pillow, a very tired Katy fell soundly asleep.

Peter, however, was wrapped in thoughts of his parents and Chimango. He and Katy had possibly just experienced more of authentic local culture and thought than his parents had in a lifetime.

He felt reasonably sure his parents had never spent a night in an African's home—eaten their food, shared their hopes and concerns, and slept in their bed.

Then Peter realized he probably had to backtrack. This was likely not totally true. His father had slept in Chantal's house—in Chantal's bed. He had probably eaten Chantal's food and even taken a dump in her toilet (this image reminding Peter that he had to fix in his mind the way to get to Chimango's latrine behind the house in case the unaccustomed diet produced any unwelcome outcomes overnight).

Peter dragged his mind back to his parents.

No—his father's deception was completely different. Paul Volman had made his way to Chantal's bed by unknown means. But he had done so with one aim: prurience. Peter's father had fled his wife's bed for that of Chantal for licentiousness—for licentiousness and perhaps fantasy. For, Peter had no doubt, his father certainly must have lusted after all the beauties of the village who, for so many years, he considered as forbidden fruit. Prohibited objects of his lust if, for no other reason than he himself had pitched a tent of hypocrisy as the *white father* who was the guide who safeguarded his flock on their voyage to redemption—not the trespasser who sought carnal satisfaction. Paul's canon had been (publicly) clear: the women were untouchable.

From the pulpit Father Paul excoriated his congregation about the immoral behavior of some. He hammered on the dangers to the Divine Soul of depraved and course acts. He declaimed to the wanton that God's Grace would save them from their moral turpitude if they could only follow His Word.

And the more Paul's words pummeled his parish, the more Paul (so Peter envisioned) dove into Chantal.

It was staggering.

But, as Chimango had said just that evening, it was what it was.

As sleep swept from his limbs into his gray matter, he left consciousness wondering what his parents would think if they could see him at that very moment in time.

The next day, as promised, a car with three people appeared on the road below Chimango's house by ten o'clock. They unloaded two spare tires from the trunk (they called it a "boot")—confirming that Blessings, true to his recounting, had relayed all the pertinent details including the nature of their problems and the requirements for finding a solution. The driver would then carry Katy and Peter to Lilongwe while his two compatriots followed after changing the flat tires (that they called "punctures").

Katy and Peter gave Chimango a big hug, happy to see that Blessings had come to say goodbye and forfeiting a hug for a manly handshake with the boy who was nearly a man. They had no real way to thank their guardian since he refused categorically any financial compensation—calling it *baksheesh*.

They highlighted how much they had appreciated all he had taught them; how he had cared for them. He responded by saying, "Just the polite and correct thing to do."

Hence, they wrapped everything up, affirming they were, "Honored to be his students," crossing the field and getting into the waiting car for Lilongwe.

After an enjoyable few days in Lilongwe, a city kind of halfway between Gaborone and Maputo in terms of activity (or lack thereof), Peter was almost contented to be sitting on a flight back to Jo'berg and back to Koopman Farms. They had carefully swaddled their new coffee mugs (Katy sending a postcard to Olivia to thank her and say she hoped they might see each other again somehow, somewhere), adding a few pounds of Mzuzu coffee in their bag to enjoy with their new mugs, and were southbound with a minimum of fuss.

Katy snoozed in tune to the hum of the 737 while Peter thought of Chimango—contrasting his views with those of Brother Mike. The men were roughly the same age—educated and deep thinkers. Each offered a different piece, however, to the puzzle Peter was trying so hard to solve.

Brother Mike was unsure, and worried about being unsure. He knew life offered many options and he continuously tried to assess his own status vis-à-vis where he might have been in other circumstances. Peter saw this, in general, as a fool's errand. After all, looking back at "could-a-beens" truly could not change the present. Brother Mike sought validation that he was on the right course. Yet, possibly that judgement was best made by others. And, more critically, he had no real assurance that he could even have been on a different course if he wanted. Self-analysis could only do so much. Brother Mike would undoubtedly, Peter thought, die as he found himself today: a Flemish monk in Africa.

Chimango seemed to accept much more readily his condition. He unquestionably had regrets, but he did not dwell on these—he did not even mention them. He appeared to be content with what he had been and what he had become. His preoccupation, his worry, was more about his society than his personal status. He felt people had to fight to keep ahead of the flow of time and, in his view, this seemed to be a losing battle for that part of humanity with which he was affiliated.

Peter looked out the window, through the cobalt column of air covering the veld below. He wondered how to intertwine Brother Mike and Chimango? He was just envisioning a quilt, with his father's image at the center—a mosaic composed of the major reflections of each—when Katy woke, squeezed his arm, asking, "Whatchya think'n 'bout?"

"How I'm going to ravish you when we get back to the cottage."

She smiled.

The plane's landing gear began to rumble.

CHAPTER NINE

The (not so) Good Samaritan

Almost a rerun—almost

THEY WERE BOTH SURPRISED at how quickly, almost naturally, their old routine once again controlled their lives. Their trips became stories—as though they had read them in *Readers Digest*. Their lives again revolved around Koopman Farms and their cottage in Slaterville. There were periodic nights out—*Trabella Pizzeria Illovo* or other favored haunts. There were passionate—at times intense, at times solicitous—moments. There were restrained moments. During these more reclusive periods, Peter thought of Chimango. He thought of his parents. He thought of Brother Mike, and like Brother Mike, he wondered.

Then, as had happened before, the ground seemed to shift beneath his feet—like the great tectonic plates that had slid apart, creating Lake Malawi—and everything changed.

It started very innocently.

Katy was once again deeply immersed in her work of identifying new markets for new and healthful products—particularly institutional markets like schools and hospitals. Much of her time was spent away from the farm, analyzing markets and talking with present and hoped-for customers. However, she would also spend some days on-site, checking the products to make sure she was selling what was being produced.

Katy's efforts had already produced good results and Mr. Koopman had, unusually heaping kudos on Katy, expanded his operations—among other things, building a second warehouse devoted principally to the markets Katy developed.

Everything seemed to be, as Peter liked to say, "Copacetic."

Then there was the slip that led to the shift that led to the tumult.

Katy was making a routine visit to what was now referred to as "Building Two," checking on, she thought, crates of fresh vegetables destined for primary schools in Pretoria. However, she noticed, alongside the fresh produce, were cartons of canned goods and five-gallon tins of cooking oil. Regrettably, as it turned out, she carefully inspected the other items, noticing the expiration dates were three or more years old.

Katy with her positive, at times naive, outlook, was sure this was merely a mistake. She immediately went to Mr. Koopman.

"Excuse me, Sir," she said, trying to maintain the social correctness that seemed to be embedded into the staff of Koopman Farms and nearly everywhere else, "do you have a minute?"

"Of course, my dear, what is it?"

"Well, as I do from time to time, I was in Building Two looking over the things going to Waterkloof and Brooklyn primary schools, to make sure we were sending items according to the most recent agreement, updated only last week."

"Of course."

"Well, Sir, I had contracted with the schools for fresh produce—fruits and vegetables—as always."

"Of course."

"So, you can see, I was surprised when the team leader getting the order together showed me a pallet with not only fresh produce but also canned fruits and vegetables as well as tins of corn oil."

"Of course."

"But this wasn't what I'd arranged."

"Of course."

"Of course?"

"Katy," Mr. Koopman said, smiling paternalistically, "you're probably not aware, after all, you're only doing part of the work, but we have larger arrangements with these institutions, building on your excellent efforts."

"OK."

"OK?"

"Well, I don't know. I guess all that's being prepared is, therefore, in line with your overall contract with the schools?"

"Of course."

"Well." Katy was now not sure whether or not to proceed and, if so, how to do so, "I sure it's a mistake—I know the guys on the floor don't look real closely all the time—but I noticed the dates on all the processed foods were far, far out-of-date."

"Damn! Those guys! You know how hard it is to get good help! I'll take care of it immediately."

"Well, I didn't want to bother you . . ."

"Of course. Dear, not to worry. So happy you've noticed this. You're always such a big asset to us. Many thanks!"

Katy exhaled.

Katy recounted to Peter the exchange with Mr. Koopman. Peter was sure it was, as their boss had explained, solely a slip-up by the crew—never imaging it was, indeed, Katy who had slipped.

After all, Mr. Koopman had generally been a good employer. Even if aloof, he had basically been friendly and, at times, sympathetic to his American team. They had no reason to think anything other than agree with the boss's diagnosis that this was utterly human error.

Nevertheless, several weeks later, Katy was back in Building Two checking on an order for Milpark Hospital that had just been modified. To her dismay, it was a repeat of the earlier school orders—the palate being prepared had quantities of canned goods and cooking oil that had expired a long time ago. This was not just a slip-up by the team. This was something else.

Katy did not go to Mr. Koopman but discussed the issue with Peter that night. They were both reluctant to do anything—say anything. Hence, they did nothing.

Things began moving in circles.

Checking on an order for Willowridge High School, Katy had the identical experience. Talking it over with Peter, they came to the same conclusion: this was no fluke.

Soon after, this all happened again regarding orders for the Mohau Child Care Center and the Mothwa Haven Old Age Home.

It was clear. This was the way (with a smile) Mr. Koopman did business.

Then the ground slid more.

While examining a pending shipment to the Avil Elizabeth Home for the Handicapped, Katy noticed the same discrepancies. Then, she saw a heap of old packing paper in the garbage bin near the pallet. She pulled this out, reading a warning stenciled in big red letters: "CONTAMINATED WITH FURAN—DESTROY. NOT FOR HUMAN CONSUMPTION".

Apparently, it was not only expired foods—it was contaminated and condemned foods.

This was not a minor blunder, this appeared to be intentional recycling of potentially toxic foods—recycling to those most vulnerable. Something must be done.

But Katy had no clue what to do.

That night she and Peter brainstormed. The best pathway they could see was to talk with Mr. de Woordvoerder at Orange River Foods. Peter's first boss in South Africa had always been understanding and, after all, he was generally in the same business. He would know what to do.

Over the next several weeks Katy went to work with a small 35-mm camera in her bag, making her inspections in Building Two during lunch breaks and taking pictures of any irregularities. She and Peter then made an appointment to see Mr. de Woordvoerder.

They were greeted with a warm smile and a hearty handshake when they entered Mr. de Woordvoerder's spacious office. After pleasantries, they placed a manila envelope with the photographs on Mr. de Woordvoerder's polished desk and Katy began, "I'm not sure, Sir (again, thinking the more honorific sobriquet appropriate), but there may be a problem that could affect many."

"Happy to help, dear. Please go on."

"Part of my work is to routinely check orders that are part of the marketing packages that I put together for Mr. Koopman." Katy paused to swallow. "I first noticed that more items than those for which I had contracted were frequently included in the orders. Then, upon closer examination, I discovered these additional items were often from expired stocks—some even contaminated stocks that were to be destroyed."

"Most unusual."

"We've talked with Mr. Koopman, but he indicated anything out of the ordinary was just the periodic human error that sadly occurs—he assured us all was fine. But all isn't fine."

"So, I see."

"Still, we don't know what to do."

"You've done the right thing. Leave this in my hands. I'll take care of it and fill you both in later. I am so happy that you've confided in me and so appreciative of your efforts."

This was clearly a sign that the deed had been done—they had delivered their message. With a bit more reservation than had been demonstrated upon their arrival, they all bid each other a good day.

Ten days later, a burly SAP officer came to the cottage and asked—ordered really—Katy and Peter to come with him in his Land Rover to the Central Police Station. While they both considered it disconcerting that they were not being directed to the closest police post, they accompanied the officer without any degree of angst—assuming this was undoubtedly a follow-up to their discussions with Mr. de Woordvoerder (never fully realizing how true this assumption had been—Peter forgetting for the worst that old adage, "Assumptions are the mothers of all screwups").

Nevertheless, Peter's nerves tightened when the Afrikaner Officer, as he opened the vehicle door for the two young people, cited *Exodus* 5:9— "*Make the work harder for the people so that they keep working and pay no attention to lies.*"

They rode in near complete silence—the officer irritatingly humming *When the Saints Come Marching In* under his breath. When the Land Rover pulled up under the station's *porte-cochère*, they were met by two other officers—one male, one female.

Katy was instructed to go with the awaiting female officer while Peter was accompanied by her male companion.

Peter was mutely escorted by his chaperone to an inner space—whether an office or an interrogation room, he could not tell—where another older, more portly SAP officer was seated, showing clear impatience and irritation at the young man's arrival.

With apprehension, Peter plainly saw things were not going well.

The seated man did not rise as Peter entered—he made no effort to introduce himself. In a monotone, he merely stated, "There are some problems with your papers."

Peter had no reply, fixing his eyes on a corner where he saw a small spider devouring a fly—thinking himself the fly.

"Young man, what do you have to say?"

"Sir, I am unclear of the issues—I don't know what to say."

"You are an American?"

"Yes."

"You are legally here?"

"To the best of my knowledge."

"How is it you are, in fact, here?"

"I was traveling and ended up in Johannesburg. I was then, purely by chance, offered a job. My employer assured me he took care of all the formalities, giving me a residence card." Peter reached into his hip pocket, removing his wallet and, from this, the aforementioned South African residence, or ID card. He put it on the desk in front of his churlish interrogator.

"Well." The seated officer frowned. "We have reason to believe this card was based on false information. Moreover, we have reason to believe you were involved in the theft of construction materials at a site in Bredell."

"I?"

"Yes."

Peter was incredulous.

"What of Katy?" he asked, trying to find his footing.

"Don't worry about her. You've enough in front of you and she's her own problems."

"But both our immigration issues were settled by our employers— me initially by Orange River Foods and she by Koopman Farms—we've copies of all the papers."

"As I've said—there are irregularities and reasons to think, in your own case, there's even been criminality."

"This is ridiculous."

"Say what you like, but right now you're in our hands." Miraculously, the door opened, and an officer appeared. Peter's questioner concluded, "Kindly take this gentleman to his cell."

≈

For the first time in his life, Peter was in jail.

He was locked up.

He spent several days only seeing the exercise area and the cafeteria.

Then, one day he was guided to another bleak room where another man was seated at a table. This time, however, the man stood when Peter entered; introducing himself as Frank Schriever from the US Embassy.

Peter was confused.

Frank explained, "The embassy was contacted by the parents of Katherine Madsen—apparently they had a call scheduled with their daughter (Peter had no idea) and it never happened, raising worries on the home front."

With a smile, Frank added, "It happens all the time."

He then went on, "Anyway, we finally found her here being held by the police over concerns about the documentation used for her residence permit. To a large extent, these were unanswerable questions with potentially severe repercussions for both the young lady and the embassy. Since she was a volunteer, unregistered in our list, I might add, the path of least resistance for all was for her simply to go home—she did—unhappily, but nonetheless, she's gone. As we were in the midst of making her arrangements, she would not leave us in peace if we didn't promise to help you. She insisted the two of you were wrongfully apprehended due to her own discovery of illicit matters regarding sales of spoiled foods.

"We don't get involved in local concerns like that—we can't. But, since you're also an American and probably in the same hot water where Katherine found herself, we did agree to try and find you and see if we could help you, too.

"They had you buried more deeply than your friend.

"And I'm sorry to say, our preliminary look-see indicates you're in more serious problems. Troublesome immigration affairs can nearly always be resolved by having the problem removed—the person in question just goes.

"But you're accused of stealing things. This is much more challenging.

"Now we've made contact and we'll see what we can do. Sadly, however, it's not just a question of them opening the door and you leaving the country as it was for Katherine. This one isn't going to be easy.

"All I can say is that you need to be patient and you need to know we're trying."

With that, without even asking about Peter's condition nor his take on his situation, Frank shook his hand and left the dreary room.

It was days later that Peter was called to the phone—Frank just telling him that he had nothing to tell him.

Peter was in jail, and this didn't seem to be changing very quickly.

Peter's *moxie* (as his father used to call it) was tested every minute of every day.

He stoically cycled through the exercise area and the cafeteria, back to his cell—thankful, at least, that he did not have to share this damned enclosure with one or more other inmates—perhaps a cramped and begrimed cubicle more tolerable accommodation for an American prisoner not wanting any roommates.

He tried to keep his mind blank—to control his fears and to steady his inner self—repeating, as his mother had taught him when he couldn't sleep as a child, "Calm, serene, tranquil."

This didn't work.

His mind raced. His imagination worked overtime. He was overwhelmed.

He needed discipline.

He forced himself to redo his travels since leaving Kpando—step by step, second by second, he revisited each site, each person.

As his mind traveled, he tried to revisit the principles that had pushed him out his parents' door. He tried to re-examine religion, faith, trust, love, hypocrisy.

He tried to get grounded.

The four corners of his cell remained—strangling him—claustrophobic for someone who had never had claustrophobia—but his mind began to quieten.

Then, a guard came to shepherd Peter to another room, Peter assuming this was Frank's follow-up visit (those woebegone assumptions). He was, accordingly, very surprised to see Sir Horace Barthley sitting at the dingy table in the forlorn room—Peter recognizing him from the original photograph he and Dabi had seen in the paper in Nigerian as well as seeing him way back when at O. R. Tambo.

He took a seat in the heavy metal chair as the guard exited and closed the door behind him. Peter stared at the man across the table from him—having no clue what to do.

The individual with the long, meticulously styled lustrous alabaster hair (almost bizarrely set-off by a nearly coral-colored complexion

that had not been visible in the original photograph in the *Tribune*, but
that Peter had noticed when he had first seen this man in the flesh at
the Jo'burg airport) before whom he had apparently been brought had
one of those indistinct ages that could only be called "oldish"—more of a
portrait than a person. He was nattily attired in what Peter guessed was
a *trachtenjanker* (Peter had absolutely no notion of why he recalled this
name)—a kind of Germanic forest-green sport coat of what looked to
be a felt-like material—adorned by a prim red tie over a sparkling white
shirt. Recalling his dress in the snapshot in the *Tribune*, Peter was not
boggled by the man's dress—he obviously chose his clothes for effect and
not for practicality.

Clothing aside, the man was sitting there, saying nothing, riveting
Peter with his dark eyes that reminded Peter of pieces of coal reportedly
used for eyes of snowmen (Peter had never made a snowman).

Having to do something, Peter opted for the minimum, "Yes?"

"Gosh boy." Horace smiled, showing lots of straight, white teeth,
"that's no way to greet a visitor. What'd your Mama teach you?"

Ignoring the barb, Peter repeated more emphatically, "Yes?"

"Boy, this isn't a 'yes' situation—I'm here to help you."

"Yes?"

"OK, OK . . . I suppose you think you're entitled to an explanation."

"Yes."

"OK, OK . . . I know you're in trouble . . . you're possibly in big
trouble. Now I don't care. I really don't care. Anyone can get in trouble.
I'm honestly not here because you're in trouble. I'm here because you and
I, we've got some mutual friends. You've been around Jo'burg a while and
people have noticed. You're cleaver and you're, so they say, a hard worker.
That's why I'm here to help."

"Yes?"

"Son, you make things hard."

"Yes."

"Son (almost as though he knew Peter hated being called 'son'), I
can help you. I can. But I don't have to."

"Yes."

"Well, damnit, do you want me to or not?"

Peter recalibrated. He was so far relatively neutral as regarded this
man; not a very good reputation from the tiny part Peter had seen, not
the most appealing of personalities. Yet, all the possible negatives apart,
he really, really didn't like his current situation and had no real faith that

it would get any better than it was if something drastic wasn't done. And he himself had no tools to take the drastic action that would change the *status quo*. What did he have to lose?

"OK, please tell me more."

"Fine." Horace exhaled deeply, as if prepared to dive into deep water. "Like I said, I don't have to do this. I'm no boy scout. I'm not trying to help my 'brother' (this last word almost spat out). Don't you go think'n, 'Good ol' Horace, he's a swell guy, spends his time helping the wronged— a real good Samaritan'. This ain't the case."

"OK."

"I'm a businessman. And I ain't that kind of businessman who says, 'Mankind is my business.' I'm a REAL businessman. I'm doing business to make money. That's that."

"OK."

"I get around. I know people. I can get things done."

"OK."

"I'm not a charity."

"Understood." Peter chose to modify slightly his nearly monosyl-labic replies which appeared to have no effect, as Sir Horace seemed to be talking more to Sir Horace than to Peter.

"But I am always looking for good hands—especially expatriate hands who aren't all tied up with local stuff—politics, finance, families."

"Good."

"Foreigners tend to get right down to business and that's what I need—someone who gets right down to business. Boy, do you get right down to business?"

"Yes."

Peter was back in his cell.

Sir Horace had said he'd get involved. He'd said he'd be back soon.

It was now two weeks. No word from Sir Horace or Frank.

Then, once again, a guard appeared to usher him into the bowels of the jailhouse. At his destination, the dank and disheartening room (he was never really sure if he was always going back to the same room or if there were always different rooms—horrid places all looked alike), he found Sir Horace, clad in a maroon checked sport coat bedecked with a bright yellow bowtie, sitting as though he were waiting for the train—impatient and irritable.

With no formalities, the older man gruffly began, "Sit down boy, sit down."

Peter did as he was told while the guard bolted the door from the outside.

"I didn't want to come today—you're taking up far too much of my time. My time is valuable—very valuable. You're getting to be a pain in the ass."

Peter only halfheartedly smiled.

"Still, like I said before, I'm looking for good people—by damn you better be worth the effort. Take care, son, I'm doing a lot for you and you are fully expected, I dare say required, to do a lot for me. We're not just talking about packing vegetables here. We're talking about real serious stuff. We're talking about big money and sometimes big responsibilities. I hope you're up to it . . .I hope you're worth all the extra effort?"

Peter kept smiling.

"But I warn you now—stop me if you're not ready to get right down to it—you'd best say so now—right now! I don't truly care who you are or where you come from. I just care about what you do—what you do for me. Is that clear?"

Peter's smile got a little bigger.

"Of course, I know you're an American. But don't think for a split second that that makes you special. It doesn't. Not one damn bit. Is that clear?"

More smile.

"I don't need to say again how serious all this is. Boy, it's life and death serious. You'd best understand that!"

Sir Horace was working himself up into quite a presentation and Peter needed to do no more than smile—no more was expected (with a twinge in his subconscious, Peter realized it was nearly like watching his father unrestrainedly homilize in or out of the pulpit).

"Like I said, I don't care you're American! Why, a while back, some young American and her husband, folks like yourself, strangers in Africa, started butting into our work in Zambia and Malawi. We don't take kindly to this, as you'll soon see if you hang in there. This unfortunate lady just wouldn't let go—it was sad. It was too bad. But what has to be done has to be done and she's dead and buried now—buried back in your country, but still just as dead."

Peter's smile faded.

"The dead lady's husband, poor soul, continues to look for us, continues to stare into the shadows, to peek into corners, to look under the covers—but he's going nowhere. We—I say we because I am more than one, I am not just me, we are numerous—are deeply embedded everywhere. It is not the bereaved husband, an American—nor, for that matter, you the boy in trouble, also an American—who will be our downfall. Quite to the contrary, if we so choose, we will be your demise.

"You were in Nigeria (Peter discomforted by this announcement and the obvious implications that Sir Horace was more than he seemed and knew more than he let on), so you know what they mean when they say, 'Take time.'

"Boy, believe me when I tell you to take time with us. We don't fool around!

"Son, am I clear?"

Peter felt he needed to say something, so he managed a feeble, "Yes."

"Kid, never forget, when good people go off the rails, bad things can happen—really bad."

And again, Peter was back in his cell. Sir Horace hadn't had anything substantive to say. Peter guessed he had only come to double check on his investment—not wanting to get buyer's remorse after he'd done a lot of work.

Immediately after underscoring the rail warning, the older man had called the guard and told him to, "Take the boy home" without providing any details to Peter as to how, or even if, he was managing to arrange what was beginning to look like a growing pile of problems with the people of South Africa—or at least their police force.

Five days later, Peter was once more summoned from his cell, led by a guard, but this time along a different series of corridors that he did not recognize. Apart from this unfamiliarity, Peter presumed he'd end up in another vile room with a crabby Sir Horace or a fidgety Frank. He was, therefore, startled when the guard silently opened a heavy reinforced metal door, vigorously pushing Peter across the threshold.

Peter found himself standing in a small courtyard with a large, gated opening in the opposite wall. Situated between him and the gate was a gleaming, black Mercedes.

Unsure of what to do, he approached the vehicle. The tinted back window slid down and an arm, trimmed by a deep purple sleeve, with just the hint of a sky-blue cuff showing, beckoned him forward.

It had to be Sir Horace.

Indeed, it was. When Peter was seated in the back next to the (probably) self-anointed nobleman, the car rolled through the gates that were opening as if by remote control.

Peter was free—or was he?

Had he exchanged one cell for another—one captivity for another?

This thought ricocheted across his brain as the Mercedes gained speed on a dual carriageway while his benefactor sat motionless, saying nothing.

After about thirty minutes, Sir Horace seemed to exhale and relax in his seat. Peter thought this reaction gave the impression that the good gentleman himself was not totally confident they would succeed in getting Peter's release (or was it a break-out?). As they had now traveled some distance without event, and were accelerating along the southeast-bound expressway, all signs indicated a successful mission.

City ring roads gave way to the major N3 Highway. The Mercedes sped forward as night fell. After another half an hour, when they had cleared the outskirts of Jo'burg, they pulled into a petrol station at Villiers.

While the driver oversaw the fueling, Sir Horace and Peter went into the station's convenience store to use the facility and ease their thirst—getting people out of jail a thirsty business. After they'd left the loo, the older man gave his charge a one-hundred-rand note to buy some snacks.

Back in the car, Sir Horace slowly sipped an apple drink while Peter seemed to inhale beer and chips—Sir Horace nearly apoplectic as Peter got crumbs on his kid leather seats.

Once they were back on the N3 and refreshed, Sir Horace evidently felt the moment had arisen. Looking his passenger square in the eyes, he said, "Boy, you're all-in now."

Peter swallowed the last of the chips and tried to speak around the gob that was stuck to his teeth, "Yes, Sir, I know. And, let me say . . ."

"That's OK," Peter's newest Samaritan said, "we've already had this discussion back when you were still detainee number 145-783. You are no longer in a South African jail. But you are all-in with me. There's no more discussion—there's no more room for changing plans. It's done."

Peter, finally freeing up his mouth, but now feeling as though his throat was constricting, meekly replied, "Sir, I understand—I understand well."

"I hope you do, boy. I hope you do. There's only one way to go now, and that's with us."

The older man smiled to himself as he thought of an amusing anecdote. "It's like in your country. You've just had a brush with the justice system—hopefully a one-off. Yet, as you know, in your country some judges get lifetime appointments. You've just got a lifetime appointment. Funny, huh?"

"Uh-huh," was all Peter could muster.

"So, son, we're off and we understand each other. No going back. No more talk about how you fit. We've already taken off."

"Fine."

"OK, let me tell you some more, as I know you're probably curious. Like I told you, some say you've got talent. We're going to see how we value your skills. This means you're going to do a few things kind of temporarily—think of it like an apprenticeship—maybe like you're an apprentice plumber.

"Then, if you get good marks, we'll be able to find a better job for you—better for you and better for us. So, don't fuck it up."

"I'm ready."

"Good. We're going to Durban. We've got about another 250 miles—should be there a little after midnight. There's a little house there where some of our guys stay. You'll be with them for a while.

"We'll give you a couple of days to get your feet back on the ground after the uncomfortable routine you've just finished. Then, in a few days, my friend Josh will come to see you and get you going on your next job.

"I have no idea when you might see me again—possibly not for a long time—possibly never."

"Well," Peter started, "I just want to thank . . ."

Once more Sir Horace prematurely ended Peter's remarks, "We've said it all. Nothing more necessary. Now, like I said, 'don't fuck up.'"

With that, the old man pushed his frosted head deep into the leather cushion, indicating the discussion was over.

Arriving in Durban after a good, and he felt well-deserved nap, Sir Horace had had one final word of advice for his young charge. "Boy, before I go, I want to make sure you'll remember you're in South Africa. You're not back in Ghana or Nigeria—this is South Africa. Whatever may or may not be the case of apartheid, race is a BIG thing. You're a white kid—you've got to act like a white kid—a white South African kid.

"The other guys staying here are white guys. Do like they do. Drink with white guys, watch football with white guys—basically live like a white guy. Believe me, you do not want to stand out. And, one of the quickest ways to stand out is to forget your racial place. Remember, you're a white guy.

"Don't fuck up.

"See ya kid."

It was early morning when Peter got into a cold bed in a nondescript bungalow in the Shallcross suburb of Durban.

Peter hadn't realized how tired he was. What a surprise: jail wasn't easy. He had had to be on his guard twenty-four-seven. He wasn't sure from whom he had felt he had needed to protect himself; the guards, the other internees (he didn't want to call them inmates or prisoners—this hadn't really been a prison, it had been a jail), or the folks outside who had ostensibly put him inside—maybe all three.

In any event, he was out, and he had been able to survive while he had been in. Still, this period had drained him. He was exhausted.

He was most thankful his sponsors (he hoped they were truly honest sponsors and not pernicious pretenders) had scheduled in a few days of rest—he needed to reestablish his equilibrium.

Then, sooner than he would have like, he found himself face-to-face with Josh.

His new interlocutor reminded Peter of a magpie—his narrow face and pointed nose always bobbing from one side to the other—his eyes wide, intelligent, and continuously exploring.

Josh had the appearance and accent of a South African anglophone. However, he never indicated anything about his personal life nor his roots. He quite directly began to question Peter—asking about his origins, his training, and his priorities. This was all old ground, covered with Sir Horace. Peter thought perhaps they were trying to see if they could get the same story twice.

Whatever the justification, the cross-examination stopped abruptly after about twenty minutes, Josh then introduced Peter to the other three men sharing the house; a Freddy, a Sam, and a Ralph.

Peter had no idea if the names were real and, once again, gained no insight into his would-be companions. Nonetheless, the trio seemed to know each other quite well, all speaking English with an accent that could well have been Eastern European.

Josh left in a beat-up double-cab Toyota Hilux with the other three, telling Peter to relax and that tomorrow he'd start his new job. Peter figured this was just a double check of the new guy before they fully opened the door into their (crooked, he supposed) activities in Durban and elsewhere.

Peter had recovered most of his mental and physical self and was more anxious to be out and about than still confined.

He needed to do something—anything.

Alone, he checked out the house. It had all the signs of a wayside or a halfway house. The dust bin was overflowing with fast food wrappers and beer caps. The fridge had cheap beer and stale food—not much of either. There was a common or living room with an old TV and a bookcase that demonstrated the residents weren't much into reading. Looking over the titles, Peter was somewhat surprised to see a Betty Crocker cookbook, a Catholic Bible, an Orthodox Bible, and a copy of *Fathers and Sons* by Ivan Sergeyevich Turgenev—this latter in Russian (Отцы и дети) along with a small sampling of well-worn paperbacks that seemed to be billed as romance novels but probably were closer to pornography.

Peter, practically absentmindedly, picked up the Bible and sat on a corner of the long and sticky vinyl couch facing the switched-off TV. His thoughts had turned to Katy. This was not how it was supposed to end.

They had known that their relationship had had no guarantees. They had understood that it could burn itself out. But this was not how it was supposed to end.

He wasn't totally sure of his honest feelings toward his good friend from Iowa—it was possible he had loved her. It was possible he still loved her. He didn't know. He didn't know if he had loved Ruby or Dabi—he certainly hadn't loved those schoolgirls in UK with whom he had experimented the dawning of their adolescent sexuality.

Katy was special.

Katy was definitely a special human being. She was also special to him. He missed her. He missed her a lot.

He began morosely recalling their time together. These had been good times. They had been good together. Everyone assumed they were a couple beginning a life together.

It wasn't right.

He started to get angry. Was he angry or was he sad?

But then, if he forced himself to take a glance from higher up—from outside his soul and outside his heart—he acknowledged that this had been truthfully unexpected good luck for the honest and forthright Katy.

She had shone a light on a breach—an intentional and thoughtless, amoral, series of scandals—that those in power did not want illuminated. She had not discovered how deeply it went, nor how much the actors profited in ill-gotten gains. Yet, this was likely not a unique event. Sacrificing the poor for profit was not a new endeavor for the rich and powerful.

Katy could have uncovered things that could have ended her life— hadn't Sir Horace talked about the American lady in Zambia who'd been killed—who they'd killed (he guessed)?

Katy was lucky to get out unscathed. Katy was lucky to get back home.

Peter's mind randomly picked up images of their time together— browsing as someone going down the line of a buffet, selecting whatever looked good.

These had been good times.

He found himself fondling the Bible that he had dismissed from his thoughts. He opened the pages, flipping through, thinking of his father and how these pages had ironically formed the bases of so much of his life—of their lives.

He more stumbled into, than carefully found a passage that seemed to remind him of Katy, albeit in no way providing him the solace it evidently it was intended to supply: *Proverbs* 3:15—*"She is more precious than rubies; nothing you desire can compare with her."* Then he lurched haphazardly into two more verses: *Genesis* 31:49—*" . . .because he said, 'May the Lord keep watch between you and me when we are away from each other,'"* and *Psalm* 147:3—*"He heals the brokenhearted and binds up their wounds."*

He re-read each.

It didn't help.

～

The next day, Peter left with the others in the Hilux. They drove to a warehouse not far from the port. While the possibly Eastern European trio stayed in the van, Josh accompanied Peter into the bustling hanger with forklifts and people scurrying about everywhere. They wove through stacks and heaps before gaining the stairs that led to the office that overlooked the entire arena—seemingly, Peter thought, hanging from the rafters like a wasps' nest and just as foreboding.

Here Peter was introduced to a portly man, likely of Southern Asian origin, who Josh presented as Sai—his new boss. His corpulent caretaker offered a limp handshake and very little if any facial expression, at which point Josh took his leave, admonishing Peter to "not fuck up" (unnecessarily reminding Peter of Sir Horace).

Still expressionless, Sai called Peter over to the window, pointing to a tall man, well over six feet, with a yellow hardhat, he said succinctly, in clipped tones, "Go and see Harry, he knows what to do."

From then on, it was roughly the same routine as at Orange River Foods or Koopman Farms; things came in, things went out. Here it was just at a much, much larger scale.

Peter had spent three weeks at the warehouse, dropped off every morning by Josh as he and the other three furtive chaps went elsewhere. It was tedious and tiring, but it was better—far, far better—than jail.

Then one morning Josh again accompanied Peter into the expansive depot. He did not, however, go up to Sai's office. Rather, with Peter still at his side, he called to Harry (Peter noting how immediately obsequious the lanky supervisor became), "Hey, a word."

With downward cast eyes, Harry almost sighed as he approached, "Sir?"

"We've a forty-footer coming in this morning. Set this container in the back and let Peter deal with it first—he'll let you know when you can send in a team to completely unload it. Got it?"

"Sir," Harry muttered, as he left.

Josh turned to Peter. "Like we spoke this morning, there's some items inside this container that have circles of red tape on one end. Pull these out, find someplace to keep them and we'll put them in the Hilux this evening."

As usual, things went to plan. When Josh came by to pick up Peter, he and Peter put the labeled boxes in the back of the Hilux, a few even ending up on the pickup's roof rack. When they got to Shallcross, Josh dropped them off with a sense of urgency—the silent trio going straight into the bungalow—Peter following with a final glance at the special cargo with the red tape, he thought, shining like a beacon. The next day, going to work, all the packages were gone.

This theater would repeat itself every ten days to two weeks.

Peter never knew what was in the cartons left in the truck for an overnight pickup.

Doubtlessly, Peter very well never knew, at least precisely, what was in the selected cartons. But he knew full well these cartons probably contained smuggled goods. He had been freed from jail to become a member of a group of racketeers—criminals.

Remarkably, he recalled his father preaching—his father, looking regal in his vestments, his chasuble-alb and stole with an over-sized crucifix made of Ashante gold (this was his pride, and what was it that was said about pride?). His father would try to stretch his back to be as tall and imposing as possible when he addressed "his people" from behind the pulpit. He would stare intensely, ensure a pious moment of silence, and then try to make his voice boom all the way to the narthex of the building. He remembered his father standing there and he remembered his father reciting, to the great confirmation of his congregation, *Proverbs 22:7—"The rich rule over the poor, and the borrower is slave to the lender."*

He was, if he dared admit it, Sir Horace's slave.

More correctly, if he followed his conscious, he was the slave of someone or something much more potent and unrestricted than Sir Horace. Sir Horace was not the power that sat atop the pinnacle and enslaved people like Peter. He was only an actor—even if an important one—in the play.

Peter did not want to get too ecclesiastical or metaphysical. In his mind he did not think he had crossed over into the den of Beelzebub. He had not sold his soul. He may have sold, however, his freedom.

After nearly four months in the warehouse, as they were driving home, Josh, normally non-communicative in the car, asked Peter, "How are you with your hands?"

Peter wasn't really sure, offering an imprecise reply, "OK, I guess."

"Fine. Tomorrow there's something new. You won't be going back to the warehouse."

The next day they still headed in the direction of the port but ended up in what looked like a big parking area as opposed to a big storehouse. The paved area, enclosed with chain-link fence topped with concertina wire, was roughly half filled with a variety of small- to medium-size sedans.

Exiting the Hilux, Josh exceptionally putting his arm around Peter's shoulder as he pulled the young man's ear closer to his mouth—Peter painfully smelling the morning coffee and cigarettes (what Josh liked to refer to as his "whore's breakfast")—and whispered, "See that shed over there? Go and see Ward. He'll show you what to do. You do what he tells you.

"I wanted to fill in some blanks, because you're gonna have questions and I don't want you go'n and blab'n all about. Understand?"

Peter nodded.

"You know about this program lots of the Japanese car companies have? They take used cars back to their factories in Japan, refurbish them, and then sell them—especially here in Africa—as some kind of 'super' used car with a factory guarantee. They get top dollar. Folks like buy'n cars that have been back to the factory—like they got a second life.

"Well, and I don't need to tell you to keep this to yourself, here we fiddle a bit with the cars and then get them into the lots that come back from Japan refurbished—only these are 'refurbished' by us—we give each on a big dose of loving care (Josh smiled).

"So, do what Ward says. Don't fuck up."

Just possibly (with a capital "P" he thought to himself), Peter figured he may have found—more correctly, that others may have placed him in—his niche. It wasn't really a question of liking or disliking the work. It was what it was—but it was, in the final analysis, his choice—this or being a guest of the SAP.

Fiddling, as Josh had called it, with cars turned out to be more rewarding than spending hours and hours in yet another claustrophobic
warehouse. While he was no real mechanic, he did do well with his hands
and the rather simple "refurbishing" of the cars was well within his skill
set—each vehicle offering a little different challenge, bringing a limited
degree of variety into the monotony.

It wasn't great, but, as always, it was better than jail.

He remembered, and he was somehow distressed with himself for
remembering, that, years ago, when he had repeatedly confronted his
father, wanting more, wanting the things others had, feeling his family
needed more money, needed to do more; his father had, as was his habit,
replied with a biblical reference: *Hebrews* 13:5—*"Keep your lives free from
the love of money and be content with what you have, because God has
said, 'Never will I leave you; never will I forsake you.'"*

Peter had few concerns about being forsaken by his father's God;
after all, his father himself had indeed forsaken his God. Peter only hoped
he could be content with what he was doing.

Yet, he had to ask himself, "Why all these thoughts about God?
About the Bible?"

He guessed, and he guessed it was logical (he wouldn't go so far
as to think it was "normal"), that this recent growing preoccupation, at
times, verging on a fixation, with religion in general and the Good Book
in particular, was a result of a confluence of factors.

First, at least as far as his memories served him, God and the Bible
were the epicenters of growing up. He and his dad didn't go hunting or
fishing or hiking, He and his mom didn't bake bread or paint landscapes.
His parents had wrapped him in their religion: morning, noon, and
night—rainy season and dry season—from his birth to his adolescence.
Like it or not, this had been his primary childhood experience.

Now, fast-forwarding to the present, he was (as he tried to find himself—he smiled at the near absurdity of it) diving more and more into the
past—digging up childhood memories to try and assess their impact on
who he was and where he was going. He was finding himself, moreover,
at least of late, in situations where he had time on his hands and where
the Bible was apparently the only easily accessible distraction.

These features of his current state (ironically, he mulled) led to circumstances where he probably invested more thought in religion than he
had at any other time in his life.

It was curious.

It was uncomfortable.

Still and all, he was OK with curious and uncomfortable. But these were getting all too close to a subject that was more than uncomfortable—for him it was distressing. Was this possibly renewed interaction with religion a symptom of what had ailed his parents (perhaps his grandparents)? Was fear and uncertainty driving him to the refuge of religion? Was the sanctuary of the sanctuary a means for self-protection? Was an adherence to the rules of a devout life a shelter from imminent threats? Was a declaration of faith, an affirmation of being a believer—were these enough to allow one (even the most insincere or hypocritical) to say, "I'm a good person. If bad befalls me, it is not my fault—it is an act of God?" Was an acceptance of the Gospels (superficial or not) enough for God to be your shield—to absolve you from any responsibility—even from your own misdeeds?

Were fear and uncertainty the catalysts?

Had Sir Horace driven him where his parents could not?

It was too much to handle while fiddling with a Mazda.

CHAPTER TEN

The Letter II

The net tears

"*Kwaheri.*"

"Huh?" Peter looked up from his coffee mug in the small kitchen where the four housemates were awaiting Josh's regular morning arrival.

Their driver *cum* overseer was standing by the back door, having silently entered to stealthily scrutinize his charges. Sometimes Peter was incredulous when noting Josh's all but cat-like behavior—the cat and the magpie combined.

The thin lips beneath the prominent nose repeated, "*Kwaheri.*"

Naturally, Peter, too, repeated, "Huh?"

Josh didn't smile—he never smiled—but he came real close, "That's Ki-Swahili for 'goodbye'—you, chappie, are out of here."

"Huh?" was all Peter could manage.

"Yep, just got some new plans—orders really—the powers that be have decided you'd do better elsewhere. They're sending you north to Tanzania. Pack your bag."

Hence, within a week, Peter found himself in Dar es Salaam.

This time it was different. There was an actual business—office and all—Equatorial Management. The Managing Director was a Mr. Hong. There was a secretary (Regina), a bookkeeper (Alfred), and a receptionist (Afaafa). He had no clue as to what was "managed," but he was now part of the crew. His official title, appearing on embossed business cards, was Operations Assistant. Again, he had no clue what was "operated."

All the unknowns aside, everyone had been very helpful. They had met him at the airport, ensured all his papers were in order, immediately started the process for a residence permit, and helped him choose an apartment—they called it a "flat"— in the metropolis of close to two-million inhabitants' most populated district, Kinondoni, walking distance from the office in a neighborhood seemingly overflowing with NGOs and expats.

This was the first time in some time he'd had a personal residence. He had not felt comfortable having his private correspondences sent to the Shallcross bungalow. He now wrote to Mr. Wewege and Silas, asking them to forward all his mail to his new Kinondoni address; with no explanation as to how he found himself in Tanzania, nor how long he planned to be at this locale.

He wasn't honestly sure if he wanted his mail or not.

Work, "operations," seemed to swirl around two foci. For the first, there was continued assistance in moving cargo from Point A to Point B. The consignments fell into two categories, the disclosed and the undisclosed.

As in Durban, Peter had no idea what was in the undisclosed, the surreptitiously flagged and zealously hidden consignments of all sizes and configurations. He assumed contraband—drugs, weapons, gems, rhino horn, ivory, and the like. All the illicit items that brought big returns to dealers in illegal markets around the globe.

He was also an expeditor for the other set of disclosed items—more routine and known, dare he think "admissible," cargo. This more mundane and public merchandise was highly variable, ranging from vegetable seeds and farming tools to medical supplies or schoolbooks. These commonplace articles were moved from the port to a large garage behind Equatorial Management's office.

Peter learned—or more precisely, had already learned, but was having growing appreciation for the fact—that, whomever his real puppet master was, nothing was left to chance. This included details like locating the office in Kinondoni, surrounded by NGOs—NGOs often being minimally controlled groups with a lot of material and staff moving about. What better than to plant a tree in the forest where it merges into the white noise of the background.

The second target area for Peter's operations involved transferring—studiously transferring—the objects in the garage to carefully selected NGOs; generous gifts from the high-powered internationally-recognized Equatorial Management (a company that impressed all, but that none knew anything about) to those in the most need.

Magnanimous donations to the sick, the poor, and the vulnerable.

These gifts were not simply perfunctorily dumped on the stoops of the NGOs' offices in Dar. They were hand-delivered to the communities where they would be used by NGO staff helping the neediest. They were hand-delivered by Peter.

Peter, entering communities afflicted by drought, AIDS, locusts, or urban migration, was greeted like a messiah. He was the bringer of their salvation. The NGO workers hyped the gifts from "an international conglomerate" as a true sign that the world was committed to assisting those in the direst of straights.

Peter was ashamed.

Yet, Peter was not so ashamed as to cease and desist.

After all, this was his job. It was better than jail.

If the communities and the NGOs had known the truth, there would have been no rejoicing. There would have been no adulation. There would have been a profound sense of betrayal. There would have been tremendous anger.

The gifts were Peter's foil. Ostensibly as part of the giving process, Peter asked for the names of the recipients. He embellished his request with lies about how the managers and board of directors of the donors wanted to be able to personalize their gifts—they wanted to know who precisely was benefiting from their largesse.

As Peter moved from village to village like Père Noël (a concept not yet well adopted in rural Tanzania), he established a growing list of names of real villagers. Next to each name, from memory, he would add a few individual details in case more information was needed at a later date.

Back in Equatorial Management's office, Peter would copy the list, giving it to Regina. This ended his assignment. However, just like with the trafficking in illicit commerce, Peter's part was just a modest link in a twisted chain.

Equatorial Management had close contacts—employees really—in many ministries, including most importantly the Ministry of Public Works. These individuals would clandestinely insert some of the names on Peter's list into payrolls creating flocks of ghost employees—Equatorial Management sucking up the salaries of these imaginary civil servants.

Then, more importantly from Equatorial Management's perspective, they would make sure these phantoms were registered with the National Health Service—securing a medical ID card for each bogus soul. They would then sell these cards at very high prices to people needing health coverage.

It was all very profitable.

Peter thought once more (again surprising himself) of passages his father so loved to recite: *Proverbs* 18:21—*"The tongue has the power of life and death, and those who love it will eat its fruit."*

This was honestly not the highlight of Peter's life. The fruits of his melodramatic conversations with the bedraggled beneficiaries of counterfeit benevolent offshore millionaires were bitter indeed. More than bitter, they were rotten.

He wondered, "Was it the low point?"

No matter the answer, it was better than jail.

As Peter delivered gifts to village after village, mastering the geography of Tanzania much more than he thought he ever would, his mail began to dribble through. There were some letters from his parents—now quite dated. There was a curiously brief note from Katy, saying she was doing well back at home. There were several missives from Silas, just chatting.

And, there was another recent letter from his sister:

> *Peter* (not "Dear Peter" or even "Dear Brother")
> *I write probably the most difficult letter of my life. I am filled with pain. I am filled with rage. I am filled with frustration.*
> *My life was never supposed to be like this. But it is. I know I must accept what is before me, but it is so very hard.*
> *I know I must fight to not be broken. But it is so very hard.*
> *I know I must, as well, accept you for what you are. That is what our parents would have wanted. But this, too, is so very hard.*
> *I feel you have abandoned us—abandoned me. I feel you are on a fool's errand—chasing rainbows while others suffer terribly*

in your place. I am so furious. But I know I must accept what is before me.

So, let me not continue in bitterness, as I know you will not agree with me and will possibly throw this away before reaching the end.

This is why I write: our father is dead, and our mother is very, very ill.

As I had written earlier, it was becoming more widely known that our father was having an affair—had been having an affair for a very long time. Over the years, he had been able to keep this hidden from mother.

I do not know if the act itself was so well hidden or the fact that mother simply refused to accept that her husband would do such a terrible thing kept her from opening her eyes to what was going on around her.

However, regardless, things unwound, finally Mother did open her eyes and did confront Father. He had no choice. The truth was there, now in plain sight. He had to accept his deceit— his hypocrisy, his infidelity, his irreverence.

I am not sure what all happened. Of course, I wasn't there. From the letter I got from Kole, he told how they fought so terribly. Mother wanted to move out, but she knew not where to go. They stayed in the rectory—not speaking unless they were screaming.

There were no more services, there was no more ministration. The church filled with dust. Mother and Father turned into hate-filled creatures. Then, one day, Father went down to the lakeshore, took off all his cloths, and just swam away.

They found his body snagged on an old tree, thirty feet down, and six miles away.

When they brought the body home, Mother broke. She shattered like a crystal vase smashed by a boulder. She just sat down and refused to move for an entire day. Then she took off all her cloths and walked into the market. It was horrible. As Kole wrote all this to me, there were tear stains on the letter. It was a world crashing down.

Fortunately, the only fortunate thing I can find in all this horrible mess, the Society was very helpful. They paid my expenses to go back to Kpando. They paid all the expenses to get Father's body prepared for shipment back to the States. They even paid for a nurse to help look after Mother.

So, Peter, there you have it. Our father is gone. Our mother is also gone in mind if not in body.

I have no idea where you are. But wherever you are, know that there is no longer a home to return to in Kpando. Whatever was in the house, I gave to the Evangelicals at the Presbyterian Church. There's nothing left. The Volman's are no longer in Ghana.

There's no one to catch you—or me. We're alone.

Aunt Rose's daughter in Gravois Mills is taking care of Mother. I go to see her as often as I can. However, no one has much hope she'll ever be herself again. Once that hard shell she showed to the world was cracked, she was crushed.

There it is, my brother, laid open in the hopes that sunlight will sterilize—that sunlight will help us all heal.

I will continue my life. You surely will continue yours, wherever you may be.

We don't really even have each other anymore.

We have always been very different—shorn from different cloth as Father used to say.

I hope you find what you're looking for.

I wish you God's Love,

Lydia

Dominus vobiscum

Peter was bewildered. In his wildest imagination he never could've foreseen an outcome like this. His father may have been a lech. Still, as far as Peter could tell, he was in his own way a Man of God—even if, in many ways, an imposter. Suicide was a mortal sin to him. Being a philanderer may have meant breaking the Commandments. But killing himself—he was, by his own doctrine, damning himself to eternal condemnation. It seemed impossible to contemplate. But now it was what it was.

As he thought of his mother, he was less astonished as to her state. She had always been balancing on a foundation that was based on her complete and absolute trust in, and love of her husband. Pull out that base, and the house of cards comes tumbling down—as it had.

Peter was bewildered.

Yet, his feeling of being perplexed, he thought, was not so much precipitated by the recent startling events that had taken place and their repercussions. For some time, he had obviously fallen away from his parents. He had doubted. He had had misgivings about his parents' lives—about their professed faith—their religious fervor. His father's disloyalty and falsity had only reinforced these feelings.

Still, he was sad. He was pretty near mad.

It was not the, as he saw it, mendacity of his parents' public, private, and spiritual lives. If his recent experiences had taught him anything, it was that there is untruthfulness everywhere. Everyone lies. The lies may have been intentional or inadvertent. The lies may have been implied or blatant. But the lies were always there.

The lies may have driven him away, but he could have now accepted them as part of the human essence. In many ways, his parents were no more dishonest than so many others—than he himself. Yes, he had had expectations. He had wanted his own mother and father to be special—to be on a pedestal. But they had fallen.

All this he could have accepted as the luck of the draw. Life was, after all, in his view, much more a messy lottery than a finely choreographed concerto.

It was not their weaknesses and their perfidiousness that had angered him. These had disappointed him.

He was mad because they were gone.

He could accept them, now with clearer eyes, as flawed individuals. And, as much as they might have been imperfect, they could still have been there to help him. To shore up his life. To share their views as part of an older if not wiser generation. To be a more imperfect if better understood part of his future.

But they were gone, and he was mad.

Peter's life had taken a new and unexpected shape.

His parents had been his antipode. Their hopes for their son's life, far from Peter's own, had been, in his mind, the catalyst that had sent him on his journey. Everything he had done had been contrasted with the lives of his parents—the life they foresaw for him.

This was now all moot.

Following in the Volman footsteps was no longer really an option.

He could no longer go back to Kpando and take his father's post at the pulpit. It was not that he wanted to do this. He had had no epiphany. It was that this had always been there in the shadows as a possibility—a safe harbor if needed.

Now, even if needed, it was gone.

He was at a proverbial fork in the road—or so he felt.

He had gone to Nigeria to, as folks used to say, "find himself." He had had no plan. He had had no prospects. He had only felt he needed to get away from Kpandao—away from his parents.

Things had escalated. That first step from Kpando had become practically a perpetual motion machine. He had gone and gone and gone.

He had learned to develop incremental plans so that he knew somewhat his next steps. This had proven to be a necessity and not really a choice.

Still, he had never had—did not have—a long-term plan. He wanted to see tomorrow but had no thoughts whatsoever about the next decade.

Ironically, his buffer had been Kpando.

His safety net was gone.

He was now in possibly perilous waters—his random wandering having taken him to a spot never envisioned.

He was on slippery ground, totally unsure where a slip might lead him—push him.

Dabi used to often say, "Shit happens!"

Well, it had.

He was on his own here and now—now his own shit. He may have been a victim (at the very least susceptible) but could also have become a pawn. Whatever had been the impetus, and for whatever reasons, he had unquestionably aggravated his condition. He had made his bed. His naive searching had led to discoveries that were now harsh and even potentially treacherous.

He had unwittingly traded his links with people like Silas, Dabi, Robbe, and Katy for the likes of Sir Horace, Josh, Sai, and Mr. Hong. He was misleading himself. He was not at a fork in the road. He had long passed the divide and was on an underused and unkept track that he himself had selected—even if by default, it had been his pick.

It seemed there were few alternatives. The decisions had been taken. He had to live with them.

Thinking of Silas and Dabi, he remembered a Pidgin proverb, "*Jamb pass die, monkey chop peppe.*" A monkey would even eat hot chili peppers if that's all there was—you did what you needed to do to survive.

He had accepted an ample serving of "*peppe.*" And, when he thought of it, it burned.

At work, Peter was able to concentrate on his tasks—be they ever so unsavory.

At home, in his flat, his mind flew to new universes and old bedrooms.

He was flooded with trepidation.

It was better than jail. Or was it?

He felt he was flailing against the gods who were pushing him up a hill to a temple hidden in the clouds.

He wished he could ask his father, ask his mother.

He was whirling about a space of his own creation.

He needed perspective.

Coming home, he stopped at a bookstore and bought a Bible. It had, he supposed, helped his parents. Reportedly it had helped millions. Could it help him?

He thought back to his recent misgivings in Durban. Was it fear, uncertainty, Sir Horace, or something else driving him?

How could a Bible help—it never had before?

He'd moved through its pages many times before with little effect. Would it be different now?

How could it?

Was this simply a ready surrogate for his now absent—his now unreachable—parents?

Nevertheless, he decided he would read his Bible. If it guided his father, maybe it could guide him.

He tried to start at the beginning.

He couldn't stick to it.

He returned to his practice of random thumbing through the pages.

In this haphazard way, he found passages that seemed to describe his situation, albeit they offered little to him in terms of guidance: 2 Corinthians 6:14—"Do not be yoked together with unbelievers. For what do righteousness and wickedness have in common? Or what fellowship can light have with darkness?", and Philippians 4:8—"Finally, brothers and sisters, whatever is true, whatever is noble, whatever is right, whatever is pure, whatever is lovely, whatever is admirable—if anything is excellent or praiseworthy—think about such things."

Words! He could sieve the text and find words that possibly described his life—just as he could probably pick up Sakurai and Napolitano's Modern Quantum Mechanics (another text that back in college in

UK he had never been able to wade through) and filter out words that described his dilemmas and possibly his opportunities.

Words. It was words he twisted and misshaped every day to do what he had to do—to eat his chilis. Words were only as good as what was behind them. There was pitifully little behind his own words today. Everything was appearances. It was all part of an elaborate play. Reality was elusive. Self-deception was the currency of the day.

He so missed running barefoot over the savannah.

He was sad. He was mad.

Chapter Eleven

From the Outside In

Newcomers add to the mosaic

IN 1910, FRANZ OPPENAUER went to Mwanza in what today is Tanzania, but was then German East Africa. Having just completed his own schooling in Heidelberg, he went to teach school on the shores of Lake Victoria.

Gold had recently been discovered and activities were in full swing with the opening of the Sekenke Gold Mine. This triggered the normal series of events. First single men came to the mine. Then married men, feeling the fever, left their families at home and went to the lakeside. Then single men married, and married men brought their families, and schools were needed.

These were not just schools just for miners or just for colonialists. These were schools for all.

Primary school, *Grundschule*, was modeled after the homeland—Franz teaching third grade.

He was ecstatic. He loved teaching and the kids seemed to love him. He loved the excitement that seemed to ebb and flow through the community as gold was dug from the Earth with bleeding hands and frantic hearts. He loved being in Africa where everything, literally everything, was new and unknown (to him).

He couldn't have been happier.

Then, World War I oozed into East Africa—Germany outnumbered by Britain and outflanked by Belgium. In spite of the odds, the colony was valiantly defended by General Paul von Lettow-Vorbeck and his devoted *Schutztruppe*.

Although the East African German troops were never beaten on the battlefield (they did retreat not infrequently as they waged what today would have been called a guerrilla war), the war did not end well for the *Deutsches Reich*. By 1919 the colony had been transferred to Britain— new rules, new masters.

Franz, no longer a teacher in the German colonial service, sought other means to gain a livelihood in the country he had grown to love. He took the train to Tanga, one of the old epicenters of German governance, looking into every cranny and crevice for something worthwhile to do.

It seemed as though his guardian angel was still with him. He was introduced to an aging German couple who had a sisal farm in Pongwe, about ten miles out of town. After the loss of the war and the relatively low view of Germans by many, the couple had decided, while they were still young enough to travel and resettle, they would go to South West Africa (*Südwestafrika*) where there was a well-established, and hopefully permanent German community.

The couple was, moreover, amenable to entering into a contract with Franz's family back in the Fatherland to purchase the farm on very good terms. They, urgently, wanted out. Still, they wanted to keep their beloved farm in German hands.

It was a win-win.

Franz began immediately putting down roots. He further imposed on his family back home to get a sizable loan to modernize the whole farm. Franz also learned more about his principal crop—his money-maker. As Chimango would observe years later, sisal, too, was a crop introduced to Africa—it's origins back among the Aztec and Mayan peoples.

Similar to its uses with its originators, sisal was cultivated as a source of fiber—used for everything from paper to rope. Production in Tanzania was ticking up, making the country one of the world leaders. With better techniques and a better-trained staff, Franz was comfortable that his farm would prosper.

And it did.

Within five years he had a thriving business and was betrothed to the beautiful Helga Von Morestein—daughter of one of the wealthiest remaining German businessmen in Tanga.

Over the next decade, while their sisal harvests grew, Helga and Franz grew their family—ultimately having four children. The eldest two daughters, Frieda and Alina, were stewards for their younger brothers, Emil and Johannes—eight years separating Frieda and Johannes.

By the time young Johannes was ten, the planet was hoping for an end to a second world war and Franz was hoping to find someone to take over the rigorous day-to-day management of the farm.

Fortunately, Frieda, as comely as her mother, accepted an offer to marry Matteo, one of a dwindling number of young German men still living in Tanga. Matteo, for his part, was as thrilled about the possibility of overseeing a sisal farm as he was about the possibility of marrying Frieda.

It all worked out well.

Even though Matteo assumed the overall oversight, he, under Franz's tutelage, ensured there were places at the table for Alina's husband Tobias (Alina soon following the trail blazed by her big sister) as well as Emil.

Franz had foreseen that Johannes, too, would stay on the farm. However, the young man felt the homestead was already full—maybe overflowing. As the country had just become a United Nations Trust Territory, with his farm background, he was able to get a mid-level position in the central government's department of agriculture. Following his new assignment, he was the only member of the family to leave home ground and move to the capital, Dar es Salaam.

Johannes' differences or quirks did not stop at his career choice. To the stupefaction of his entire family, two years after arriving in Dar, he married Edina, a young lady of the Wachaga tribe, coming to the capital from the slopes of Mount Kilimanjaro. After a suitable period of getting settled and (successfully) building bridges with both their families Johannes and Edina had a daughter, Evelynn—the name, according to her mother, meaning "life."

Edina was not a well-worn resident of the restless fast-growing capital. She was and always had been a girl from the village. Her grandfather was an advisor to the paramount chief and her father a member of the committee of peers that participated in the running of village affairs. She had come to the city to visit her cousin who was in nursing school. She had literally run into Johannes when the young man hurriedly left a tailor's shop in the main market, not watching where he was going, colliding with the lass as she admired the myriad of market wares. He offered her a cup of tea to apologize for nearly knocking her into the gutter. And, as they say, the rest was history. There was a magnetism that entrapped the two, overcoming any other cultural, social, or ethnic forces. Two people who should have been opposites in all ways found a nearly immediate oneness.

Their personal attraction aside, it was Edina and not Johannes who was the most reticent to head down a trail that could lead to a serious relationship. While she freely and happily acknowledged deep new and foreign feelings—good feelings—she was overcome by her surroundings and her inner thoughts.

She was uncomfortable in the city. She was disquieted by the push and pull. She missed the pastoral tranquility of home and the emotional tightness of family.

Moreover, although she was not at all intimidated by what others might call "the white man's ways," she in no way wanted to give the impression that she was a poor native girl chasing a rich foreign patron. While she was unintimidated by what others might think of her with a white man, she was concerned about what she herself thought about a mixed union and its chances for survival in an often-unsympathetic world (not that she was looking for sympathy).

It was only through time that she realized what Johannes had noted from the onset, their special and strong bond was something that superseded more oft-used considerations employed to justify becoming a couple. While it sounded maudlin and contrived, Johannes was finally able to help Edina understand they truly had a very extraordinary relationship that should not be squandered.

Convincing their respective families of this rare and valuable alliance that supplanted time-honored norms of behavior and standing was no easy task. Again, it was not the rigid Teutonic mindset that was the most challenging to change—it was those living on the steps of Mount Kilimanjaro—it was they who were the most difficult to convince that Edina should not just come home and marry a nice boy from the village but should join her life to this son of colonialists who was better suited to the boroughs of Europe than the savannahs of Africa.

When all the formalities, obligations, and adjustments had been addressed, including both traditional and civil marriage ceremonies, Edina
and Johannes settled into a small house in Machimboni, on the south
side of the bay formed by the Kizinga River that was the Port of Dar
es Salaam. They were less than ten miles from downtown. However, the
commute could easily take more than an hour due to the congestion afflicting the rapidly expanding urban center. The house was, nonetheless,
in a calm and safe neighborhood not far from the beach where Edina
could feel almost as tranquil as in the highlands near Mount Kilimanjaro.
It was a reassuring harbor where they could start their family.

They were elated with the birth of Evelynn.

She was perfect and she was theirs.

As the years inextricably swept by, Evelynn grew from the perfect
baby into a radiant and resourceful young girl. She did well at school and
was a thoughtful member of the household.

The family trio did everything together. They went to the beach.
On weekends, they went to the mountains of Morogoro. Johannes helped
with homework and tutored his daughter in German. Edina ensured her
little girl had a profound and respectful understanding of her Wachaga
roots. Edina took them to the village at least once a month, grounding
both mother and daughter. Johannes also arranged for Evelynn to go to
Pongwe several times a year to renew bonds with her German relatives as
well as learn about farming—a subject dear to his heart.

Evelynn transformed, seemingly overnight in her parents' eyes, into
a stunning young woman with a flawless amber complexion, hypnotic
obsidian eyes, and long, generally braided hair. She was generous, even
selfless, and steadfast to her family and friends. She was happy.

When his little girl finished secondary school, Johannes was able to
arrange a job for her as an extensionist working with woman's groups—
working on the coast with women farming seaweed. It was fascinating.
Evelynn thoroughly enjoyed her job and the people.

She stayed in a government guest house in Bagamoyo during the
week, each weekend taking the fifty-mile bus trip back to Machimboni.
Every Friday night, over savory home-cooked dishes, a mixture of Bavar-
ian and Bantu cooking, she would regale her parents on all the week's
goings-on—her parents breathless at the wonderful things their little girl
was doing.

One Friday night she came home and did not talk about the seaweed
farmers. She talked about Arvin. This young man she had just met was,

as her parents guessed, German. He was a businessman—more correctly, a businessman in waiting, as he had only finished his studies three years earlier. He worked in the chain of industries and operations that dealt with processing seaweed. He'd come to Tanzania to see first-hand where his products came from—to go to the source, as it were.

The harvests from Tanzanian waters were most often purchased by Indonesian brokers who shipped the product to plants in Asia for initial processing. The semi-refined material coming from this first step was then sent to different places for different uses. In Arvin's case, his employer (he called it his company) refined the substance further, into a fine white powder that was used in confectionary products.

Arvin lived in Dortmund. And he'd invited Evelynn to come back with him to visit one part of her homeland.

Edina and Johannes' reactions were immediate and palpable. It was only Edina's hand on Johannes thigh that prevented an instantaneous, possibly frantic, reaction to his daughter's proposal—or, better put, Arvin's proposal. In place of a spontaneous eruption, there was more of a gurgle.

Johannes knew that in his mother tongue Arvin meant friend of the people, and he had no doubt what sort of friendship the young scoundrel had in mind for his little girl.

"Dear." Johannes swallowed hard to calm his thoughts and his voice, "you don't even really know this man, do you?"

"Well, we've only met. But he has spent a week at Bagamoyo, and we've spent a lot of time together. After all, dad, you've told me so often how you fell in love with mom in the blink of an eye. It must be inherited."

"*Kichimbakazi*," Edina said, using her pet name for her daughter—Evelynn was fluent in Ki-swahili as well as English and German. "Finding a great man is a wonderful thing. It can happen in a second. It has happened in a second. But it can—most often does—take a long time—a lot of trial and error. And it's those errors that we're worried about."

"There's no need to worry, Momma."

"We know, *msichana mdogo*," Edina continued, "you're a good girl. You know right from wrong. You know how to behave. Still, everyone is not like you. You—we—have to be careful not to be too trusting too soon. The world is full of all kinds of people."

"This is just a visit."

"But who knows what more."

"It's a visit. After all, I'm half German and have never seen this other half."

"True enough, but there are many ways to get to Germany."

"But this is an opportunity now-now. I can't miss it. Who knows when it will come again?"

The discussion—the debate—continued long into the night. There was little consensus, but the strong bonds and close ties they all felt for each other kept the tone civil. Tempers never flared. No one stomped off in a huff. Still, no agreement was made as they all went to bed.

Edina and Johannes talked softly together until sunrise. They knew too well there was no surefire control. Evelynn was a young woman, and she would do what she decided she must do. All they, her parents, could hope to do now was to provide some guardrails.

They contrived what they hoped would be a satisfactory compromise. Uncle Günter, Franz's senior brother, had been one of the main backers of the sisal investments. Günter and Franz were close. Günter lived near Hanover where his children had now taken over his banking interests—the elderly gentleman semi-retired. Through Franz, they could contact Günter who would surely agree that Evelynn could come on holidays for a visit. Edina and Johannes had some small savings. They could arrange for their daughter to go to her second homeland, as she desired, as was correct. Then, if she were there and she wanted to visit Arvin, at least she would not be beholden to him and she would have some local family support if she needed it.

Over breakfast, the parents made their pitch. Evelynn, always the levelheaded young adult, could find no fault.

The beautiful Evelynn was going to Germany—following the stem back to the roots.

No one had imagined it. It hadn't even been a consideration. It was a holiday, not a relocation. Yet, it was sixteen months before Evelynn returned from Hanover to Machimboni.

She did not return elated. She did not return dejected. She did come back as a more reserved and pensive woman who smiled and laughed less—who, with her head held high, was more introverted and somber.

Throughout her absence, she had written at least weekly to her parents. Edina and Johannes had also had regular contact with Günter or his family, insuring there were no hidden problems. While all the outward signs raised no warnings, it was unclear why she kept extending her stay.

Fortunately, Günter and his wife Rike had a big house with plenty of space. Evelynn had her own room and was free to come and go as she chose. She could even regularly dine with her great uncle and aunt if she wished. It was a good arrangement— Günter assuring Johannes that everything was fine.

Nevertheless, when Evelynn returned, Edina and Johannes knew everything was not fine. While their daughter did not say much, and they did not force the subject, they sensed that she was carrying a burden that would someday be shed.

It was weeks later when that day came.

When the dam did break, it was not a flood—more of a dribble.

Evelynn recounted how she had, as all expected, met with Arvin. She had done more than meet with him. She had loved him. She had passed sensual and passionate days with him. They talked of marriage. They talked of their future.

At first her world was divided between Günter's home and Arvin's apartment. Then, as their ardor became more controlled, they began to go out to Arvin's favorite haunts—bars, restaurants, and discos. They began to meet Arvin's friends. At first, people just stared and snickered. This changed as they were more frequent habitués in different establishments. The more they were seen, the more people seemed to be overtly antagonistic. The more it became clear to outsiders that this was not a one-night-stand, but some sort of continuing liaison, the more these observers became flagrantly racist. Before too long, others were openly calling Evelynn "*der Nigger*" and "*schwarzer Affe.*"

It was terrible.

Initially, Arvin would try to sooth Evelynn's nerves, saying people would get used to them. It was nothing. As the insults continued and redoubled, Arvin began to blame Evelynn, saying she was ruining his friendships. When she would point out the obvious, that it was these so-called friends who were throwing all the insults, he would get angry. He would tell her she had to adjust. After all, she was in Germany now. She couldn't expect people to act like Africans. Germans were definitely NOT Africans.

It was horrid.

Then it got worse. Arvin began hitting her—accusing her of all manner of things and slapping her or locking her in his bedroom. She fled to Günter's. She convinced the kind old man not to tell her parents. Not to go after Arvin. Not to make things worse. She only wanted to stay with him and his family until her physical wounds healed. Then, with her psychological wounds, she would go back to Tanzania.

Here she was—home.

Edina and Johannes did not want to, did not want their daughter to dwell on the bigotry and meanness of one's fellow human beings. They, as a mixed-race couple, knew all too well the malice and boorishness that people showed towards mixed races here in Tanzania—the situation many times worse in Europe, they imagined. They wanted their girl to get on with her life, having learned a caustic lesson, but ironically, at the same time, having had a chance to see her second homeland and meet heretofore distant relatives.

It was time to move on.

Fortunately, Evelynn had done well in Bagamoyo. Her direct supervisor, Mr. Kaali, a loutish man from another era, used to say to Edina and Johannes when they visited, while the couple shuddered and bit their tongues, "Go figure, your gal's got brains as well as good looks."

This ill-mannered and sexist (perhaps a foreshadowing, in retrospect) notion aside, Evelynn had proven herself to be a hard worker with an agile mind. Thus, when her ordeal in the northlands was over, she had little difficulty finding a job with the extension service—even landing a promotion. When she went back to knock on the ag service's door, she was unexpectedly, but gratefully, rewarded with an offer for a post of area supervisor (of, among others, Mr. Kaali, ironically) in Pangani, further up the coast.

This was not a leap to the top, but it was a move up. Pangani was about a tenth the size of Bagamoyo in terms of population, while her work area would actually be larger. Moreover, she would be further from home. While most littoral folks told her she was just going a little ways up the beach, it was far. If she took the unmaintained coastal route, it was a 350-mile trip from Bagamoyo, requiring nine hours—by the faster inland route, it was less than 200 miles and still about a five-hour drive. Surprisingly, to her, it was only 225 miles, but seven hours, from Pangani to Dar and her family (from Bagamoyo it had only been two hours).

Once she got settled in Pangani, benefiting from government housing and a government pickup truck for work, she arranged with her parents to visit them once a month—still needing to reach out to her progenitors to feel grounded.

Nevertheless, sooner than she had imagined, she had an established routine that was becoming a ritual. She enjoyed her work and she loved going home. She still shied away from testing the social milieu for any masculine companionship.

Pangani, at the mouth of the Pangani River, was a busy place. It was only seventy miles from the Kenyan border and due west of Pemba Island. It had a long history of being busy. For years it had been under the rule of the Sultan of Zanzibar and a major slave port—slaves sent to Pemba to work on clove plantations. The town had also been the starting point for excursions in the other direction—caravans west, into the interior seeking slaves and other riches. As the resident population grew, there were farms of sugarcane and coconut along the riverbank. Much of Evelynn's work was overseeing agents working with these riverside farmers.

These riverine farms provided a special challenge. Farming was changing. Like other parts of the coast, sisal had been an important crop, but its local cultivation was waning due to high costs in accessing markets. Sugarcane was also losing ground as its profitability was increasingly questionable. There were efforts on some farms to shift to growing betel nut—more correctly, for Evelynn's work, the Areca nut. This stimulant was widely savored, especially across Asia, with India a major consumer. Prices were good. Raising the Areca palm (reportedly originally from the Philippines) was no great jump from raising the more traditional coconut palm (also, apparently, of Asian origins). And it was less work than the bothersome sugarcane.

However, trying to look at the bigger picture, Evelynn learned that the addictive Areca nut was also reportedly carcinogenic—seriously affecting the health of many heavy users. To her (albeit, not to all in her service), this raised the issue of the social license in promoting this crop that could be a disease-causer. Yet, this was a sensitive subject. Farmers felt they could make money with Areca and it was politically untenable to simply take a contrary stance.

Nonetheless, Evelynn would not just drop it as many of her colleagues advised. She enquired, helped by the aegis of her parents, as how best to address such a delicate issue.

Ultimately, she received some advice that appeared to be the right key for the lock she was trying to open. There were a number of multinational agencies and institutions that studied the wider impacts of various activities, among them agriculture, including the farming of specific crops. These respected groups of experts were able to assess tricky topics—giving an external, objective scientific basis for decisions taken by local leaders. It was the implementation of the old adage; an expert is someone who is fifty miles from home. And importantly, these groups came with their own resources, requiring only an official request to initiate an initial fact-finding mission.

This could, Evelynn felt, work. The leadership in Dar would not reject a request for additional analyses as long as someone else paid the bill. After all, ties with multinationals often hopscotched from one activity to another—a good relationship might well lead to substantial funding at some point in the future.

Evelynn was able to draft a letter and get official sanction for support from EHT, the Ecumenical Humanitarian Trust—a Swiss-based group that, according to Evelynn's sources, had a long record of evaluating the pros and cons of different agricultural enterprises. Within three months, Evelynn received a visit from an EHT staff member based in their Geneva headquarters. She introduced herself as Paula Patterson, a cultural anthropologist.

When Evelynn looked askance at Paula's professional *bonafides*, the visitor quickly explained that she was part of a larger team—EHT called it the "Mixed Assessment Team," MAT for short. MAT covered a wide variety of disciplines including horticulture, ag engineering, marketing, and others. However, for a first look-see type of mission such as the present, experience had shown that it was often useful to have the lead-off investigator be someone with a rather broader base—someone like an anthropologist.

Obtusely, this seemed to make sense to Evelynn—she and Paula thereafter prepared a plan as to how to approach the issue of Areca nuts in Pangani.

Paula and Evelynn developed a close working relationship and a rather warm personal bond even though Evelynn was still somewhat in a recovery phase as regarded interpersonal relationships. By design, part of

Paula's work was in Dar, interacting with staff at the central government level as well as both being informed by, and informing decision-makers.

In Dar, Paula would boldly (or shamelessly, depending upon whom you asked) stay at the Golden Tulip City Center—a pricey four-star hotel that offered the amenities she had grown to appreciate, even if these were embellishments to which she had not grown totally accustomed (when submitting her travel claims, she would almost flippantly reply, if queried about her accommodation costs, "people of standing have to stay in places of standing").

After a late afternoon meeting at the Ministry of Agriculture, Paula was having a drink with her host at the Breakpoint Pub, not far from her hotel. After the second pint arrived, her ministry contact, Jephter, called out to a youngish white man entering the bar, "Hey Peter, come on over."

A thirtyish clean-shaven, brown-haired man of average weight and height, hearing the beckoning, turned toward their table, offering an enchanting smile. Seeing Jephter, he strolled in their direction. Paula noticed the man, a bit younger than she (maybe, just maybe, more than a bit younger), moved with a certain grace, yet simplicity.

"Jephter, my friend, long time no see," the stranger announced in a voice that was perhaps a little louder than necessary, extending his hand for a vigorous shake.

Jephter, indicating an empty chair at the table, replied, "Peter, please have a seat—I owe you a beer."

Then, turning to Paula, Jephter made the introductions. "Paula, Peter is one of those guys you see all around. He works for a local NGO or something and is here in Dar just as much as up-country, in villages all over the place."

"Nice to meet you, Paula," Peter enjoined, "like Jephter says, I work for Equatorial Management. We do a lot of different things, among them serving as a conduit for donations aimed at needy folks in villages across the country."

This was not the beginning of a steamy romance, but it was the beginning of a casual friendship between two Americans who had chosen the life of the expatriate, but who enjoyed hashing-out a laundry list of hometown topics with someone from the homeland (for Peter, a homeland he'd never even visited—rather a contradiction in terms).

Paula explained a wee bit of her work, taking care not to get too far in the weeds—emphasizing more her position with EHT and her French boyfriend's current work in Burkina Faso than the assignment she was currently undertaking in Tanzania. After a few more beers and an animated discussion about China's rise in Africa, each went their own way, Paula and Peter exchanging cards as they separated.

EHT had contacted Paula while she was in the capital, asking her to follow up on a number of issues unrelated to Areca, but linking to EHT's broader program and plans for Tanzania. To take care of all of her now diverse assignments she had to extend her stay by six weeks and then divide her time between Pangani and Dar. This meant more nights at the Golden Tulip and more drinks at the Breakpoint Pub. With some misgivings about being indiscreet, given she was in a serious relationship, she would call Peter when in town to see about a drink at the pub. The two would meet, enjoy the beer (commenting how it was so much better than American brew—which Peter had only tasted at a specialty bar in Accra) while tearing American political personalities and others on the public stage to shreds—more vehemently as the beer consumption increased. It was an amusing pastime enjoyed by both with no strings attached.

As the end of her mission approached, Paula arranged to go with Evelynn for a wrap-up debriefing in the ministry. All went well and afterwards, to celebrate, Paula invited Evelynn to the Breakpoint—having already informed Peter she would be at the pub that evening.

Peter arrived about half an hour after the ladies. There were formal introductions, then, as Paula noticed (happily, she supposed), there were some sort of fireworks between Peter and Evelynn—some sort of magnetic attraction that was palpable. It was nearly as though Paula was no longer at the table. The two younger people saw only each other, Evelynn seemingly completely forgetting her troubled relationships and, on the spur of the moment, ready to dive into a new and hopefully better pairing.

Peter and Evelynn left together. The next morning when Paula and Evelynn had their final meeting, nothing more was said. Paula flew back to Geneva hoping the two young people would be able to form a happy relationship—the troubled world needing all the happiness it could find.

Peter and Evelynn had sensed the attraction—they had sensed an immediate seductive pull bringing them together. Peter and Evelynn had been mesmerized with each other. Peter and Evelynn had been fascinated with each other.

While Peter very likely had had some biblical passage flashing through his mind, Evelynn, closer to her roots, had thought of Friedrich Nietzsche, " . . .*if you gaze long into an abyss, the abyss also gazes into you.*"

She, and maybe he, had felt the abyss was close. But the fascination had been far too seductive—a force of nature, or so it had seemed.

It had been inevitable.

That first night, they had gone back to Peter's flat.

What, not very long ago, she had understood to be the impossible, was now the possible—Evelynn was in a new relationship—with a man.

Evelynn would still come home once a month to see her parents. However, she began coming to Dar one or two more times a month to see Peter. Both had busy schedules and there were frequently long separations with rousing reunions.

At one point several months into their relationship, Peter and Evelynn were back enjoying a beer at the Breakpoint Pub. As always, they were fully absorbed in each other. They could, in fact, have been almost anywhere as, most of the time, they were oblivious to their surroundings.

During one such period of oblivion, Peter looked up over the rim of his glass, breaking his stare deep into Evelynn's eyes, seeing a khaki sleeve leaving a partially exposed heavy gold bracelet. Sweeping his gaze higher, he was shocked, really flabbergasted, to see Sir Horace standing at their table.

Feeling he had no other option; Peter motioned his clandestine master to an empty chair at the table. He then introduced the good gentleman, wearing a belted bush jacket over a rose-colored turtleneck, as an old business associate from South Africa. He finished his introduction saying, "Evelynn, dear, just like me, you never know when Sir Horace is going to pop up."

Evelynn was polite—possibly overly so. Peter could tell—but he was unsure of his boss's perceptions—that Evelynn fundamentally, almost organically, did not like the older man in the pink turtleneck. "Pleasure, Mr. Barthley. Oh, excuse me, Sir Horace." Evelynn seemed almost compelled to interject, "is that 'Sir' a bequeathment from the House of Windsor? I've never met a knight before."

Sir Horace, sly operator that he was, appeared to sense that he did not want to antagonize this young lady—he did not want to even stir up her imagination. There was much to be gained from anonymity and he did not really need an obviously very intelligent young woman on his case. He decided some version of the truth was better than a complete falsehood that could set a trap for him later. Thus, he parried Evelynn's thrust adroitly (as could be expected).

"So kind of you to ask, my dear. I guess in some sense I might be a knight—I definitely think of myself as chivalrous. Yet, my title is not from the British Royal Family. It is not even from the Order of the Immaculate Conception (he added with a wink). This notwithstanding, I have indeed been bestowed the Royal Order of Sahametri by the King of Cambodia. So, I believe you can say the 'Sir' is real—I helped the King out of a fix, and he felt I should receive some compensation in terms of an honorary title to honor a good deed."

"So," Evelynn chimed in with a wink of her own, "we shan't hold the Queen responsible."

"Not at all," was the modulated reply.

There wasn't much more chitchat. It did not really feel like a chatting moment. Sir Horace sipped his whisky and soda while the young couple nursed their beers. There was an occasional attempt to ask about the weather or the traffic *en route* to the airport, but mostly the trio just tried to act as though they were sucking up the ambiance to balance their id.

With an empty glass, Sir Horace stood up, formally and politely taking his leave, as nearly an after-thought reminding Peter he'd see him on the morrow.

Peter and Evelynn ordered more beers but said nothing about their departed third party.

"I think he's pusillanimous." Evelynn almost pouted, sitting cross-legged in a fetchingly chic see-through green negligée.

"Who's what?" Peter nearly cooed from his bower in the rumpled bedding on the other side of the bed—the deep wine-red sheets Evelynn had given him bunched up around his waist.

"That old codger friend, or whatever, of yours. I don't like him. He's pusillanimous."

"OK. Sure, he's truly special. Not even sure I know how I feel about him. But what the hell is pusillanimous (Peter stumbling over the vowels and consents unaccustomedly spilling from his lips—wishing his lips were pressed against Evelynn's)?"

"Chickenhearted."

"Well, aren't you the one with the big words," Peter scoffed with a smile, as he lunged from his recess, grabbing her across her chest.

After a rerun of the amorous acts of earlier in the evening, Evelynn felt pulled back to the same subject. "Peter, who is he? I really don't like this Horace Barthley—don't trust him. He gives me the creeps."

"Don't worry *chérie* (he loved throwing his grade school French at her). Do you see him lurking anywhere? He's not in our life. And, between us, I agree—he's creepy."

Creepy or not, lurking or not, Sir Horace was an inexorable part of Peter's life.

The next morning, he found his scowling master seated in his office at Equatorial Management. The aging Cambodian knight could only, very atypically, with no genteel preface (be it ever so bogus), blurt out a coarse, "What the hell is this all about?"

"This?"

"Don't be smart with me, kid! This is all about 'don't fuck up,' and it seems, in more ways than one, you're fucking up big time."

"Not your problem."

"What's not my problem! You're my problem. All of you! One hundred percent of that shabby carcass of yours belongs to me. Twenty-four-seven! And don't you ever forget it! Who drug your lousy ass out of jail, huh?"

"I do your bidding, but my off-time is my time."

"You really think that. You fool!"

"Who do you think . . ."

"Enough! I own you. Full stop!"

Peter could not react.

His boiling-over boss continued, "You don't have a private life. Don't lie to yourself, thinking you do. I know what you eat, where you sleep, and who you shag. You're mine!"

Still no reaction.

"Now, this time you're lucky. Normally, I'd tell you to dump that damn half-caste bitch on the spot. Normally, if you didn't dump her in the ditch, I'd have my boys chop off your balls and jam then down your pitiful throat. But it just so happens she might fit into my plans."

Peter bridled but said nothing.

"She works up the coast near the Kenyan border (it was not a question, but a statement). I have items I now regularly need to get across the border. In your role, as you like to think of it, of Père Noël, I need you to take my items to Pangani. My guys will take the stuff off your hands there. You can easily insert (a wink) this into regular visits to poke your raggedy *métis*. She'll love it. You clear?"

Peter could only grunt.

Sir Horace practically bounded upright and was out the door with one final admonition shouted over his shoulder, "Don't fuck up!"

Peter was shaken.

For some reason, startlingly, another of his father's passages blazed through his brain: *Revelation* 6:6—*"Then I heard what sounded like a voice among the four living creatures, saying, 'Two pounds of wheat for a day's wages, and six pounds of barley for a day's wages, and do not damage the oil and the wine!'"*

What was the cost of a pound of his flesh?

CHAPTER TWELVE

Existential Gymnastics
Keeping fires burning

PROVERBS 1:26-29—*"I IN TURN will laugh when disaster strikes you; I will mock when calamity overtakes you—when calamity overtakes you like a storm, when disaster sweeps over you like a whirlwind, when distress and trouble overwhelm you. Then they will call to me but I will not answer; they will look for me but will not find me, since they hated knowledge and did not choose to fear the Lord."*

Peter put his Bible down.

He was screwed.

The despicable (his mother would have called him horrid) Sir Horace had him by the balls and knew it.

They both knew it.

He was the guide who had led himself to this point. He had no one else to blame. He alone had chosen the direction and he alone now had to live with the consequences. It had never been a question of fearing or not fearing the Lord—although it might have been a question of following or not following his parents' advice.

He had never hated knowledge, but had always wanted to, insisted on interpreting it in his own way—probably to suit his own needs or biases.

Now he was where he was.

He could no longer be sure it was better than jail.

But it was what it was.

He had been infuriated by Sir Horace's harangue. His mind had flared, and his heart had fumed. Yet, he knew he could do nothing.

He could do nothing about Sir Horace nor the old man's hold over him. Nonetheless, he could do something about his life. Regardless of Sir Horace's proclamations, Peter did have his own life. Sir Horace knew amazing things about him. Sir Horace knew things Peter thought were well-kept secrets. Still, Sir Horace did not know all. He was certainly not omnipresent. Peter retained, or so he thought (so he hoped), control of his relationship with Evelynn. This was a priority. This needed to be safeguarded.

Peter's first concern was to make sure things were in good shape with Evelynn. He had lied, telling her Sir Horace was not in their lives. The elderly and execrable creature was, obviously, very much so. All the same, this was not the time to correct the lie—to tell the whole story of Sir Horace and his outrageous crew.

Peter was sure he could balance the two forces simultaneously—especially since they overlapped. Sir Horace wanted him to make regular trips to Pangani and he wanted to see as much as possible of Evelynn. Synergy—it was partially odious, but nonetheless a symbiosis.

Within three weeks of his ignoble leave-taking, word came from the repulsive reprobate through Mr. Hong that there was a consignment for Pangani. The items in question were already loaded into Peter's company car, a long-wheelbase Land Rover. Evelynn was in the field, but Peter was able to leave word at her office that he, unexpectedly, had work in Pangani and would be there the next evening.

Symbiosis.

For the umpteenth time, a new normal seeped into Evelynn and Peter's lives. She now came to Dar as often as weekly if Peter were in town. Peter then saw her in Pangani every four to six weeks.

They were happy. They enjoyed each other. Neither was ready to call what they were experiencing love. They considered themselves simply good friends.

They were friends and they were busy.

Paula's initial efforts had opened the door to a greater collaboration with EHT and MAT. Agronomists, engineers, and market specialists visited the river's farmers—these visits coordinated by Evelynn, but the farm level work covered by her agents.

Overall, the joint team working with the riverside farmers undertook a wide variety of studies to look at crop options that could be as profitable, if not more profitable than Areca nuts. The aim was more money in farmers' pockets with less risk of marketing potentially harmful products. It was a big task and a busy time.

Peter was busy, too. He had more and more materials to shuttle about the large country—his back feeling the miles he accumulated as the Land Rover bounced and shook over endless county roads. It was increasingly difficult to find time to personally follow-up on the subsequent actions to be taken at the Ministry of Public Works and the National Health Service. Others now had to take care of the minutiae and making sure the names he had harvested were satisfactorily inserted into payrolls and health programs. But he still had to provide the overall oversight—ultimately, it was on his shoulders.

He felt pressured—both from his vertebrae and the job.

In spite of all this, it was not all work and no play. Peter and Evelynn increasingly spent more time together. They took long weekends on the Kenya Coast. They climbed Kilimanjaro—Evelynn recounting her clans' history as they ascended. They even splurged and took a ten-day vacation to the Seychelles.

It was all good.

Then, in recognition of all her hard work and her efforts to really make long-term improvements in local farming systems, Evelynn was promoted. She moved higher up the totem pole, now responsible for a cluster of seven districts. She also moved physically—from Pangani to Mwanza.

This was a major displacement. Not only did it push Evelynn away from her beloved and accustomed coastal plains, but it also pushed her farther from Dar. She was now 700 miles to the northwest, on the shores of Lake Victoria. It would take her nearly twenty hours to get to Dar.

While both her parents and Peter (individually, since the young lady had still not done the introductions) applauded the overdue promotion, all were exasperated with the distance their girl now found herself from home and hearth (Peter thinking his burning heart provided the glow of a hearth).

In truth, Evelynn was, in many ways, as exasperated as her home team. She welcomed the advancement, could well use the additional salary, and was delighted that she (as a mixed-race female) was able to climb the civil service stairway with relatively few impediments. However, her real professional pleasures were in the field. She enjoyed feeling the raw earth beneath her feet. She relished talking with farmers who always knew so much more than she did. Rain or heat, mud or dust, she was at her best when she was out of the office and on the farm. Now it was office, office, office.

But it was what it was.

It was just impractical for Evelynn to keep making frequent treks to Dar—the distance was too far. While she still made the Herculean effort to see her parents at least once every three months, she now relied on Peter to use his imagination and his good office to figure out how the two of them would stay together.

Peter gladly accepted the task. It took a good chunk of manipulation, but he managed.

Peter kept his two-bedroom flat in Kinondoni paid by Equatorial Management. At the same time, he proposed to Mr. Hong that, given the amount of time he was on the road, that this company investment would be better used if it were spread over more folks. In short, he proposed that instead of being his personal residence, it be a kind of guest house. After all, Equatorial Management had a lot of visitors and one of the bedrooms could comfortably accommodate these transients. Given the price of hotel rooms in the city, this would help the company by providing accommodation closer to the office. If this was agreeable (it was), moreover, Equatorial Management should then rent a small economy flat for him in Mwanza so that he would not have to spend so much time on the road but would have a base in the west of the country—a base were they could even store more of his cargo rather than taking it up-country one Land Rover load at a time.

Peter had never told Mr. Hong about Evelynn. He had never taken Evelynn to his office nor made any effort to introduce her to his colleagues. Even so, he knew painfully that that old fart Barthley knew all too well of his sweetheart—although he had no indications the old bastard had told Hong. Then again, why not?

What did it matter? He spun his proposal.

Whether to placate Peter or because it seemed to make sense, Mr. Hong bought into Peter's suggestions and soon he had a very barebones flat in Mwanza that he could share with Evelynn on his now increasingly regular visits west.

Everything seemed back in order. Appearances can be deceiving. Nonetheless, Evelynn and Peter were once again rocked by the breeze of complacency. If Peter's father had been around, he might have cautioned his son to dig out his Bible and read *Jeremiah* 6:14—"*They dress the wound of my people as though it were not serious. 'Peace, peace,' they say, when there is no peace.*"

It had now been months and months since Sir Horace had made his unwelcome appearance. Peter's assignments had been tweaked but remained basically the same. Then, the specter reappeared.

Peter was in Iringa—about halfway between Dar and the northern end of Lake Malawi—a town of roughly 100,000 in the highlands of the Ruaha Valley that had been a German military center during the colonial period. While a good-sized and well-kitted-out community, it was a long way away from most places.

Peter was, furthermore, staying at his favorite place, right next door to Ruaha National Park, at the Mabbataa Makkali Luxury Tented Camp— fifty miles (one and a half hours) from Iringa town. Yet here Sir Horace emerged from the flock of Safari-goers. He blended in well with shorts over spindly legs and an olive-drab sweater against the cool temperatures of the high altitude.

Peter was enjoying a stout G&T with fresh home-grown limes when he felt a hand on his shoulder. He had to stifle a laugh as he turned to see his master, thinking the only thing lacking for the old man to be part of Richard Francis Burton's excursions in the 1800s was the pith helmet.

"So, kid," Sir Horace said, kind of gurgling, "how's it?"

Not wanting to reward the devious elder with any sign of surprise at his presence in the Ruaha Valley, Peter simply replied, "OK, how about you?"

"Could be better."

Peter did not take the bait. There was no reply.

"See you're still shagging that wretch. Haven't got enough yet, huh?"

Still no reaction.

"Boy, you can clam up as much as you like, but I've warned you. You know the risks. So far, I've kept my distance because, though uncalled for from my seat, your hormonal dalliances have, up to now, not rocked my boat."

Nothing from the other side.

"Honestly, son, boys, girls, or sheep—I flat don't give a shit what you shag as long as my business stays my business and does good business."

Silence.

"I'm not, hear me, NOT saying, 'so far so good.' If you'd done as I'd advised and dumped that bitch on the rubbish heap, then it'd be so far so good. You're still playing with fire and my fatherly advice is that you're likely to get your fingers burned."

Peter malevolently stared at his fingertips.

"I shouldn't have to repeat myself. You're a big boy. And you're my big boy. Just do as you're told."

A sullen Peter only continued to stare at his hands.

"OK, youngster, my youngster, I'm not going to take up your time here at this lovely lodge with these delectable G&Ts and all the equally delectable tourists—boys and girls—with whom to talk business. When you're back in Dar, you'll find that your assignment has changed some. I trust this won't upset your apple cart too much—I know where there's a will there's a way and your willy is always looking for a way. Oh heavens, please excuse my vulgarity—so unexpected from an apparent blueblood such as myself (bowing theatrically). Such language obviously unaccustomed to a chivalrous man of my position—a most chivalrous man, and a cockney lad from Clerkenwell to boot (he added with a toothy smile—a snicker really)."

The old man's hand squeezed Peter's shoulder with surprising and painful force. Then it was gone. When just a step away from Peter's bar stool, Sir Horace, as always felt compelled to turn and repeat, "Don't fuck up."

Then he was gone, absorbed into the khaki-clad throng that had just exited from the dining room where the tourists were fed *en masse* like dairy cows going back to the barn.

∾

Peter spent a few days longer than necessary at the lodge. He was troubled. He was obviously potentially in trouble, perpetually it seemed, with Sir Horace and his gang. This was worrisome. Yet, this was, by now, a given. This was a constant battle to try and lead some semblance of his own life while still being the marionette of powerful forces that truly held his fortunes in the palm of their hands.

He surmised, indeed, he believed, that he was not under their microscope as much as they tried to let on. It simply wasn't practical. It probably wasn't possible. But this was only a question of degrees. If they knew sixty or eighty percent of his goings-on, it didn't make much difference. He wasn't free—not at all.

He wanted to tell all to Evelynn. He wanted to tear it all open. Let the two of them see what best to do. He wanted to, yet he knew he could not. They, he and Evelynn, had started their relationship based on his lies. Sadly, their continued existence as a couple, to him, seemed based on these same lies—their connection sadly balanced delicately on these fabrications.

Were he to tell all, she would almost certainly say she understood. She would offer to help. As clever as she was, she probably could help—a great deal. They might just get through this dreadful conundrum where he had unknowingly (but he knew he should have known) exchanged one prison for another. However, they would come out on the other side with Evelynn knowing her relationship was based on lies. Once the scandalous situation within which Peter had found himself was settled (if it really could be), once the high-octane efforts of salvation were one and done, his dear Evelynn would most certainly look back over their bond, see it as built on falsehoods, decide this was no way to establish a life-long rapport that required confidence and honesty. The truth would doom him. The old fart was terribly correct—Peter was owned by these foul people and had little recourse.

This was his fight.

He need not, should not bring Evelynn into the melee.

Peter still had more stops. The endpoint on this tournée was Mbeya, about equidistant from Lakes Rukwa and Malawi and over 200 miles southwest of Iringa. Once he had disposed of all his gifts and plucked all his names, his now empty Land Rover rattled and banged even more over the 500-mile and sixteen-hour trip back to Dar.

All told, it had turned out to be a complicated and long journey. He took a (company-paid) day of rest (but not, as his father might have wished, a Sabbath; a day of rest and worshiping and reflection) before mustering the energy to see Mr. Hong.

Once seated (uncomfortably) in front of one of his (too) many bosses, Mr. Hong offered him a cup of green tea from the apparently bottomless pot that was always by his side. As the two sipped the bitter brew, Mr. Hong eyed Peter closely—almost as though it was the first time the two had met.

Putting his nearly empty cup on its saucer, Mr. Hong broke the silence, "So, Peter, how was the trip—productive I hope?"

"It was fine, Sir. Managed to do what I had planned to do. I gave all that I picked-up to Regina when I came in this morning."

"Wonderful, son. We always count on you."

Peter just nodded.

"Heard you ran into our old friend in the South (it was not a question). He'd passed through here a while ago and we'd had a chance to update our program. Guess he must have told you?"

Another nod.

"Well, first let me say, you've been doing a good job—and I told Sir Horace so. He seemed preoccupied about your private life, but I told him you did what needed to be done. I have no complaints."

This solicited a halfhearted smile and a soft, "Thank you."

"No thanks. It's true. You're doing fine. The old gentleman seemed very concerned, but I think I was able to allay his worries. Between us, I don't think he likes women—it's just not his thing."

A nod and a subconscious recognition that, as expected, his immediate supervisor had known, and undoubtedly still knew a lot more than he let on.

"Anyway." Mr. Hong seemed to be tiring of circular discussions. "The big bosses have decided we need to expand—our contribution, according to them, to the greater good has not been good enough. They want us to do more—of course, so they can get more. But, alas, I am but a small cog."

A nod.

"Straight to it then. It's been decided that we need to grow. This means widening our scope and our staff. A new guy is arriving to do what you've been doing. You're now the show pony to show our new swelling activities—like it or not. THEY have spoken."

Nothing.

"Let me get to the good part first. Your replacement will be arriving this week. We'll take care, here in the office, of his briefing. You don't need to bother yourself. In fact, it's been arranged that you take three weeks off to rest and get ready for your new assignment.

"About the new job. First, it's here in Dar. You'll stay in your flat—it's going back to more of a residence as opposed to a guesthouse. I don't know what will happen in Mwanza—that'll depend on how your replacement works out. But you'll be back alone in your cozy flat . . . no more intrusions . . . pretty nice, huh?"

"Swell," Peter gave a muffled reply.

"Now, the job. Like I said, it's here. It's mostly dealing with transit agents and folks in the port. The story is that 'the company'—whatever that is—is investing in large-scale farming in Malawi and Mozambique—mostly maize. They'll be bringing their produce by road to Dar to consolidate and for forwarding to their clients in Europe and elsewhere.

"Boy, this is a coat-n'-tie job. While you're off resting up or doing whatever it is you're going to be doing (he winked), you need to see our tailor and get some proper clothes. I've asked Alfred to draw out half a million for you to do some careful shopping. It'll help everyone out if you're a little more dapper. Jeans and sneakers are fine for the village, but here you're now top-drawer. You're the show pony.

"Be off now. When you're back, we'll go into the details of your new job."

A handshake, an open door, and Peter was heading back to his flat, unsure of what lay in store.

Peter spent a restless day questioning his next steps. In the end, it was as clear as it always had been that he had one good move: go see Evelynn.

He'd already agreed with himself that he could not tell her all the sordid particulars of his work and employer or employers. But this history was now, as important as it was, background to their present situation.

They needed to look at now-now—leaving the past in its own unopened box (at least for the moment, he reassured himself).

They were now a long distance apart and he no longer had the means through his work to make regular visits. Was their bond strong enough to withstand extended periods of separation?

Strong or not, was this what they each wanted?

They now needed to assess their positions (he smiled to himself at the possible *double entendre*). They needed to do this together (another smile, another *double entendre*).

Peter had no car. He'd always used the office's Land Rover (this had been a very flexible arrangement).

He called Evelynn's office and left word he was coming by train.

The Tanzania Railways Corporation dated back to the German period when, in 1905, the main line west, the *Mittellandbahn*, started with typical Teutonic ardor; the rails reaching Kigoma on the shores of Lake Tanganyika in 1914. The 300-plus mile northward branch from Kigoma to Mwanza was overseen by the British—completed in 1928.

Over the years, rail travel had improved—but only so much.

Still, this was a logical, if arduous choice of conveyance. With a high degree of unreliability and an amazingly low top speed, the trip to Mwanza took the major part of four days—Tuesday to Friday sitting on a train—what a way to spend your vacation (or furlough).

The Mwanza urban and peri-urban areas, accommodating nearly two million inhabitants along a squiggly shoreline of Lake Victoria that followed Mwanza Gulf, were Evelynn's new realm. She had foregone the offered public housing in favor of a personal monthly indemnity for private accommodation. She rented a lovely home on Capri Point between the yacht club and Hotel Tilapia. With Peter's unheralded arrival she, as the regional supervisor, had approved her own request for five days leave—unsure really how long Peter was staying nor why he had come in such a seemingly haphazard way.

The bother of public transportation aside, Evelynn was delighted to see Peter. The two spent an exhausting weekend in each other's embrace before Peter even dared broach the topic of his new, but still unclear, assignment.

Monday morning, the spent lovers enjoyed big mugs of Kigoma coffee, sitting in lounge chairs on Evelynn's veranda, looking across the Gulf at the Port of Mwanza, as Peter hemmed-and-hawed about his new job. He didn't have much to say other than he would no longer be able to regularly cycle through Mwanza while on the job.

He explained about Equatorial Management's plans to expand. He mentioned that he was being replaced and that his boss had nothing but good things to say about the job he had done. He had, in fact, done so well that they were now moving him up to a more responsible position that dealt much more closely with their major economic partners. It was, as his boss had pointed out, a coat-'n-tie job—the office even paying for the coat and tie.

He did not mention Sir Horace. As far as Evelynn still knew, the odious old man was just a colleague—nearly a random acquaintance. It was not the time, as he had already convinced himself, to delve into his more shadowy relationships. Moreover, while he surmised that the obnoxious Sir Horace had had a big role in his move to a new job, the aged bastard seemingly ready to do almost anything to throw up roadblocks between Evelynn and himself, there was no proof that these changes were totally orchestrated by his elderly overlord. He knew from experience his masters were subscribers to the tactics of keeping all their targets moving and off-balance—no one stayed too long anywhere. Even without Sir Horace's meddling, it was highly probable that he would have had to move on to something different. At least it was a different job and not, as last time, a different country.

With an ample degree of time-honed stoicism, Evelynn understood all too well that it was what it was. As always, they had the choice to carry on or to shut things off. They chose the former.

They spent the next four days enjoying each other's company and wracking their brains as to how they would revise their schedules to be able to still see each other on a normal basis—whatever "normal" was—they had no clue.

The only choice they could come up with was to meet at least once a month somewhere accessible from both Mwanza and Dar. The best options were either Singida or Dodoma. The first was a regional capital of over 100,000 residents while the second was ostensibly (since 1973) the national capital approaching half a million inhabitants albeit the effective seat of government and power remained in Dar. Both cities were approximately equidistant from their home bases—travels (not by train) that could realistically be accomplished and still leave enough quality weekend time to take pleasure in each other.

The remedial plan had been born if not inaugurated.

It was time to use their remaining hours ensuring they were fully satiated in preparation for a possible extended period of abstinence.

They made good use of their time.

Friday afternoon they had taken a stroll, ending up at the Mwanza Point Bar near the Lake Ferry Terminal. As they savored their second pint, they met Joe Thompson.

Chapter Thirteen

A Robin Hood

Lesson or omen

Joe Thompson had wandered into the Mwanza Point Bar looking for information. He heard the American twang in Peter's voice (as much as Peter tried to disguise it and cover it with the English-English of his studies).

"Excuse me," he politely interjected, as he approached Peter and Evelynn's table, "I wonder if you might help?"

"Of course," they both answered in unison.

"Honestly, I heard the gentleman's American accent and thought maybe my fellow Yank would be a good advisor."

"Happy to help, if I can," Peter replied coolly, but in his best American tones—choosing not to take exception to the, from Peter's viewpoint, querier's likely blatant conclusion that Evelynn was NOT an American. Everyone always jumped to conclusions, especially when skin color was involved—and so it seemed had the outsider, the scrutinizer himself ancestrally closer to Evelynn than he.

From all appearances, totally unaware of any potential boorishness, a smiling Joe Thompson unraveled his tale. "I'm hoping to take the ferry to Bukoba but hear that it's been broken-down of late. Don't want to spend all my time waiting for something that's not coming, huh?"

"Well." Evelynn pleasantly picked up the lead (also oblivious, or choosing to seem so, to any discourtesy), "first let me do what this Dumbo didn't, and make the introductions. I'm Evelynn and he's Peter.

I'm the one who actually lives here, so I may be the best to answer your question."

"Excellent." Joe's smile grew to cover much of his lower face, appearing to melt into his thick week-old beard growth, "I'm Joe, Joe Thompson from Detroit. I'm just mucking about these parts but have all too often sat waiting for something that never came. So, I learned to overcome my gender's reported abhorrence of asking questions and try to learn as much upfront as possible.

"The guys at the terminal said the Bukoba ferry has been down for some time but some of them thought they'd heard it was back up and running. Figured I'd best check."

"No problem," Evelynn coolly stated as she called to the barman—she obviously a known client. When the publician, Evelynn called him Prosper, came over, Evelynn passed on Joe's query. Prosper then left to confer with some folks at the bar, who in turn carried their commission to the outside world.

As they waited for news of the Bukoba Ferry, at Evelynn's insistence, Joe shared a welcome beer and his story. The pair of Mwanza regulars found the tale both riveting and touching—possibly even foreboding.

The newcomer, like a troubadour of old, unfolded his tale with ease and no small amount of drama, even without lyrics.

He was the son of an auto worker, Paul Thompson. He was a son of Detroit. His grandfather had come north from Dixons Mills, Alabama, in Marengo County, where he, as his father before him, worked in a gristmill dating back to the 1820s.

Grandfather, as many coming from the South, settled (or was settled) in the segregated Black Bottom neighborhood of the municipality that came to be called "The Big D" or "Motor City." In the 60s, when Joe was just a kid, his family, still living in his grandfather's house, was forced to move by what was called "urban renewal." His dad said this was just the white folk taking what they saw as valuable property and grabbing it for their own benefit.

Whatever—probably was just another rip-off. Anyway, the family moved to the North End neighborhood. This was only a few miles from the Fisher Body Plant 21 where Paul worked—less than a ten-minute commute if you had a car, more than half an hour by bus, if like Paul, you took public transport.

Joe attended Northern High School. The school, with a majority minority student body, had been flagged as a troubled institution for years. Just before Joe's arrival, students had walked out to protest the poor quality of education when compared to schools in white areas of the city. Although the school had produced such products as Aretha Franklin and Smokey Robinson, Joe never felt he would be an alumnus of prominence—he felt he'd be lucky to even graduate.

School was a mess. There were gangs. There were drugs. There were unbridled hormones. And there was schoolwork to boot. There was also a smorgasbord of high school sports and (sanctioned) extracurricular activities.

Somehow Joe survived.

He was agnostic about sports and not a joiner—be it a gang or Photo Club. He also managed to, in spite of his opposing personal interests, plug away at the always irritating schoolwork to be able to graduate just a little below the middle of his class.

However, his major attribute was that he looked much older than his teen age. While he himself was a moderate drinker, he was able (generally) to buy a six-pack without getting carded. This turned out to be a major boon. It endeared him to a wide swath of the booze-swilling student body, allowing him to iron-out peer pressure and other forces that often diverted teens into the ditch. It also apparently made him "a catch" for the girls.

He always had a date, he was left alone by the gangbangers, and he could get a beer when he wanted one. What more could one ask?

He just wasn't too into the books.

The whole school thing seemed like a major waste of time. He had better things to do.

But, ultimately, it was all over, and he found himself, like so many minority youths, working at a minimum wage job and happy to have a job to go to. His inauspicious position was cleaning up for a company, Upper Midwest, that dealt with warehousing in-transit food—fresh, frozen, and canned foods. The warehouse was located across from the GM plant in Warren. Like his dad, from the North End family home, he could have made it to work in less than half an hour if he had had a car. It took him three times as long by public conveyance.

It was hard work. It was a hard life. It was a dangerous life. There was widespread substance abuse. There was rampant racism. There was growing, all too often lethal, violence in poorer neighborhoods—now called ghettos by no small number of outside observers. There was even HIV greeting many adolescents. Numerous young African American men from his world were either dead or in prison before they were thirty-five.

Somehow Joe survived.

While Evelynn and Peter attentively followed Joe's story, they realized their erstwhile balladeer, minus the melody, was not a grandstander—far from it. As he regaled them in his past, his focus was the where's and somewhat the how's. There was little about the who's and even less about himself. In spite of this, what might be called self-effacing reticence, it was clear to both of them that their guest possessed an extremely keen mind and an acute intellect.

As Peter was to remark later, "He was one smart cookie."

Evelynn and Peter knew there was a story within the story. Still, accepting that this inner work would likely not expose itself—at least not at this sitting—they continued to concentrate on Joe's tale.

Joe continued.

Upper Midwest was big. They reported their warehouse complex to have an interior surface area of over 300,000 square feet—that was nearly seven acres under their roof. Joe felt he needed roller skates to get around.

Get around he did, even without roller skates.

The huge distribution center had specialized areas to handle any and all foodstuffs. Joe would come early or stay late just to amble about, looking high and low, seeing eatables he had never imagined. Everything was there.

After Joe had taken in the grandness of his space—both in terms of sheer size and in terms of spectacular inventory—his mind slowly began to put on different filters as he looked about his job site. There was a lot more here than clean up.

He began to appreciate that Upper Midwest serviced a wide spectrum of clients. There were crates and crates of candy bars, chips, and bottled spaghetti sauce for big box-store customers. There were canned vegetables along with fresh produce for small- to medium-scale grocers as far away as South Dakota. And, what he hadn't noticed at first, there was a whole market basket of high-end items destined to up-scale bodegas and restaurants. There was Russian caviar. There were French truffles.

There were hermetically packaged holiday sweets from Germany. There were boxes and boxes of very costly food items. There was *casse-croûte* from France, endive from Belgium, smoked bush meat from South Africa, Rambutan fruits from Thailand, and seasoned olives from Tunisia. There was everything—everything for the gastronome's plate.

Joe dug a little deeper. These warehoused gourmet foods were really, really expensive. It was a treasure trove fit for a king's larder.

Joe's mind began to use different filters.

Here was a treasure in front of his eyes as he was shackled (or so it felt) to a broom.

Joe took a number of shortcuts as he described the evolution of the processes that ultimately moved him from floor sweeper to entrepreneur. He undoubtedly intentionally left out several of the critical steps that allowed him to (legally or not) make this transition.

Nevertheless, as he summarized, with the help of a bevy of other carefully selected disillusioned employees, he managed to knit together a very effective team that moved about the giant facility doing more their own business than Upper Midwest's. In off hours, in secluded corners and shadowy workstations, they were able to switch foods. For most of the expensive stuff, there was a low-cost cousin—white mushrooms for truffles, asparagus for endive, cherries for Rambutan. Once one knew the real lay of the land, it was easy. Boxes could be changed. Labels could be changed. Waybills could be changed. With a little imagination, soon the high-end inventory was more suitable for a ghetto soup kitchen. Then, to make up for the changes, Joe and his group added items they had purchased at several local discount groceries. They would then take the delicacies they had harvested and sell these directly to their own epicurean buyers across the Midwest.

Joe and his guys became masters at the switch—magicians of the marketplace.

Surprisingly, there were few repercussions even when the switches had been discovered. Of course, the established Upper Midwest contractors did not know there had been a switch. When the wrong product was received, they complained to the warehouse. Warehouse management responded and reacted in a standard fashion. Mislabeling and human error were not all that uncommon. These were simple mistakes. The items would be replaced conforming to the original order and in line with their contractual obligations.

In fact, Upper Midwest had an insurance policy that assisted them with such concerns, so they were not out of pocket for any significant sums.

Joe and his group, additionally, did not hit the same customer very often. Thus, random mistakes seemed a plausible excuse. No one went looking in the corners or shadows of the warehouse for an explanation.

Joe and his band then expanded from Upper Midwest.

They diversified from foods.

They began using their capital reserves to buy farm implements from around the region. With some steam cleaning and thick coats of good quality paint, these machines soon looked new enough to fetch a much higher price—even if the new owner was soon dissatisfied with his proud new tractor and came looking for the scammers who had now vanished in the wind.

Joe's boys also targeted bottled water. They ordered some fancy bottles, filled them from the tap, and sold them as imported spring water from Switzerland—the dew of the Alps. They made a bundle.

It was a thriving, if illicit, business.

Then Joe tried a new filter.

He looked beyond US borders.

As he studied the landscape, he found there were tons and tons of food aid sent overseas by the government and civil organizations. Yet, as could be easily imagined by the pragmatist, these goods were not tightly controlled—often intentionally. There was a lot of leakage.

The ultimate suppliers, whether public or private, were in the game of spending money. Tomorrow's budget depended on spending today's allocation—and spending it fast. This often led to overpaying for items— sometimes to enable kickbacks, but frequently just because everyone was in hurry.There was a large margin of error. Haste (as Joe's mother had often told him) made waste, and there was a lot of waste in the system— waste for one being profits for another.

This was all at the origin.

At the destination, food aid channels were even more chaotic. There was theft. There were aid items used as *Bakschisch*. There were items lost to floods, tornados, vehicle accidents, and road-side bombs. It was a mess. It was a mess where Joe saw an opportunity.

Without further belaboring the point, Joe underscored that he had managed to metamorphose from a near high school dropout into a wealthy international merchandiser—sadly, and he didn't dwell on this, also an international actor sought by authorities in several countries.

His new Mwanza colleagues should have no concerns; however, he was on good terms with all in Tanzania and across East Africa—most of his dabbling in the aid market having taken place in West and Central Africa. With a wink, he said he certainly was not the *bien venue* any longer in Congo.

Joe took a gulp of the sweating beer Evelynn put in front of him and continued.

"We all did pretty well with our sleight of hand. As we were all kids from The Big D, we decided we needed to payback part of our good luck. We took fifty-one percent of our profits, giving this to local community organizations to help with youth centers, hospices, homes for seniors, clinics, and the like. Over the years, these endowments turned out to be quite a pretty penny.

"Over these same years, our operation has recast itself. We're no longer insider buccaneers in Upper Midwest. We pretty much shaped ourselves into a diverse black-market supplier. We don't get involved in drugs or arms. We definitely do not engage in human trafficking. We tend to focus on food and agriculture-related matters but are open to most anything that does not cross our red lines.

"For a bunch of kids from the streets, we've become pretty sophisticated. We established a company in Luxembourg that funnels money to a couple of NGOs in the States from where the money can transparently move to the organizations we support in Detroit. It's kinda neat!"

Joe took another big swallow of beer.

"Wow," Peter offered, "you're a real Robin Hood!"

"Not sure," Joe parried, "you know it well, like everybody around here, you just do what you have to do."

Evelynn smiled.

Peter returned the serve. "OK, I agree. We all have our challenges— some a whole lot worse than others. Like the man said, 'Life ain't fair.' But still and all, you've managed a pretty unprecedented thing—or so it seems to me. Tempting the system to truck you off to jail while you manage to make a lot of change for yourself and your group, all the while getting support back home to those the most in need. Pretty remarkable."

"Well, sir," (Peter raised his head to object to the 'sir,' but then thought otherwise) Joe said, seemingly to try to wrap things up, "to me it's all a roll of the dice. So many kids from my high school are now dead, behind bars, or in really bad shape. I certainly was no better a student than they. My family wasn't all that different from theirs. My home wasn't all that different from theirs. Somehow the gods smiled on me when, at the same time, they smiled on far too few in the North End. The luck of the draw."

Evelynn looked up and interjected, "Now Joe, we'll see if your luck holds. Here comes Prosper with news of the ferry."

It turned out the Bukoba Ferry was running, the next departure in just three-quarters of an hour.

Joe bid his small audience goodbye and headed to the terminal to get a ticket. He was a long way from Detroit.

As Joe left the Mwanza Point Bar, Peter had a flashback, as so often but still so surprisingly, to his father's preachings: *Genesis* 12:1-3—*"The Lord had said to Abram, 'Go from your country, your people and your father's household to the land I will show you. I will make you into a great nation, and I will bless you; I will make your name great, and you will be a blessing. I will bless those who bless you, and whoever curses you I will curse; and all peoples on earth will be blessed through you.'"*

Peter knew his father had hoped to forge a great nation of follow-ers—alas, ending up as a drowned corpse—fish food. He imagined Joe had no such religious ambitions. The man from Detroit, who had indeed also left his home and family, Peter's latest model for humankind, seemed to have no lofty expectations. He certainly didn't seem as one who would see the world bathed in blessings due to his efforts. Still, he seemed to be blessed himself somehow—protected somehow. And, somehow, he seemed to be doing real good deeds—while at the same time helping himself (some would say, to others' wealth).

As Joe evaporated into the blaring midday sun that soaked the bar's entrance, Evelynn looked seriously at Peter. "Do we have the luck of the draw?"

Peter had to jerk himself back from Abram and rerun Evelynn's question before he could feel grounded enough to engage. "Who knows, we've done OK so far—haven't we?"

"Peter, think about it. We've been like a water drop on a hot griddle. We've been jumping up and down; jumping into each other's arms, jumping into bed, jumping on top of one another. We've been jumping about. We've loved, we've laughed, we've enjoyed. We've never planned."

Peter felt the weight close in. There was too much behind the curtains—curtains that could not be drawn. But there was all too much to lose. She was special. They were special. He needed to find an elixir to get them back into each other's arms—back into bed. It was a long shot.

"*Chérie*," he started tentatively, "we really have done OK. You know all too well—it's not been easy. Both of us are moving targets. Still, we have managed to get this far—still jumping on top of each other not all that infrequently. We've done OK so far."

"So far! How far is 'so far?' We've been floating with the tide and hoping it'll take us where we want to go. Look at Joe. He says it's the 'luck of the draw,' but see how much he's planned—how much he's organized. He was in a lot tougher straights than we've been in and he stood up, saw the system stacked against him, and found a way to do what he needed to do—not just for himself but for others—his 'guys' and all those his charity helps. If he stopped today, he's got a legacy. What's ours?"

"Yeah, I ain't got much—you're right. But look at you. Look at all the farmers you help. Look at how you did such great work getting dangerous stuff off the market. Look how you've rocketed ahead—you, too, having faced tough straights and sometimes a system the seemed set against you."

"Don't flatter me . . ."

"It's the truth."

"Maybe. But it's not the point. Even if I've done some things, it's us that I'm talking about. What have we done? What will we do?"

"Sure. You're right. If I was a normal guy we'd sit down now-now and lay out our life together—day by day if we wanted. But I'm not that guy. I'm sorry. I'm still the same guy you first met in the bar with Paula, but I'm not THAT guy who can sit down a look ahead with confidence. You know. My job's been changed—right now as we speak, it's changed, and I don't even know all the details. What should I do? Should I quit and come here to serve beers at the Mwanza Point Bar? Should I become a ferryman to Bukoba? Should I write to Paula and ask her for a job? *Chérie*, I am what I am and the job I have is the job I have. It is what it is. Whether or not I'm thrilled with these circumstances, there isn't a lot I can do unless you've got some magic fix?"

"Alright Peter. I do know the situation. I know reality's a bitch. But I also know we can't keep going like this. If we can't sit down today, when can we? Sometime, somewhere, somehow, we need to take a clear look at tomorrow and the tomorrow after tomorrow. We have to."

"I agree."

"So?"

"So, I agree, and I know we have to do some better planning. Let me get my feet on the ground with my new assignment and then we we'll find the sometimes, the somewheres, and the somehows to sit down and take that look—that passionless look—at tomorrow."

"Humm. OK."

This was followed by a warm smile and squeeze of the hand.

They went back to Evelynn's and jumped into bed.

After the weekend, Peter took the long train trip back to Dar. He thought again of Abram. Did he want greatness? He thought not. He wanted stability. He wanted peace. He wanted Evelynn.

He was already missing her tender gaze. They had agreed to meet in Singida in ten weeks, giving him ample time to get used to his new work. But this would be a long haul. Many a time, twenty-four hours was a long time to be separated from his *Chérie*—ten weeks was a terribly long haul. He remembered from his astronomy class, on a good day, he could almost make it halfway to Mars in ten weeks—but he couldn't get to Mwanza.

Feeling as though he was walking in the haze of illness as he had in Bouar, Peter warily made his way back to the offices of Equatorial Management and to a seat in front of Mr. Hong to hear his destiny. Like a battery-operated toy puppy, he had come for Mr. Hong to put in a fresh battery, give him a push, and send him in a new direction.

After all the build-up, it was rather anticlimactic. Other than being locked down in Dar and lassoed into a coat and tie, the job was pretty much as described when he was first advised of the (mandatory) change.

Equatorial Management's partners were engaged in considerable international trade, as Mr. Hong explained. Much of this had to do with buying and exporting agricultural products—both processed and unprocessed—to ports around the world. The trick, of course, with food-stuffs, was to move fast. Things could spoil—especially in the roasting heat of Dar. If containers—everything was containerized—didn't move quickly, there were large losses—losses the bosses did not accept.

The job was essentially to flag containers coming into the port by lorry and then do the needful so that these containers were placed on ships as quickly as humanly possible. Dar was seen by Equatorial Management and its colleagues as a friendly port: people operated under the principal, "You help me, I'll help you."

Help took many forms and needed to be targeted to specific individuals who could do the most to quicken the normally painfully slow and needlessly complex steps of getting merchandise into and out of the port.

Peter needed to learn what to do, with whom to do it, and when to do it. His not inconsequential experience in facilitation notwithstanding, it was a steep learning curve.

He would actually have a desk in the Equatorial Management offices, and indeed was expected to report to the office every morning at eight o'clock sharp. But that was about all Mr. Hong hoped to see of his young American employee. Once he'd picked up the day's dossiers and got the keys for a company Corolla, he was expected to be out of the office—generally in and around the port.

For the first few weeks, Hong wanted Peter to work with Darweshi. This new co-worker had been an Equatorial Management expeditor (Peter had no idea how many there were) in the port of Dar for twenty years. He was retiring. Peter was not exactly taking over his job, but Peter would largely be dealing with the same people with whom Darweshi worked. Hong, therefore, wanted Darweshi to build strong links between the American and all his Dar port contacts before he left the company and left the city to become a pensioner in his home village of Gwara, not far from Lake Natron.

Hong wanted Peter, in spite of his position as an outsider, to be able to quickly ingrain himself into the local environment such that everyone thought of him as a fixture—someone who'd been around a long time. Darweshi's charge was to lay this foundation. Then, after his mentor had departed, Hong wanted Peter to give his new best friends (the Darweshi entourage) generous gifts for the upcoming holiday of Saba Saba.

Hong needed Peter to be an unremarkable but very effective port agent. And he was in a hurry.

Darweshi proved to be a great guy. He readily accepted Peter as a *rafiki* (friend in Ki-Swahili). He openly and candidly shared his port experiences and contacts. It seemed in no time at all Peter was (for better or worse) acknowledged as one of the endless streams of agents, facilitators, and scalawags that seemed to flow through the port's portals.

After six weeks with Darweshi, and after Saba Saba, Peter felt ready for his new job and ready to soon (for all too short a period) jump ship for a few days to go west to Singida and hug Evelynn. He was ready to suck in her very essence—hoping it would be the potion to find not only love but also the wider stability and peace they both sought so hungrily.

Back in the heat and humidity of the port after the cool freshness of the West and the equally cool freshness of Evelynn's lustrous skin, Peter felt he was entering an oven when he exited his air conditioned Corolla the first day back on the job—back on the job alone, without Darweshi's reassuring hand on his shoulder. It was all up to him now.

That morning as he'd picked up the files and the car keys, Mr. Hong, with a beaming smile, reminded him (as if he needed reminding) that he now oversaw millions of dollars of merchandise. No slip-ups were allowed.

The pressures aside—and, there were many: the work, the heat, and the separation from Evelynn—Peter honestly felt he was up to the assignment. All the time he had spent bouncing about the country, visiting villages, talking with headmen and farmers, dealing with the unknown—all this had given him both much improved people skills and significantly improved self-confidence (hopefully not an overdose of the latter).

In fact, if he was honest, the conditions more than the work proved most challenging. It was not the physical environment; not the searing temperatures nor shirt-soaking humidity. It was not even peeling back the layers that covered all the possibly shady actions that were taking place under Peter's perview. It was the operational environment—the operational culture. This was the first time he had had an eight-to-five, put-on-a-tie job. He didn't find it appealing.

Being jostled for hours and days at a time as he zigzagged across the hinterland was probably less professionally enriching than trying to see how he could deal with each and every arriving container as though it were a labyrinth and he alone had to find the way through. Yet, when he was jolted about the Land Rover, swallowing dust and sloshing through mud, he was doing it on his own time. No one was looking at him—he had no clock to punch. He wasn't much of a clock puncher.

He had never lived a life of routine. He had always managed to structure each day as he wished. Now he got up at six-thirty, after breakfast and a quick walk, he got to the office at eight sharp. By eight-thirty on most days he was sitting in rush hour traffic trying to make headway to the port. It could even take several hours before he exited the Corolla, leaving his sport coat in the back seat and rolling up his sleeves, very much in contravention of the dress code Mr. Hong had suggested (Peter thought of it as a tiny act of defiance).

He would then spend whatever time was necessary to locate the shipments highlighted for the day's efforts and then reach out to the individuals involved, giving them immediately a small stipend for a beer after work, and ensuring them that there was more to come at the end of the month.

So far, it all worked smoothly. He had the confidence of his contacts and his contacts had the means to move things through quickly. Everyone was happy. Everyone except Peter who, although he appreciated the increased salary, was still feeling as though he was operating on a leash held by some unknown and unwanted force.

He would then recall that rather than a leash, he could be finding himself in a jail cell. Maybe things weren't all that bad.

Some days Peter would have to run his legs off, his shirt wringing wet by evening when he was still chasing a container. Other days, and there were more of these, he made his morning appearance, ticked-off all the day's tasks, and was done before lunch. Understanding that his desk at the office was basically for show, he needed to find a refuge for these out-of-the-port hours.

He found the answer at the Durban Hotel on Uhuru Street. It was a discrete distance from the port (ironically only 400 yards from the Central Police Station) so he could meet his contacts there if they needed to have private discussions or make some not-to-be-publicized transactions. It was also a place where Peter could have a cool beer (or two or three) in cool and relatively untraveled surroundings that he found to be a welcome sanctuary. He could spend up to several hours quietly sipping beer before he headed back to the tumult of the port to make a final status check before going back to the office to handover the updated files and turn in the Corolla's keys.

At the Durban retreat, Peter sensed a peacefulness. The pandemonium of the day and of his life seemed parked outside.

On one occasion, he was beginning his second beer when he was heralded by a, "Hey son."

He turned and was stunned (although he knew he shouldn't have been) to see an obviously tipsy Sir Horace, attired in a light blue Safari suit, ambling his way.

It was clear the old geezer had had more than Peter's pair of beers. He was a little unsteady on his feet, but Peter feared he was anything but unsteady in his mind. Beer or no beer, the old asshole kept control.

"Son-of-a-bitch," Sir Horace practically slurred, with a down-home Cockney accent, "who'd have thought I'd find you here. What brings you to sample the hospitality of the Durban, young son?"

"Hi," was all Peter could, or would muster, as the buzzed old-timer flowed onto the once luxurious scarlet tuck-n-roll Naugahyde seat across from his target.

"My boy." (Peter wanted to yell, '*I'm not your boy*') The aging imbiber, slouching in the deep seat, continued as though Peter had not even acknowledged his presence, "I'd have thought you'd have been out there sweating your ass off in the port doing our business—keeping the bills paid. But, indeed BUT, I find you here boozing. That should be grounds for dismissal, don't you think?"

"What's up?" Peter asked, knowing full well that neither his overlord nor the nebulous forces that controlled the whole show cared a damn about who did what as long as they got the results they wanted—the results they required.

"Drinking on company time, son. That's worrisome."

"And?"

"Well, ya know, it just ain't right. You're on the job. Not only are you not doing now-now what we pay you to do, but you're setting one helluva bad example to these poor local folks who should be seeing white guys like you as sterling examples of how to excel, not how to get drunk—that they know full well how to do, huh?"

"So?"

"I am your boss."

"I don't owe you anything. You know god damn well I do my work. You know god damn well I do my work well. I certainly don't owe you an explanation. You toss me around like I'm your personal property and you get your pound of flesh."

"Boy, you are my personal property—I've told you so many times."

"Yassa boss. OK, I'm taking a break. Fire me. Please, fire me!"

"Kid—cheeky kid, nonetheless—you've got work to do."

"Yes. And go check. Everything is fine. Everything is on target. Your stuff is coming in and going out just like you want. So, get off my back!"

"Tsk-tsk. Such cheekiness. Son, is that any way to speak to your elders? Did your parents bring you up to talk that way? You know better."

"Hump."

"No, really. You can be civil. Remember how much I've helped you. I saved you. Don't forget it!"

"Sure."

"Boy, you may be frustrated. We all get frustrated. A few good beers might help wash some of the frustration away—why I've had more than just a few enjoying the ambiance at this fine establishment. I understand why you might be here, too. But remember, you've got a job. You're the employee. I'm, so to speak, the employer—the *bosi mkuu* like they say over there in the port."

"Go check if you think I'm not doing my job."

"It's OK, son. Have another beer," Sir Horace motioned to a waiter to bring two more bottles and settled himself deeper into his seat.

There was silence. Peter finished his second beer and immediately assaulted the bottle offered by his taskmaster—a small reward, in Peter's view, for massive suffering.

The bottles seemed to quickly empty and Sir Horace ordered another round.

There was silence.

It was then startlingly broken.

"Did your mother have mementos?"

The question took Peter aback—totally unexpected—totally out of context.

Nevertheless, Peter thought back to that house next to the church in Kpando—the only home he really knew. The only home of which he had significant memories. His father had always insisted the home remain spartan. After all, they were white missionaries in Africa—as he constantly reminded them. They had not come so far to live in comfort.

They should've stayed in the US if they wanted comfort. They were doing God's work. God did not want His chores cluttered up with all sorts of unnecessary items competing for space in His home.

Her husband's attempts to enforce an ascetic lifestyle notwithstanding, Peter recalled how his mother had tried, as she called it, to "Gussy-up the place." She had several nice pieces of Kente cloth she had been given in Bole. One was a wall hanging and the other an afghan on the couch in the living room. She had a pair of rough-hewed wooden figurines she had bought at the Kpando market when they had first arrived. She had a few porcelain knickknacks that she said came from her mother. She had some framed photographs—old sepia ones of people unknown to Peter. And, as Peter recalled, most important to his mother, she had a small polished wooden chest. On special occasions, she would show the contents to her son. On other occasions, when Peter passed her bedroom unnoticed, he would catch a glimpse of her wistfully staring into the box—her eyes moist. She told him the box contained bits of jewelry and "women's things" going way back to her great-great-grandmother.

In spite of her husband's puritanical aspirations, Lynn had tried her best to make her home a home for herself and her children if not for her husband.

Alas, Peter had no idea of what had happened to these keepsakes—possibly Lydia had managed to recover them. And even if she had, who knew what they really were—what they really meant.

"Hey kid, what the fuck?"

Peter's reverie was exploded by Sir Horace's bawl.

"Uh, yeah. Yeah, she had some," he belatedly replied to the old man's surprising query.

"Of course, she did." The errant nobleman continued, seeming to ignore Peter's detachment, "everybody's got something—something that is special—something that they alone prize—whose story they alone know. It's always like that. People are like that. We're scavengers—just like the rats. We want little morsels. Maybe these little morsels are real things we touch and enjoy or maybe they're just memories—but they're ours.

"Look at me (Peter did not), I've got a lovely wardrobe—but that's not my memento—my treasure. Boy, do you know what my treasure is?"

Peter gave his *bosi mkuu* a vacuous look.

"I'll tell ya youngster. I'll tell ya now—right now. My memento is my life. How do ya like that?"

Peter stared at a spot in the corner of the room.

"My story is special. You take care. My story is special."

Peter looked at his shoes.

"You look at me and see a funny old man. Maybe I am. But I tell you, if I'm funny, I'm also rich. I'm also powerful. But that's not my story. My story is that I'm also a brother."

Peter looked like he was following an imaginary fly buzzing about the room.

"Do ya want ta know?"

Peter continued with the fly.

"Great. I'll tell ya . . ."

Then, for reasons unknown, Sir Horace told his tale:

"My older brother and I were born in Romania during the period of the Soviet Union. I was christened Horaţiu. My brother, nearly two years my senior, was named Răzvan. Our family was poor—really poor—dirt poor as buggered paupers—someth'n you'd know nothing about, I'd guess. When I was six, our parents, to their great stupefaction, had twins. There were now simply too many mouths to feed. It was a big fuck'n problem, I tell ya.

"Our parents were devout Orthodox Christians. They beseeched their priest to help, to find a way whereby they could all survive. If they went on as they were, surely some members of the family would perish. They could not feed and clothe the entire household, including an ailing grandmother.

"Somehow, with no fuck'n authority at'll from the Church nor the bloody State, the priest reached out to his confrere in Hungary who in turn contacted a confrere in Austria—these guys were everywhere. The upshot of all this networking was that two families were identified, one in the US and one in the UK, who were looking to adopt a child and were willing to adopt one of us.

"It was a terrible decision for our parents, and probably for their priest—you can't imagine, fuck'n terrible, or so they said. But nevertheless, at the age of eight I was adopted by a family in London while my brother, then almost ten, was adopted by a family in Chicago. Our lives changed completely. Regardless of how different things were, however, we stayed in contact, my brother and I. In god damn Anglophone worlds, I was now flip'n Horace and my brother was Robin. Who would believe this shit?

"In spite of our efforts to keep connected, it was a quarter of a century before we actually met face-to-face again in New York. That meeting was indelible—even a dope like you can appreciate that.

"And ya know, by the time I was thirty, I began to notice that my frick'n hair was turning white and that my frick'n skin was pale—and not due to the god damn damp and dreary English weather, either. When I made enquiries with the doctor, the best guess of the local medical establishment—geniuses with their heads up their fat arses if you ask me—was that there had been some latent albanism in our family tree and this accounted for my light complexion—often verging on rose-colored—and my white hair (now worn long in more of an ivory thatch).

"A few years later, when we met in in New York, to my total fuck'n astonishment, my brother was my mirror image: alabaster hair and coral skin. Those god damn genes were strong.

"We were, it turned out, brothers in more than genes and complexion. We seemed to see life in the same bloody way. Perhaps it was our Romanian roots, but we both knew we had to fight our way to the top. We'd both seemed to have learned that we could show no quarter—you have to be fuck'n ruthless to stay at the top of this heap of shit in which we had found ourselves.

"My brother, however, having, I guess, been raised by a less contentious, more comfortably placed family, was suave—polished. Some would even say he was flip'n dignified. I guess you could say my personality has other charms.

"Still, when you scrape-off the affectations and peel-off the crap, we were brothers to the core. Blood and history combined with our Patzinak heritage held us tightly together.

"When we met for that first time after so many years, Robin, who had been able to follow Romanian events more closely, informed me that our family's damn fortunes had amazingly reversed. Our parents had cut their ties to the god damn Church and jumped headlong into local fuck-all politics. Our father had even become a pretty high-ranking member in the local communist party. The blasted family was doing fine.

"It was, in fact, due to our father's god damn connections that a few years later Robin and I were contacted by a Ukrainian group offering us both fuck'n jobs. These weren't jobs in the same place. They weren't even jobs in the same bloody company. But they were positions in the same blooming global conglomerate—they were in the same massive heap of shit.

"My brother, Robin McCandless, moved to a high-up position in Delpro—a really big transnational. I, as you can plainly see, have had the misfortune to be saddled with worthless blighters like yourself."

As Sir Horace wrapped up his tale, Peter had two reactions. First, the aged bandit was still keeping his cards close to his chest. Peter had no greater idea of for whom he was really working than he had had before the venerable man began spinning his story. Second, with all due respect to Joe Thompson, given the type of work Peter himself was engaged in, he was sure that Robin McCandless was no Robin Hood.

Sir Horace seemed to exhale deeply as if to calm his soul (or remove stale air after a long diatribe), almost as some do when they have just entered a church and are preparing for a religious experience. He then whispered, nearly inaudibly, "If I'd gone to Chicago maybe I'd have been a big boss, a *bosi mkuu,* at Delpro."

Peter took this final feeble narration as the end of the current Sir Horace tirade and the culmination of the Sir Horace story—a story Peter had been dismayed to witness. He was nonplused not so much for the short story itself, albeit he had found this illuminating. He was more puzzled that Sir Horace had even told him the tale. He and the old fart were definitely not chums. And whatever he was or was not, Sir Horace was calculating. Little if anything happened by accident. Peter wondered truly why had his master shared so much (in truth, probably not all that much, but anyway it was something)?

When Sir Horace left the hotel, opening the front door and leaving in a beam of bright light almost as though he were ascending to who knew where, Peter was unsure of what had just happened. Albeit the sullen grouch had, as always, taken pains to unabashedly tell Peter who was the boss, exceptionally, his vociferations had not been harbingers of new and unwelcome changes in Peter's life. Quite to the contrary, they had cracked open a small door into the old man's history if not his soul. Peter was still troubled why his master had chosen to share. Why offer snippets of his background? Why then and why there?

Sir Horace and his brother Robin—quite a pair.

Yet again Peter recalled the scriptures his father so relished: *Proverbs* 17:17—*"A friend loves at all times, and a brother is born for a time of adversity."*

Peter remembered (strangely, he thought) the words, but not the context. He thought his father had undoubtedly twisted this to underscore how, between his two offspring, the son was the most challenging—the most headstrong. Maybe he was right.

Looking through a different portal, Peter could also now interpret this as insightful regarding his present situation. He had a sister, but someone from whom he was distant in so many ways. Had he had a brother, would this person have been his touchstone? Would this person have helped him with his current adversity?

All this was neither here nor there. Things were what they were.

Still, old Sir Horace did have a brother. Did he or would he turn to his brother for help? Or did he see his brother as the root cause of any or all adversity that was afflicting him?

Who could know the goings-on in that aged head of the malicious Sir Horace?

His thoughts tripped over one another.

He, Peter, needed to be in the present. He had an unfinished beer and that was his present challenge.

Draining the bottle of the now tepid brew, Peter was unsure if he now needed to change his refuge. Certainly, his overseers knew where to find him.

To hell with them. He liked the Durban.

Peter went back to the port.

Sir Horace did not appear again over the coming months. Peter spent hours, days, it seemed months in the port. Merchandise came in and under his stewardship, it left promptly. Everyone seemed content. Everyone except Peter (and, he hoped, Evelynn). They maintained their periodic rendezvouses. The bonds that joined them, in spite of the separation, remained strong. As before, a new rhythm was adapted and adopted. Life ebbed on.

CHAPTER FOURTEEN

Shrouded Corridors

Turning over stones

ECCLESIASTES 2:17-19, 24-26—*"So I hated life, because the work that is done under the sun was grievous to me. All of it is meaningless, a chasing after the wind. I hated all the things I had toiled for under the sun, because I must leave them to the one who comes after me . . . A person can do nothing better than to eat and drink and find satisfaction in their own toil. This too, I see, is from the hand of God, for without him, who can eat or find enjoyment? To the person who pleases him, God gives wisdom, knowledge and happiness, but to the sinner he gives the task of gathering and storing up wealth to hand it over to the one who pleases God. This too is meaningless, a chasing after the wind."*

Peter put his Bible down.

He was pretty sure, if his father's God was around, He was not pleased with Peter's toil.

He, Peter, was not all that pleased with his toil.

As far as the eating, drinking, and satisfactions were concerned—these were generally feeble attempts at covering-up his frustration. He drank too much. He ate too little. He found rare moments of satisfaction when with Evelynn. Yet, most times, dissatisfaction reigned.

His apartment, where he now sat with a cup of tea (at least he had good Tanzanian tea) awaiting the time to walk to the office, was no shelter. He had made his deal and he was sticking to it—but it chaffed his very soul.

His job was lackluster, to say the very least. He did what needed to be done and got the results he was paid to deliver. And, he had to admit, he was paid pretty well.

Still, he had no clue what he was really doing. He was pushing products down an assembly line. He was a tiny cog in a big machine—having no idea of what the products were. As he scrutinized, as he did often (all too often), his situation, he felt ignorance was bliss. He was relieved he did not know the products he was pushing.

He could always claim innocence of the crimes that were probably being committed. This would be, of course, a sham. He knew all too well of Sir Horace's felonious doings—even if he only saw the silhouettes, unable to see, from his vantage point, the precise images.

He had no real excuses. He was a hoodlum just like all the folks with whom he had been linked since Sir Horace broke (so to speak) him out of jail.

The deal was done.

Peter spent considerable time in introspection—probably an unhealthy amount of time. But, outside his unchallenging job, unless he was in a bar (he would say, "having a few beers," others would say, "getting drunk"), he had little to occupy his ever-active mind. It was only in those moments shared with Evelynn when he felt some level of normalcy seep in. Yet, he had to accept he was honestly realizing more and more that this "normalcy" was truthfully a deception. Nonetheless, it was a deception he welcomed.

As his voice echoed off the hard surfaces of his functional but grim flat with the functional but grim company-supplied accouterments, it was even uncomfortable to talk to himself.

It was a frugal setting.

It was, he realized, the type of setting his father had wanted for his family in Kpando. It was a good backdrop for his father's hoped-for ascetic lifestyle.

Peter then inadvertently jumped outside his own thoughts with a tangential recollection of his father's asceticism. When at home (which he spiritually and intellectually separated from the church, the Home of God—albeit the rectory was truly part of the church complex), he would persistently rant about the need for abstemiousness. He would endlessly spout-off on the social ills of materialism, the rare opportunity they had to be so close to real authentic humanism, and the heretical risk that diabolic idolatrous commercial agents would try to force them to put material things before God's divine offerings—all this couched in the tenet that if they, the family, felt this was not so, then they, the family, should be back in Missouri—home of the almighty dollar and not the Almighty.

Then, when in church, things were different—very different. Humble and abstemious Paul Volman would enter the sacristy and valiant Father Paul—God's Warrior—would exit. And he was dressed to the task: fine linen cassock, brilliant white starched suplice, stole of the finest Kente cloth, all accented by an over-sized chain and crucifix of pure Ashante gold.

When behind the pulpit, Peter's father felt like he was walking in God's shoes. Raising his voice, stretching out his arms, swelling his chest to make the crucifix sparkle—he embraced the congregation as their emissary with Paradise and their salvation from the poverty and drudgery of today.

That was then. This was now. It was all gone. There were, to use that old bastard Sir Horace's own words, no mementos. He had nothing—absolutely nothing—from his childhood, from his home.

He had left for Nigeria thinking he would walk about a bit and then go back to Ghana, go back to Kpando, go back to his family. He had taken nothing except a few changes of clothes.

After all, he could always go home; home to the mission, home to his father's God, maybe even home to his new place at the head of his father's congregation. There had always been a fallback.

He had no idea what he would have done had all this happened—if he had "fallen-back." If he had gone home. If he had reunited with his parents. What would he have done?

His father had always said he had the makings of a fine preacher. His mother had always remained silent.

What would he have done?

He had no idea.

Would he really ever have wanted to follow in his father's footsteps as his father had felt he followed God's? He doubted it very much.

Right now, those lives, those people, those places from his other life seemed dust-covered and murky. He did not even have a picture of his parents nor his sister as a keepsake.

He remembered, growing up, when he would move about with his father, attending various religious (Peter called them "Bible-beater") meetings and events, every small village, every hamlet would have a photographic studio (*Pascal's Fine Photos*—a name that stuck in his brain as an example he had seen somewhere, sometime—he couldn't remember where or when).

These photo studios weren't complicated. They generally amounted to some guy (it always seemed to be a guy) with an aged ratty thirty-five-millimeter camera and a few trays of developer who took black and white snaps of clients—clients in their market-day best, clients just married, clients with new babies, clients in coffins. To memorialize important times and people, almost everyone invested a few cents for a five-by-seven black-and-white picture of their life.

Peter had no pictures.

He had scoffed at these second-rate run-down ill-equipped studios. Now he wished he had gone in each one and had had his picture taken with his family or others with whom he might have been sharing the moment.

Peter's bag of souvenirs was empty—he had no mementos, maybe not even his life which did not seem to be his own.

Peter thought he would not have been a good preacher. If his ecclesiastical hopes were tied to having inherited his father's skills, then he was sure he would have been a terrible preacher. His father, in the final analysis, had not done well. There was no reason to hope the son would do better even if he wanted to (and he did not).

Still and all, Peter had inherited from his father some of those personality traits that had entwined his father as he stood in front of his congregation. Peter, like his father, came across as a basically good guy—someone with whom, in whom one could have confidence. Moreover, both father and son thought quickly on their feet. By virtue of this attribute, they were each comfortable speaking to a large group as easily as soothing a small, distressed family—even though they often gushed drivel.

Paul's drivel (though he would have been mortified if anyone had ever called it that) was aimed at convincing a community that he was the key to their redemption—in so being, the key to his own.

Peter's drivel was no less contrived, although possibly less self-centered. He was, by his own admonition, a grifter. He was able to cajole and exhort. He was able to get people to do what he wanted them to do (generally speaking—the women in his life, especially his dear Evelynn, proving to be more challenging)—even if this required some special persuasion in the form of a gratuity (large or small). But (and it was a tiny "but" that Peter clung to in order to rationalize his often-repellent behavior) Peter did all this not for his own benefit but for the benefit of *them*. *They* were that entity, whatever it truly was, represented by the odious Sir Horace. He was inescapably Sir Horace's organ monkey.

He had fancy clothes, a big smile, a friendly handshake, some clever words, and a small chain affixing him permanently (so it seemed) to the organ grinder.

Peter, to his own chagrin, realized the traits that made someone a good flimflam man (a good organ grinder monkey) could also make someone a good preacher. In some cases, maybe the two weren't all that far apart.

He found rereading, nearly in spite of himself (possibly, he thought, as some form of masochistic contrition), as seemed to be the case of late, a Biblical passage that he could recall indistinctly from his father's many, many sermons—even when only preaching to the family:

> *2 Timothy* 4:2-5—*"Preach the word; be prepared in season and out of season; correct, rebuke and encourage—with great patience and careful instruction. For the time will come when people will not put up with sound doctrine. Instead, to suit their own desires, they will gather around them a great number of teachers to say what their itching ears want to hear. They will turn their ears away from the truth and turn aside to myths. But you, keep your head in all situations, endure hardship, do the work of an evangelist, discharge all the duties of your ministry."*

Peter realized he sat on both sides of the equation. He preached the words—the words handed down by Sir Horace. And he told people what they wanted to hear, wrapped in fictitious packaging, to transmit this word to its intended audience—be they customs officials or village leaders.

While Peter's mind was so engrossed pondering many and diverse thoughts about his past, his body was active (even if not as active as he might have wished) in the present. He was in the port rain and shine—day and night. Whenever there was a shipment needing shepherding, he was there. Generally, his ample expediting budget was more effective at accelerating service than his elegant cajolery—he was even making great strides in fawning over key linchpin personages in Ki-swahili. With tributes and tips, he was getting containers promptly shifted onto awaiting ships with no troublesome checks or inspections.

Peter's work, the work of the shepherd, became monotonously efficient.

The tedium and the frustration that were growing inside him were only moderated by his regular but still too infrequent visits with Evelynn. He began insisting they add on days—turning a romantic weekend into a bawdy four- or five-day pursuit of oneness and forgetfulness.

Evelynn did all she could from her side to extend their unions, reciprocating in all ways to his emotional, spiritual, and physical needs—she, herself feeling many of the same pressures.

They were still managing to hold it together. They were still managing to hold themselves together.

Then everything changed.

Evelynn's work had been shifting more and more to small lacustrine communities in the Mwanza area where the families split their energies between fishing and farming. Her outreach team had collected meaningful data and derived broad-based recommendations for how such families could plan both of these main activities to optimize each while minimizing the toll on the family trying to balance two such fickle enterprises as farming and fishing. Her group had elaborated innovative extension packages that truly led to positive results.

These successes were met with accolades by the Dar leadership. They were replicated along the country's inland shorelines. They also caught the attention of the East African Community which began evaluating how these packages could be disseminated across a multi-country region.

As the flag of success flew over Evelynn's Mwanza offices, it caught the attention of many. One such observer was Paula Patterson, watching the action from her Geneva offices as part of the Mixed Assessment Team at the Ecumenical Humanitarian Trust. These types of widely applicable socio-economic improvement packages were the subject of much of her work—the outcomes from Evelynn's efforts so far were quite impressive.

Paula remembered Evelynn as a smart, dedicated, and dynamic young woman. She was exactly the sort of candidate Paula sought for the EHT Internship Program. Through this fully funded award, a participant such as Evelynn could hone her skills and gain exposure to a far wider tableau while making real contributions to EHTs efforts.

Paula reached out to Evelynn.

Peter went ballistic.

At the end of the day, after astute discussions with her family and topsy-turvy exchanges with Peter along with consultations with her peers and superiors in Mwanza and Dar, Evelynn packed her bag and headed again to Europe—this time on a very different assignment.

There was a huge hole.

Evelynn was gone.

They'd promised to stay in close contact. She'd invite Peter to Geneva when she got settled. She'd try to get home for Christmas or New Years. And it was only for three or four years. They'd already managed to survive a long period of separation—this would just be a little longer and a little further.

They would keep it together. She vowed they would keep it together.

Peter didn't know if Evelynn honestly felt they could endure—overcome all the constraints. He, for one, was highly doubtful. He'd gone through relationships—burning, aching relationships. But there were unavoidably, inextricably stresses that partners applied to their alliance. All too frequently, the relationship could not survive—it could no longer bend. It broke.

He would try. He knew Evelynn would try.

Hopefully the liaison would weather the rigors of time and space.

There was still a huge hole.

Peter recalled the weddings his father had officiated. There was always that same passage: *Mathiew 19:4-6 "Haven't you read," he replied, "that at the beginning the Creator 'made them male and female,' and said, 'For this reason a man will leave his father and mother and be united to his wife, and the two will become one flesh'? So they are no longer two, but one flesh. Therefore what God has joined together, let no one separate."*

Even without a formal marriage, he and Evelynn were truly united. They were, in so many ways, one flesh. While he, and he believed she, did not see this as a relationship created by God, they each knew it was special. It was rare. Now, whether or not joined by God, they were separated by continents, by miles, and by cultures.

It was a huge hole.

Always the pragmatist, Peter carried on.

Days merged into a slurry that percolated between his grim flat and his lackluster, now very, very routine activities at the port. It was like a never-ending, uncomfortable bus trip. A trip where the destination was the beginning. Around and around the days went.

At the end of a particularly trying period, writing unfulfilling letters to Evelynn and surveying unfulfilling work at the port, Peter was exalted (as he sarcastically saw it) by another unannounced and unforeseen visit by the nasty old Sir Horace. This time it was a visit to his flat.

"Hey kid," the old man started, "sorry to interrupt your evening— kinda expected to see you here with a couple of off-the-street sluts as I hear your normal pook has fled the coop. Sorry, I guess, for your pain— but I sure as hell warned you about that high-yella bitch."

Peter bridled, but with supreme effort, held his tongue—leaving to go to the fridge to get some beers to cool his mounting anger.

"Anyway, whatever, good riddance." Sir Horace continued without missing a beat, "someday, you ungrateful sod, you'll learn to take me seriously. I know stuff."

Peter handed his master an opened beer bottle—accepted obviously begrudgingly as not the posh libation his guest often preferred—the faux nobleman generally choosing other more sophisticate potables more in line with his perspective of his status in the greater scheme of things.

"So, son." He picked up after a theatrically difficult swallow of the cheap local brew, "I didn't come here to see who you're shagging. Like I always tell ya, I plain don't give a fuck. But ya know what I do give a fuck about, don ya? Money. Your work is my money. But I'm not a bad man. You know that. Huh? Ya know, when I get my money and know someone's helping me, I like to share. I'm really a nice guy at heart—trust me. Know what I just did? I told Hong to give you a nice raise. Don't thank me. You work hard. You get things done in the port. In fact, you've done so well, and seem to have so much time available to hang onto the bar at the Durban Hotel, that we've decided to spruce up your job a little."

Peter noted the reference to "we," but said nothing. Rather, he rudely turned his back on his patron and went to the fridge for another beer—the first having vanished in a few gulps to try and cool his exasperation at the very presence of his despised overseer.

"Son." Under the brim of his fedora, that set off his pink calico shirt and pressed khaki pants, the oldster winked maliciously at Peter. "We figure you've got time on your hands—especially since your hands are no longer up that *métis* bitch's nickers—so we want you to add to your dossier. We want you to become an 'in-and-out' man. You can thank me again. Since you're not getting in any bedroom pumping, we figure you need to do some in-and-out in the port. You'll now be covering some incoming goods as well as keeping ahead of our shipments out."

Peter remained impassive.

"It's just as much for your good as ours," Peter's elder resumed, "an idle mind is the devil's playground and all that crap. What's more, you really don't have to do anything different. Hong will add the paperwork in your morning file. You may have to make a few new contacts at the port, but you can figure out all the nuts n' bolts. However you manage is fine—just manage."

A stoic Peter went for another beer.

"Now pay attention, youngster. For the outgoing, you can wash your hands quickly of the charge—out of sight, out of mind, and all that crap. Incoming's different. I'll be your stuff. I'll be your responsibility. You'll have to look after it until you get it onto the lorries, we'll arrange to take it wherever we want it to go. Is that clear?"

Peter offered a "Humpf."

"Great. It's all arranged. 'Course kid, never forget, 'don't fuck up.'"

He was gone as seamlessly as he had arrived—a nearly full beer bottle on the end table next to the chair where Sir Horace had just been sitting.

Peter had no idea of what was in store. But it probably wasn't for the best.

In spite of Sir Horace's assurances, things had changed considerably. The authorities we not so concerned about what left the country, especially when it was transit goods. If they could get their slice of the pie as the cargo moved across their plate, that was about all that was required.

Goods coming into their country, however, were a different thing—a very different thing.

First and foremost, the financial enticements to cooperate increased by more than an order of magnitude. Peter's partners realized full-well they were in added home turf jeopardy—the compensation needing to increase proportionally.

Second, there were a whole lot more partners. It was no longer simply a question of making friends with a few critical people in the port. Goods coming in and then leaving the port for the broader national territory fell into the domain of many public agencies.

Peter spent weeks in the dark and shrouded corridors of ministries, departments, and directorates checking on procedures, paperwork, and opportunities for expediting these overloaded processes. Peter met people. Peter brought secretaries chocolates and clerks cigarettes. Peter took people out for a beer, sometimes, for the serious candidates, accompanied by *nyama choma* (spicy grilled meat). Peter collected examples of piles of forms to be filled and certificates to be obtained.

It was a morass. The entangled corridors and walkways of the ordinarily dingy government buildings melded into a jigsaw puzzle that he was ultimately able to piece together. After what felt like far too much effort, he finally was confident that he knew enough and had strong enough contacts to begin moving Sir Horace's affairs out of the port whenever they might arrive.

He didn't have to wait long.

Within a month of his informing Mr. Hong that the groundwork was laid, he received his first notification of an incoming container. Unavoidably thinking back to Sir Horace's disgusting offhand comments, Peter had the pump primed. He was able to move the consignment of farm implements through all formalities and into a warehouse apparently under Hong's prevue within a week. However, he was still the responsible person until the container was loaded on a lorry for transit to a destination outside Tanzania.

This was more learn as you go. But there was not a lengthy delay and soon the transit container was loaded on a flatbed by Hong's people and headed to unknown parts, starting by taking the highway north.

As forewarned, incoming was more difficult than outgoing.

At the city limits, the truck was pulled over for a random check. The driver did not have enough cash on hand to deter the curiosity of the police at the checkpoint.

Things had not gone well.

The driver called Hong.

Hong called Peter.

Hearing the police were holding the lorry and driver, Peter took a large cash advance from the office, got in the Corolla, and headed to the checkpoint.

It took several hours, requiring all the company cash Peter had drawn as well as all of his own that he happened to have in his pocket. Even then, he was only able to break the lorry free with the assurances that the goods were destined for Burundi and therefore would not be in any way a matter that would affect Tanzania.

This eye-opening series of events was caused by scrupulous officers opening several of the wooden crates labeled "farm implements," finding arms and ammunition inside.

This could have been a major, major problem.

There could be no repetitions.

Peter had a heart-to-heart with Mr. Hong—knowing he was only the mouthpiece for those higher up.

They needed another tactic.

Peter fundamentally was shocked and opposed to any arms trafficking. It was quite simply wrong. Still, he did not have the luxury of imposing his values on on-going operations. He was not only a small cog; he was an involuntary actor—he was a slave to Sir Horace's system. As such, it was in his self-interest—it was necessary for his self-survival—to find a solution.

Peter felt he—*they*—did enough business (be it clandestine) in the port that he could get things out and in without undue surveillance. Yet, once outside the relatively controlled environment of the port, there were no assurances at all (as the first shipment had clearly demonstrated).

Peter's solution was inelegant—requiring additional time and money. Nevertheless, with no guarantees, he felt it might work. It would certainly work better than a full-frontal attack.

They would need to procure a warehouse close to the port and under an ownership with no links to Equatorial Management. Here, at the "new facility," as it grew to be called, they would unload and release the container. They would then re-load the "farm implements" or similar contraband—splitting the consignment into several mid-sized lorries. They would put their merchandise at the front of the bed and then fill the whole bed full of agricultural products. This could be bagged animal feeds, bags of coffee, crates of vegetables, even hunks of meat. At any checkpoint outside the port, it was highly unlikely the officials would unload the entire contents of the trucks. If they did, they would again be in trouble.

Sir Horace and whomever else was at the helm seemed to go along with Peter's plans. Incoming shipments were suspended until the near-port facility was arranged, including a fleet of suitable used fifteen-ton trucks.

Peter added a codicil to his plan before sharing it with Mr. Hong. He made the case that as he was a known employee of Equatorial Management as well as a well-known personage in the port, his responsibilities for the incoming shipments should end as soon as the items were onboard the company truck and leaving the new near-port facility. There should be, could be, no more chasing an outgoing truck to a police checkpoint to try and bribe the company's way around a very serious obstacle.

No one flagged this as a contentious piece of the proposal, so it seemed Peter had been able to minimize his personal risk in this very risky (and unsavory) business.

A new equilibrium was established.

Evelynn's letter-writing skills, as probably should have been anticipated, far exceeded Peter's. She wrote regularly, with clear affection and homesickness. However, as the weeks glided by her letters began to dwell more on her work in Geneva. While she found the city itself somewhat overwhelming and very expensive, the work had captivated her. She was hooked. Progressively, there were more attestations of the wonderful work and fewer protestations of their disjoined love. In spite of her objections, she was being swept away.

This realization (long hidden in the corners of his mind), pushed Peter to submerge himself more into his own work (and drinking).

As ordained by his master, Peter was now doing the "out and in"— refusing to use his lord's terminology "in and out."

Most shipments were still outgoing. The incoming were dispersed as discretely and quickly as possible among the new fleet of old trucks— vanishing over the hills—undoubtedly to the bane of those on the receiving end.

Peter did not inspect every arrival.

It wasn't his job.

In fact, he was tacitly dissuaded from doing so.

He did not need to know, did not want to know the full venal details of all the merchandise that transited through his hands.

Nevertheless, inevitably, as one of the primary actors at the "new facility," he did catch more than fleeting glimpses of numerous shipments. These were not all arms. Even so, there were a fair number of arms shipments—apparently most destined for the Great Lakes region. There were also crates that appeared to really be farm implements—or some sort of implements. There were also cartons that appeared to be pharmaceuticals (medical or recreational, he supposed) as well as cigarettes and whisky. There were bales of soft goods—likely textiles. A good portion of the consignments were labeled for addresses in East Africa or the Great Lakes, but some were for as far away as Zambia (apparently by going back down Lake Tanganyika—quite a circuitous route).

Whatever Peter saw, he tried to quickly forget.

It wasn't part of his job to keep inventory.

He attempted to envision himself as someone on an assembly line. Things moved from left to right, or from right to left, but everything just moved past him—barely (he hoped) inoculated with his fingerprints.

Peter would make periodic visits to the government corridors to make sure the wheels were still greased, while spending most of his time, as usual, in or around the port.

He and Evelynn remained in what they tried to consider as close contact. Peter made no efforts to expand his social life—even if temporarily.

He was back on the merry-go-round moving him from apartment, to office to government corridors to port. More stops than before, yet still the same vortex that seemed to spin him around in a state of continual frustration.

After an average gyrating day, Peter was enjoying a cool beer in the refreshing shadows of the Durban Hotel's bar. He felt more than saw someone approaching him. It was not a second run of the terrible Sir Horace, however. It was Joe Thompson.

"Hey, remember me?" he asked, with a full-faced smile and an outstretched hand.

"Sure, trust you made it to Bukoba," Peter countered.

"Did, indeed. Can I buy you a beer?"

With that, the duo took a table in a quiet corner; Joe methodically told another tale as Peter enjoyed his seeming never-ending offers of beer.

Joe recounted in minute detail how, from Bukoba, he had gone on to Uganda and then to Lake Edward, for some reason feeling he should explore opportunities around the major lakes of the region. While the rationale was unclear, apparently Joe thought there were potential profits to be made acting as a liaison with fishing communities. This brought back stabs of memory, both of Evelynn's work around Lake Victoria as well as his own initial work in the villages with Equatorial Management.

Joe portrayed laboriously how he had then made a slow arch to the south and east. He had continued his link to the lakes by following, after Lake Edward, Lake Kivu from north to south, zigzagging between the Congolese and the Rwandan shores. At Bukavu, he had followed the Rusizi River to Uvira, taking a boat across to Bujumbura.

At the mention of Bujumbura, Peter took a mouthful of beer, recalling with poignancy his discussions with Brother Mike on the terrace. He hoped the old monk was doing well—better than he.

"Boy," Joe offered, bringing Peter back from his reminiscences, "I really enjoyed that city—it's great. Ever been there?"

"Yeah."

"Well, it's a gas. I had a swell time. Thought about going all the way to Mpulungu, but that's really a long haul. Too much for me at that time. I just went down the lake as far as Kigoma and then headed back here to Dar."

"That's nice."

"It is. I'm glad to be back."

"You live here, in Dar?"

"Well, sorta. I move around a lot like I told you and your girlfriend— by the way, where's she?"

"She's gone overseas for an internship."

"Oh, that's tough on you."

"Good for her though. I'm managing."

"She's a fine lady."

"She sure is."

The conversation then transformed into more bromidic chitchat for another half hour when Joe impulsively looked at his watch, announcing he was late for a meeting, and fled into the flare of the afternoon sun.

Peter was still left feeling he only had a piece of Joe's story. This not-withstanding, he had scored a lot of beer and it had been better than his usual solitary "hanging onto the bar" as Sir Horace had so lovingly called his drinking habits.

Thoughts of his master seemed to have spawned the emergence of the old man. The next day, as Peter made his accustomed stop at the office for the day's file of actions, Mr. Hong exceptionally came out of his office to greet his favorite port agent (as he liked to call Peter), in a mild state of agitation, indicating that Peter should first go to the meeting room where someone was waiting for him.

Before even taking his seat at the small conference table, Peter knew his nemesis had arrived once again. No forewarning, no clue of the mission. It was his curse, and he could only bear it.

In a violet polo shirt that offset his alabaster locks, Sir Horace scarcely looked up at his protégée, as he reportedly now liked to call Peter, slid onto a seat as far away from his overseer as possible.

"'Bout time you got here," Sir Horace sneered.

"Office just opened, huh?"

"Who cares? Been here for an hour. You should be early—especially now when there's no muffin in your bed to keep you under the covers."

Peter had learned to tune-out most of the old man's rants, staring vacuously at the map of Tanzania on the wall above Sir Horace's head.

"Pay attention, kid. This is important."

"Humpf." Peter made a barely audible reaction, his eyes still on the map.

"Seems like everyone's your fan. They got big things in store for you."

Peter again recorded the "everyone" and the "they," remaining to-tally unsure who his bosses were and where the graceless Sir Horace fit in the true scheme of things.

"I was happy to get you into the in-and-out work." His interlocutor loutishly grinned. "But the decision has been taken that you need to focus more. Looks like you've passed muster for dealing more directly with our incoming shipments."

In his mind, Peter traced the margins of the Serengeti's Lake Eyasi on the map.

"Get this straight, youngster. You'll not be dealing with any more outgoing stuff—OK? We've already got someone else on this. You don't need to do any more—just leave well enough alone.

"If you look closely at the file you just picked up—know you're probably too cock-sure to even check it out before you leave the office—you'll see a new collection of items needing your attention. They're all incoming.

"This gets more complicated, so pay attention—I know how quickly your mind diverts to poontang if you don't concentrate. Some of the shipments will be for Equatorial Management. These will follow Hong's regular pathways—sure hope you already know these. Other shipments will go to what I hear you dummies here call the 'new facility.' Now there's even some others that will go to Vijibweni, on the other side of the harbor. You're the conductor of the orchestra now. You get stuff where it needs to go. Is that clear?"

Another "Humpf."

"Hong will fill you in on anything else. I'd love to sit here and shoot the shit with you til the cows come home, but I'm a busy man. I gotta run. So, as always kid, don't fuck up."

Sir Horace seemed to float out of the room. Peter was not fully sure what had transpired nor how it would affect him. As always, his life was unlikely to be made easier by Sir Horace's most recent arrangements.

He went to the port to his new job in the same old place.

What Peter was soon to appreciate was that things had changed. The routine was not the same. When he now dealt with incoming consignments, it was not in the context of the process he had only recently put in place. He retained oversight of the shipments up to the final destination, including even dealing directly with the receiving client.

This did not mean that he rode in the lorries carrying the merchandise. This meant that he was given a list of destinations and clients with instructions. He was to visit these places and people soon after the items were scheduled to arrive to ensure satisfactory delivery—also, in some cases to place new orders, in others to ensure final payments (he had no idea if the list covered all the clients involved in a given shipment, or just a subset selected by the overlords—and, of course, this knowledge did not matter as he was just a tool in their toolbox).

In the end, he was once again away from Dar about as much as he was in the city. However, this time, he was not in the hinterland. This time he was painfully learning all the intricacies of the regional airports as he flew from Dar's Julius Nyerere International Airport to Entebbe, Kigali, Nairobi, Bujumbura, Lusaka, and even Kinshasa, Addis Ababa, Juba, and Mogadishu—the consignments that fell through his hands obviously covering a very wide network.

He had left the drab corridors of government offices for the throbbing and tumultuous concourses of East African airports.

Peter would arrive at his destination to be met by a complete stranger. He had no idea if his greeter was an employee, a contractor, or simply someone picked up off the street. Whatever the arrangements, made by unknown and invisible parties, Peter was helped through immigration and customs—advancing as though a high-level diplomat. He was then accompanied to a four or five-star hotel (if such was available) and handed a large manila envelope with all his contacts and schedules for his visit as well as the tickets for the next leg of his journey. In effect, each trip was like coming into a totally dark room, never knowing who would turn on the lights and what the lights would reveal.

Over and over, when the lights came on, the images revealed were those of greed and narcissism. Undisclosed shipments going to unseen clients for covert purposes were not recipes for positive and constructive actions. The customers served by Peter's lords were all, each and every one, undoubtedly engaged in corrupt and illicit enterprises.

Peter never knew those with whom he interacted at the various destinations. His intermediaries were certainly not those controlling the situation. His liaisons were the agents of powerful individuals who were cloaked in secrecy—at least hidden from the eyes of an outsider such as Peter (a fact for which he was eternally grateful).

Peter would normally not spend more than two or three nights in any one place. His instructions identified contacts for discussions his masters wished to have regarding new shipments or settling accounts on existing consignments. He would ask the prescribed questions, record the answers provided, accept any sealed envelopes offered, and then consider that part of the job closed.

At times, he would be contacted unannounced, ostensibly by clients. These self-declared customers, or more precisely, their agents, indicated they had been apprised of Peter's visit and they had a communication for him to carry back for senior management. He was, in effect, a roving mailbox.

Half Peter's life seemed to be occupied by waiting for planes to take-off or land. The other half was back in his old haunts in and around the port. For yet another period, a new cadence quickly became ordinary.

What was possibly extraordinary was that, as he traveled, Peter carried, what was now becoming a rather worn copy of the Bible. This, in all like-lihood, would have been considered as extraordinary by his parents. It would, moreover, probably have been considered as extraordinary to all who knew, or had known him (Lydia, Kole, Wanda, Silas, Dabi, Katy, Evelynn, and certainly the wicked Sir Horace). But it was the most ex-traordinary to Peter himself. This book had been, maybe continued to be, he thought, the curse of his personal life—the downfall of his family. Yet, in some perverse way, it almost seemed to him to be at the talisman of these failures and something he now indescribably kept close at hand—possibly an attachment like Hamlet's to Yorick's skull.

His ragged tome was not his father's copy. It was not a family heir-loom. It was just his cheap off-the-bookstore-shelf copy. Still and all, this soon became a memento for his duffel bag as he meandered about—perhaps that needed memento to which the noxious Sir Horace had referred—who knew.

He did know something, however. This now nearly omnipresent addition to his travel bag was not, and he reminded himself regularly on this point, because he had found religion. He had not picked up his father's mantle. He had not had a transformation—an epiphany. This was definitely not the case.

Religious faith aside, he was sure his Bible had become a sort of touchstone. This was not because Peter had learned that the book pro-vided wise and true insight into man's nature. This was not even because Peter saw Christianity as a deceit that had ruined his family as it may have many other families. This was not from a "know your enemy" mindset. It was simpler. This book had been the epicenter of his father's life and the life of his grandfather before him. It was in some strange way his inheritance. Peter candidly yet erratically thumbed through the pages that had held so much meaning for his family—trying to see if he could understand why it had so consumed his forebears.

It was during one such perusal, while waiting in his overly plush hotel room in Kinshasa, that Peter noted a passage he considered appropriate to his current commission. This, he felt, was not prescriptive, but matter-of-factly descriptive—illustrating, if not his own situation, maybe the circumstances in which his bosses found themselves, whether they knew it or not:

> *Ecclesiastes 5:10-15— "Whoever loves money never has enough; whoever loves wealth is never satisfied with their income. This too is meaningless. As goods increase, so do those who consume them. And what benefit are they to the owners except to feast their eyes on them? The sleep of a laborer is sweet, whether they eat little or much, but as for the rich, their abundance permits them no sleep. I have seen a grievous evil under the sun: wealth hoarded to the harm of its owners, or wealth lost through some misfortune, so that when they have children there is nothing left for them to inherit. Everyone comes naked from their mother's womb, and as everyone comes, so they depart. They take nothing from their toil that they can carry in their hands."*

Peter wondered, could there be solace in this old book, even if different from the intended purposes presupposed by others?

CHAPTER FIFTEEN

The Lions' Den

Dire straits

In his hotel room, Peter, with little else to do, was back thumb-ing through his book—his anathema. Practically at random, he read: *Matthew 6:24*—*"No one can serve two masters. Either you will hate the one and love the other, or you will be devoted to the one and despise the other. You cannot serve both God and money."*

Peter had two masters. He did not, to the undoubtable shame of his father's spirit, consider God as one of his masters, however. His masters were those pulling Sir Horace's strings and his own soul. He certainly could hate and despise one. He could not, sadly, love or be devoted to the other. The other was kept in a small box, locked tightly against the realities of today.

Peter had changed. Or life had changed Peter. He had no long-term plans. He no longer assessed his own actions. He no longer felt deep con-nections to (any) others. He lived in the moment—not because he found the moment to be so fabulous, not because the moment was so special. Frankly, the moment was all he felt he had.

While not classically religious—*not at all*, he would say—he did be-lieve the essence of existing was composed to two parts: the spiritual and the corporal. The jury—his jury—was still out on the question of whether or not the spiritual portion was linked in any way to any sort of higher power (not the power and spirits as typically defined by Christianity, of that he was certain). The corporal component was all too real (as demon-strated by his beating and illness, if nothing else). He now poured all his energies into his corporal self—like, he thought, a mud turtle from Volta Lake (what the Ghanians speaking Twi called "*akyekyedeɛ*") closing up in a defensive action. He locked out his spiritual self—not knowing where it went nor what it did when it was driven from its host.

When Peter thought of his current state, he was reminded of a work he had had to read in Lit Class in the UK: Jack Williamson's 1947 novelette, *With Folded Hands*. The story described a world where "mechanicals" or "humanoids" (robots) took over human functions. Like a mechanical, his human functions had been taken over by Sir Horace's overlords. He had become their cyborg.

Robot or not, in many ways, his life had become robotic. He could now navigate the port of Dar with his eyes closed—moving stoically through a nebula of humidity and monotony. Incoming shipments moved smoothly along the pathway he had so well lubricated. Be that as it may, he could not just assume things were going smoothly. As Sir Horace had said (one of the few of the old man's utterances with which he agreed): "Assumptions are the mothers of all bloom'n fuck-ups."

He had to make regular appearances at the port. He had to see, face-to-face, his co-conspirators. He had to offer small *zawadi* (Ki-swahili for gift), even if only some cigarettes or chocolate bars. He had to, again thinking of the disgusting discourse of his master, keep the pump primed.

As with the port, the region's airports became a blur. He ebbed in and out like a never-ending tide. From airport to a they-all-look-the-same hotel room then back to the airport. As a drifting mailbox, he rarely had any exchanges of any substance with those with whom he was in contact at each of his assigned destinations. He was purely a vessel.

At one point, when assuming this role of company utensil in Kigali, having made his contacts, he sat poolside at the Hôtel Des *Mille Collines,* enjoying several *Primus* beers in the climate they called "Eternal Spring." It was truly pleasant and relaxing. And he needed to take this opportunity to relax as his next leg was to get back to Nairobi on transit to Mogadishu—certainly his least favorite and the most incendiary of all his routine destinations.

This particular visit had been more bracing than most as he had been able to leave the Rwandan capital—in some ways, he was discovering, all capitals, like all hotel rooms, looked just the same (this observation bringing a poignant flashback of Katy and their tour of southern African capitals). He had hired a car and driver and gone south to Butare, nearly to the Burundi border (into, he reminisced on the drive, the terrain of the memorable Brother Mike—knowing he had neither the time nor the liberty to try and find this thoughtful friar). Here, his company (or his czars) had clients and, exceptionally, Peter knew a tiny bit of their activities since he had been closely involved when one of their consignments had been badly damaged when in transit in Dar port.

The Butare company, apparently run by folks originally from southern Asia, surreptitiously produced a variety of pharmaceutical products in a small jerry-rigged "factory" in their garage. It was reportedly a shoestring but profitable operation.

Butare was also the site of a government-run pharmaceutical company that made a relatively limited assortment of medicaments that addressed the twenty major illnesses in the country—common ailments like malaria, intestinal parasites, and cholera. All efforts were taken to control the quality and distribution of these locally formulated medications. They were made to international specifications and sold at a subsidized price to ensure they reached the poorest segments of society.

Control was necessary. For many years, pirated pharmaceuticals fabricated in Asia to no standard whatsoever (often dangerous to the health as opposed to restoring health) had flooded African markets in general and Rwandan markets in particular.

The Butare supplies were an effort to replace faux imports.

Ever scheming, Peter's clients now managed to circuitously address some of the control measures and keep at least part of their former market share. In their garage they produced sham products with organic powders and flours of no medical value that they purchased, undoubtedly at very special prices from Peter's taskmasters. They then were able, by pushing the ever-present buttons of venality, to clandestinely intermingle these counterfeit drugs with the supplies leaving the government's Butare plant.

It was unconscionable.

It was Peter's world.

It was surely, through the eyes of people like his father, the road to Perdition.

These were transgressions that could in no way be washed away by guzzling beer at poolside at the *Mille Collines*.

His woolgathering was severed by an unexpected greeting, "Hey, Pete, how you like those big *Primus* bottles?"

Peter refocused, seeing Joe Thompson coming across the pool deck in his direction.

"What a surprise. What brings you to the thousand hills of Rwanda?"

Peter extended his hand to grip Joe's outreached palm, trying to smile as broadly as his greeter, explaining, "Equatorial Management has partners in development across the region. We have kind of a network—exchanging strategies and success stories. I'm basically the liaison." It was a memorized retort that often came in handy.

"How about that," Joe replied in a rather off-the-cuff manner, as he settled into the lounge chair next to Peter's.

"Yep, get here from time to time."

"How about that."

Peter needed to break the loop. "How about yourself?"

"Yeah. Remember back in Dar I had told you I'd spent some time around the lakes, including Kivu? I'm back following-up."

"Great. Well, the climate sure beats the hell outta Dar."

"That it does."

"Kinda relaxing after all the chaos of the big city."

"Yeah. 'Course, there's a lot going on here. The calm exterior hides a real volcano ready to blow its top—and I don't mean Karisimbi or Bisoke."

"How's that?"

"Lots of ethnic tension. Been around for a long time. A real delicate balance for years. Now a bunch of folks who fled to Uganda way back when have come back here and that, among other things, has upset the equilibrium—that and the new cries for 'democracy'—there're now what they call political parties all over the place—to me, they're more like football teams. Lots of tension just below the surface."

"Well, you seem pretty well informed for a lake guy."

"Oh, it's really just history."

"Huh?"

"Yeah. This problem goes way back. You otta read up on it. Been well documented. Like I say, it goes way back."

"Huh."

"Yeah. The original folks who lived here ages ago were kinda peaceful hunter-gatherers and potters. Then folks started following rivers. Ever heard of such a thing?"

"Not sure what you're talking about," Peter said, perhaps a little too defensively as someone who had been a follower of rivers—rivers that had brought him ultimately to the poolside of the *Mille Collines*.

"Yeah. Sure. Skipped a few steps. Sorry."

"OK."

"Yeah. Ya see, this country sits atop the headwaters of two of the Continent's major river systems: the Congo and the Nile. So, I guess it makes some sorta sense that folks follow rivers. Don't know?"

"Makes sense to me."

"Yeah. Well, that's what happened, anyway. Folks moved up the Congo and folks moved up the Nile. These were different folks. Ethnically and culturally very different. The Congo-side folks were farmers. The Nile-side folks were herdsmen. And do ya know what happened?"

"Nope."

"Yeah. Well, the farmers and the herdsman dropped down like a lead balloon on the poor potters. The local folks got pushed to the side by the newcomers. Then the newcomers wanted to see, among themselves, who was the boss. Know what happened?"

"Nope."

"Yeah. Well, in general, the herdsmen were a hellava lot better warriors than the farmers. The long and short of it was that, for ages, the herdsmen and their kings oversaw the farmers as their vassals—often overseeing them with severity and brutality. The poor potters were just pushed aside in the ditch. Quite a story."

"Sure is."

"Yeah. Then, just to wrap up this quick tour through the past, with the arrival of the colonialists, the herdsmen were left in power next door in Burundi while the farmers—ex-serfs—were put in power here in Rwanda. This asymmetry—remember there's about four-times as many farmers as herdsmen—was an antecedent for the pot that has been simmering for so long and may soon boil over."

It was Peter's turn to say, "How about that."

"Yeah. Quite a story. 'Course there's others on the outside who are trying to pull and push to see how they can make a buck if the pot does boil over. There's always vultures waiting in the wings."

"'Course."

"Yeah. Anyway, just saw you here and wanted to say 'hi.' Had no idea I'd get myself carried away into the backstory of today's fragile times in the thousand hills—makes all the bedlam at Northern High back in Detroit look like a cakewalk."

"Scary."

"Yeah. But who knows?"

"Yeah."

"Maybe we'll all get lucky?"

"Yeah. How about a beer?"

"Yeah. Thanks anyway. I gotta run. Maybe we'll catch-up later."

With that, he was gone.

Soon, Peter too was gone. Gone from the thousand hills and the lovely weather, now awash in the aseptic florescence of the transit area of Nairobi airport. His connection to Mogadishu was not for another four hours. Today, as too many times to count before, he had walked the concourses of the terminal, malingering among the shops selling souvenirs, electronics, and booze; he gawked at the congregate of multicultural journeyers who swirled about (rarely gawking back). He had walked until his feet hurt. He had then, as had become his custom, retired to the small café at the extreme end of the hallway where he could sit at a relatively quiet table and enjoy a well-brewed cup of good Kenyan coffee.

As he sipped the aromatic Arabica, he let his mind roam.

He was deeply engrossed in a small group of Chinese excursionists at a larger table across the coffee bar (they seemingly drinking equally good Kenyan tea). He thought they might be headed to Chinese construction sites in Zambia, Chinese rice farms in Sénégal, Chinese textile factories in Lesotho, Chinese irrigation schemes in Burundi. They could be heading anywhere because the Chinese were everywhere. While it might take some time for them to control the world, they were damn close to controlling this Continent.

Oh well, Sir Horace probably already had lots of Chinese partners.

Just as he was about to refocus on his unpleasant master, he heard a chair at his table scratch the floor as someone, an uninvited someone, joined his personal space. He turned around to be surprised again—a second time in so many days. With a big grin, Paula Patterson slid into the orange molded plastic chair next to Peter.

"They used to say," she started, "that you can meet anyone on Princess Street in Edinburgh. However, of late, I've decided you can meet anyone at Nairobi Airport. Peter, how are you? Good to see you."

With that, after minimal chitchat, Peter got Paula to recount all she could, all she felt comfortable recounting, about Evelynn. Peter drank the tale like savoring a fine glass of Pinot Noir.

Evelynn was fine. She was enjoying her work. Paula even went into considerable detail about the various activities and projects where Evelynn was now an integral, often a critical, part.

The crucial details for Peter were that, as far as Paula was willing to say, Evelynn did not date—she still spoke often and with great emotion of Peter. And, less positively, with all her engagements, Evelynn had, with senior management's blessings, extended her stay for at least another year—AT LEAST another year!

Peter recovered.

"That's great. Thank you so much for the most appreciated update," Peter inserted with what he hoped was a calm voice while "another year" bounced off his cerebellum.

"You know, Peter." Paula smiled. "She really loves you."

"Thanks again for all the support. We write all the time—but there's only so much you can put on paper. Your first-hand news is so welcome."

"And, my friend, how about you? What shall I tell Evelynn when I get back into the office tomorrow?"

"Oh, yes. Please tell her everything is fine—everything is really terrific." This last word with special, perhaps overly effusive, emphasis.

"I'll really have to say more than *terrific*."

"Of course. Well, inasmuch as you see me here, clearly, I'm now traveling much more outside Tanzania than inside. Before I spent most of my work visiting communities around the country, as you may recall. We've expanded. We now have partnerships all cross East Africa and I am the one who follows-up on many of these joint actions. This means lots of travel—lots of airports. Evelynn should be happy she's not having to sit in Dar to wait for my plane to land—because it seems as soon as it lands, I take off again."

"I'll tell her."

"Well, don't scare her, either. Now that I know she's another year to stay outside, I'll make sure I talk with my boss so that when she's ready to come home we can be together—I'll do all I can to arrange to have less travel and more time at the *nyumbani*," he replied, using the Ki-swahili word for home that he knew Evelynn would appreciate if Paula remembered to tell her.

"Not to worry. She'll be thrilled we had a chance to talk."

With that, the conversation took a dip, sweeping through a variety of pedestrian topics before Paula's flight to Geneva was called.

As they separated, Peter gave Paula a big hug that he asked her to pass on to Evelynn, when reporting that he was "terrific."

After Paula had left, Peter thought of being terrific. He remembered, as so frequently these days, one of his father's oft-spoken verses (never quite sure how he managed to recall all these passages—maybe because he had been bathed in them since birth): *Proverbs* 27:1—"*Do not boast about tomorrow, for you do not know what a day may bring forth.*"

Shortly thereafter, his own flight to Mogadishu was called.

This was his least favorite destination. The *Zeytatuun Palace Hotel* was rated five-stars, but the hotel and the climate (the Somali capital having routine temperatures ranging from eighty to ninety-plus degrees) were a far cry from Rwanda and the Hôtel Des *Mille Collines*—about as dissimilar as one could get. Moreover, if possible, the company's clients were even more shrouded in namelessness than usual. He literally saw no one and nothing of the activities with which he was supposedly liaising.

It was infamously recounted that, between the harbor and Lido Beach, the slaughterhouse dumped goat, sheep, and cow blood into the sea—attracting sharks (to the horror of any on the beach). But Peter knew, if even half the stories were true, that the blood of more than Halal butchered meats washed into the sea. The city and the lands there-about were deluged with violence and death.

Peter wondered what role his masters played in all the pandemonium.

If there was money to be made, regardless of the volume of blood that flowed, they would be there—in every nook and cranny.

This called to mind Joe's alarms about potential violence and mayhem in Rwanda. Peter had no doubt that if the pot did boil over, his principals would be there stoking the flames.

It was distressing.

It was dangerous.

He sequestered himself in his hotel, feeling the world around him was rapidly falling apart. Any communications he brought with him were left at the reception for pick-up by unseen ghosts. Any issues or decelerations needing his attention or the attention of those up the ladder, were similarly left at the hotel's front desk.

He spent forty-eight hours feeling tethered to a cramped space in a precarious parish—feeling a persistent sense of agitation—feeling like

Daniel in the lion's den. Going back to his Bible that both infatuated and exasperated him, he checked the text just to make sure:

> *Daniel 6:16—"Then the king commanded, and Daniel was brought and cast into the den of lions. The king declared to Daniel, 'May your God, whom you serve continually, deliver you!'" and, Daniel 6:22—"My God sent his angel and shut the lions' mouths, and they have not harmed me, because I was found blameless before him; and also before you, O king, I have done no harm."*

CHAPTER SIXTEEN

All's Well

Maybe not

PETER AWOKE IN DARKNESS. His head was full of cotton wool. He was discombobulated. He thought he heard the palms blowing in a July thunderstorm in Kpando. He thought he heard bats scratching about in the attic. It took a moment before his brain clicked on. There were no palm trees. There were no bats.

Gradually, he realized he was in his bedroom in his flat—the first time in some time that he had been home. A sign of his extended absences the fact that he knew not where he was when he was home.

That last thought struck an awkward note.

There was the pragmatic. There was the emotional.

Practically, here and home were one and the same at this point in time: Dar es Salaam, Tanzania.

Still, was this his home?

He was a voyager like Saint Paul, but that was where the resemblance ended.

He was a tiny part in an ignominious puzzle. And not a puzzle of religious fundamentals—although this too was truly a puzzle (at least for him).

He thought of his mother—a tangent to his normally paternalistic recollections. While she followed the path blazed by her spouse and shared his zeal, she cast a wider net. Albeit Christianity was at her soul and her nature, she tried in many ways to support this devotion with other elements that, to her mind, made an even stronger case for her husband and herself being right in their strict beliefs and narrow priorities (though Peter was pretty sure she saw these as neither strict nor narrow).

She fancied herself a student of the classics (a hobbyist at most, Peter thought). Student or not, during his childhood, there had been a maternal dusting of the odd quotes and passages from the Greek classics that were nearly randomly mixed with the ever-present preachings from the Bible.

Peter knew his mother had been particularly fond of one of the Delphic maxims at the Temple of Apollo—*Know thyself*. Then, according to Mother, Plato took things one step further, writing, "The essence of knowledge is self-knowledge." The position of the Classics was, as mother put it, that we all had to know ourselves before we could know anything else.

She employed this logic to defend her spouse's often myopic view of the world—seen only through his particular prism of Christianity. To her, her Paul was wisely correct in concentrating on his interpretation of the verses—first as these shed light on his own being and then as they illuminated the lives he was trying to redeem.

Peter could see the words as if written on the old plywood blackboard in the garden in Kpando when his mother reviewed their lessons—*know thyself*.

Yet, to him, the words were not justification for monomania. The words were in truth the filter through which he had to view his life since leaving his parents in Kpando—what now seemed like several lifetimes ago. If the ancient Greeks had it right, his journey was handicapped from the onset. Without knowing himself thoroughly, he could not have hoped to know others—to know nature—to know the world about him. All the faces, all the people, who had populated this journey with him were only partial, incomplete consorts. He should not have hoped to appreciate them fully without first fully appreciating himself. He couldn't find himself through his journey but rather should have found himself and then undertaken his journey.

If the ancient Greeks had it right?

Right or wrong, what was self-evident was that Peter was still a long way from finding himself. If he had to wait to find himself before he could find others, he would have a long wait coming.

～

Back in Dar was not, however, the time for soul-searching—for deep thoughts and deeper concerns. He had a lot to do.

His recent trip had been a long one. He had to attend to the port. He had to see Mr. Hong. He had to prepare his reports and deliver the missives that he, ever the attentive messenger, had accumulated along the journey.

He had to keep busy.

Busy he was.

It had taken nearly ten days before Peter was satisfied, he had attended to all the things requiring his attention—clearing up any *shida* (as difficulties were called in Ki-swahili) and pushing forward his masters' agendas. Now he was caught up and satisfied he had left no loose ends before, during, or after his most recent *safari*.

Then there was another assignment. This was effectively taking a step back. There was an "errand," as Mr. Hong called it, in the south of the country and his replacement was fully engaged up north on the Lake's shore. So, as kind of a "cherry job" (again, Mr. Hong's words), Peter was to make a quick run down the coast to Mtwara to deliver some rice processing machinery. Actually, a pair of lorries were delivering the machinery—what seemed to be about a whole factory—and Peter was meeting them there for the inspection of the purchases and the signing-off by the purchasers—all very routine.

In truth, it did seem to Peter like a relatively easy task that could be done at his pace and not the helter-skelter tempo of an airport or a capital city. Mtwara, the capital of the region of the same name and the home of a deep-water port on Mikindani Bay, was a straight shot south of Dar—about 350 miles on the B-2. All things considered, it was an uncomplicated, and even possibly relaxing, trip.

The road was good, the scenery pleasing, and the encounter with the clients surprisingly painless even if tedious (Peter wondering if his masters had sold *bona fide* new equipment or, as Joe Thompson might have done, pushed truckloads of outdated material with beautiful fresh coats of paint).

The assignment lived up to expectations. Peter was underwhelmed. While he had arrived with two lorries of hardware, as it turned out, there were a lot of bits and pieces that were still awaited to get everything up and running. But this wasn't Peter's chore. Others from Equatorial Management's crew would come to assemble all the parts and get the rice processing underway. Then, once he had the green light, Peter would come back for a final check.

It was all straightforward.

Dare he think it, it was practically by the book.

For accommodation, he went a short distance outside Mtwara to the little community of Mikindani to the Old Boma Hotel where he had booked a room for the night. The colonial-era establishment was top-rated (and high-priced) for a reason—it was luxurious. There was a spa and a most enticing bar. It was a great place to top-off a nothing-to-it chore.

Peter was indeed relaxing.

The skies were pinkish purple. The fuchsia sea lapped gently at his legs—or was it the surge of Lake Volta—a force pulling him to deeper waters, far from the tangerine sands of an eroded beach.

There were the woeful cries of seagulls. No, these were the tear-doused wails of children—children in pain—children in anguish. Their shrieks ricocheted off the mauve clouds like a gyrating pinball off a rubber bumper.

Peter could feel more than hear the vibrations.

Wait. There was a boom. Was it the surf? No, it was the boastful reverberations of his father at the pulpit. His father, old and wasted, seagrass in his hair, dressed in the uniform of a Roman legionnaire. His father, barely able to hold to the sides of the podium, a lectern encrusted with blood and dust, screaming to the skies. The sightless eyes, bulging from the parchment membrane masking a cranium partially gnawed away, fixed on the heavens.

His father swirled about with amazing speed. His head exploded as he faced the presbytery. Bits of skull floated into the air, swirling about the sanctuary lamp. Then, in a cloud of chartreuse vapor eddying about the altar crucifix, a withered and haggard version of his mother fell to the flagstone floor.

There was a gut-throbbing whine.

His mother slithered between cracks in the stones.

The lamp erupted into jade flames.

The crucifix melted into a pool of mercury, oozing from the alter.

His sister swept the floor clean.

Lydia then carefully deposited all the sweepings in a massive head-pan—too heavy for her to lift. Dabi and Katy appeared, helping Lydia, somehow now their sister, position the pan on her head—her crown covered with a swatch of intricate Kente cloth. The three ladies then walked out on the tangerine sands to the fuchsia sea.

Then, they were gone.

The world churned.

There was darkness.

There was nothing.

There was whiteness—a white-out. He thought, it must be like in an Arctic storm.

Was he in the Arctic?

He didn't know. He wasn't cold. Or was he? He was hot now, but it seemed he had been cold. He knew he knew nothing of snow, the Arctic, and real cold. He had seen a tiny amount of snow in the UK but was otherwise totally unfamiliar with the winter wonder.

Was he covered with snow?

He didn't think so.

Things were moving; big things.

Strangely, he recalled his mother telling him a story about the Mothman—the red-eyed flying man seen in West Virginia—a creature made legendary, according to Mother, by a book that was a cult favorite in the 70s.

Was his mother a cultist?

Was she, in truth, a moth creature?

Had he been carried away by moths?

The white shadows circled about him.

There was darkness.

There was nothing.

Again, there was whiteness. But this time, his senses had more-or-less returned. He could see that, once again, he was in an unfamiliar bed in an unknown room—most likely, he knew, he was in a hospital. But he had no idea why nor where.

A sister appeared, bedecked in flowing white vestments that he first mistook for his father's clerical robes. She came to his bedside, felt his forehead, and offered him a drink of refreshing water from the white metal table beside his white metal bed.

Seeing her wide-eyed patient, the sister intoned calmly, "Don't worry. You're alright. You'll get better. Just rest."

He tried to speak, but his throat felt as though it had been flayed.

"Don't try to talk," she continued, seeing his puzzlement—near fright. "you're at Saint Benedict's hospital in Ndanda."

Peter's eyes grew even wider—questioning.

"You collapsed at the bar in the Old Boma Hotel."

Complete bewilderment.

"You have malaria—but, of course, no one knew it at the time. But, of course, they knew you were a *muzungu*—a foreigner—and they had to be careful.

"The hospitals in Mtwara are considered by many to be mediocre. When the hotel physician recalled that there had been numerous outbreaks of cerebral malaria, the hotel manager opted to bring you here, to us. This was no small doing as we're over two hours away from the hotel. But we're glad he did. You were really sick. You've been here more than a week.

"So, welcome back. You have had a rough time—a very rough time—delirium, high fever, chills, and more delirium. It has been difficult—but it's better now. Rest and drink lots of water. It will be alright."

Then she was gone.

Some unknown time later—Peter didn't know if it was hours or days—he awoke more aware of the here and now, at first thinking the sister's visit had been a dream until he took stock of his surroundings and the crucifix over the head of his bed. His new reality was truly that he was somehow or other again in a hospital. It might as well be Saint Benedict's. It might as well be malaria.

As he took in his surroundings, absorbed his reality, he realized how fortunate he had been. Whether Angola, Central Africa, or here in southern Tanzania, when he had been hit, and hit hard by serious health issues, he had been able to avoid the inadequate and even wretched dispensaries and clinics that accounted for most of the health care offered to the majority of the population. He had luckily (but perhaps not unexpectedly) managed to find himself in well-equipped and well-staffed hospitals capable of getting him back on his feet—be it ever so slowly.

He remembered what Dabi had said when he had told her of his Good Samaritan along with the doctors and nurses in Luanda: "The cassava today fit be gari tomorrow." Or, as his Nigerian colleagues had so often cautioned, "No condition is permanent."

On the one hand, this was encouragement that illness or ill tidings will not last forever—better times are ahead. On the other hand, however, this was an admonition that these better times, too, were ephemeral and would not last forever. Dabi, as so many he had met along the way, had learned (or been forced to accept) a tactic of taking life one day at a time.

Still, he was tired of days in hospital.

Nevertheless, it took a few more days before Peter was able to get up, bathe himself, and realize, as he stood up, how weak he had become. He was able to call Mr. Hong who admitted he had been in a panic. However, he had contacted the Mtwara police to see if anyone had stolen Peter's vehicle. The officers had tracked it to the Boma and the manager had recounted how his *muzungu* lodger had become terribly ill and been sent *post haste* to Saint Benedict's. In short, the company knew of Peter's illness—although their inaction and apparent indifference were inescapable.

Hong's only instruction, with no "get well soon," was to get back as soon as possible.

It was a full month before an enfeebled Peter presented himself in Hong's office. It was another month before Peter, under doctor's orders (otherwise, Peter was sure they would have immediately dispatched him back to Mogadishu or somewhere equally glum), was able to start work again.

There was the mandatory check-up on the port. All was fine.

Hong's unruffled assignment for Peter was not Mogadishu—it was Ethiopia. And, it was not, this time, just another visit to the capital—at least not to the national capital. Peter was to go to Arba Minch, the capital of the Gamo Gofa zone in the Southern Nations, Nationalities, and People's Region of this complex country—a city over 300 miles south of the nation's capital of Addis Ababa along the A7 highway, located between lakes Chamo and Abaya. The incredibly fast-growing city of nearly 50,000, a city that had not even existed several decades ago, was now home to a large textile industry and the Water Technology Institute.

Hong provided a dossier that explained Peter's assignment. In some ways, this was simply a much more extravagant and strenuous (for Peter) version of the recent Mtwara assignment. According to the file, the World Bank was planning a very large project to help local farmers process fruits and vegetable to reach higher-paying markets in Kenya and across East Africa. One of the major target crops was red peppers—hot chili peppers. These were to be processed into high quality hot sauce for the urban consumer.

Peter's task was to meet with the concerned parties and offer, on behalf of his masters, his services to provide all the necessary machinery to process and package hot sauce.

It was straight forward. Peter knew how to make friends and influence decisions. He was to use these now well-honed skills to ensure that he was the principal—no, the sole—supplier of everything the hot sauce project might need.

It was more of the same.

Yet, from the onset, it was clear that the triggers for success would be different from those in the port of Dar. He needed to move carefully, assessing each step. It would take time. Still, Mr. Hong did not seem to care how long it took as long as the required results were achieved.

On arrival, he spent a few days in Addis, staying at the Hilton, checking with the Bank's head office, getting a feel for what public agencies were involved, and basically trying to understand how things worked. He then booked a room at the Haile Valley Resort in Arba Minch, rented a car, and took the A7 south.

He had thought his lodgings were named after Haile Selassie, Emperor of Ethiopia from 1930 to 1974. However, apparently, his room was not in honor of the Emperor but in honor of Haile Gessoes—famed long-distance runner and Olympic gold medal winner.

He initially booked his room for a week. He was now in his third week. It was indeed a slow process. Like the country, this job was complex.

On the eve of his fourth week, he was in the resort's bar, wondering if he would ever be able to convince those needing convincing. He was just about to order another Harar Beer when he felt someone tap him lightly on the shoulder. Swiveling on his barstool, still amazed that he was still surprised, he saw Sir Horace attired in a forest-green blazer overlaying a cream turtleneck; all on top of precisely starched and creased khaki slacks and highly polished henna-colored loafers.

Enjoying the consternation in Peter's countenance, the old man could not resist piling-on. "So, Old Sport, you didn't think you'd see me here, huh?"

"Sir." Peter was never really sure what to call his *bête noire*. "I would not be surprised to see you anywhere, including the gates of hell."

"Now son." Sir Horace tried to look stricken in spite of the twinkle in his eye. "Is that any way to talk to someone like me who has done so much for you? Why, I've made you what you are today."

"Yes, you have definitely done that—for better or worse (I should think the latter, he thought but did not say)."

"So, what say you buy me a drink—you're flush staying in a luxury hotel with an open-ended expense account."

After his master got his flavor of the day, Chivas and soda, and he himself had a fresh beer, the newcomer stepped immediately into the subject that had made him fly to Addis and then take a small charter to this, according to him, outpost on the edge of nowhere. "We all hope you're making good progress."

Peter gave a lackluster nod.

"I know Hong emphasized this, but this a really big job. You know, 'don't fuck it up!'"

Another listless nod.

"Just between you and me and the lamppost, you're sitting on the brink of a major new area of investment for us—for you. 'Cause, if we do well, you do well—huh?"

The ho-hum responses continued.

"There's really big agricultural projects sprouting up—excuse my pun—all over the place. It's all a racket anyway. So, we want to get our slice of the pie. And you're the one serving this up right now. So, 'don't fuck up!'"

Peter ordered another beer.

"Boy, you've gotta run with this. I mean it. You'll remember I spoke of my brother and his company, Delpro—swell guy—great company. Well, while we sit here on the West side of the Rift Valley, good ol' Robin and Delpro, bless their hearts, are trying to engrain themselves into projects down the Valley in Samburu. They always like to follow my lead, huh?

"Now, we may be family—one big happy family, of course—he's my brother, after all—and a superb person, as I told you. Our organizations may even overlap—at times, a lot. We may even see many of the same people sitting on the perches above our heads. Nevertheless, we're all in a *laissez faire* society! And, damn it, right now, there's only space for one top dog and I intend to be that puppy! It's on your shoulders, kiddo. Is that clear?"

In the subdued barroom light, Sir Horace's face had become almost plum-colored. Really, Peter observed, with the emotion and the burden of time, he was more like a prune than a creaky Cockney (the idea made Peter smile an honest smile that he had to hide from his controller given the gravity of the situation).

Sir Horace was, in his own dramatic way, painting a serious portrait that, unavoidably, and by no choice of his own, put Peter right in the thick of things—things he would undoubtedly rather have avoided.

Peter understood, as Sir Horace would likely have put it, his knickers were now in a twist—the knot tightening.

Peter felt he needed to at least grunt his assent as the senescent senior droned on.

"Delpro—tremendous portfolio—maybe they'll be part of our wider international community. We may both serve some of the same gods. But don't let anyone mislead you. It's the ground game that counts. All the high-level chess they play at the summit would go nowhere if there were not gains on the ground. It is those grounded teams that have the advantage, that get to call the plays, and make the dividends. We need to be there at the forefront. This is not the usual compromise and sharing. This is all out competition for the highest stakes. And, once again I say, you're at the center of everyone's attention right now. Make us all proud and you'll make yourself rich. I can guarantee it. Fuck up, and you'll be shoveling shit til your hair turns gray."

Peter tried to give a little less antagonistic grunt.

"From the highest echelons, you're under the microscope. But I don't tell you this to scare you. I know you can do it. You've done things just as tough as this before. The job's really not that difficult. Still, the impact will be felt far away and for a long time. So, think before you jump and please, as I always advise, 'don't fuck up.'"

Peter ordered another beer and a Chivas for his overlord as he saw his tumbler was nearly empty. He then put on his biggest (most artificial, he thought) smile and, after all Sir Horace's oration, said, "No problem."

The elderly would-be gentleman drained his second glass in two gulps, holding Peter's eyes in a steely stare. "Kid, this is no longer the minor leagues. You've past the threshold and it's deadly serious."

"I hear you," Peter softly acknowledged.

"So." The venerable conniver smiled (or snickered, Peter was never sure) in turn, as he pushed back from the bar and stood up. "Bring the hot sauce home. Don't come back without it."

Then he was gone.

Whenever Sir Horace turned up, Peter's blood pressure shot up.

He was, ironically, just as nervous when he did not see the old fart for an extended period—wondering what had happened. Then, when he did see his raunchy and time-worn head honcho, his pressure rose as the presence of the geriatric grifter never bode well.

He, once more, was disturbingly reminded of the verses his father had spouted without end: Proverbs 22:24-25—*"Make no friendship with a man given to anger, nor go with a wrathful man, lest you learn his ways and entangle yourself in a snare."*

Peter was genuinely in a snare.

Yet, as it turned out, Sir Horace's appearance was just a blip on the long slog required to reach any level of understanding and visibility where he could leave a fingerprint. A month turned into two-and-a-half, but eventually Peter did manage to get to where he could leave a mark—to where he needed to go. He had (through skill or luck, he was never sure) woven an intricate tapestry that put his principals at center stage. He had, using Sir Horace's metaphor, set the table so that his masters could not just get a piece of the pie, at least as concerned Arba Minch, but the whole bloody thing.

With the pieces in place, he returned to Dar, tired but satisfied he had done the needful. His controllers had nothing about which to complain.

Nonetheless, there were no expectations of praise nor gratitude. His first day back in the office, he was sullenly and matter-of-factly given another dossier for another agricultural project; this time in eastern Congo. Like the old man had said, ag projects were flourishing.

Things began to escalate—undoubtedly much to the joy of senior management, but much to the burden of already overstretched junior staff. It became unavoidable. Mr. Hong, with his directors' blessings of course, had to expand the office and hire new staff. Equatorial Management was now becoming truly equatorial. The Dar workstation covered all of East Africa as well as some parts of the Central Region of the Continent.

Peter was, though with no personal satisfaction, still the centerpiece.

His efforts had been reflected in a sizable salary increase, if not in any specific personal recognition for his exceptional achievements. Still, it was work he did not enjoy—promises he knew that were often slight-of-hand. Methods that could easily backfire. And he remained the sole occupant of the center ring—the lights shining brightly on his face—others ensconced in the shadows.

As the ag project segment of Equatorial Management's program proliferated, Peter became the point man and in charge of cleanup. Much like the template from Mtwara (which he and probably nobody else ever imagined would turn out to be a template), there would be an initial contact when all the arrangements would be made (above and under the table). Other Equatorial Management folks would then take over getting all the services and materials in place. Peter would then return for the accounting. Going over the deliverables, verifying that all parties were satisfied, and, most importantly, getting signatures for final payments.

One of the most challenging sites, surprisingly even more so than Mogadishu, was southern Sudan. Here there was a dreadful civil war that pitted the south's Peoples Liberation Army against the central government—fighting, among other things, against the *sharia* law the Moslem government to the north wanted to impose on the mainly Christian and Animist southern communities.

This seemingly never-ending conflict had led to wide-spread famine. The area was inundated with food relief and agricultural projects. It was, therefore, an ideal place for Equatorial Management—by default, a place where Peter spent more time than he wished.

Given the endemic strife, the vast majority of projects were managed by local NGOs as opposed to large national or multinational agencies. The outsized transnationals often funded the NGOs in the background, but the boots on the ground and the on-the-spot decision-making was done by homegrown groups—groups with whom Peter had relatively quickly established good relations.

Community actors, frequently doing business without any form of government or other oversight, all welcomed the supplements Peter generously offered. Spreading the wealth spread Equatorial Management's influence. Soon the company was engaged in multiple actions, supplying overpriced goods and services while putting down roots to inveigle themselves into other areas where war presented not only terrible suffering but also considerable opportunity.

Given the high visibility of the political trauma being experienced by southern Sudan, funds flowed in to feed the famished. There were some medium-scale cereal-growing projects where Equatorial Management was able to make some serious earnings. Still, these were dwarfed by a series of impressive oil seed ventures—ventures where Equatorial Management contrived to control the entire value chain, making hefty profits at each step.

A big part of the oil seed activities was the sale and installation of a number of seed presses and bottling factories. Peter was advised of the arrival and set-up of the equipment—only learning much later that it had all come from Ukraine. Using Joe Thompson's techniques, Soviet-Union-era machinery with thick coats of shiny paint (all covered with Sir Horace's fingerprints, Peter thought) was supplied across a swath of the countryside where large tracts of sunflowers were being planted. Even the oil seed planting materials, Peter learned, were of Soviet origin.

For a while, everything went well. Village shelves were stocked with good quality local cooking oil.

Then, as if a house of cards (which in many ways it was), the equipment began to fail. Bumper harvests from the selected high-performance plants rotted. The value chain transformed from supplying oil to amplifying anger. Everyone was furious.

Peter was pulled off a trip to Uganda to get to Juba as rapidly as possible to sort out the affair before its negative impact pushed ripples through all the other actions where Equatorial Management now had planted its flag (and these were many).

While dealing with homegrown groups had had its advantages in terms of finagling the company's way into lucrative on-the-ground machinations, it also now had a real disadvantage. Local folks wanted local justice.

Large donor organizations might possibly write-off losses and simply blackball malefactors. At the most, they would bring some sort of legal action against the corporate headquarters, not the employees in the field.

No so with resident community organizations.

They wanted justice.

They wanted vengeance.

They wanted retribution—even if it was a pound of flesh.

And Peter was in the center ring.

When Peter returned to Juba, he was met at the airport (Mr. Hong de-crying the urgency and hiring a plane to hastily ferry his representative from Entebbe to Juba) by police. He was taken immediately to the central police station. He was locked in a cell.

There were no questions.

There were no formalities.

It was matter of fact.

It was a week before Peter was allowed out—and then, only to go before a judge. He asked to make a phone call. This wish was granted and, to his great surprise, the call to Dar went through. He spoke with the receptionist, Afaafa, who transferred him to the secretary. However, Regina said Mr. Hong could not take his call.

He then implored the judge to be able to contact the US Consulate. As Peter was traveling under a US passport, the judge apparently felt he could not refuse, and Peter was once again talking to a secretary—this time a Department of State employee. Yet, to his total dismay, the Con-sulate official informed him that they had been advised of his presence in southern Sudan and apprised, by staff in Washington, D.C. nonetheless, that he was traveling under fraudulent papers. The Consulate would be visiting him in jail. But this would only be to decide if the US Govern-ment wanted to add charges to those already lodged against Peter.

This was horrendous!

Peter had no idea what to do.

The judge, however, knew exactly what to do.

He scheduled Peter's trial in six-months' time, politely apologizing for the busy docket, and sent him back to his jail cell to wait.

Just as for Saint Peter, not that our Peter was anywhere near saintly, peo-ple everywhere denied any knowledge of him or his affairs. Here there was no crowing cock to remind people that they did in fact know Peter, had in fact worked with Peter. There was no repentance—there was no backpedaling. There was only denial.

When questioned by authorities in the run-up to the trial, Equato-rial Management, partner NGOs, even hotel operators and barmen all claimed to have only seen, never known, this stray and furtive man—this white man--this *rajul 'abyad* (XXX XXXX in Arabic). He was a pretender and a crook. No one knew him.

Peter could mount no defense.

He could not defend himself.

He could only thumb his Bible—as always seeing it as reading material (the only available reading material) to occupy the time—nothing of any spiritual value nor emotional comfort.

Nonetheless, he read passages—looking through them like through cellophane, as he gazed back over his journey. Often, his eyes returned to Proverbs; this always brought a smile to his lips as a proverb was generally linked to wisdom—a character he had sorely lacked. The Book of Proverbs, especially selected verses from chapter seventeen, seemed to merge into a description of his life—an explanation as to how and why he might find himself where he did. With no small degree of consternation, he frequently re-read these passages:

> *Proverbs 17:1, 4, 8, 16, 20, 23, 25—"Better a dry crust with peace and quiet than a house full of feasting, with strife . . . A wicked person listens to deceitful lips; a liar pays attention to a destructive tongue . . . A bribe is seen as a charm by the one who gives it; they think success will come at every turn . . . Why should fools have money in hand to buy wisdom, when they are not able to understand it? . . . One whose heart is corrupt does not prosper; one whose tongue is perverse falls into trouble . . . The wicked accept bribes in secret to pervert the course of justice . . . A foolish son brings grief to his father and bitterness to the mother who bore him."*

Peter was brought before the bench for the high crimes of larceny, extortion, and fraud—the US Consulate charitably declined to press any charges. He sat in a stifling courtroom for ten days as a parade of individuals passed before the black-robed rotund judge who would define Peter's future. The witnesses, all for the prosecution, described in minute detail how this unknown white man had appeared and with sweet-talk and lies convinced them to embark on tasks that were doomed to failure—tasks only lining the *rajul 'abyad*'s pockets with ill-gotten gold and worsening the conditions of poor people already horribly scarred by war and famine. It was a complete travesty of justice.

The judge was visibly moved—and not by Peter's innocence.

Peter was sentenced to fifteen years in Borh Prison, 125 miles north of Juba along the White Nile.

Peter was shattered—shattered and imprisoned.

Against the wishes of his parents, he had claimed a rite of passage. He had not claimed the ritual for incorporation into his community; killing a marauding leopard or building a house for his soon-to-be wife to become a vetted member of the greater whole. He had arrogantly claimed his imagined postpubescent right to find himself. He had incautiously traveled the breadth of a continent trying to discover what he wanted to be when he grew up.

He now knew—a prisoner.

He remembered the Ashante proverb the kids had recited when he was growing up: "By the time the fool has learned the game, the players have dispersed."

CHAPTER SEVENTEEN

Locked up

How bad can it get?

PETER, BORN IN THE valley of the White Volta, was in jail on the banks of the White Nile.

It was terrible—it was traumatic.

It wasn't fair. It wasn't right.

But it was real. He had fled jail to be jailed

The son of Paul had fallen off the face of the Earth.

At least, he thought he had. And, at least, he thought it was a gift (if he dare use that word) that he was in southern Sudan and not regions to the North where *sharia* law might have already cost him his head. Here Christianity was common. Here they had allowed him to keep one possession with him in his cell: his Bible.

He began to seriously fear his attachment to the Good Book was akin to his father's ardor for that text. Yet, he was still confident that the words were mere pastimes. To him, it was a book like so many others. It was just a book, but it did have nearly an infinite collection of passages that seemed to apply to a multitude of events—whether rightly or wrongly.

He read at least one passage every day—not wanting to go too fast—wanting to savor it like a sweet pudding slowly dissolving on the palate. He found numerous appropriate, if not soothing, verses. Some of his most often read and reread (he would not say, "cherished") were in Psalms: *Psalm* 146:8 *and* 9—*"The Lord sets prisoners free, the Lord gives sight to the blind, the Lord lifts up those who are bowed down, the Lord*

loves the righteous. The Lord watches over the foreigner and sustains the
fatherless and the widow, but he frustrates the ways of the wicked."

Still nothing changed.

He was locked up.

Painfully, he recalled Evelynn's frequent warning, "*Hajuliki mwema na muovu.*" She translated it as saying, "You can't tell a good person from a bad one." He had certainly known the bad and was paying the price. He was afraid—very afraid.

CHAPTER EIGHTEEN

A Sinner's Wares

Noblesse oblige

SIR HORACE WAS NOT afraid. He was angry.

He, of course, had followed Peter's misadventures from afar.

While he honestly liked the young man, he felt no remorse for his minion's dire straits. Peter was just one of his many tools.

It was too bad the Sudanese activities had taken a hit. They had been very promising and would be difficult to resuscitate. Maybe that damn Peter deserved to be in jail again—he'd spoiled a very profitable portfolio of ventures.

Peter's real innocence in the matter—he having had no role in choosing the equipment to provide for the oil press project—was not even a thought that entered Sir Horace's head. Someone had fucked up. Things had turned to shit. It was time to move on.

But the old man's pragmatic approach to the volatility of his investments—more truthfully, the investments of his own masters, although he saw these projects as "his"—was not what made him angry.

He was angry because of the lopsidedness of the playing field—there were always the vultures and the assessors ready to swoop in on any spilled crumbs—taking advantage of any vulnerabilities.

In many ways he regretted (regrets were things upon which Sir Horace did not often fixate) having told young Peter about his life's story—about his origins, about his childhood (albeit, very briefly), and about his brother. Back in Arba Minch, he probably shouldn't have told the cheeky little shit about his brother—at least not about Delpro. But what was done was fucking done. Who would try to dig up the secrets? Who would give a fuck?

The geriatric nobleman's indiscretions aside, because what could that incorrigible punk do buried on the banks of the Nile, he was even more irritated, maybe furious, because he had lost any momentum for overtaking his brother in terms of villainy. The playing field had tilted. He had sworn, brother or no brother, to become top dog. He could taste the sweet bouquet of success becoming acid in his mouth. Once again, through no action of his own, Robin had won.

This wasn't, naturally, just about who'd have the most nefarious operations in the Rift Valley. It wasn't ultimately about who had the most power or money. Both brothers knew all too well they themselves were just maggots in a great heap of putrefaction. They weren't the down-in-the-gutter shit-on-your-shoes soldiers of the organization. But, from 30,000 feet, they were just as much expendable pawns as those in the carrion-filled trenches.

He and Robin had a high degree of freedom and were handsomely rewarded for their successes at beating the system. But each had his own boss. Each was on a leash of varying length.

Above their own masters, there were undoubtedly, as rumored, more and more layers in the never seen and never understood organization.

Horace, and for that matter Robin, had few options in terms of looking up into to the clouded architecture that ultimately ran everything. They could look down to the labyrinth of scurrilous acts and actors under their purview. They could also look sideways—brother to brother.

Horace imagined he loved his brother. Yet, he was intuitive enough to know he was unsure if he knew anything of love—brotherly or otherwise. Those days when they had been together were so, so long ago. He doubted he really knew his sibling. Moreover, and more to the point of his angst, whether the luck of the draw or a bad omen, he had always felt his big brother had been favored and had had the better chance by being adopted in the US and not the UK.

Their paths had never strayed far apart and today they were basically equals in planning and implementing misdeeds. They even collaborated often on scandals and delinquency.

Possibly, Horace ruminated, this was just human behavior—the younger brother always trying to outcompete the older. Maybe. For whatever reasons, he did want to outdo Robin. For all that, he wished his brother no harm, no ill will (knowing, if outside forces intimidated them, the brothers would band together into one fierce fraternal unit). He just wished him a little bad luck so that Robin's follow-back could shine a bit brighter.

For now, shining (or, at long last, overshadowing his blessed big brother) through his own exceptional (as he saw them) efforts in Sudan was no longer possible.

Damn that fucking cocky kid locked up on the Nile.

Sir Horace was back in South Africa, sipping a daiquiri at the bar of the Marriott Hotel near O.R. Tambo Airport. He was waiting for a new youngster—a bright upstart pointed out by unsavory colleagues in London.

Horace was pragmatic (and hardly phlegmatic, he thought). He assumed, he had to assume that the once up-and-coming Peter would never see the outside of Borh Prison. And so much the better. While he had been frugal in how much he had divulged to his hireling, the kid was sharp. Maybe worse, the kid had a lot of connections. He was likely able to interpret much more from the scant information shared with him. He gleaned a little and extrapolated a lot. That had made him a valuable tool. It also made him a potential threat if he were ever to walk freely again. But now there was little chance of that.

So, Sir Horace had to start to backfill. He needed new people to slowly move into places where Peter had been so effective. No one was irreplaceable. Still, Peter would be hard to replace. Nonetheless, replace him he would. His meeting at the hotel was the first step in the process.

Much to his frustration, the newcomer's flight had been delayed by several hours. Sir Horace was stuck at the hotel bar.

Accepting he had to modulate his drinking to be able to carefully evaluate this in-coming neophyte, he oh so slowly savored his drink while he let his mind float freely about the nearly empty bar.

He and Robin had been lucky. There had been a multitude of potential pathways that could have brought them to despair and even premature death. Having stayed in the Romania of the Soviet Union as Horațiu and Răzvan had been, fortunately, a nonstarter. Then, years later reconnecting with their family, now with western educations and contacts, had led to openings in Ukraine's massive criminal network. Their unique biographies had pole-vaulted the brothers up the ladder of the alternate economy run by powerful and clandestine figures. Delpro, Equatorial Management, and an entire ever-changing web of cloaked enterprises gradually—with the blessings of the higher-ups—revealed themselves to the brothers.

They had found their calling. And, it turned out, they were both very good at what they did.

In those early years with the organization, the intertwined narratives of the two middle-aged men of Patzinak heritage had proven to be mutually reinforcing. Although they engaged in, at times, cutthroat competition, they always managed to keep their fraternal bonds intact. To the outside world, they were the two pearly haired, rose complected men from Eastern Europe—this moniker remaining in spite of their lives and accomplishments in the UK and the US.

However, between them, there was a continual tug of war—at times playful, at times deadly serious—but always there. This competitiveness was not to determine who could be seen in the best light for their common masters. They knew they each did good work and there was no need for play-acting or theatrics. This rivalry was as simple as it was elementary: each wanted to outfox the other—feeding their egos and not their careers.

Horace knew this was nothing about good versus evil.

There was no moral high ground.

There was no right conquering wrong (or the reverse).

At least between the brothers, there were no illusions. This was doing what they wanted to do for their own enrichment with full knowledge and forethought that they were outside the law—they were rogues and malefactors.

There was no contrition for sins committed.

There was no political or religious ideology in which to wrap their ignoble deeds.

They had been kids fighting to get out of Romania. They had been kids fighting to stay afloat in the UK and the US. They had been young men trying to get a foothold in new careers. But they were now old men, old well-to-do men who could have left the game years ago but who stayed in because they enjoyed the rush—they needed the thrill—they wanted to keep competing with each other.

Almost reluctantly, Sir Horace ordered another drink as his thoughts shifted gears—moving from Robin to the organization. He really had no clue how big it was. He didn't know how vast its holdings were. He was unaware of who sat atop the global dung heap that was the conglomerate of crime called the organization. He just knew it was.

The topic was taboo. No one asked about the organization. No one enquired about the who's, the where's, or the how's. Just as for some God was an omnipresent unseen presence, so was the organization.

Sir Horace and Robin never discussed the subject—not even when alone in some isolated alcove. They matter-of-factly accepted it as being there and they themselves as being small parts of a very big whole. There was nothing more with which to concern oneself.

Nevertheless, in the backrooms of his mind, Sir Horace did wonder. He wondered who? He wondered why? And, most perplexingly, he wondered how?

Whatever it was, it was massive. It had roots and arteries everywhere. It cut across oceans; it permeated governments and industries; it infiltrated villages and megalopolises. In his mind's eye he could only envision it as a great dark cloud that enveloped the globe.

A worldwide smog of sin.

Amorphous and omnipresent as it might be, it was still driven by someone. There was a person at the helm. Hidden deep in the vapors, there was someone who was in control—from all his indications, in very tight control.

It was an enigma.

Yet, none of this could be told to the young man he was about to meet. The new Peter needed to be kept in the dark. With time, he might or might not discover more. But for the moment, ignorance was salvation for a newcomer.

The thought of Peter brought his reflections full circle. He imagined the young man in a hellhole on the Nile.

Well, he nearly spoke out loud to himself, "Better him than me—I kept telling him not to fuck up."

Chapter Nineteen

Blue Skies

Do walls a prison make?

PETER VOMITED.

He vomited until his guts ached.

He vomited until tears seeped down his grime-encrusted cheeks.

Prison gruel was practically inedible. Prison hygiene was nonexistent. The only concession, the only gift—as the Prison Director had magnanimously called it—was that Peter was in a cell by himself. Somehow authorities did not feel comfortable putting a *rajul 'abyad* in the general population.

Peter was allowed into one of the prison's courtyards in the morning before the temperatures became unbearable—at least to him. This was repeated before sunset as the earth cooled to meet the night. When outside, he was with a group of mainly aging prisoners—apparently a group the overseers felt posed no danger to a defenseless white man.

His yard-mates showed no compunctions about mixing with a *ferenghi*—an outsider—a foreigner. Prison was a great equalizer. They all wore the same putrid rags, ate the same rubbish, and shat in the same buckets. With all that, what importance was a little difference in pigmentation?

Peter and his co-inmates would sit in the shade of the few trees that inhabited the yard, communicating in a hodgepodge of sign language augmented by word scraps from English, French, Arabic, Ki-Swahili, or languages totally unknown to Peter. Their exchanges were the bases of

human existence: family, health, survival. None proclaimed their innocence nor planned for tomorrow—they were only trying to survive today.

When Peter was not enjoying his sorties to the yard, he was cloistered in his cell, overloaded with oppressive thoughts that made those
late-night weighty deliberations he had had with himself in his flat in Dar
seem like child's play.

Here there were no mental guardrails. Even though he tried to
curb his free-wheeling mind, he could not. His brain sloshed to-and-
fro, grasping ideas like a drowning man grasps flotsam. He moved from
frenzy to hysteria to dread.

He thought of his parents—of his family. Did they love him? Had
they loved him? Did he love them?

Had he been a welcomed son or an encumbrance to two people who
felt they operated by divine right?

Had he been a good son? Or had he been an embarrassment?

Should he have stayed at home? Should he have followed in his father's footsteps as his father had followed in those of his own father?

Would he, should he become a father himself? Was not he ill-qual-
ified and unsuited to be a parent—perhaps as his own parents had been?

What did he know of his sister? Had he been a good brother? Could
he be a good brother?

What of love?

Did he know love?

Had he loved Ruby, Dabi, Katy, or Evelynn?

Did he love them?

Could he love them?

Could he love at all?

His father had ended it all—should he do the same? He could probably hang himself with his rotten and ragged bedding if he really tried.

His mother had gone crazy. Was he going crazy?

The world was crazy. Why shouldn't he be crazy too?

His brain sloshed and swirled.

He missed everyone. He longed for anyone.

He found himself clinging to his sole possession—his Bible.

He found himself, in strange ways that made him feel very uncomfortable, seemingly relying on the Bible as his father had.

He saw himself sinking into its words while still not fully grasping
their meanings—their impacts.

He worried he would be sucked into the morass—he would be parasitized by verses and thoughts he did not truly understand.

Was he brainwashed?

Had his father been brainwashed?

Was the Bible friend or foe?

Ultimately, he found his Bible to be of little help. It was more like pouring acid on the wounds of despair and solitude. As a perfect example:

> *Ecclesiastes 4:9-12—"Two are better than one, because they have a good reward for their toil. For if they fall, one will lift up his fellow. But woe to him who is alone when he falls and has not another to lift him up! Again, if two lie together, they keep warm, but how can one keep warm alone? And though a man might prevail against one who is alone, two will withstand him—a threefold cord is not quickly broken."*

How he longed to have Evelynn by his side to lift him up, to keep him warm, to talk with him, to comfort him.

He was in hell.

Probably, he guessed, this was his destiny.

If his perdition was of his own making, was his torment a result of the weeping stone walls that encased his body or the raving thoughts that encased his mind?

Was there a route from the inferno?

Was there a way to quench the agony?

Could he find peace?

Where could he find peace?

He could not, in spite of himself, put his book down. What else did he have to do?

He found himself careening through its pages, like someone lost in a forest (and he was, indeed, lost).

He would randomly lurch from chapter to chapter, verse to verse.

Some selections he would read, other times he would stare at the pages until the words began to move.

Then he stumbled upon a passage not so much of hope or solace, but of redress, even vengeance (at least, in his interpretation):

> *Psalm 69:18-24—"Come near and rescue me; deliver me because of my foes. You know how I am scorned, disgraced and shamed; all my enemies are before you. Scorn has broken my heart and has left me helpless; I looked for sympathy, but there was none, for*

comforters, but I found none. They put gall in my food and gave me vinegar for my thirst. May the table set before them become a snare; may it become retribution and a trap. May their eyes be darkened so they cannot see, and their backs be bent forever. Pour out your wrath on them; let your fierce anger overtake them."

He was truly a captive—unlikely to be rescued. Yes, he was also a sinner. Still, he was the sacrificial lamb of Equatorial Management and all the hidden masters that sat above this depraved company. He had been thrown into the abyss to sink or swim—but to sink or swim on his own accord with not the slightest intervention from those who truly controlled his actions—those who pulled the strings. To have these puppet masters, these crooked controllers, these heartless souls listed among the unrighteous—to have them blinded so as not do no more harm—this would definitely be justice, even if it meant he remained in captivity.

At the end of the day, Biblical verses or not, in the words of that pompous asshole Horace, Peter had "fucked up." Or, more to his tastes, he had simply been fucked.

There was no salvation.

Not from a book.

Not from a god.

He would melt into dust like everything in Borh.

He would never feel the blue skies and soft breezes of freedom again.

He continued to paw at his Bible—the book now almost unrecognizable, with a permanent layer of filth and numerous frayed pages (pages, thin and supple, that he had so far managed to safeguard from more disgusting use when he had recurrent bouts of diarrhea). But it was more a talisman than a comfort.

A day did not go by where Peter did not leaf through the pages of his tattered Good Book. Yet, as always, in spite of the horrid conditions and the constant depression, it was not a pathway to finding God—not a conduit to discovering the "delicious truths," as his father had called them; truths of comfort and liberation offered by Our Father in his Great Book.

It was just a book and his only possession.

He was like a dog guarding his bone. Even if his corroded teeth could no longer gnaw at its core, even if he could no longer hack away at the most rock-like parts, he would guard it with all his being because it was his.

This was, after all, the book that was the essence of his parents' universe. It had been their basanite throughout, and, by default, the yardstick for his own childhood.

Nonetheless, it was just a book.

He sought answers.

He sought explanations.

He sought hope.

He found a diversion—a way to pass the time—and he had an abundance of time.

As opposed to the typical random Biblical events that had been spouting up in his thoughts for a long time, he decided to try to systematically categorize in his mind his parents' favorite (or at least most often recounted— proselytized really, Peter concluded) verses. He then tried to match the quotation with a specific memory of his family. He wanted not to forget. It was so easy to forget.

He recalled his father often telling his mother she had the patience of Job. So, of course, he skimmed through the pages to find Job. These were, in truth, passages that he thought, with a stretch (a pretty good one at that), just might, unlike so many others, somehow be indicative of his misery:

> *Job 6:11-13—"What strength do I have, that I should still hope? What prospects, that I should be patient? Do I have the strength of stone? Is my flesh bronze? Do I have any power to help myself, now that success has been driven from me?"*

This all tracked intrinsically with Peter—the verses seemed after a fashion applicable to him and his present heinous situation. Hope was being driven from him. He recalled his father referring to Job as a righteous man and a wealthy landowner—none of which obviously applied to himself. Still, Job's words described how his faith helped him persevere:

> *Job 27:2-7—"As surely as God lives, who has denied me justice, the Almighty, who has made my life bitter, as long as I have life within me, the breath of God in my nostrils, my lips will not say anything wicked, and my tongue will not utter lies. I will never admit you are in the right; till I die, I will not deny my integrity. I will maintain my innocence and never let go of it; my conscience will not reproach me as long as I live. May my enemy be like the wicked, my adversary like the unjust!"*

Job, as Peter read, seemed to have found God—found his God. Had he truly found faith? Did he find vengeance? Were these compatible? Was his devotion to save his soul or his life? Peter did not know. Job refused to admit his accusers were right. Job professed his innocence. He declared himself as having a clear conscience—free of wrongdoing.

For Job, it seemed patience had paid off.

Could he, Peter, have such hopes?

Peter thought not.

Moreover, Peter thought he was far off from finding his God.

Still, maybe, as he really had no choice, he would be able to find patience.

Peter did not know if it was patience.

He was no longer sure what patience looked like.

Are you patient when you are refused to go anywhere, do anything?

He thought not.

It was not patience, it was endurance.

Yet, as his body forcefully endured, his mind roamed.

He wanted to seize his memories. He wanted not to forget.

His chaotic (often panicky) solitary thoughts were not solely self-centered. His twisting ruminations were not solely whirling about the Good Words in the Good Book. He also thought in broader strokes about his life in Africa—a place those of his country of nationality thought of as a backward and a pagan world.

In spite of the uneducated biases and the views of the Continent in the frame of a Tarzan movie, Peter knew—he deeply understood—how lucky he had been to have been able to see, to touch, to smell, to taste so much. He had tried so hard to live his life.

Now, imprisoned by four walls and even more formidable unconscious barriers, he relived this life.

He saw, touched, smelled, tasted.

He wondered.

Had he really seen, touched, smelled, and tasted?

Had he looked without really seeing?

Had he touched without really feeling?

Had he inhaled without really smelling?

Had he eaten without really tasting?

Yes.

He had somehow flown above the surface.

Was it white privilege?

Was it American arrogance?

Was it youthful ignorance?

Was it naivety?

Was it the artificial life of a tourist?

What had it really been?

Peter had a wealth of questions. He was flooded with questions.

Where were the answers?

How could he find answers within four walls?

He could not find them in the Good Book.

He could not find them in his soul.

He could not find them in his heart.

He could not find them in his mind.

Where could he find the answers?

Would the old men under the tree in the yard have the answers?

His brain was exploding.

He felt the waters of Lake Volta lapping at his ankles.

He felt a push.

He felt a pull.

How much time had passed?

Peter had no idea.

Like a flea crossing the Adomi Bridge back in Ghana, he could not see the other side—he could only see the expanses of today and tomorrow lying before him. He could only go ahead, one small footstep at a time. Thinking, hoping, trusting that at some point—some still unknown and unseen point—he would reach the other side of the bridge.

Earlier than usual, his guards came to escort him—he assumed to the yard for his afternoon outing. However, they took a different route through the maze of prison pathways, taking him to a small and musty room with a rickety table and two rickety chairs—no windows—one door. They manhandled him into one of the chairs, gruffly saying, "*abaq ealaa wadeik*" (ابق على وضعك)—although English and Arabic were the working languages of southern Sudan, and his keepers undoubtedly knew he was an Anglophone, they persistently ordered him about in Arabic—this time telling him to "stay put"). They then left, locking the door behind them.

Peter stared at the dust motes. He followed them on their journey through the mildew-full air, thinking if he could sail so, he would be long gone. He was following one such floater, with his back to the door, when he heard the portal open and then heard, in American English, "Far cry from pool-side at the Hôtel Des *Mille Collines*, huh?"

He snapped around so fast his neck hurt.

There was Joe Thompson, crossing the room and taking the second chair at the table as the bolt slid shut on the door and the guards disappeared.

"Who'd have thought we'd meet in a prison on the White Nile?"

"Joe?"

"Yep. You're not dreaming—I promise."

"Joe."

"Yep, just stopped by to say, 'Hi.' You up for a chat?"

"Joe."

"Indeed, rub your eyes. It is I—not the Ghost of Christmas Past, but the next best thing."

"OK."

"OK. So now I think you're with me. Wanna chat?"

"But how'd you . . ."

"Don't worry about the how's now-now. Just tell me, do you have time for a chat? Seems like you've a lot of free time—but I'm not sure. Thought I'd check."

"Yea. Sure. Talk."

Peter's lips were sticking together with heavy globs of white mucus, so Joe called a guard and asked for some water. Apparently given the visitor's status, the guard returned with a sealed bottle of spring water and two clean glasses—items Peter had not seen for ages.

Peter greedily gulped three glasses of water and then inhaled deeply before he was able to sit up straight, look Joe in the eyes, and say, "Go ahead. I'm all yours."

"Great. Now, let me tell you a few things just so we don't get our lines crossed."

"OK."

"Here I'm working for a schoolbook company that subsidizes school supplies for kids in tough places—places like Sudan. So, remember that— I'm here with schoolbooks."

"OK."

"But let's be frank. You've seen me before in different places—wearing, though you may not have noticed it, different hats."

"Sure."

"Well, I won't trouble you with the details, but I do wear lots of hats. My employer is a tiny piece of the massive government of the United States of America that wishes to remain anonymous. It suffices to say that I'm involved in a lot of things and I come to see you in regard to these things."

Peter nodded.

"Peter, this is important. I'm not your buddy here to see how you're doing in lockup. I'm not your chum to see how I can break you out. I'm here on business. Do you understand?"

"OK.

"Not 'OK.' Do you understand?"

"Yes."

"Fine. So now that we're on the same page, let me explain some more. My business brings me here because I think you might be able to help me. As in any business, there is quite possibly a *quid pro quo*. If it turns out that you can help me, I might—*might*—be able to help you. Is that clear?"

"Yes."

"Great. Let's get to it. First some more water. This might be thirsty business."

Joe again called the guards, briefly exchanged a few words through the door, and promptly three more bottles of water appeared.

Peter drained half of one immediately.

"OK, Peter, let's dig in. Do you know one Sir Horace Barthley?"

There followed a lengthy, and at times prickly, interrogation. Joe wanted to know all about Peter's relationship with Sir Horace—he wanted to know ALL about it—the smallest details.

Although Peter had not seen his ostensible master since before his imprisonment, he had been the old man's minion for years. He likely knew more, even if he wasn't aware of all he knew, about the miscreant nobleman then most others. Furthermore, Peter's animus toward the aging scoundrel meant he was uniquely placed to tell tales from which others would flee.

Peter could be the ideal informant.

He could also be a damaged asset who, at the end of the day, was of little help.

Time would tell.

Three more water bottles were brought in to signal a sort of halftime break. Then Joe picked up where he had left off, "Do you know a Robin McCandless?"

"No," Peter replied, fighting the fatigue that pressed down on him after more thought and talk than he had done in a long time, "Sir Horace referred to him, he's the old fart's brother I think, but I've never met him—don't think I've ever laid eyes on him."

"OK. Well, just to provide a little context so you don't think I'm only pumping you without trying to make sure you're at least understanding the broader context, Sir Horace and McCandless are brothers. The story Sir Horace told you is true. McCandless is the key figure in many activities in the US and around the globe. Most of these are through a company called Delpro. Have you ever run across or worked with Delpro?"

"No. Again, I've heard the name mentioned—in no special context—but I've never dealt with them in any way—as far as I know."

"OK, what can you tell me about Equatorial Management?"

The inquisition continued.

At one particular point in the discussion, Joe abruptly stood up, stretched, and announced, "That's fine for now."

"But . . ." Peter tried to intervene.

"Don't worry. We'll pick this up later."

Then he was gone.

Peter was back in his cell.

Peter was back in his routine.

Peter was back in his wild thoughts.

Joe's visit seemed like a dream.

Had it really happened?

Then weeks or months later, time had no benchmarks, Peter's move to the stifling mildew-covered room was repeated. Again, he was visited by Joe.

Joe was all smiles. "Last time, Peter, we talked about a lot of stuff. When I got back to my hotel, I tried to summarize our discussion—sending this recap to my colleagues. They liked it. They've given me the go-ahead. Know what that means?"

"Nope."

"Well, it means good news. My colleagues are well placed. They know how to get things done. They've started looking into your case. You've got some powerful folks against you. Your adversaries have invested in a lot of *baksheesh* with a lot of well-situated Sundanese to keep you exactly where you are—keep you here for a long, long time. They've built a pretty strong box to keep you in—to keep you out of the way and under control. However, my colleagues may be even more influential. They're trying. We'll see how far we can get."

"Hmmm."

"So, let me go a step farther—off the record, you know. You've heard of the witness protection program—like where the FBI whisks you away to the wastelands of Utah with a new identity—putting you on ice until they decide if they need you in some sort of legal maneuver or another?"

"Uh-huh."

"So, my people do the same sort of thing—not exactly the same, and maybe not in exactly the same way, but we try and identify people who help our cause and take care of them until or if we need them. It's really a pretty good deal."

"Uh-huh."

"So, this is on the table. This is an option."

"An option—that means there are other options, huh?"

"Well, we've always operated with a number of scenarios."

"Then you could just walk out that door today and that's that—nothing more—I just rot here?"

"Remember, I made it clear that this is business. Businesses do things that are best for the businesses. I just can't tell you now what the best move will be and for whom. What I've shown you and told you is that there is interest—if there wasn't, you'd never have seen me again after my first visit. My colleagues are engaged. I think this is a good sign. You'll simply have to be patient."

As he spoke, Joe could see Peter's frustration, his near panic. Joe knew patience was not one of Peter's attributes. He had come prepared—he hoped.

"Peter," he said in a calm voice, "no one ever said this was going to be easy. Christ look how long it took you to get this messed-up. We're looking for common ground here. If needed, my colleagues have provided a brief entrée to them, so you'll know you're not just dealing with me. I'm just the guy in front of you. Behind me there's a whole buncha folks."

Joe handed Peter a crisp and neatly folded sheet of A4 paper.

Peter read—thinking back to the letters from his sister, wincing at the memories. The letter was handwritten in a neat and precise script:

> *Dear Peter,*
>
> *My name is Rodney Mills. I start by telling you my name because I tell NOBODY my name—certainly not people in your situation. I tell you my name to try and underscore the seriousness with which I view our relationship with you. I am one of those behind-the-scenes people who knows a lot and can get a lot done. I say this not to brag, but to assure you that you are dealing with people who can do things, but who remain in the darkness.*
>
> *My team, my colleagues, and I have been working for years on examining issues that involve many of the groups and companies you know. You've been in the trenches, and we've been watching. While you may not know all that you know, we are sure you know a good deal. It is with this confidence that we are willing to try and help you. This is not charity. If we do help you, and I honestly believe we can, you must help us. That's the way it works. You've gone through this once before—you know the dance. And I can promise you that this time the outcome will be more satisfactory than the first time.*
>
> *So, Peter, if you're ready to be our partner, please let Joe know. He's a good fellow and he is trying to do all he can to help you, as am I. I hope someday we can meet in the flesh.*
>
> *Sincerely,*
> *Rodney*

Peter refolded the page, handing it back to Joe who put in his shirt pocket as he held is gaze on Peter.

Peter was uncomfortable.

Who the hell was Rodney Mills?

Who pulled his strings? Probably the same assholes who yanked that ol' bastard Horace's leash.

Who to trust when all were to fear?

It was just another shit-storm brewing.

Peter was in prison.

Peter was troubled.

Peter found this totally unsatisfactory—but it wasn't like he had any other choice. He had to go ahead with Joe. After all, if he failed, what could his enemies do to him—he was already in prison—he was already a lost soul.

He and Joe had another long day of questions and answers, Joe leaving with Peter's commitment (if given with great uneasiness), but no apparent plans nor any explicit way forward.

It was, to Peter, cruel and unusual punishment to toy with him—to build up his hopes only to dash then and then build them up again.

The cycle was repeated twice more. Each time there were long lists of questions about Equatorial Management, Sir Horace, Peter's travels, Peter's partners, Peter's life. After each session, it seemed as though Peter's replies were distilled and analyzed by those in the shadows and a new set of questions filtered for the following session when the process was replayed.

After the fourth session, Peter felt emptied—he had nothing more to offer. He had given all and he still had no inkling as to what, if anything, Joe had in mind.

When Joe left this time, Peter felt he would never see him again.

CHAPTER TWENTY

The Seeker

In search of rectitude

RODNEY MILLS HOPED PETER understood his note. He hoped the incarcerated young man appreciated the seriousness of both his situation and the offer Rodney was making.

To say Rodney was aware of the seriousness of the actions involving Peter was to make a major understatement. Rodney had been totally absorbed by the misdeeds of the so-called organization for years.

Rodney was a lawyer—a Harvard-trained lawyer at that. He worked for the Division of Enforcement of the Security and Exchange Commission. He had started with this group right out of law school as a member of the Task Force team headed up by chief investigator (the agency called them analysts) Hal Schleider.

Hal had a nearly revered reputation. He had been with Special Forces in Vietnam. During the war he had migrated to the CIA in the Central Highlands, working with the Montagnards. He moved into Cambodia as part of the Studies and Observation Group, staying until bombing started in 1970. Then, as an experienced and talented senior operative, he began taking assignments all across the globe. Hal had finally found his niche when he landed with the Security and Exchange Commission where he was the focal point for high-level international corporate criminality. Here he sought to identify the culpable with unparalleled dedication and fervor up to his untimely death—a death, Rodney recalled, that was not from natural causes and that was still an unsolved case itself.

Hal had become nearly obsessed with his assignment. Initially, he had slowly, like someone tasting an unfamiliar soup, immersed himself in the Task Force's work: identifying leading offenders of the Security and Exchange Commission's federal security laws on the global stage. The team was to do all possible to limit if not eliminate these rapscallions.

The more he dug, the more he found. Then, completely unexpectedly, his investigation had lurched forward due to the terrible misadventures of his nephew Eddie.

Eddie was a surveyor. He worked overseas when his wife Samantha was on the staff of an international NGO supporting refugees. Eddie had undertaken several assignments in Europe and Africa for an American firm named Delpro. These commissions had led to his uncovering a number of questionable practices. When he began to aggressively query his findings, Samantha was killed in a tragic accident in Zambia that was, in retrospect, no accident, but an effort to get Eddie to leave well enough alone.

Eddie had left Africa and, heavy-heartedly, secluded himself at his family home on the Pacific Coast. Yet, no matter how hard Eddie tried, it appeared he could not tear free of Delpro. As he haltingly emerged from his mourning, he began to take a few jobs around home. To his astonishment, he eventually uncovered that these local actors were also tangled in the tentacles of Delpro. This felonious and furtive company seemed to be doing ill everywhere. Eddie reached out to his Uncle Hal. Ultimately, Hal's nephew became a prime witness in the first case against Delpro.

Hal had begun to think they were actually going to be able to halt Delpro's ostensibly limitless influence. On a number of crucial occasions, Eddie had witnessed a man with a remarkable mane of alabaster hair that off-set a pink complexion engaging with individuals he knew to be lawbreakers. With Eddie's help, Hal had been able to piece together many parts of the riddle, the uncle-nephew duo greatly assisted by hundreds of hours of work by Hal's able team. Finally, Hal was ninety-eight percent sure the incongruous man from Eddie's tales was Robin McCandless.

Appallingly, Hal unexpectedly died before he could apprehend McCandless—a death, like Samantha's, that was not due to an accident nor natural causes. Before his death, Hal had been able to track McCandless to a cloistered villa at Candy Point, at the confluence of the Potomac River and Chesapeake Bay, on the Virginia-Maryland border.

With Hal's death, Rodney had taken over as chief of the investigation. Rodney had been Hal's deputy. Rodney had also been Hal's lover (this latter point, a well-concealed confidence).

Rodney had picked-up where his paramour had left off. This included working with Eddie to try and build an air-tight case against Mc-Candless and Delpro.

They continued to make progress and Eddie was convened as a witness to a grand jury that ultimately indicted McCandless.

However, the subpoena was brought in absentia. As authorities closed in, apparently McCandless had tried to flee across the river to St. Mary's in Maryland. It was reported the boat had exploded mid-channel; McCandless' body was recovered in the wreckage.

McCandless' body had been dismembered and burnt to a cinder by the explosion. Nevertheless, the remains were officially identified based on dental x-rays as being those of McCandless. Rodney had serious doubts. He redoubled his team's efforts and prepared a second related case for the grand jury. Eddie testified a second time. Indictments were delivered a second time—this time against Delpro.

Grievously, by the time there were warrants to enforce, there was no longer any Delpro of record. Eddie had confirmed there had been offices of Delpro in California in Menlo Park. He had also confirmed they had been formally involved in numerous legal matters regarding financial misdoings and land expropriation in the West. He added they had been the owner of record for a variety of enterprises that Eddie had been able to identify, including sawmills and cattle companies.

All this notwithstanding, miraculously, after McCandless' exit (to the grave or elsewhere), Delpro seemed to vanish from US shores. There was still ample evidence of overseas' activities, but no trace was left in the US of A.

This had forced Rodney to bend the rules and to take an open, and formally domestic investigation to new shores and new lands. Given the delicate nature of these enquiries, the most expeditious and prudent method had been to use an intermediary. Rodney felt lucky to have been able to find Joe Thompson as his foreign agent.

Now, through Joe, he had Peter.

For Hal it had all been about Delpro. Rodney now understood it was much larger—much more complex—than Hal had envisioned. There was apparently something called the organization.

Through the feedback from Joe's shadowing of Peter, Rodney began getting snapshots of the bigger picture—be they ever so disjointed. A map of Peter's travels over past months showed, if nothing else, how vast an area was covered by just one operative and how varied the tasks assumed by this steward of powers hanging beyond the horizon.

Still, Rodney honestly had no idea what effectively constituted the organization. There was a new and increasingly popular term: "deep state." This neology was used by a growing number of people, including several in Rodney's business. In fact, it was used frequently enough that Rodney had decided to try and understand to what it referred. As best as he could deduce, it was a variant of the Turkish *derin devlet* that related to a collusion in the 1990s between the Turkish military and criminal forces in a dirty war against their common enemies. Rodney wondered if the organization was a present deep state collusion between crime and government.

Rodney had, of course, heard organized crime referred to as the "underworld," some also called it the "Black Hand," but he was uncomfortable with these existing classifications. From all indications, the organization was much wider and deeper than organized crime—at least the organized crime of yesteryear. He was equally reluctant to use the often bantered "deep state," still unsure himself as to its true implications.

Before becoming totally involved in this case, Rodney had worked on some similar organized crime issues. One of the biggest cases targeted Semion Yudkovich Mogilevich, a Ukrainian-born Russian considered by many to be the boss of bosses of the Russian mafia syndicate. A criminal Don who, while on the FBI Most Wanted List, was still at liberty—still openly doing business. He was reportedly closely associated with the Solntsevskaya Bratva crime group. Thinking back to this case, Rodney's mind focused on the word "bratva" (братва). Being a bit of a polyglot, Rodney knew some translated this word as meaning "lads" in English. That was it, he baptized the organization as bratva—the lads— for internal work and reference purposes.

Bratva became the centerpiece of Rodney's world.

The newly-christened Bratva Task Force—BTF for short—was still managed from the same offices where Hal had started his investigation, in the south of the District of Columbia, not far from the Maryland state line, in a nondescript office building among a row of 1950's brick apartments along Blue Plains Drive, near the Potomac Job Corps Center. The stodgy exterior belied a modern and bustling interior that was home to some of the country's top investigators and analysts.

The BTF team, following Rodney's intuition, was unable to definitively confirm Robin McCandless' death. The remains found in the boat's wreckage had ultimately been handed over to the gentleman's estate—reportedly cremated and enshrined in a family mausoleum. Although no one could tell Rodney's crew where this crypt was located nor if there were surviving family members.

A total lack of current details notwithstanding, the team was able to bore into the history of McCandless. With tenacity and a superb network of sources, they were able to follow his trajectory backwards all the way to Romania and his life as the youthful Răzvan. As they followed the worn threads, they began to see more and more of Horațiu or Horace.

A spinoff group started expressly examining Horace—the Sir Horace to be found in the popular press across the globe. He was totally visible and invisible at the same time. He sought the spotlight and, through a never-ending series of strange events, always seemed to have his name in a local newspaper somewhere or other. Yet, in spite of this public openness, it was never clear what he did, where he worked, nor what he had been doing at the time that he had made the news. He simply seemed to drop out of nowhere and then return to oblivion.

With a dead-end for older brother Robin, BTF refocused on kid brother Horace. It became a "now you see him, now you don't" act of prestidigitation—the, as they learned, doubtful nobleman, popping up in the most bizarre of places at the most bizarre of times.

Through this surveillance, they came across many of the old gent's associates, including Peter. It was a big job. BTF ran background checks on all known contacts. Peter stood out only because he was one of the few without an extensive criminal record. No one was able to explain why he was part of Sir Horace's squad—but there he was.

Rodney's considerable resources began to probe as intensely as possible into Peter Volman. In spite of their remarkable efforts, there were a lot of big holes in Peter's story from the time he graduated from school in the UK until he had had his run-in with authorities in South Africa.

But these deficiencies did not seem too important. They were able to tie Peter to Robin McCandless' brother from the time Peter was sent to jail in Jo'burg.

Rodney's sleuths and seekers had been everywhere. While Joe Thompson had been the overt face of the BTF team's scrutiny, there had been a variety of concealed observers following Peter's movements, noting his acquaintances, and recordings habits. Paula Patterson and Evelynn, among many others, had made the list of Peter's connections. As a result of being flagged by BTF, oversight of Paula had been extended to Geneva. The watchers had also closely followed Evelynn's romance with Peter and even followed her to Geneva where she had met up with Paula.

After careful review of a myriad of data points, the BTF team had been able to declare that Evelynn was still very much a person of interest as she had a very close and, from all indications, authentic relationship with their target. Paula, however, was relegated to a much less prominent category—someone who could be a factor in validating some of Peter's potential statements, but not a party directly involved in any of the transgressions.

Rodney's file on Peter was very thick and growing.

Rodney knew all too painfully he was only seeing a tiny slice of the picture. Hal, with Eddie's help, had managed to push the door open to get a larger glimpse of the group's—the lads'—reach. It had been and certainly continued to be vast. There were legitimate businesses intertwined with slavery, prostitution, drugs, fraud, murder, and more—much more.

But when the line broke with Robin McCandless' apparent death, the door had slammed shut. The newly-minted BTF team was only now beginning to be able to budge it—to open it—just the tiniest crack. They needed more information. They needed more sources. They needed more leads. They needed more facts.

They needed collaborators (yes, thought Rodney, "*collaborateurs*") to gain any forward momentum.

They looked everywhere. They followed Sir Horace. They followed Mr. Hong. They followed anyone who had come up on their radar. Rodney had even personally reached out to Paula. Still, as his team had already concluded, she knew no specifics about the brothers, Delpro, nor any of the elements central to the case. She had a lot to offer about international fraud, extortion, and even racketeering. But Rodney doubted any of these concerns were directly relevant to the present case.

They needed first-hand information.

They needed Peter.

CHAPTER TWENTY-ONE

Resurrection

Finally a destination

A LONG TIME PASSED.

Peter wasn't sure how long—just long.

Late one afternoon the guards came and, as they did not take him to the yard, he assumed he was going to the musty room to see Joe. However, the corridors they followed did not seem at all familiar. They zigzagged through prison byways for more than ten minutes before coming to a heavy steel-reinforced door. Here, the guards opened the door, pushed Peter out, and slammed the door behind him. It was nearly a rerun of his memorable yet lamentable exit from the South African jail with Sir Horace.

In truth, it was practically a repetition of his earlier escape from Jo'burg except for the fact that this time the car waiting for him was not a gleaming black chauffeur-driven Mercedes but a well-worn and some- what the worse for this wear dust-covered Mazda 929 with Joe Thompson at the wheel—the *déjà vu* aspects of the current situation evading Peter whose mind and body were fully occupied elsewhere.

Peter rushed to the car, his legs feeling like rubber. He jumped, hur- riedly, into the front passenger seat as soon as Joe opened the car door, asking no questions when Joe dropped the car into gear and slowly left the prison's parking lot.

After a quarter of an hour, Peter's muscles relaxed.

Joe could feel the unwinding.

He turned to his passenger, the recent detainee dressed in rags, with a smile, saying, "Look in the back seat."

Peter glanced partially around, thinking his new chief might have thoughtfully brought a change of clothes to replace the purulent prison garb that was literally adhering to his skin. But, from his limited vantage point, he could see nothing unusual in the back seat—no parcel—nothing special.

"Go on," Joe prodded, "take a good look."

Peter then completely twisted around in his seat to fully see the rather cramped rear area. There, directly behind him, in the shadows, was Evelynn.

She leaned forward, squeezed Peter's hand and whispered in his ear, *"Qui ne risque rien n'a rien"*[1]

They were off—rushing down the road under a cobalt sky.

Joe was a good driver. And he knew where he was going.

He drove south out of Borh, following the Nile, stopping at the first small village, only twenty miles along the road (but requiring over an hour to cover that distance on the unmaintained tract).

As soon as they had left the prison, Peter had moved to the back seat to be close to Evelynn—to absorb her presence (while she, with great endurance, absorbed the foulness exuded from his rags).

They all rode in silence.

Then, at the village, Joe pulled over and opened the boot where there were indeed clean clothes for his charge and a basket with some canned drinks, fruit, and sandwiches.

Peter did his best to scrape off the encrustation from the prison that had entered his very pores—donning clean garments for the first time in he didn't know how long. They then sat on the hood of the Mazda and picked at the food, saying little.

There was so much to say. But the time didn't seem right.

Likely, they were all worried their extricating of prisoner Peter might still go awry. They all felt they were in danger—but didn't know how imminent. Certainly, arrangements had been made. Still, they all knew how easily these could backfire—how quickly fortunes could be reversed.

---

1. Nothing ventured, nothing gained.

It was more a time to hold one's breath than to try to catch-up. There were palpable feelings of urgency and jeopardy.

Quickly, it was then back in the car and back on the road. Joe continued south to Juba as Peter slept in Evelynn's lap. They crossed the city in the deep hours of night, Joe somehow migrating through the several police check points by showing a package of documents laced with a generous number of 500-pound South Sudanese notes.

They then left the sleeping capital by the A43, heading west to the border with the Congo and the town of Yambio—a 240-mile, seven-hour trip. Here there was a small airport with a small Cessna waiting to carry the trio on the two-hour-flight to the discrete Wilson Airport in Nairobi. In their flight, they had avoided the massive and ever-bustling Jomo Kenyatta International Airport—not knowing who might be in Peter's pursuit. Kenyatta Airport was the major hub for East Africa. Peter's stalkers, if there were any, could very likely set up in the airport's arrivals hall thinking that sooner or later their escapee would pass through its doors.

Joe, however, felt much more conformable about departures than arrivals—reasoning they were looking for someone running to Nairobi, not leaving. Therefore, within hours of landing at Wilson, the threesome was at Kenyatta Airport checking-in to a Kenyan Airways flight to Dakar—checking-in, as far as Peter could determine, with no tickets nor passport. Yet, checking-in, nonetheless.

With what seemed to be unmatched speed, Peter soon found himself whisked through departure formalities, airborne, and heading back to West Africa. He had asked for the window seat, Evelynn sitting in the middle, and Joe on the aisle.

There was still only pragmatic conversation. Nerves were taut. Fatigue weighed like heavy flagstones on all their heads.

At cruising altitude, from 37,000 feet, Peter stared down through the pooling blue sky, through filamentous whips of clouds to the shadows of land moving beneath them. But he did not look at the screen in the cabin that traced their travels. Instead, in his mind, he relived his own odyssey from Kpando that had finally ended in Borh Prison.

He thought back to Silas and Dabi. He moved through time, trying to retrace his steps. He called forth images of Kele, Abeo, Raul, Robbe, Brother Mike, Mister Khan as well as Messrs de Woordvoerder, Wewege, and Koopman. To this mix, he added Katy, Chimango, Josh, and the trio of Freddy, Sam, and Ralph. Then, of course, there was Mr. Hong and the office crew of Regina, Alfred, and Afaafa with Darweshi in the port. And through it all, he could not (unfortunately, he lamented) forget the despicable Sir Horace.

His voyage had not only been long and geographically complex, it had been populated by an amazing sliver of humanity. Now it was just Evelynn and himself—who knew where Joe really fit in.

Gazing at the blur rushing by beneath him, but seeing nothing, he concluded, somewhat to his own surprise, that it had all been worth it. Given the simple choice of stay or go, he had done what he had to do. There had been horrors. But there had been many wonders. Wondrous places. Wondrous people. Wondrous happenings. He had nearly lost his life. He had nearly lost his sanity. He had, at least temporarily, lost his freedom. But it had been worth it.

Landing at Aéroport International Léopold-Sédar-Senghor, the baggage-less triad quickly navigated through immigration and customs. This, in spite of the fact that Peter had no ID nor travel documents, and no one seemed to ask Evelynn for any formalities, Peter unsure if she had her passport, health card, and other items generally demanded at ports of entry.

Joe seemed to effortlessly navigate the crowded airport, basically never stopping his forward motion until they were seated in a cab at the airport's exit—Joe, in passable French, telling the driver to take them to the Pullman Dakar Teranga, a 5-star hotel at the western tip of the city, at the end of the promontory that pierced into the Atlantic like a Zulu *assegai*, in view of Isle Gorée.

Entering the luxurious hotel, Joe asked Peter and Evelynn to take seats in the lobby while he took care of all the needful. They watched as he discussed with the receptionist, signed some papers, and talked to the bellman—who promptly disappeared and then reappeared at Evelynn's shoulder with two mid-size suitcases.

By this time, Joe was back in the lobby, sitting on a lavender brocade wing chair across from his charges. There was a visible change in his demeanor, as though some of the flagstones had been removed.

Though near exhaustion, he smiled at his travel mates. "Welcome to Dakar."

Peter and Evelynn could only offer half-smiles unsure how much they should celebrate and how much they should worry.

"I think," Joe continued, "we're far enough from the banks of the White Nile that that lovely Horace or his bootlickers won't be able to follow—at least for now."

This last bit added by Joe bothered them, both Evelynn and Peter tensed, but kept their awkward smiles on their faces—speechless.

"I know," Joe said, trying to be calming, "this has been one helluva run. We're all tired, hungry, and filthy—some more than others.

"You'll be happy to know that we'll be able to rest here for a while. You can thank the very kind Rodney Mills—I am but his proctor.

"Hoping that you would want to accept his invitation, Rodney and his outstanding team, present company excepted, made the multitude of arrangements for you to be able to get from there to here—both of you. They've dealt with the big-ticket items like getting Master Peter out of prison and Mistress Evelynn back at his side. They've also paid attention to detail, from greasing the skids for you two to be able to enter Sénégal without visas or any other paraphernalia, to purchasing necessary personal items and changes of clothes that you'll each find in your suitcase the bellhop kindly just brought.

"So, here's your keys." Joe put two nondescript plastic cards on the end table next to the divan where Evelynn and Peter were perched in front of him. "We all need to rest. Rodney's crew has reserved a lovely room for you guys, so go and take a break. Use room service if you like— it's all covered. It's Tuesday afternoon, in case you don't know. I'll call up to your room Thursday afternoon and we can meet by the pool to see what's next."

For all the fuss and build-up, when Evelynn and Peter got to their room on the sixth floor, it really could have been any room in any nice hotel anywhere. There was a clean and comfy king-size bed, a rather cramped Formica-covered workspace, a small veranda through sliding glass doors with a pair of chairs for peering across the Atlantic, a large shower with a modern vanity. All this was bathed in a kind of orange-red light that reflected off the wallpaper, bedspread, and curtains—all in the sort of setting-sun, tangerine tint.

It was nice. It was sure as hell a lot better than a cell in Borh.

They instinctively opened their suitcases after surveying their room. Both were impressed by the thought that had gone into assembling a collection of toiletries and clothes suitable for each. They were touched by the obvious personal effort and would have been more so if they weren't so drained.

They arranged their new wardrobes. Then there was an awkward moment of "what's next?" They knew each other so well. Yet they were at a point where somehow, they were nearly strangers. It had been so long—so much had happened.

Evelynn and Peter had displayed very little in terms of emotions since Peter had jumped into the Mazda in the prison parking lot. They had held hands, they had hugged, but they had said little.

It had all simply been too overwhelming.

Now, awash in an orange-red tinge, they felt as though they were melting—melting with relief and melting into each other.

The first order of business was to get Peter scrubbed and scoured from head to foot. Evelynn insisted on personally, very personally, over-seeing the work and the two had a most enjoyable shower followed by gentle and almost hushed lovemaking in the big bed with the sheets so freshly laundered they crinkled under the slow motions of the couple's reunification.

Exhaustion then took its toll and the lovers plunged into a deep and dreamless sleep, only awaking the next morning, hungry for breakfast, hungry for each other. While they waited for room service, Evelynn in-sisted they shower again to make sure the last remnants of Peter's incar-ceration were washed away.

They had another enjoyable shower.

As they sat on the tiny veranda sipping their coffee, the nearly crumb-free plates from their breakfast stacked on the room service tray, it seemed like the time had come. There was finally space to talk.

"It must have been horrible," Evelynn said, tentatively trying to get a conversation going.

"It was." Peter wanted to stop there, there was where he would have stopped for anyone else, but this was Evelynn, so he continued, digging deeper. "I'm not sure how I managed to come out sane, if indeed I'm sane."

"Ahh, *chérie*, at least from initial indications neither your sanity nor your virility is in question."

Then more seriously, "But there is no way you are not scarred. No one could go through what you've gone through and come out as they went in. It's terrible."

"It was tough," Peter admitted in nearly a theatrical underplaying of events, "but it's over and that's the most important thing—that, and once again being next to you."

"I don't want to pick at scabs—scabs that are probably just now forming—but I think it's a miracle we're even together today."

"I don't want to dwell on it now, it is too fresh," Peter admitted, "but you know the strange thing? Really the kind of truly frightening thing that happened?"

"What?"

"I had a Bible. Me, Peter, with a Bible. Amazing. Truly unthinkable. I had begun thumbing through the book I saw as my antithesis—a book that had, I felt and still really feel, helped ruin my family. But there I was, the one possession allowed by the guards, with a Bible and nothing else—not even much in the way of clothes.

"I began haphazardly browsing the pages that were so familiar to me from afar but so foreign up close—pages of which I had no real personal knowledge. I aimlessly jumped from chapter to verse, as I skipped about, realizing my father would've been furious at this practically irreverent treatment of The Book he held so dearly and which was so fully categorized in his mind that he could tell someone immediately which words from which verse applied to that person's condition.

"Despite my almost careless nibbling of the text, I honestly did read the passages upon which I landed. I didn't just read these arbitrary words, I read and reread them to try to fully comprehend their meaning—their impact. Besides, what else did I have to do?

"Basically, as you see me here before you, I can say I really tried to understand, to feel the inner meanings of those words. Yet, the messages so crucial to my father continued to escape me. I found many of the stories themselves an acceptable way to pass the time—of which I had an abundance—but this was just like reading any story. I even found the way some feelings, some strategies, some directions were stated to be interesting. In some cases, I found that these statements even reflected things I had seen—feelings I had felt—feelings I still felt. But I could not take any of these observations the next step to assign any divine or holy aspects to the words. I guess I just didn't get it."

Evelynn was not sure how to reply so she offered an unsatisfactory, "Well it's not for everyone."

"Anyway," Peter picked-up, "my Bible, like my rags, became so soiled I could barely read the pages. Still, I must confess, in the face of great pressure, I did not use this book that seemed to weigh so heavily on me to wipe my bum."

"Well, we'll take note of that," Evelynn again ineffectively chimed in.

"And ya know," Peter went on as though Evelynn had not intervened, "since I obviously didn't know where the guard was taking me—didn't know I was on my walk to freedom—my Bible was left in my cell. Certainly, someone is using it to wipe their bum now. Never let a good resource go to waste in prison.

"And ya know, I don't think I'll rush out and get a replacement. I think it's OK now." Silently, to himself, he added that phrase that appeared so frequently in discourse in Nigeria, "Who knows tomorrow." Dare he think things were OK?

There was an uncomfortable moment of silence, the discussion seemingly having concluded, but the next on the list of topics not immediately popping up to take its place.

Peter took a large swallow of now tepid coffee and asked his most pressing question, "All that aside, my dear—my very dear—Evelynn, how the hell did you end up in the back seat of that Mazda?"

It was Evelynn's turn. She summarized quickly and succinctly how things had gone well in Geneva. Paula was a great person, and the work was fantastic—or so it seemed. As evident by her multiple postponements of her return to Tanzania, she was having a wonderful time and, she felt, learning a lot.

Throughout her assignment, she had been Paula's apprentice. Paula had mentored her. Paula had advised her. Paula had sent her on missions where she saw things she thought she would never see. Paula had shaped her into a professional—a qualified professional.

Then, as Peter knew all too well, good things turned bad. Paula uncovered inadvertently deep corruption in the trust. Nothing was as it had appeared. The entire operation was potentially a fraud—a house of cards that could possibly come tumbling down due to Paula's discoveries.

While Paula's revelations could not be undone, the Director General immediately did all he could to get her out of the way. Applying extreme coercion, he managed to convince her to publicly say she was accepting a new job offer in the US—the true aim to get her the hell out of Geneva and as far away from EHT as possible in return for a very, very hansom financial settlement. All this, of course, wrapped up in an airtight nondisclosure agreement so that the DG had as much cover as he could manage under the unpleasant conditions Paula had crafted.

With Paula's return to the US, Evelynn as Paula's disciple, was un-wanted baggage. At the earliest possible moment, her contract was termi-nated, she too benefiting from surprising financial generosity as long as she went away and kept her mouth shut.

She continued, now that she had completely captured Peter's atten-tion, "I found myself back in Dar. But I was really in no hurry to do anything. I was tired. EHT had been exhilarating. But it had also been fatiguing. It required being on the go all the time. Nothing like the last seventy-two hours, but still I was happy to get home and to be able to do nothing but relax with my family."

"I surely can understand that," Peter piped up.

"It was nice, and I spent lots of days just doing nothing. It was fun. It was necessary.

"Now, I don't want you to think I wasn't thinking of you. I was. I called your office and tried to get in touch with you. Afaafa, who's always been so kind to me, told me you were on an extended assignment out of the country but that she would send you word that I had come back to Dar and that she was sure you'd be getting back to me in the near future.

"When I didn't hear from you, I called the office on two more oc-casions, but basically got the same story. Finally, knowing how you are sometimes and how your business operates, I figured you were in a far-away place and out of contact with the office crew, so all I could do was wait. At least they knew I was back in town and I was confident they'd ultimately get this news to you.

"In the meantime, I had to think about my own situation and a pos-sible future job—accepting that sooner or later I'd have to get back to work.

"I was still debating with myself whether or not to see about go-ing back to my old government job or entering the broader international job market given my newly found international experience. I was really suffering over the debacle. Then, suddenly it fell off the table. I was sur-prised—really, I was dumbstruck—one day when Joe Thompson showed up at my parents' home. He had to remind me of our meeting at the Mwanza Point Bar. Otherwise, I would never have known who he was.

"But, as you know, he's a charmer, and with no concerns, I invited him in for a beer. This was a good decision, but boy was I unprepared for what followed. Joe told me that you were in prison in South Sudan. Without going into too many details, he described your real relationship with that nasty Sir Horace and explained how you were the fall guy for some of their recent failed operations. He explained how this position potentially made you a threat to them. As long as you were locked away and forgotten on the banks of the White Nile, no one would care. But if you got out and started spouting off, you could do damage to a lot of people. This, Sir Horace and his syndicate, wanted to avoid at all costs.

"Joe illustrated how one man's problem was another man's opportunity. You were Sir Horace's problem—apparently a big problem. But you were also Rodney Mills', and through Rodney, Joe's opportunity—by the looks of this room, a big opportunity. As Joe outlined it, they were convinced you knew a great deal—some things you maybe didn't know you knew. You could really help them in their investigations of Sir Horace and the much larger organization. All this was, of course, only if you were willing to cooperate.

"However, and Joe now came to the crux of his visit to see me, if you did decide to cooperate, Sir Horace *et al* would be merciless. They would do all they could to destroy you. And, with the loss of your parents, the only other person with whom you were close, as far as they knew, the only other person where they could get leverage over you, was me. If you cooperated, I was in danger.

"This I understood. This I understood all the more clearly having just gone through something much less worrisome with Paula. This was a problem. Joe then, ever so generous, offered the solution: if they were able to get you out, I'd go with you wherever they decided we should go. In short, I agreed.

"I talked to my parents. I couldn't risk putting them in jeopardy by telling them the whole tale, so I concocted some story, Joe helping with completely made-up correspondences, that I had been offered and had accepted graduate studies in the US. My folks think I'm studying at the University of Chicago. Joe and I began meeting at the Breakpoint Pub. I felt like we were true cloak-and-dagger agents. I'm sure patrons of the bar were sure we were an item. But we were, in fact, just planners.

"Joe kept me up to speed after he began seeing you in prison. He laid out the hoped-for timetable. We dreamed-up some new letters from Chicago to convince my parents of why and how things were evolving as they were—me being on very short notice to leave the country—not something my folks readily understood nor particularly liked—but they supported me and accepted all the nonsense, as they saw it, for the advancement of my career, as they saw it. The next thing I knew, I was in the back seat of the Mazda."

All the talk had made them hungry, and not for food.

The big weighty questions had been answered.

They knew there was still a lot they did not know. But they knew there was a lot of time to fill in all the details. They contentedly spent the afternoon and following morning alternating between ecstatic love-making, ravenously devouring excellent room service, and sitting on the veranda engaging in free-form chitchat.

Then Joe called and they all met at the pool.

"You two look a little more rested," Joe started off, with a twinkle in his eye.

With sangfroid, in unison, Peter and Evelynn replied, "It was a long trip, we were quite tired."

"Well," Joe followed-up, eyes still twinkling, "let me offer you each a good cold beer to start off our poolside chat."

After the drinks were served, Joe unfolded a sheet of A4 paper, handing it to Peter.

Joe's charge read silently:

> *Dear Peter,*
>
> *I am glad to know you are reading my second letter. This means you have decided to help us, and to allow us to help you. This also means that all the preparations my team made have not been for naught. You are now one of us. We hope you can appreciate this situation and the seriousness of your decision. We likewise hope you continue to have the courage to stick with this decision.*
>
> *It will not, we want to underscore, be easy. We are engaged in a very complex and multi-layered fight. As we believe you have experienced, this is a fight against some very bad actors. This is a fight that adversely touches many innocent victims. This is a fight where you can play a pivotal role.*
>
> *However, we are still not sure how best you can serve all our causes. We know you are a valuable asset. We know you want to do the right thing. But we have to be strategic. We have to employ our resources for maximum advantage.*
>
> *To boil all this down, this means two things: (1) we are counting on your continued cooperation, and (2) we are, at this point in time, unsure where or when we need to avail ourselves of your services.*

This means, from your perspective, you are, probably again, in a waiting game. All the while, as you have seen all too personally, you are at risk every day from these same bad actors. We honestly believed your dear Evelynn is also at risk.

Our plans at present are to find a place where you and Evelynn can be comfortable and safe—a place where we can contact you when we are ready and from where you can assist on a timely basis. For the sake of security, I will not articulate our plans in this missive—we never know who reads what.

Therefore, you will be getting all your further details from Joe Thompson. I can only add that you and Evelynn can have complete confidence in Joe. He is a good person who has your interests at heart as well as being a stout proponent of justice and doing the right thing. Please take all Joe tells you very seriously. Please trust in what he proposes. In the future, you will be in regular contact with our representative who will be able to get messages to Joe or me very quickly, providing you with feedback equally promptly.

I thank you for agreeing to help us and I wish you well in this new phase of your life.

Sincerely,

Rodney

Finishing, Peter handed the paper to Evelynn, then fixed Joe in his stare, "So, it seems you've something to tell us."

Joe politely waited for Evelynn to finish reading before he shifted the conversation to himself. He then built on Rodney's lead. "I have naturally read Rodney's letter—we've all read it as he intended. There's no need to go over what is clearly spelled-out. There's no need to emphasize what we all already know. This is dangerous. This is high stakes. This is serious. There's no going back.

"But there's also no reason to overly dwell on the past nor to fret about the future. All we really have is the present. It is what it is.

"Now here's what Rodney didn't say. Tomorrow morning I'll be leaving you. My close personal responsibilities are over as of then. Until then, if you have any misgivings or questions, you'd best ask them quickly.

"Tomorrow, before I leave, I'll introduce you to Paulino, he'll be your new shepherd—your herdsman. Paulino will fill in all the blanks, but what you need to know now is that, with the oversight of Rodney's team, it has been arranged you will continue from here to Cape Verde. All the necessary arrangements have been made. Paulino will be with you throughout. And it is important that you understand, as Rodney indicated, we have no clear timetable. No one, not Rodney, not Paulino, not I, can know how long this complex affair will continue. We simply don't know. You have to understand this. You have to know that we don't know. You can't begin asking, 'When are we leaving?' 'When is it over?' We don't know. You don't know. This is the beginning. That's all we know.

"So, think about all these concerns this afternoon and evening while you're resting," the twinkle was back, "and make sure you both understand the seriousness and the unknowns about what is just beginning."

With that Joe order more beers and asked, "Do you know the story of Isle Gorée, just there, offshore?"

Peter and Evelynn had stayed poolside for about another hour, talking about the slave trade and the shores upon which they sat being the last glimpse of home many people saw as they were crammed onto ships from what was now called the "House of Slaves" on the island.

They had a light lunch, discussed everything and nothing, and then went to their room. Rodney's letter combined with Joe's homily had had a discernible effect on them both. This was serious. While they were asked to make one last assessment of their options before tomorrow's meeting, there really were no other options. The bridge for going back had been burned. Evelynn had now a perpetual cloak of guilt by association. Sir Horace and his underlings as well as his superiors were not the forgiving kind. For them, the best solution was the simplest and the most permanent: remove the couple—wipe the slate clean.

There were no options.

Tomorrow they would go where they would go.

They hoped Rodney and Joe had their shit together. They seemed to. So far things had honestly been relatively smooth, and they had no reason to doubt the sincerity of their present overseers.

It was done.

They spent the rest of the afternoon in romantic play, their couplings becoming more energized, more surefooted, as they came to the realization that they were now together for the long haul—more rambunctious as they renewed their intimate knowledge of each other.

After another delectable room service dinner, they went to bed, falling immediately asleep in each other's arms. Then, in the pit of darkness, there was a knock at their hotel door. They awoke, noting it was after three o'clock in the morning. Even though Peter tied to hold her back, Evelynn went to the door, not opening it but asking, "Who's there?"

A husky voice of indeterminate gender, in muffled tones replied, "I need to talk with you."

"Who's there?" Evelynn repeated.

"Open the door," was the brusque reply.

"I'm calling the front desk," Evelynn reacted sternly.

There was silence.

The night visitor had left.

They slept fitfully for the remainder of the night, not enjoying each other's affections in the morning as they had planned but repacking their suitcases and going down to the hotel restaurant for breakfast, no longer sure if they were safe in their room.

They then waited in the lobby until Joe appeared, accompanied by a middle-aged man of short but stout frame with a head full of straw-colored hair that nicely accented a deeply bronzed complexion.

Seeing them, Joe and his companion quickly came to the divan where the couple were seated—reminiscent of their arrival at the hotel.

Shaking hands, Joe introduced Paulino, their new "most important person."

After the two men were seated, Evelynn, with no preamble, shared her concern about the night visitor, "We had someone come by our room about three this morning. It was strange. I don't know if it was dangerous?"

Joe looked at Paulino, saying in Portuguese in a muted voice, "*Eles tiveram um visitante desconhecido durante a noite. Você tinha um homem no saguão, ele viu ou ouviu alguma coisa?*[2]"

Paulino shrugged.

Joe frowned, "*Provavelmente um bêbado, mas isso não é bom. Verifique e modificaremos nossos planos.*[3]"

"OK," Joe looked back at Peter and Evelynn, trying to smile, "we have a backup in case something gets messed up. This is all probably nothing, a drunk at the wrong room. But we can't take any chances. Get your bags and go with Paulino. I'll take care of everything here and then watch your back.

---

2. They had an unknown visitor in the night. You had a man in the lobby, did he see or hear anything?

3. Probably a drunk, but this isn't good. Check and we'll modify our plans.

"Paulino will take my car—we were originally planning on going straight to the airport by taxi, but that's changed—it's parked outside. You'll drive about five hours south and cross over into The Gambia— Paulino will have all the necessary papers, don't worry. You'll have bookings at the Sunbeach Hotel, on Cape Point, outside Banjul on the west side of the River Gambia. This is a place we can easily lockdown if we need to. Don't worry. Paulino has it all down pat.

"You'd best get moving, you've an unexpected road trip and I've got loose ends to tie up. Not sure when we'll see each other again but know we will."

With that he gave Peter a hug and then shook his hand, doing the same with Evelynn, and then departing to the front desk. Paulino accompanied them to their room, looked everything over, and then helped them get their suitcases to the car.

They were off—again.

The road south was uneventful, Peter and Evelynn mostly dozing on each other's shoulder. At the border, they stayed in the car while Paulino talked to the Sénégalese officers. A short hop and then the ritual was repeated with the Gambian officials. Then they were in The Gambia.

Paulino explained the tactic, "If people, the wrong sort of people, know you're in Dakar, they'll be watching the airport. We'll stay here four or five days until I get the go-ahead from Joe. Then we'll fly to Cape Verde, connecting through Dakar but never leaving the transit lounge. Everything will be fine."

It was more or less an extension of their hotel stay at the Pullman Dakar Teranga except that the bed was not quite so comfy and the room service not quite so delicious. Peter attributed the difference to a slackening in hotel management. Evelynn thought this was because they were just getting more settled in their routine and little things were no longer all bright and shiny.

Whatever the comparison between hotels, the major difference was that Paulino had a room down the hall. This was, they realized, in part to assure their safety. Still, it imposed a need for a certain level of social decorum. Peter felt obliged, during their unplanned vacation on The Gambian beaches, to devote some effort to his escort. Accordingly, they would have a beer at the bar every day at teatime—Peter maintaining beer was far better than tea for the constitution.

It was during these quotidian encounters that Peter learned, drop by drop, Paulino's story (his companion already knowing his own life's tale from A to Z).

Paulino's grandfather had been scion of a line of mixed Portuguese and African lineages going back to the 15th Century when Portugal had occupied the volcanic islands that became Cape Verde as a slaving outpost. As a youngster, his granddad had signed on for a pittance as a cabin boy on an American whaler. He, along with a good number of Cape Verdians, finally settled in Boston as transplants from the whaling industry.

Paulino had grown up in a bilingual, bicultural home where he felt as much Bostonian as Cape Verdian. He had been lucky enough to go to college and graduate with honors with a degree in economics. Professionally unsure of his calling, he had moved through a number of positions in public service before he literally fell into Rodney's camp. From that time, he had never looked back.

Paulino added that he was very thankful for his current assignment. Although, over the years, all his family had either died or left Cape Verde, he still knew his roots were in the hard, volcanic rock that held the islands above the Atlantic's pounding surf. He was now going home, and he assured Peter that he would do all he could to make him as well as Evelynn feel at home on the windward islands.

Peter hoped, for Paulino's and their own sakes, the old adage, "you can never go home," was incorrect.

After four nights in the outskirts of Banjul, Paulino got word from Joe that they had not been able to identify any suspicious characters searching for Peter. No one had been seen with any known links to Sir Horace or other abettors from the old man's darker side. They had had to conclude that the night visitor had indeed been some befuddled lost soul—albeit Joe didn't really buy into this outcome. But there were no tangible reasons to maintain everyone on high alert.

Things should move forward.

Paulino, Evelynn, and Peter boarded the short afternoon flight on Orenair to Dakar, connecting on the same carrier to Praia, the political capital of Cape Verde on the island of Santiago. Paulio explained on the plane that Joe had altered the plans a bit out of an abundance of caution.

Since they were nearing their final destination, it was critical that this location be concealed to the outside world—only a select number of Rodney's team in the loop.

Joe was ninety-eight percent sure there were no followers, no moles from the organization. But they couldn't be too careful. Therefore, as a final way to circle back and make sure there were no sentinels from the other side, Peter and Evelynn would once again stay for a few nights in a local hotel. This time it would not be a gaudy four- or five-star affair, but a small secluded auberge where they would not leave their room.

Paulino would meet a crew on the ground and, in the relatively sparse population of Santiago, they would comb the island to make sure there were no threats. These were all Cape Verdians who could move invisibly about the capital and the island as a whole, examining every nook and cranny for anything out of place, anything suspicious.

They were very good at what they did.

It took a full three days, but Paulino was able to report to Joe that there were no problems. He then delivered the same message to the shuttered couple. He told Peter and Evelynn they would be able to walk about the city a bit the next day and then the following day they would take an inter-island flight to São Vincente, the second most populous island with slightly over seventy-thousand inhabitants.

Landing on São Vincente, they were met by one of Paulino's retinue, the quartet immediately traversing the major port city of Mindelo, continuing twenty minutes to the northeast to the fishing village of Salamansa—a hamlet of just over a thousand on the wind-swept shores of the Atlantic. Then, with dramatic fanfare, Paulino announced to his wards, "Welcome to your new hometown!"

They continued through the village to a whitewashed house that was indistinguishable from its neighbors. "This," Paulino smiled, "is your destination, your new home."

Peter and Evelynn did not know how to react. In many ways it felt like they were at the end of the world. It even felt a little like they were now both in prison. Yet, they were together. They were somehow free. And, hopefully, they were safe.

Paulino led them through the varnished front door into a neat home that looked on the inside just as you thought it would when you were on the outside. There was a small but adequate kitchen, a combination living and dining area, two bedrooms, and, surprisingly, two full bathrooms. The house had been furnished with just as much attention to detail as had been devoted to packing their suitcases. It was nice. No, it was better than nice. It was great—their first home.

Evelynn prepared some tea as the pantry was already provided with the essentials, and the four of them, including Paulio's colleague who had met them in Mindelo, sat around the dinner table and listened as Paulino presented the rules of the game.

"First," Paulino began, as he sipped his tea, "let me introduce formally Aleixo. He will be your direct contact and your principal assistant. He lives in Salamansa."

With the introduction, the young and agile Aleixo got up from his chair and shook hands with Evelynn, then Peter. In rather strained English, he grinned, "Happy to meet you. Happy to be with you."

"Now," Paulino continued, "we've all got to make sure we know what's going on."

The straw-haired Cape Verdian was the center of attention as he outlined (what Peter would later call chapter and verse) the situation and the arrangements, "We all know this is going to be difficult.

"I am ultimately your link to Joe and Rodney. Aleixo is your link to me. He will never be far away. To start with, he should be your link not just to me but to the world all-together. Whatever you need, let him know and he will see about supplying your requirements—to the extent possible, from suppliers here on São Vincente, but, if need-be from wherever.

"Now, as you've just set foot in your new home, let me assure you that the same kind people who helped kit you up in Dakar have also taken the liberty to get you set up here. The kitchen should be well-equipped, and the pantry fully stocked. You should find additional clothes in your wardrobe and additional toiletries in your bathroom. In the middle compartment of the sideboard, you'll find two notebook computers complete with most of the necessary software. You have a landline telephone. There is a television as you have probably already noticed but reception is limited. However, it has a built in DVD player and there is an assortment of DVDs in the TV stand.

"In summary, we hope you will find all you need. If not, Aleixo is here to help. He will also, I should add, have the names and numbers of doctors, dentists, barbers, or other skill sets of which you may be in need.

"So, the practical issues addressed, let's talk a little about the 'how's.' For the first few months we want you to basically quarantine yourselves in your home. You can, naturally, go out for walks, go to the beach, stroll where you wish. But just the two of you. Do not engage people. If someone seems to want to be friendly, just wave and cross the road. Stay to yourselves—it is important.

"Please, do not make any phone calls other than to Aleixo—think of the phone as a walkie-talkie to him, not a line to the outside world. We have intentionally not provided WiFi access. If you need something let Aleixo know.

"You must keep off everyone's radar!

"When we are comfortable that your location is known only to us, we will begin to relax things a bit so you can have somewhat of a more normal life.

"For now, it's Aleixo or no one."

It had sounded easy.

In fact, it had seemed the simplest thing in the world.

Evelyn and Peter had just been reunited after a long and painful separation. They had just faced many unpleasantries, both together and separately. They had just made the decision to join their lives into a new and single life.

They had lost time to make up for. They had stories to tell. They had loving to catch up on. They needed to absorb one another.

It sounded easy, but after a month of twenty-four-seven absorption and immersion, it didn't seem so easy. They began looking for options to have some private space—some personal time.

For Evelynn, it was probably easier. She had been involved in a number of projects, had had extensive professional experiences over recent months. She could, from memory, write technical articles that could be—that should be—of interest to the wider community of those involved in international development even if published at a far-off press under obscure authorship to protect the source.

Peter felt he could only write about the inside of a cell at Borh Prison and that was probably not of much interest to anyone.

Thus it was that every afternoon Peter would go for a long walk on the beach while Evelynn began writing.

Peter couldn't help thinking back to his walks about Kpando—about his walks along the shores of Lake Volta. It looked like he had come full circle. It had taken years, but the troubled (what he now saw as) young-ster from the lakeside was now the troubled adult on the seashore.

Walking was good because it gave him exercise—it gave him fresh air. It invigorated him. Yet it also gave him too much unstructured time to think—to construct mental snares as if to catch himself. He needed something more.

Fortunately, Aleixo spontaneously provided the solution.

Peter and his usher were having a beer at the dining table when Aleixo began telling his companion about the good ol' days. This, Peter thought, from someone nearly young enough to be his son. Nevertheless, it was interesting to hear about how São Vincente, and Salamansa in particular, had evolved over recent years.

In his remarkably good, but heavily accented English, Aleixoa lamented, "We're a fishing community. Commercial fishing is everything to many families here—they know nothing else. But catch is falling, supplies are getting harder to get, compared to just a few years ago, people are really having a hard time.

"My family were not fishers, so we've managed to avoid many of the difficulties. My family were shopkeepers. But, like all on the islands, the sea is everywhere—the sea is everything. Even though my family did not earn their livelihood from fishing, they were still inextricably tied to the sea. My father used to go surf fishing every Saturday. Every Sunday my mother prepared his catch—big, beautiful, fresh pieces of the best the sea had to offer."

This struck a curious note for Peter, "Do people still surf fish?"

"Oh yes. It's still very popular. Although, I must be honest, the fish people catch today are nothing at all like my father caught."

"I imagine not. Still, could you get some fishing gear for me?"

"I'll look into it."

The seed was planted.

A few months later, Peter and Evelynn had a visit from Paulino. Over the ubiquitous beer, their visitor, after exchanging all the pleasantries, asked, "So how is it going?"

"We're fine, "Evelynn happily replied, "we feel like we've finally established a routine that fits us—keeps us close but not so close we mash each other's toes.

"Aleixo is wonderful. He's such a big help to us both. He's helped me set up a kind of cottage business (she laughed at her own sort-of pun). I write a number of articles for popular magazines—some more technical than others—always writing under a pseudonym. Aleixoa then sends my work to your colleague in the States who has a list of publishers to whom we offer my material. I've had five pieces published in recent months and been paid well for each—actually, as you certainly know, your man in the States has been paid on behalf of my ananym, but it all finally filters down to me. Works fine."

Peter felt he really couldn't top his dear Evelynn's accomplishments, so he simply added, "I've found I may have a talent for fishing."

Paulino displayed sincere satisfaction that the couple had been able to adjust—that the couple was still a couple. He knew it was challenging and wanted to offer all possible encouragement. "Well, I've really popped in to give you a quick update."

"You and your update are most welcome," Evelynn said, assuring him.

As always, it was down to business for Paulino, "We've been watching everything very closely. We have no indication that anyone who shouldn't knows you're here. Let me caution, this news is more to comfort your worries than to provoke any major changes in lifestyle. You've done very well and should be complemented. But don't change now. Keep going and I'll keep updating you as we have news."

After a quick beer with his people in Salamansa, Paulino was up and nearly out the door when he turned and said, "I nearly forgot." He put his hand in his pocket. "Rodney's also sent you a new letter."

Paulino handed Evelynn the single sheet of folded A4, shook both their hands, and was out the door before they could say anything.

Evelynn read the brief note, handing it to Peter. It was succinct:

> Dear Evelynn and Peter,
>
> Paulino told me he was coming over to São Vincente to see you both, so I thought I'd take the opportunity just to drop you a quick line. I really have nothing to report that you have not already heard from Paulino—he is doing a terrific job. We are now confident that you are safe and well-hidden from view. But, of course, we cannot let our guard down—we need to be ever-vigilant. I know the measures we are asking you to follow can be stressful, but please bear with us.
>
> While we are comfortable in assuring you that you are secure, we have honestly lost our oversight of the old scoundrel Sir Horace. We know your departure from Borh sent waves of panic through many parts of the organization. We do not know how these might

have affected Horace's role in the goings-on. We must assume he is still a critical person of interest and that he has gone to ground temporarily in the aftermath of your rescue and disappearance.

All this is to say that things are now no clearer than they were a few months ago. I can guarantee my team is working as hard as they can to develop the materials we need to be able to see justice done. And we are making progress. But this is still very much a work in progress, and I cannot, unfortunately, give you any specifics as to when or where we would hope to call upon your kind services.

I can only ask you both to continue to be patient and again assure you that you are both well protected and considered as among our highest priorities.

I know things will work out well for us all.

Thank you for your sacrifices.

Sincerely,

Rodney

Peter knew there was really nothing more to say.

It was time to go fishing.

Final thoughts—or are they?

SURROUNDED BY WATER, PETER had indeed become an avid fisherman. Somehow the sport that had eluded him on the shores of Lake Volta captured his attention on the wind-swept shores of the Atlantic. Maybe it was the chase; now being the chaser and not the chased. Maybe it was the menu. Avoiding the offshore waters where tourist fishermen ardently sought marlin, Peter discovered how to maneuver the shoreline to snag grouper, snapper, Mahi Mahi, and even the occasional barracuda—all most welcomed on Evelynn's table.

Between outings, Peter wandered the beach, staring at the writhing sea, wondering about where he had been and where he was going. His reflections were interwoven with images of all those with whom he had shared the road. Unavoidably, and sometimes uncomfortably, effigies of his parents intertwined with snippets of their faith would take center stage. He would recall his father's love of the Good Book—even if somewhat hypocritical. Even without his dog-eared and dungy Bible in hand, he continued to remember those passages favored by his family. He would inescapably think of the words of another Peter, another fisherman (but not the surf fisherman of our story), and one of the most prominent spokespersons of his time:

> 2 Peter 2: 18-22—*"For they mouth empty, boastful words and, by appealing to the lustful desires of the flesh, they entice people who are just escaping from those who live in error. They promise them freedom, while they themselves are slaves of depravity—for 'people are slaves to whatever has mastered them.' If they have escaped the corruption of the world by knowing our Lord and Savior Jesus*

Christ and are again entangled in it and are overcome, they are worse off at the end than they were at the beginning. It would have been better for them not to have known the way of righteousness, than to have known it and then to turn their backs on the sacred command that was passed on to them. Of them the proverbs are true: 'A dog returns to its vomit,' and, 'A sow that is washed returns to her wallowing in the mud.'"

The Peter of our story, the son of Paul of our story, has accumulated a crust of mud that will not easily wash off. So far as we know, however, he has not returned to his vomit.